THE SEARCH

"He that falls in love with himself
will have no rivals."

— *Benjamin Franklin*

CONTENTS

1 PRIDE

Friday evening

He could never forgive himself.

However, if his wife might forgive him, then he could live with the guilt for the rest of his life; guilt was all that he deserved. Looking at his wife used to bring him delight and meaning in life, but now it brought him a hollow feeling of remorse and shame. He had to tell her. He could only bear the burden for so long.

When they got married, he'd promised himself never to make her cry, and during seventeen years of marriage, he had never once broken that promise. He was convinced his wife had never shed a single tear because of his actions. However, she was bound to cry this time, and so was he. He had ruined their relationship for both of them. He didn't have a good response to the question that had been haunting him for the past couple of days.

He was a man.

That was the short and simple answer.

He was a man with too much macho pride, and he was afraid of losing his masculinity. That was the only answer he could come up with, and he knew it wasn't good enough. He felt nauseous. He wanted to cry, scream, and throw up, all at once.

How could you have been so stupid? he asked himself.

"You want to get some enchiladas?" his wife suggested and looked over at the café counter. "Or are you full?"

The thought of eating made him even more nauseous, but he knew she wanted him to help her finish the enchilada she now eagerly hoped to taste. His wife had a strict policy about not wasting food, and she made sure they never threw away any food at home. She said it was disrespectful to the rest of the world.

"No, I got some room left, but I can't finish a whole one," he said. "Perhaps we can share one? If that's all right with you?"

She left the table as soon as he finished the sentence. Seeing her leave frightened him. His chest started to hurt as he thought of the pain and agony that awaited.

They'd met in college in Vancouver where he was the foreigner, and she was the domestic student who struggled with the language. The attraction wasn't love at first sight, at least not on his part. But eventually, he was struck by how authentic she was, and how she presented herself to others. She didn't pretend to be perfect or try to hide her flaws. The impression she made on him was always genuine. She never wore fashionable outfits or fancy lingerie. Her clothes never defined her; they only kept her warm and comfortable.

When they started dating, she insisted on paying for herself because she didn't want him to do anything on account of his being a man. As husband and wife, they would share every burden equally. She didn't demand anything more or expect anything less from him. She made him feel special. She told him what a good man he was. He liked himself better when he was around her—she brought out the good side of him.

Her prince, she called him, as she pretended he was the frog she'd kissed as a little girl. *'It took you a long time to find me, but it was worth the wait,'* she'd told him. Not until years later did she reveal that she'd actually kissed the frog when visiting relatives in America. *'So, you kissed an American frog?'* he'd asked her. *'And now you're married to an American you met in Canada.'* What he said had rendered his wife speechless and her eyes wet. That was one of the happiest days of his life.

His wife used every opportunity presenting itself to tell the story to others, and she did it with great pride and enthusiasm. She started to introduce him as *'the prince, formerly known as frog.'* She wanted to name their son Prince Junior, but he wouldn't let her—the schoolyard was tough enough to begin with.

She made him feel like the man of her dreams, the best husband in the world, her husband, and that's all he ever wanted to be. All she expected from him was his honesty, nothing more and nothing less. The thought and memories brought a tear to his eye, and he made sure to wipe it away before she noticed.

His wife returned to the table with a smile almost as big as the enchilada she carried. Seeing her smile reminded him of how beautiful she was. Even if the feeling of remorse cast a shadow over her image, her beauty still amazed him. She had aged so gracefully. The lines only highlighted her face even more, framing and emphasizing her beautiful portrait.

"I love you."

The words sounded wrong. Even though he said those particular words every day, they sounded different this time, and she must have noticed, because she didn't return the favor at once.

"I love you too."

Tears started gathering in the back of his eyes.

"I'm going to use the restroom," he said, and swallowed a tear.

"Okay, but hurry back before nothing is left."

He never used the urinal unless he had to. He enjoyed many things in the company of other people, but urinating wasn't one of them. As he stared down at the toilet bowl, he felt as if he were looking down an abyss. The view reminded him of his recent recklessness, and of his stupidity.

Not only had he betrayed his wife, he had also forsaken their children. He had protected his manhood when he should have protected the welfare of his daughter and son, and the safety of dual parenting. He suddenly realized his wife might replace him with another man, and even worse, that man would have access to his children.

He closed the lid out of habit, only to open it again a second later. He fell down to his knees and threw up the meal he'd just consumed at the airport café. The smell of stomach acid and urine burned his eyes, and again, he asked himself the same question.

How could you have been so stupid?

When he returned to the café, he noticed his wife playing with his phone, and how her facial expression had changed drastically. He wasn't used to seeing her angry, but this time she appeared to be furious. The light from the screen emphasized the feeling in her face. Her eyebrows were low, and her lips were narrow and thin. Her eyes focused on the screen, and she never blinked.

As soon as she spotted him, she put down his phone, and gave him a bleak smile.

"Is everything all right?" he asked.

"It's nothing. Never mind. Let's enjoy the enchilada while it's still hot," she said with an absent look.

"I'm sorry I took so long," he said. "I thought you started without me."

His wife remained quiet, and her expression stayed the same: She looked absent.

"Are you sure everything is all right?"

She took her eyes off the food and glanced at his phone with eyes of rage.

"It's this video that's going viral. A group of men beating a transsexual to death," his wife said and shook her head.

"Oh. Where was this?"

"I think somewhere in South America," his wife replied. "You know, I'm actually afraid of leaving the house these days.

In case, some guys decide to beat me to death for wearing too little makeup. Like if I don't look feminine enough that day or something. To think some men could deprive another person of his life, just because the person's appearance didn't appeal to them."

"The good outnumber the evil ones," he said.

"What?"

"The majority of men would never think of hurting a woman, or anyone else for that matter," he said. "Some really good men are out there. Don't you forget that."

"I know. I married one of them," his wife said. "Where is this coming from?"

"You said you're afraid of men on the street," he replied and shrugged his shoulders. "I don't want you to be afraid."

His wife took a few breaths before answering.

"No, I mean what scares me is society in general. It's so violent these days."

Her French accent had become apparent, as it usually did whenever she felt nervous or uncomfortable. He made sure to give her a moment to compose herself.

"Are you afraid of *women* beating you to death?" he eventually asked.

"Touché," his wife said in a perfect French accent, and she put her hands up as a sign of surrender while a look of resignation crossed her face. "That's French," his wife added.

"What? Surrendering?" he asked, and stuck out the tip of his tongue.

"No, the word. Wiseguy."

"I know what touché means."

"Oh, do you now," his wife said. "So, what does it mean?"

"It means the other person is right. Which is probably why I don't hear it very often," he responded, with a smile.

"I agree. You aren't right very often. But that's only when you use the word. What does the actual word mean?"

His wife had a mischievous smile, and he knew what she was up to. She was going to get back at him somehow or other.

"I don't speak French."

"So, you do *not* know what touché means?"

"Touché." He pronounced the word slowly and raised his eyes toward the ceiling. "I guess it sounds a bit like *touch*."

Her look of disappointment confirmed his guess was right.

"But that doesn't make any sense," he added, and tried his best to look clueless.

His wife's smile returned, then she made a stabbing motion with her knife.

"What?" he mumbled, and actually did feel clueless.

She moved her knife to form the letter Z in the air and made a swishing sound.

"What are you doing?"

"I'm Zorro," his wife said in a silly accent. "Touché comes from fencing. You know, before they had those electronics in the swords. Touch, as in you touched me. To let your opponent know they got you. Touché, as in you won a point."

"Touché," he said, and awarded her with a wink.

His wife always had a charming way of educating him, and she always maintained a glint of humor in her face. Even when she criticized him, she always did so in an amusing way. The words were negative, but the experience in itself wasn't. This was one of the things he admired most about her, and why he loved her so much. He couldn't imagine living without her.

He felt a lump growing in his throat.

He noticed a man across the room who appeared to be praying. The sight reminded him of his wedding vows, and the remorse and shame he now felt toward his wife. Looking at her made him feel vulnerable and weak, and once again, he reminded himself of how stupid he was.

A stupid man, he added to his thoughts.

"What?" his wife asked.

Just then, he realized he was staring at her.

"You're so beautiful. So, lovely."

She turned her eyes to the table, and her face began to grow red. “We better get a move on. They start boarding in an hour, and this girl is going to do some shopping.”

He hated the airport environment, and that combination of stress and constant waiting. Waiting in line to check in, waiting in line to go through security, waiting in line at the gate, waiting in line to finally enter the airplane, only to wait in line to find the right seat—standing still, with all cylinders firing.

He never felt as lonely as when he walked around the airport now, even though his wife was right by his side. He was the only one who knew the truth, and the person he was hiding from was also the person he felt closest to in life.

After an hour of deputized shopping, they arrived at their gate just in time to get some seats in the waiting area. He was out of breath, he had a throbbing headache, and tears had once again started to pile up in the back of his eyes.

“Save a seat for me,” he said, and sniffed. “I’ve got to use the restroom again.”

As he sat on the toilet, he reacted to the sound. The sound was off, yet it came as no surprise. He was used to the sound by now. The view, however, was beyond his disbelief. There was so much blood, and this time the blood was thicker and darker.

He had convinced himself that he just had a tear, and that would explain both the pain and the blood. And the rock-hard stool was probably due to dehydration. He’d made sure to drink plenty of water, and he’d reduced the amount of salt in his diet.

However, the idea of the humiliation of a rectal examination was what had kept him from seeing a doctor. He knew he was in trouble, but he didn’t want to admit it. He felt he was confronting a line he might have to cross, and his manhood prevented him. Ignorance hadn’t just ruined his life, either. His pride had ruined their lives. When he finally did cross the line, he’d prepared himself for the expected treatment, but all he got was '*sorry.*'

Sorry you didn't come in sooner.

Sorry, it's too late. We can't do anything now.

He had to tell his wife as soon as they got home and hope she could forgive him, so they could spend the last remaining time together filled with something other than sorrow and grief until death would them apart.

How could you have been so stupid?

He couldn't fight the tears anymore, as he thought of the ramifications of his actions—or more accurately, the lack of action. His chin started shaking, and seconds later, he was sobbing loudly and endlessly, while gasping for air.

When he returned to the gate, he noticed his wife had begun her mental exercise, and as always, she had her glasses on. He loved the way she looked when she wore her glasses. They made her look sophisticated, but also slightly nerdy in a charming and cute way.

"How's the exercise?"

"I'm struggling with the hard level," his wife answered. "Can you help me?"

"If you're struggling, then how am I supposed to figure it out?"

He noticed a trace of a smile in her face.

"We can help each other. Come on, it's fun."

"Counting to nine over and over again is fun?" he asked in disbelief.

"It's good for you. Besides, your brain could use the exercise." His wife ended the sentence with a wink.

"I'd rather have a carrot."

His wife tilted her head down and forward, and looked over the frames of her glasses, with a deadpan look on her face.

"First of all, a carrot can only do so much. Eating healthy is good, but you still need to exercise your brain," his wife claimed. "Secondly, I think you're confusing carrots with hot dogs, which is understandable, considering they have the same shape and size." She gave him a big smile. "I hate to break it to you, but you don't eat any carrots and hardly any vegetables either, and whenever we have fish, you moan for the rest of the day, and then fry some *carrots* as soon as the kids are in bed."

Do you know how cute you look in those glasses?

He smiled, then he leaned in toward her and briefly kissed her mouth.

"Okay, let's see what we've got here," he said, and focused on the book in her lap. "That's a lot of numbers. At least with a crossword puzzle you earn some knowledge. With Sudoku, all you do is count to nine."

"Sudoku isn't about counting. It's about applying the rule of elimination in order to find the answer, and that's the fun part," his wife said, and then tapped the page. "This leaves me clueless. I have no idea."

No, you have no idea how cute you look in those glasses, do you?

"I think it has to be two," he said, and swallowed another tear.

"I think you're right. It has to be two."

His wife suddenly turned her focus to the counter by the gate. "Perhaps we should get in line. They always start boarding the passengers with the highest row number first."

"Yeah..." He frowned. "Why is that?"

"They do it to save time. So the passengers with the lower row numbers don't block the aisle for the rest of us."

"Wouldn't it make more sense to board all the passengers with window seats first?" he suggested. "I mean, now, people have to get up to let the others in, and by doing so, they block the aisle for the rest of those finding their seats. Boarding window-middle-aisle, would save more time, am I right?"

She patted his chest gently.

"See, that's what you get from solving Sudoku."

"Sudoku boarding," he said, making her laugh.

She looked up at him and gazed into his eyes, and once again he began to feel tearful. She looked so cute with her glasses on, and this time, her glasses had slipped down her nose, just a little bit, but the sight was enough to break his heart.

He decided that he would tell his wife the truth as soon as they got back from the funeral.

26 C

2 LOVE

Friday evening

As the yellow taxi kept circling the tall building, the gentleman in the apartment on the top floor was still staring at the ceiling. But he was almost finished.

The people who lived in the tall building didn't need to go to work. Even though the majority of them probably had jobs, they didn't need to earn a living. The concerns of those living in this building were only of the petty kind. They had the sorts of problems with no actual impact on their quality of life. One might say the residents of the tall building lived "carefree" lives.

The building itself was a stunning Art Deco-inspired tower, which rose above all the other buildings in the neighborhood. The building had its own spa, and a gym area with a swimming pool for the residents to enjoy. Several exclusive restaurants in the neighborhood offered fine dining experiences, each one specializing in their own cultural cuisine. So, therefore, the residents of the tall building, always had outstanding dinner options of their choice. Many designer fashion stores and luxury retailers were in the neighborhood as well, and most of them understood the shopping experience itself to be a priority and offered their customers champagne and strawberries while the customers were making their selections.

As the yellow taxi once again turned the corner of the building, once again the driver must have noticed no person waiting at the entrance of the building who matched the specific description given to him. That was because Dr. Sherman was still lying in his bed and staring at his ceiling, though he was almost finished.

The bedroom was the main reason Dr. Sherman had bought the apartment. Even if it didn't have an en-suite bathroom, it did have a magnificent view of Seattle and the Pacific Ocean. The good doctor loved to sit on the balcony and admire his view. He would watch the people below on the street, who were so tiny and small that to him they looked like toys in a sandbox.

Dr. Sherman had bought the apartment for some measly three-million dollars a few years before as more of an investment than a place to live. He figured the apartment would increase far more in value then the cost of owning it, even if the apartment had a hundred-percent mortgage. The apartment also gave him easy access to many of his patients.

The main reason Dr. Sherman had earned his doctor's degree was in order to please his father, and most importantly to get access to his grandfather's trust fund. He quickly discovered, though, that he had no desire to help people with their illnesses or discomforts. Just the mere thought of what people expected from a doctor made him sick to his stomach. He did, however, put his doctor's degree to good use, as he became a private practitioner who specialized in discreet house calls. Free of charge, he'd visit his patients and prescribe them the medicine of their choice. He was basically a drug dealer with a doctor's degree.

If any of Dr. Sherman's patients actually needed medical care, he'd recommend a specialist he was associated with, not only earning a small commission on the side, but also, more significantly, relieving him of the ordeal of actually engaging in doctoring. However, if the patient was an attractive female, he would try to put his education to good use and help his patient—or at least give the impression that he tried.

Dr. Sherman prescribed and delivered all the medicine personally, but more notably, he sold the medicine to his patients for ridiculously high prices. He, in some sense, had his own private pharmacy located in an apartment building that he indirectly but actually owned. His childhood friend owned and ran the pharmacy, and the owner of the building was on paper the doctor's wife's stepbrother, who thought signing a particular document made him the co-owner of a local basketball team. The deal also included season tickets and a huge variety of supporter gear. His wife's stepbrother was so pleased with the deal that he, in fact, kept his promise not to share this information with his younger and much brighter stepsister.

Technically, the doctor didn't charge his childhood friend any rent. Even though his friend paid the rent each month, the doctor gave it all back in cash, so his friend got a free business space and the benefit of deducting the cost of the rent on his income taxes. In return, Dr. Sherman had access to his friend's pharmacy, and he could come and go as he pleased. He only paid normal retail price for the medicine he prescribed and sold to his patients at a premium.

The rent income from the apartments in the building pretty much covered the cost of owning the building, except for maintenance and cleaning. However, that expense was a small one, and the good doctor always made sure to pay the janitor and the cleaning lady in cash, so he wouldn't be on the hook for any benefits or employee taxes. Since his patients always paid him in cash, the doctor always had plenty of it, and he made sure to pay for their medicine in cash as well.

Dr. Sherman's wife was a very fortunate woman. She had all the privileges anyone could ask for in a carefree life, such as a personal maid, a personal driver, and most desirably, a credit card without any spending limit. The doctor's wife knew he'd bought the apartment a few years back, and Dr. Sherman was sure his wife knew for what purpose he intended to use it. But his wife didn't seem to care about what he did as long as he did it with discretion.

Mrs. Sherman's husband was the true definition of a perfect gentleman, and he was now almost finished.

Dr. Sherman could easily afford a pedicure, but like most men, he didn't care about the welfare of his feet, or the welfare of other human beings. His toenails were as dirty and disgusting as they were long. The big toe on his right foot had a minor infection of some sort, just where the nail attached to the skin of the toe, and all of Dr. Sherman toes were drenched in the usual sweat. Combined with today's growing infection in his big toe and a slight but distinct smell of fungus, this all resulted in a disgusting odor of human decay.

Dr. Sherman's bedroom had a luxurious wall-to-wall carpet with an oriental design, and even though the fireplace was fake, it still created a 'harmonious environment with a natural glow.' Above the fireplace, a gigantic television was mounted on the wall, and it probably had all the features one could possibly need, but none of that mattered since the television was off. Even if the television had been on, it probably wouldn't have made any difference at this particular time, since it was moving up and down against the wall, leaving any potential viewer with a shaking image.

Dr. Sherman was usually finished by this time, but for some reason he'd lasted longer than usual. As the television kept moving up and down, now at an even faster pace, the young woman above his naked, sweating and frankly stinking body reassured herself that the good doctor was just about to finish. Dr. Sherman's bedroom had no clocks, but she was certain she was running out of time. She feared her legs would cramp before Dr. Sherman was finished. She reminded herself that Dr. Sherman had to finish.

Wait, are you holding back for my benefit?

She considered if perhaps she had overestimated Dr. Sherman's self-knowledge. Was his fear of reality so strong that he could delude himself to such an extent he might actually believe she enjoyed this ordeal?

Do you really think a man like you could ever give me an orgasm? I can barely notice you.

"I'm almost there, babe," she said in a shaky voice.

She grabbed his hairy legs, and started to move her neck back and forth, as she picked up the pace.

"You can do it. I'm almost there," she said, moaning.

She thought about all the money and how she would spoil herself when this was finally over. The adrenaline added to the excitement of her upcoming reward.

I'm almost there. It's not far to the finish line.

"I'm almost there. Don't give in, babe," she said, and kept moaning.

Then she clawed her nails into his kneecaps and shook her legs as if she were spasming. She twisted her toes apart with her feet on his stomach, and then she made a loud gasping sound, followed by an even louder moan. She exhaled, pulling in her abdominal muscles and brushed her hair behind her ears.

Dr. Sherman was, apparently, finished.

"Thanks, babe," she said. "I needed that."

"My pleasure," the good doctor responded in a tone of satisfaction.

She took a deep breath, and as she climbed off him, she created a strong but silent internal cough. Dr. Sherman's moaning confirmed her strategy had been successful.

"Sorry about that," she said, and tried her best to look sweet and innocent. "Don't move, or you'll get it all over the carpet. Just stay still. I'll get you a towel."

While she walked across the bedroom, she made sure to have her hand between her thighs, to emphasize to Dr. Sherman what was at stake. While he watched her leave the room, she felt certain the good doctor was calculating the cost of removing semen from his expensive wall-to-wall carpet. As she ran toward the bathroom, she peered into the hallway and made sure her purse was still on the console table—she noticed the envelope.

She turned the water on at the sink in the bathroom, and then quickly ran into the hallway. As anticipated, the purse snaps were so tight she had difficulty opening them, but that was also the reason she'd chosen this particular purse. A purse with a zipper would be easier to open, but it might encourage Dr. Sherman to leave the envelope inside her purse, as he'd done on a previous occasion. She'd hidden the card in one of the sleeves of the thick sweater she'd folded tightly and placed in the bottom of her purse.

Now, she gently opened the sliding door to the hallway closet, trying to make as little sound as possible, and then she placed the card between a pair of his shoes. That way, it could appear as if the card had fallen out of his jacket, and even if he'd already discovered that his card was missing, he might well have failed to see the card between his shoes. Of course, Dr. Sherman probably hadn't noticed his card was missing. She knew he didn't use it every day, and the card had been missing for less than twenty-four hours. But the further she analyzed the situation, the less she cared.

I only took a small amount. He'll never notice, and even if he did, what's he going to do about it? Call the cops? I don't think so.

She had obviously overestimated Dr. Sherman's intelligence. He'd almost caught her when she took the card from his jacket last night, but the good doctor was dumb enough to believe she only wanted to smell his jacket.

She took a couple of towels from the bathroom linen closet and moistened one towel in lukewarm water, before she returned to the bedroom. As instructed, Dr. Sherman was still lying in his bed covered in his own semen.

"Took you long enough."

"What?" she responded and pretended to be surprised by the remark.

"I said, it took you long enough." A look of annoyance stared directly at her.

"I was waiting for the water to get warm," she said with a sad expression, and then held up the moistened towel for him to see.

"Oh, yeah..." Dr. Sherman's look of displeasure quickly turned to a micro-expression of guilt.

She wiped away most of the semen with the dry towel, and then used the moistened towel and gently caressed his lower body, making sure his navel was free from all the nasty liquid. She noticed him staring at her breasts.

"See. No harm done. Nice and clean," she said.

Dr. Sherman looked suspiciously at his stomach.

"Nice job, lady."

"That's what I do."

She winked at him, but he didn't notice, because he was staring at her breasts again. Suddenly, she felt a chill running down her spine, as she realized Dr. Sherman could get another erection just by staring at her.

"I gotta run, babe," she said. "I got a taxi waiting."

She could feel him staring at her as she bent over to pick up her garments which he'd so randomly spread across the bedroom floor. She went into the hallway and quickly put her clothes on. She didn't bother to put on her socks or underwear, instead placing them in her purse, before putting on her thick sweater.

Suddenly, Dr. Sherman's disgusting naked body emerged into the hallway, and as he came toward her, his sweaty feet left footprints across the marble tile floor.

"You look hot."

"Thanks," she said, and smiled wide.

Dr. Sherman started to laugh in his distinctive way. His laughter sounded more like a silenced sneeze than a laugh, a never-ending series of muted sneezes and gasping chuckles. She couldn't stand his laughter, which was probably the worst of all his disgusting characteristics.

You sound like a pig gasping for air.

"I always look hot," she added.

"I was just about to say that," the doctor claimed. "You stole my line."

"Snooze, you lose."

"But I wasn't fast on the trigger either, was I?"

"You were amazing, babe," she said as she looked him in the eyes and smiled. "You rocked my world."

She bent over to pick up her shoes. As she put on her second shoe, she lost her balance, causing her head to eventually collide with the closet door.

"You're all right?"

"Yeah, I'm all right," she moaned.

She felt a small lump on her forehead. "I'm not used to wearing low heels. And my knees are still shaking from the orgasm you gave me. So, it's really your fault."

Still on her knees, she turned her head around and stared directly into his naked crotch, as he seemingly had come to help her up. His distinctive laughter caused his genitals and his oversized stomach to shake right in front of her.

Can you even begin to comprehend how repulsive you are?

Can't you see the mirror beside you?

"Is that for me?" she asked, as she stood up and then reached for the envelope, and got some distance between herself and Dr. Sherman, who answered her question with a single nod. She put the envelope in her purse without any hesitation.

"Can you help me with the taxi, babe?"

The little twitch across Dr. Sherman's face revealed that he was slightly insulted. He knew she had an envelope with cash, and that she could easily pay for the taxi herself. But after some hesitation, Dr. Sherman went to the closet and fished out a crumbled hundred-dollar bill from his jacket. He gently grabbed her left hand, placed the bill in her palm, and closed it.

"Always the gentleman," she said.

"So, I see you next week?"

"Only if you want to."

"I got a lot on my plate right now, but I'll call... I mean,

I'll e-mail you over the weekend."

Before she left, she made sure to kiss the good doctor on the mouth, not only to show her appreciation, but also to remind herself that she wasn't a prostitute.

As the yellow taxi, once more, passed the entrance of the tall building, the driver must have been relieved to see a person in front of the entrance matching the description given to him: A smoking-hot blonde with a beige purse.

She saluted the taxi driver and then threw her cigarette onto the sidewalk.

The first thing she noticed upon entering the vehicle was the taxi meter, and that her ride had so far cost her about seventy dollars.

"Thanks for waiting for me. Not a lot of people would do that," she said. "I hope you can forgive me?"

The driver seemed to check his rearview mirror for sarcasm, but she made sure he didn't detect any.

"As long as you showed up, then I have no problem."

"There are people who just don't show up?"

"Some people."

"That's so disrespectful," she said. "Not only do they waste your time, they steal your gasoline as well."

The taxi driver seemed to be nodding in agreement.

"I only have cash," she said, and then ground her teeth in the rearview mirror for the driver to see. "Two hundred-dollar bills."

"Okay."

She rolled her eyes as she heard the taxi driver's inconclusive response, but she made sure the driver didn't notice.

Then, it suddenly hit her.

An emotional wave, swept her off her feet and slammed her down against the rock-hard ground. Suddenly, she felt lonely, vulnerable, and small. But she anticipated nothing less. She was used to it by now. But sex without chemistry was no different from a hangover, and a small amount of alcohol would incapacitate a specific part of her brain, therefore relieving her of the regret of chemical-less sex, and the guilt of potentially creating the wrong offspring.

She decided to have a drink as soon as she got to the airport.

She knew what love was.

Love was a misinterpreted neurological reaction, caused by the release of neurotransmitters as the brain detected an individual who matched the mental impression of a childhood role model. "Love" was no more than a simple urge to remain with one's parents as a child in order to ensure one's safety.

Love is nothing more than emotional ripples from a childhood past, for fools to explore and for imbeciles to enjoy.

Her heart rate slowed down and she began to feel more at ease.

To her annoyance, the taxi driver probably had plenty of change, because he didn't stop the taximeter when it reached one-hundred dollars.

Seeing the airport entry gates made her nervous about the flight, and she decided to have a smoke before going into the airport. A drink was what she really needed, but this was her last opportunity to smoke before the flight. She noticed the sign as she took out her last cigarette.

She spotted the woman almost immediately. She could tell by the way the woman walked that this person lived an unremarkable life and was going to cause a problem for sure —an assertive, know-it-all who had to meddle with other people's lives at every given opportunity.

"You can't smoke here," the unremarkable woman barked at her.

"We're outdoors, aren't we?"

"You can't smoke by the entrance. Read the sign."

The unremarkable woman with gray hair, and who could stand to lose a few pounds, then pointed toward the sign on the wall.

She refused to turn her head to look at the sign. "Do you

even work here?"

"No, but I can get someone who does if you don't obey the rules."

"What the hell is your problem, lady?" she hissed, and then stomped on her cigarette. "Get a life!"

"Those are the rules."

What is it with people and their constant desire to interfere with other people's lives? Is their self-esteem so low, they have to seize every opportunity they can to point out the flaws of other people in order to feel better about themselves?

She needed a drink now more than ever, and she quickly made her way to the nearest bar. On the way, she spoke out loud to herself.

"Those are the rules," she said in a demeaning and whining voice.

Any woman would notice the pathetic loser sitting at the end of the bar, and judging by the female repellent force-field surrounding him, it appeared that all of the female customers did notice him and made sure to order their drinks from the opposite side of the bar. The spotlight enhanced his lonely and vulnerable personality and also emphasized his qualities as a human dartboard. She gave him a small but polite smile as she approached the bar and pretended to contemplate what drink to order.

"What's your poison?" the loser instantly asked her.

She pretended not to hear him, but made sure not to ignore him. The question, however, made her think of a past encounter with a Norwegian man. When she'd asked if he was married, the man responded by claiming he was having a detoxification—meaning he was going through a divorce.

Apparently, the Norwegian people used the same word for married as they did for poison. She thought the fact was amusingly coherent. The word in question was the same word as "gift" in English, which in retrospect turned out to be very ironic, considering the Norwegian man was definitely not a gentleman.

"What's your poison?" the loser asked once more.

"I beg your pardon?" she responded in a flawless British accent.

"Can I buy you a drink?" The loser had a startled look.

"I suppose you *may* buy me a drink. I was just about to order a double brandy."

"Double brandy it is. Bartender! A double brandy for my new friend!"

The loser made eye contact with her, and then swallowed once in what appeared to be an attempt to hide his nervousness.

"So, you're from England?"

"Wales," she said, and looked him in the eyes.

Her answer threw him off long enough for the bartender to serve her the drink she so eagerly wanted. *Bullseye*, she thought, as she congratulated herself. Then she raised her glass in salute to her defeated opponent.

"You, my good sir, are a true gentleman," she said in the same flawless accent.

She was gone as quickly as the brandy was. Then she went and treated herself to a dubious meal at a Chinese food stand before finding her gate.

The waiting area there was almost full, and people had begun to form a line in front of the counter. It wouldn't be long before they boarded, but she still saw no sign of him. She began to wonder if he'd cancelled, but then he might have notified her by e-mail. She logged into her e-mail account using her cell phone to check whether she had a message from him, and to her surprise, she actually felt disappointed when she discovered the empty inbox.

Despite the alcohol, she still felt nervous about the flight. The alcohol didn't erase the mental image of a horrific crash scenario. She tried to reassure herself that the odds were in her favor, and the likelihood of a fatal outcome was slim. But as she stared out the terminal windows at the alarmingly empty cockpit, her intuition told her not to get on the plane.

Suddenly, she hoped he wouldn't show up as planned, and then she would have no reason to be on this flight. She could just go home, relax, enjoy her own company, and sleep in her own bed. She began to ponder how to exit the departure hall and what the procedure was for leaving. She assumed she had to check out of her flight before leaving the airport.

But then she saw him. He conspicuously paraded his way down the departure hall, and unknowingly imitated an oversized penguin. Staring at him almost caused her to throw up the outsized fast-food meal she'd just consumed. As anticipated, he was dressed for the occasion, and obviously deceiving himself into believing the layer of clothes on his back could ever compensate for the cruel miscalculation of nature. The chewing gum didn't remove the bad taste in her mouth, or the horrific memory of having sex with such a repulsive man.

As he approached her, she made sure to turn her head away from him. She didn't want anyone to understand the two of them were an item. She'd worked briefly as a temp at the airport during the summer, and her biggest fear was that a former colleague would see them together and realize what kind of person she really was.

"Hi," the *penguin* disobediently said.

With a short, stiff smile, she glanced at his chest for a brief second, only to acknowledge his presence. She noticed the coffee cup in his hand. Despite her numerous appeals for him not to greet her in public, he'd once again ignored her request. But she caught no condescending or gasping expressions from the rest of the passengers, so she assumed no one had noticed.

And why would they? Why would anyone believe such a beautiful person as I would ever be with such a dreadful person like him?

His only outstanding quality as a human being was his desire. But his desire was also his greatest weakness, and when she had explained to him what love was, it had only increased his longing to treat her as a gentleman would.

Love is when you give, without expecting anything in return, she'd told him.

32 D

3 GUILT

Friday evening

As the blade of the fantasy knife penetrated his skin, he tried his best to imagine the sharp pain it would have caused.

That excruciating pain.

A woman wearing high heels walked past his table, and he was distracted by the sudden smell of perfume. A spicy floral mix of violet and roses. He closed his eyes completely and tried to focus even harder on the sharp pain each time the imaginary knife pierced his skin. He reminded himself that his life was unpleasant. He was alive, breathing, moving, but no more than that.

It's not like I'm enjoying life.

His brain started to respond, and he felt the level of discomfort dropping. As the feeling of guilt decreased, he decided to give it another chance. 'It' being the delicious apple pie he'd purchased at the airport café. He thought his choice was as obvious as the sales pitch. He glanced at the counter and read the sign once more.

As American as apple pie can be,
made with local apples grown
right here in Washington state

The scent of coffee and fresh apple pie defeated the smell of old perfume in a one-sided air battle, and the floral mix never had a chance. Though the scoop of ice cream served on top of the pie had almost entirely melted, and the pie crust had turned wet and soggy, nonetheless, the taste was sweet and delicious. The amount of sugar and fat sparked his brain to reward him with a solid dose of dopamine, leaving him with a sensation of joy, and therefore, indirectly, increasing his level of guilt and self-loathing. As he finished his coffee, the imaginary knife frantically stabbed his neck, slicing his arteries, crushing his larynx, and bringing him a sense of relief.

A young, female employee passed his table, and he noticed how the young woman glanced at him just as she passed his shoulder. He then observed a happy couple across the room sharing what appeared to be an omelet. They seemed quite content together and enjoying each other's company. The man couldn't take his eyes off the woman. Suddenly, the young employee came toward him, her eyes focusing on the floor as she approached his table.

"Did you enjoy your apple pie, sir?"

He wasn't sure how to answer that question. "It was delicious."

"Will there be anything else?"

"No, I'm fine, but thank you just the same."

The young woman quickly cleared the table, and as she did, she bit her lower lip and exposed her teeth. She suddenly leaned in toward him, close enough for him to feel the heat of her body.

"Four customers are at the counter waiting for a table, so maybe..." The waitress trailed off.

Now he noticed the group of people by the counter, holding their trays of food and waiting in despair to eat.

"Oh, you want me to leave?"

"If you don't mind?" the waitress asked with an apologetic tone.

"No, I don't mind."

As he gathered his few belongings, he felt as though the rest of the customers were watching him, judging him, and wondering what he'd done wrong. On his way out, he felt as if his old high school coach had substituted another player for him, and he now did the walk of shame and was relegated to the bench. He left the café with a feeling of rejection and insignificance. He felt as if he wasn't worthy of doing business there. But the feeling of guilt was gone, and so was the imaginary knife.

He arrived at the gate early and found many seats available, so he selected a seat the furthest away from the counter, one with the back against the wall. An old man was sitting on the row opposite him, with a beard as white as his hair. The old man must have been at least thirty years older than he, but despite all the wrinkles on his face, the old man still looked quite healthy and elegant.

He noticed a woman and a young child entering the waiting area. The young boy was obviously upset, screaming and crying as he tried to break free from the woman's firm grip. The boy finally broke free, but the chase was over within seconds after his escape. The scene reminded him of all the times he used to chase after his mother, begging and pleading with her to stay.

He closed his eyes, and bowed his head, as he thought of his own childhood. As a young boy at his most vulnerable age, his mother would suddenly and for no apparent reason, threaten to abandon him. '*I'm leaving you and I'm never coming back*,' she would yell. He remembered running toward her in the hallway, and how terrified he felt of his mother reaching the front door before he could get to her. He used to grab onto one of her legs, holding on as hard as he could, knowing she would be unable to leave for as long as he managed to hold on. '*Please don't leave me, Mommy. Don't go. I love you*,' he would scream, at the same time crying tears of despair. Then his mother would wipe the tears off his face and comfort him, caressing him with hugs and kisses, and perhaps offering him some candy or ice cream. Then, suddenly, his mother was happy again, and they would enjoy each other's company, watching television together, or going for a walk together. He promised himself never to let her out of his sight, making sure his mother was always within his reach. This promise was hard for a young boy to keep, and as soon as he devoted his attention elsewhere, he would hear the shouts from the hallway, and his chase for survival was back on again.

His mother's threats of abandoning him never ceased, but as he grew older and became more independent, his fear of abandonment decreased. His mother would stand in the hallway and shout endlessly, and sometimes she would actually leave, but she'd always come back, and when she did, she would be furious at him, accusing him of being a bad son and not caring about her.

When he finally became a teenager, his mother had lost all interest in him, and they hadn't spoken since. All these years as an adult, he always thought his mother suffered from depression. But lately, it had come to his attention, that his mother wasn't depressed. On the contrary, she thought she was perfect.

As he opened his eyes, he now stared directly into the eyes of the old man, both of them fixated on each other's eyes. He felt that they were having a staring contest.

Eventually, the old man gave him a clever smile, got up from his seat, and slowly came toward him. The old man sat down next to him, extended his index finger, and put on a huge smile.

"I know what you need, son."

The old man reached into his bag, moving its contents around, obviously looking for something. Then the old man took out a sweater, and gave it to him to hold. The sweater had a distinctive smell, but at the same time was almost odorless. The thought of butter suddenly appeared in his head. The old man eventually found what he was looking for. He reached into his bag and took out a couple of bananas, and holding onto one of the bananas encouraged him to break off the other.

"Here you go, son."

He was reluctant to accept the fruit as he knew it wouldn't be good for him.

"Go on, it's good for you," the old man stated.

He felt as he didn't have any choice but to accept the kind offer.

"Thanks."

"It will get your blood sugar up. Trust me, you'll feel better."

He felt they were having a nice moment together, he and the old man, eating their bananas in synch with each other. He felt as though they were breaking bread. And at the same time, he felt the compulsive urge to injure the old man. His mind urged him to defend himself from the threat that harmed him. He needed to strike in order to remove the pain. The level of guilt was high before he received the kind gesture from the old man, but now the level was so unbearable even his imaginary knife had lost its edge.

Do you have any idea of how much pain you're causing me? How much this hurts?

"Don't you feel better now?" the old man asked him.

He didn't know how to answer the question, so instead, he just smiled and raised his eyebrows. Then he took the banana peel in the old man's hand and made his way over to the trash can. He told himself not to ruin the moment for the banana man, and not to excuse himself and walk away as he usually did, as it would only make him feel even guiltier.

"So where are you going, son?"

"Alaska."

"I know you are. So am I, and it says so on the screen."

The old man pointed toward the gate monitor.

He smiled and raised his head in acknowledgement to the old man. He was well aware the old man expected a more specific answer on the subject, but he wasn't going to give him one, because he knew exactly where he was going.

North of Anchorage was a small town called Willow with just a few thousand residents. The town only had the bare minimum of necessary retail and public resources. On the outskirts of Willow, there used to be a house, a barn-red and white house, a house that could easily fit into a children's tale. The yard had several apple trees, and even if most of the house residents enjoyed apples, the only purpose of the trees was to attract the thieves, and every apple thief paid the ultimate price as they were shot and killed, all year round.

The house itself wasn't important. In fact, he had no idea if the house was still there or if anyone was living in it. He'd lived in the house at a young age, only for a short period, but for enough time for him to hate everything that reminded him of that house; he even hated the color red.

On the north side of the house was a small canyon, leading into the deep forest. Even after all these years, he could still picture it in front of him, convinced he would find the path that led to the cave, where he had spent so many hours. The cave was actually a large crack in the mountain, wide enough for a teenage boy to enter, but not too narrow for an adult to penetrate. He was convinced he could still squeeze his way in. The cave was his final destination on this trip; it was the end of his journey.

He thought the old man looked sad and disappointed with his lack of response, and felt as though he should engage in a conversation with him. He started to stress as he tried to think of something to say.

"Are you visiting your family in Alaska?"

"Sort of. I'm going to meet my son, but it's for business purposes. He's trying to land a new deal up in Anchorage, and he has a meeting tomorrow and asked me to sit in. We supply hotels with various breakfast accessories, mostly jam and marmalade. You know, those small containers you find in a basket at the breakfast buffet."

"So, you're the owner of the company?"

"I still own a part of the company, but I'm retired now, and my daughter and son run the company, but I founded it and built it from scratch—You know, you remind me of my son. He's also a strong, tall man. He's very popular with the ladies, perhaps a bit too popular. I keep telling him to find a courteous woman and get married and start a family."

After a short pause, the old man gave him a curious smile.

"I don't see a wedding ring on your finger, son."

"No, I'm not married."

He looked at his left hand and extended his fingers. He felt surprised by how old his hand looked. He was used to his face growing older, but he'd never noticed that his hands were aging as well. He couldn't help but stare at his thumb, puzzling over the lizard-like skin surrounding it, and all the visible veins on the dorsal side of his hand.

The old man must have noticed the distress in his expression.

"I wouldn't worry about that, son. I bet women are standing in line to meet a handsome man like you, and before you know it, you'll have a family of your own."

He kept staring at his hands, making sure they weren't moving, even though his mind instructed them to. As his level of adrenaline and testosterone rose, the compulsive urge to strike the old man grew stronger. His mind pleaded with him to defend himself and to strike the threat, which caused him harm. However, he was very used to having such emotions and his mind couldn't deceive him anymore. He tried to focus on the exchange with the old man, but he quickly realized he'd lost the tread of the conversation.

Is the old man talking about marmalade?

As he drifted away again, he began to wonder how the old man would, indeed, react if he actually were to strike him. Here he was, being kind to a complete stranger, sharing his food with him, and then suddenly, and for no apparent reason, that person rewards his benevolence by punching him in the eye. The image actually brought a smile to his face, and the old man must have noticed, because he suddenly stopped talking, and the staring contest was back on.

"I know what you're thinking, son," the old man eventually said.

For a brief moment, he felt scared and exposed.

"Marmalade is just a different kind of jam," the old man said and shook his head. "No, that's where you're wrong. You see, jam is made out of berries, basically. All jams are pretty much the same. It's just the number of berries or sugar that varies with each product. Marmalade, however, can be made from a variety of different berries, fruit, spice or herbs. And one could make it with or without the pulp, and even use the peel of the fruit, providing the peel is cut properly, that is."

He gave the old man a nod in recognition of his wisdom about marmalade.

"That's why we're so competitive. We've got the best marmalade. So, when you get the chance, you should try our orange marmalade. The secret is cardamom and pears, and of course, orange peel, the peel is important. That's *Lady Jane Marmalade*. Jane is my mother, and she helped me with many of the recipes. She's still alive by the way, ninety-three years old."

"Perhaps it's due to the marmalade," he said, making the marmalade man laugh.

Then the same man continued his story about the impact marmalade had had on his family history. This time the old man spoke with even more enthusiasm.

As the number of people in the room grew, so did his urge to escape reality. He could see the *box* in the corner of his eyes.

At a young age, he used to seek refuge under his bed, sliding the blanket all the way down to the floor, and in the darkest corner under the bed, he would curl up with a pillow in his lap, with nothing to do but to count the time and wait for another day to pass. The solitude gave him refuge. At times, when he had no such place to hide, he created an imaginary box in the corner of his eyes.

He could see the box now in his peripheral vision. The lid was open. All he had to do was to acknowledge its existence, and the box would consume him and all his content. However, this time, the box started to shake, and it slowly disappeared.

"You're falling asleep, son."

The old man gently shook his shoulder and brought him back to reality.

"Sorry about that."

"Don't be. I know you're tired, and I know I talk too much. In fact, I think that's why my son wants me to attend tomorrow's meeting. Once I get started, they'll give in just to end the meeting."

"I think I'll go and splash some water in my eyes."

"You want me to save your seat?"

"No, I'm fine. They'll start the boarding soon anyway."

"Well, you have a pleasant flight then."

"You too, and thanks for the banana."

"Don't mention it."

"Lady Jane Marmalade," he pronounced clearly, as he got up and left.

In the corner of his eyes, he could see the old man's face light up with joy and enthusiasm. Behind his back, he gave the old man a discreet wave, as he kept walking.

He had no desire to splash water in his eyes, but he decided to do it anyway. If anything, it would erase the lie he'd just told the old man when he excused himself.

When he returned to the gate, he noticed that a young woman now occupied the seat next to the marmalade man. She was perhaps in her late twenties, and she appeared to be taking an interest in the exchange with the old man, or at least she pretended to do so. Perhaps it was just a way for her to distract herself from the mobile phone in her hand, and trying to convince herself that she didn't have an addiction.

The sun had descended and was replaced by the peaceful darkness of the night. The reassuring glow of the landing lights illuminated the airstrip and gave him a sense of relief, while the thought of what would come next gave him a morbid feeling of accomplishment, and for a brief moment, he actually felt happy.

Soon it will all be over.

He noticed the happy couple from the coffee shop was waiting at the same gate as he was. They appeared to be mutually solving a crossword puzzle, and once again, they seemed very contented together, smiling and leaning in toward each other. This time, he noticed their wedding rings, and he began to wonder if the happy couple perhaps was on their honeymoon, which he thought could explain their overly affectionate feeling toward each other.

Seeing the two men in pilots' uniforms made him feel both meek and vulnerable. He felt as though his life was in the palms of their hands, much as a patient would feel when greeted by the surgeon before an operation. He had no other choice but to trust the pilots with his life and only hope they'd carry out their duties and nothing more. The emotion puzzled him, and he couldn't understand why he felt vulnerable, as he had nothing to lose. Suddenly, he felt insecure about everything, and his intuition told him something was wrong. He shouldn't be on this flight, and he shouldn't proceed with his plan.

Except for their matching uniforms with white shirts and black ties, the two pilots were remarkably different from one another, not only in their physical appearance, but also in their behavior. One pilot was tall and muscular and showed no interest in the passengers—if anything, he appeared to be trying his best not to notice them. The pilot looked furious, but at the same time absent, and his pulse was hammering on his neck.

The other pilot was shorter and much more inelegant, and he obviously loved the attention the uniform brought him, as he proceeded through the waiting area with a big smile. This pilot seemed to be paying extra attention to a particular woman, but she showed no interest in him. The woman appeared to be about twenty years younger than her unwanted and unappealing suitor.

Don't embarrass yourself, buddy. The uniform can only do so much.

As the pilots marched along to their responsibilities, he noticed a female employee had appeared behind the counter, signaling that their boarding the plane was imminent. He noticed the old man was still in his seat, but his young neighbor had left her seat, as were the rest of the passengers about to do, thereby leaving the old man with the entire row for himself. The marmalade man showed no interest in rising from his seat; he wasn't about to join the stampede.

Looking at the old man made him think of the men he'd served with, and the nickname they gave him. He also thought of the man he'd killed in battle.

"May I help you, sir?"

He flinched. "What?"

"Do you need help scanning your boarding pass?"

He realized he was holding up the line. After some hesitation, he slowly placed his boarding pass onto the scanner. The beeping sound from the machine confirmed that his plan was still in motion.

When he entered the plane, a beautiful female flight attendant greeted him with a smile, and he pretended not to notice her. She appeared to be about the same age as he.

He placed his blazer in the overhead storage bin and sat down in his seat. He tilted his head back and as he closed his eyes, the first word that popped up in his head was "marmalade."

31 C

4 JOY

Friday evening

The sign reminded her of the jacket she wore. The jacket he'd bought for her birthday. He'd forgotten to take the tag off, so she knew where he'd bought it and how much he'd paid for it.

MIND THE GAP

Her heart rate increased as she stepped out of the bus, and took in the scenery. She experienced the excitement only an airport could bring. The feeling was one of liberty along with a thrill of defying the laws of nature. She rarely got the opportunity to fly, but when she did, she felt like an explorer. She was intrigued to discover the adventures of life, and she was open to new ideas. She had a very relaxed attitude toward life and what might lie ahead.

On her way into the airport, she noticed the golden retriever by the entry. Her first impulse was to pet the dog, but then she noticed the sign that told her not to. The dog didn't want to be disturbed. The dog was working. Then her mind began to drift away, as it usually did.

Who picked up after a seeing eye dog? Did the blind man pick up? How could he know where to find the object? Did the dog give him some kind of signal? Did the blind man use the cane to locate it?

The chain of thought made her feel guilty, and she told herself to stop drifting before her mind spun out of control. But it was too late, and in her next mental image, the blind man was on his knees, with his face close to the ground, and he kept sniffing as he attempted to locate the target.

Stop that. It's not nice to make fun of other people, and especially people with a disability. How would you like it if people were laughing at you? Think about your loan application. The bank employees are probably laughing at your expense.

She made a pledge to herself to pick up after a seeing eye dog if ever the opportunity presented itself. Then her mind drifted off again as she began reflecting on the symbiotic relationship between a person and a dog.

What did dogs make of all this? Did dogs understand the law and structure of society? Could dogs be that perceptive? Or were they oblivious to why?

I sure do enjoy walking with you. It's my favorite thing in the whole world—well except for food that is. But do you have to collect my poop every time we enjoy a walk together? Must you do that? Can't you see how embarrassing it is to me? Can't you just leave it there? What do you do with it anyway? You two-legged freak.

Her excitement grew as she waited in line to go through security. Soon she would be airborne, actually flying in the air, and seeing the world from a bird's perspective. She noticed that one of her fellow explorers took her shoes off for the x-ray machine, and just then, she realized she'd forgotten today's exercises.

Important note to self: Exercise knees as soon as you enter the hotel room.

The person who invented high heels should stand trial for crimes against humanity, and she would be a key witness. At one point, her knees had been so bad she considered quitting physiotherapy, and simply donating her knees to science.

She turned her cell phone off before she sent it through the x-ray; he still hadn't responded to her text message.

The departure hall was full of fellow explorers. A pulsating stream of people from around the world, a sea of faces, and each one looked different from the other. All of them with equal qualities, but each one with a different melody. Some were high, while others were low. Some were dark, while others were bright, but either way, they were all part of the greatest symphony ever created, and brought together in a fellow interest of exploring the world.

Seeing other people brings her joy. She was fascinated by the diversity of mankind, and was amazed by how every person looked different from another. Millions and millions of people, and every one unique in their own special ways. Then her mind drifted away—as usual.

When did the word million become so common in the American housing market? What happened to thousands?

She didn't have anything remotely close to a quarter of a million dollars, or any other fraction of a million dollars. However, she might be able to raise two hundred and fifty thousand dollars, if her loan application came through. But the chance of that happening was about the same as of her winning the state lottery. Before she applied for the loan, she actually reflected if sharing the state of her finances with anyone else was in fact irresponsible.

Could a person die from laughing too hard?

I'm sorry, Miss Davis, I'm afraid we can't approve of your loan application at this time. Unfortunately, the person who reviewed your application seems to have died from a massive stroke. You wouldn't happen to know anything about that, would you, Miss Davis?

She would crack under pressure, and especially if the temperature in the interrogation room was slightly below seventy-four degrees. And given her age, they were bound to try her as an adult—or at least until they got to know her better.

Miss Davies noticed the young couple holding hands, which reminded her to turn her cell phone back on. But she'd received no messages from him. She missed him, and she missed holding his hand. The smell of food and perfume made her both hungry and nauseous. The sight of people enthusiastically spending their money without a concern in the world reminded her of how she used to dream of wealth and the prospect of unlimited shopping. But he'd changed the way she thought. She didn't need any fancy clothes anymore, she only needed to stay warm. She didn't need to impress anyone but him.

A permanent marker is a cruel and dangerous invention, and just like any other weapon of mass destruction, it should only be put to use if absolutely necessary. Writing "8456" on the wall of a public restroom is a great misuse of power. At least the person who wrote "I HATE VANDALISM" showed some creativity. Why would anyone write random numbers on the wall of a public restroom?

8456

On her way out of the restroom, she noticed the young woman freshening her makeup in front of the giant mirror. In the past, Miss Davies would spend a lot of her time in front of a mirror. She would spend a half-hour applying her makeup to perfection, only to spend a few minutes in a store, hoping to impress some store clerk who had no bearing on her life whatsoever. Nowadays, she only wore makeup on special occasions. She must have saved years of her life by dropping the daily mirror routine. And she'd probably saved a lot of money also. Perhaps even a fraction of a million dollars.

The airport had plenty of restaurants to her liking, but they were all crowded, and she ended up ordering a hamburger and fries at a sports bar. Miss Davies noticed the television in the sports bar. The rain had interrupted the schedule, and the game had been replaced with a television show portraying an American family. Which lead to an all-too-familiar question: Why were men such idiots?

Their personalities might be different, but in the end, they were all imbeciles, one way or another. They were so incompetent that they couldn't tell a good offer from a bad one. They couldn't even operate simple equipment, and especially kitchen appliances. An average five-year-old child could outsmart most grown men. Fortunately, large numbers of them were married to smart women who told them what to do. If not, they'd most likely starve to death, or perhaps die while trying to attempt to operate a toaster.

Why didn't anyone make a sitcom about a dumb woman with a clever husband? Could it be because no one had thought of it? Perhaps she could create a sitcom. Perhaps she could write a manuscript, and sell it to a major network for a quarter of a million dollars. Or perhaps she didn't need to write a screenplay. Perhaps she could just pitch the pilot to the network. Perhaps she could star in the pilot also?

Once at the gate, Miss Davies sat down next to an elderly gentleman who she thought looked friendly and familiar. His white beard reminded her of the goat her family had on the farm. She'd named the goat Whitebeard—for obvious reasons.

Whitebeard was a stubborn goat, and he wouldn't do anything that didn't please him. One day, the stubborn goat decided to stand on the railroad tracks. Despite the train bearing down on him, he showed no desire to move, and needless to say, the train didn't swerve. The tale of Whitebeard came to a sudden end.

Once again, Miss Davies checked her cell phone. He still hadn't responded to her text message. The lack of reply wasn't like him. He usually answered right away. She started to become anxious and concerned.

"Where are you going, young lady?" *Whitebeard* suddenly asked.

"Alaska."

"I know you are. It says so on the screen."

Whitebeard pointed toward the gate monitor.

"I'm going to Alaska myself," Whitebeard added.

She felt a bit embarrassed. "Of course, you are."

"So, is it business or pleasure?"

"Neither, I guess," she said, and felt insecure about what to say next. "It's just a weekend trip. It's not as though I had a choice. If the destination was up to me, I would've chosen a warmer destination."

"August is a good month to visit Alaska."

"But it's late August," she responded uneasily.

"The temperature is just fine. I promise."

"I hope you're right," she said. "So, what takes you to Alaska, if I may ask?"

Miss Davies kept one eye on her cell phone as she listened to a wonderful tale about the love and understanding of marmalade.

Her heart skipped a beat when the gate agent eventually announced her flight. Soon, she would be defying the laws of nature. The hair on her arms stood up as she thought of the feeling when pushed back against the seat at takeoff, and the feeling of flying above the clouds and discovering a whole new world. The sudden vibration in her hand startled her, but the message on the screen did just the opposite.

Love you too. Stay safe <3

She loved him more than anything else in the world. There was nothing she wouldn't do for him.

How do you shoot a pilot?

9 A

5 HATRED

Friday evening

The man didn't have a name. He'd lost his name in a shower locker room on a cold November evening in Anchorage, Alaska.

It had been impossible for the boy to pronounce a particular name. If the boy for some reason had to pronounce that exact first name, then the boy would instead choose to pronounce the last name of that specific individual. And if the last name was unknown, then the boy would simply use a pronoun, and if necessary, combine it with the appropriate hand gesture. The name in question only contained two syllables, but pronouncing them was too difficult for the boy.

The airport is empty. I'm all alone. There's no reason to turn my head around and confirm it. The terminal is clear. I'm the only one present. I'm safe.

And I'm not hearing any voices.

As long as his shoes passed through the metal detector, he'd be all right. The airport staff wouldn't think of asking him to remove his shoes. His shoes didn't contain any metal, and there was no reason as to why they wouldn't pass through the metal detector.

Sweat isn't running down my neck. I'm not breathing more heavily than anyone else. I have no reason to be concerned about the future. I'm not going lose my legs.

He was always hot, but he always made sure to cover his skin with fabric. He only wore long sleeves. He assured himself that the note was still in the inside pocket of his blazer. But the noise was louder now and getting harder to ignore. His mental barrier began to crack. His reinforced mental *concrete* could hold no more. He couldn't ignore the voice anymore, and as usual, the voice was that of a male. The voice reminded him that he smelled bad.

He wasn't used to the outside. He preferred the inside. Trapped in his room. His room was harmless. When he was alone, he felt like a normal person. But when surrounded by other people, he felt lonely and isolated.

People can only see what they believe.

You can't see me. I'm fooling you.

"You need to take those shoes off."

His heart skipped a beat, but then he was relieved to see a hand reaching for the frame of the x-ray conveyor belt. The woman behind him was supporting herself against the rail while taking her shoes off. He made sure to turn his head away from the airport employee, hoping it would reduce the risk of enduring the same cruel fate as that of the woman behind him.

He didn't walk; instead, he wobbled. He merely shifted his weight from one foot to the other, and tried his best to put as little weight on his shoes as possible, hoping the landing would be soft and consistent. He moved slowly. Anxiety had a firm grip on him as he approached the metal detector. He made a silent and desperate prayer. The voice reminded him not to get stuck. The machine didn't make a sound. The sympathetic and artificial smile from the woman attending the machine confirmed his fear was uncalled for.

Suddenly, the voice was back, a different voice this time, but still a male voice as it usually was. This time, the voice reminded him that he had no value as a human being. But the words didn't hurt as much as the laughter. The laughter reminded him of the man without a name. That over-enthusiastic joy of witnessing another person being humiliated.

The smoke detector is wrong. There's no fire. The fire was in the past. There's no danger and no reason to be concerned. It's a false alarm. The back of my brain is deceiving me. As soon as the air clears, the alarm will silence.

Breathe. I'm safe now.

Timing was essential, so he made sure to "recharge."

The sensation created by the frontal part of his brain relieved him of the stress and fear detected by the back of his brain. The responding chemistry silenced his alarming anxiety. His mind was different now; the sweet and dark compound in his mouth stimulated it, and brought him a rewarding sensation. People were staring angrily at him, though. The chocolate bar seemed to provoke them.

His eyes sought further energy. He needed to recharge as soon as possible. Fast food wasn't an option, as too many young people were in the restaurant, and he hated to place his order. People didn't approve of his voice, since they found it too bright and feminine. The café was overcrowded. However, the kiosk had plenty of supplies with the right nutritional content. He made sure to open the door to the refrigerator with his sleeve. He had no particular reason for doing so, but merely did it out of habit, because he had done so since he was eight years old.

It was impossible for the boy to touch the same surface that the man with no name had touched. However, if the boy had to touch the surface (for example to open a door), the boy would use his sleeve to protect his skin. If his skin accidentally were to touch the surface, then the boy had to wash his skin as quickly as possible. If a sink wasn't available at that particular time, then the boy would blow on his skin until the warm indentation was no longer noticeable. The boy stopped wearing short sleeves when he was eight years old.

The all-too-familiar container had six varieties of the same product, each one the same size and shape as the others, but with different and inventive coatings. The product was easy to consume while walking and therefore suitable for a person short on time. His taste buds quickly detected the product's sweet and glazed surface. He made sure to devour all six donuts as quickly as possible before he washed them down with cold, sugary soda.

Disliking the experience would be impossible. Whenever a member of the human race was so fortunate as to obtain nutrition high in energy, that person was supposed to consume as much as possible. In order to ensure that the person made the right choice between food high in energy and low in energy, the person was rewarded with a delightful sensation whenever consuming food high in energy.

He was running out of time. The reward wasn't fast enough. He could feel it.

The architectural design was thousands of years old, and it was constructed with amazing precision by the most advanced physical engineering ever known. Electricity ran through the endless number of rooms and hallways in this amazing "structure." At the entry, the electric current was strong, and provided spectators with a bright and clear image of their surroundings. At this part of the structure, the owner was happy to share any impression to any visitors at any time.

For example: One room held images as far as the eyes could see. Another room contained the scents of all aromas the owner had ever detected. The sounds from another room were so powerful they could leave a person devastated or filled with joyful and moving enthusiasm. But the interior in these rooms wasn't by any means unique or special. These rooms were basically the same as one could expect from any other structure.

The content in the vault made the structure unique. The content in the vault contained the very essence that defined the owner. The vault had a display room attached to it, but the owner only allowed a few selected and specific visitors to view the content. The objects presented in the display room would vary tremendously, depending on who the visitors were. More than often, this particular owner would display several trophies, and despite that, none of the trophies had the owner's name on them, the owner would still describe the trophies with great pride and enthusiasm. This particular owner had access to all the secrets within the vault—except for one specific secret.

The lock to that specific secret appeared impenetrable. The lock did, however, have one flaw. It relied on an electric current, and if the owner didn't recharge in time, then the door to the secret vault would open. Despite the owner's determination never to view the content of the secret vault, he still couldn't resist looking whenever the vault of memories opened. This time, the reward was too late. The batteries had run out, and the door to the past slowly opened. And just then, the owner could see a small fragment of its horrific content.

A shower locker room.

And a man without a name.

People couldn't even begin to understand who he really was. They couldn't see the person behind all the camouflage. They were blinded by their own perception. The voice behind his back confirmed it. It was a male voice, as it usually was. This time, the voice reminded him that he was a disgusting human being who didn't deserve to be treated with respect.

You can't see me. I'm fooling you.

You only see what you believe.

But tomorrow, people would finally realize who he was. The note was still in his pocket. The consequences of unveiling himself in public sent a cold shiver down his spine. He feared his public humiliation. He started to feel shame and he knew he would feel even guiltier tomorrow. He started questioning his plan, uncertain if his statement was too strong. But he knew some people would consider him a hero.

Standing in line to use the restroom reminded him of all those times as a child when he used to lock himself into the bathroom stalls at the bus station. With nowhere to go, or nowhere to be, he would sit in solitude, isolated from the rest of the world, with nothing to do but to count the time passing him by. But he was satisfied just sitting there, because the two other alternatives were worse. He could either freeze, or go home.

His anxiety grew as he used the urinal. The smell of salt and chlorine reminded him of the man with no name, and the taste of urine.

It's all in the past. My mind is deceiving me. I'm safe now.

As he washed his hands, he was appalled by his reflection. He couldn't recognize the man in the mirror anymore. His camouflage was too thick. His own relatives probably wouldn't recognize him either. But he didn't care about them. The only person he'd ever cared about was his mother. She was the only person who ever loved him; tomorrow was her funeral.

He wasn't used to seeing his own reflection. He didn't own a full-length mirror. He was afraid of the person he'd become. A person who fantasized torturing every person who ever caused him harm. The torturing images brought him relief and got him through the day. The person he ones was, was gone. Replaced by the beast staring back at him now. The transformation was too slow for him to notice. It all had happened gradually. Nothing was left of his smile, which had disappeared a long time ago. He'd stopped brushing his teeth as a child. He couldn't stand the gagging sensation the toothbrush inflicted on him, and the foamy toothpaste only made it worse. He'd literally forgotten how to smile, how to create the actual movement of the right muscles in order to shape the correct facial expression. He was convinced his life wasn't going to get any better, and he'd never experience happiness. The past prevented him from living a good life. He couldn't alter the past, and neither could he live with the past. The injustice was too strong. The beast was filled with hatred and with the thirst for vengeance.

I'll ruin your life just like you ruined mine.

You'll be sorry tomorrow.

As he boarded the plane, he received a pitying smile from a beautiful female flight attendant. Her younger colleague, however, turned her eyes to the floor and pretended not to notice the morbid beast in front of her.

The man seated next to him spread his legs, and once again, he was reminded of the man without a name.

The flight menu offered three different package meals, all of them high in energy. He decided he'd order them all.

Just to feel safe.

1 D/E

6 LUST

Friday evening

The numbers brought her ease. They reassured her that life was predictable. As long as she followed the plan, then the numbers would prevail. It was all a matter of simple mathematics.

Two-five-seven-eight.

Today's number is eight hundred, and she was right on schedule.

Her cell phone had been in her hand for the entire ride to the airport, and she made sure the taxi driver noticed. She was wary of men, always suspicious, because she had no way of knowing if their intentions were good.

As she waited for the driver to take her luggage out of the trunk, she made sure not look at her reflection in the side passenger window. She couldn't stand her reflection. Her reflection reminded her of what a despicable person she was, and how she'd wronged her family.

In the eyes of her parents, she was nothing but an abomination. Her father couldn't stand to look at her anymore. According to her mother, her father had removed her picture from the living room wall. It'd been three years since she had last spoken to her father. This year, her mother didn't even call her for her birthday.

On a Sunday morning, a friend of her brother had apparently told her father what kind of woman his only daughter was. According to her brother, her father cried in church that day. The news had apparently broken her father's heart.

She felt as if she could collapse at any moment, and she needed three attempts to lift her suitcase high enough to place it on the weight scale. She could feel her body pulsating through the fabric of her clothes, while her head felt light and her feet were numb. The woman behind the counter sounded as if she were addressing a small child.

"Nine," the female employee said once more. "Your gate is nine C, and boarding is at nine o'clock. Do you understand, what I'm saying?"

She nodded in response. Her hand trembled as she reached for her boarding pass.

Two-five-seven-eight.

If her parents only could see the person she was, rather than the person she could be. Then perhaps her parents could love her again, and perhaps even admire her for expressing her sexuality openly and without shame. If only her parents could accept who she was, then perhaps she could love herself again.

She was never the good child. Growing up, she was always the rascal. She would lead and others would follow. But no matter what she did, her father always forgave her. But not this time. He finally ran out of tolerance, and he'd cried his eyes out in church. He was ashamed of his daughter. But she wasn't ashamed of who she was. She didn't think she had any reason to be ashamed. Yet, she felt ashamed every day. Especially when she saw her own reflection staring back at her with judging eyes reminding her that she was a disgusting person whom God didn't love anymore.

The security woman was encouraging her to join her on the other side. The metal detector didn't perceive any threat. The female employee reminded her of Jessie. She moved her tongue around in her mouth and stroked her teeth. The taste of Jessie was still in her mouth. A fresh and salty-flavored mix of Jessie's orgasm and her own saliva. The taste brought a discreet smile to her face, and a memory of how the goose bumps on Jessie's inner thigh felt when rubbed up against her cheek.

The departure hall was full of people. Most women didn't notice her, but most men did though. Men looked at her with both contempt and desire, as though they didn't know if they should be disgusted or aroused by her appearance. They enjoyed the image, but they couldn't help but despising the person. In their eyes, she was the wrong kind of woman.

Why do you care who I have sex with?

Isn't it a human right to choose who to have sex with at any time? You say you support human rights, and the right to choose, but my choice still provokes you.

Are you threatened by me?

Do I make you feel obsolete? Is that why I provoke you?

Instead of trying to stop the world from provoking you, why don't you try to stop yourself from being provoked?

And stop being such a hypocrite.

The chain of thoughts made her angry. Her face felt warm. She decided to buy yet another bottle of water. She always drank a lot of water, at least a gallon every day. She noticed the store carried bananas, but she had plenty of them in her purse. She ate at least two or three bananas every day.

Two-five-seven-eight.

Today's number is eight hundred.

She looked at the information screen to find her gate number. Apparently, the 9:30 a.m. flight to Anchorage was departing from gate nine C.

Looking at the overcrowded café reminded her of all the excuses she had for not joining her friends. Every excuse was different, but in reality, the true reason was always the same. She couldn't handle criticism, not even from her friends. Any form of disapproval would shatter her self-image, even if her friends merely disagreed with her. And if they pointed out she was wrong about something, then she would fight to the very end, trying to convince them otherwise. Her self-esteem was too low to handle a defeat. Hours of physical preparations and planning didn't make any difference. The mental barrier was too big. Her couch was too reassuring. Her self-image was too fragile. The best line of defense was to simply stay at home.

However, she was a different person when she was working. Nobody at work could hurt her, because no one there cared about her, and no one really knew her. She felt indestructible when she was working. She felt as she was always in control.

She stopped once more to look at the information screen. She'd already forgotten her gate number. She forgot things frequently. But she never forgot to eat. Her next meal was always on her mind.

Two-five-seven-eight.

Today's number was eight hundred.

On her way to her gate, she noticed a man coming toward her. He was staring at her. He was a grown man, although his face resembled that of a child. He passed her with his eyes wide open and with an enthusiastic smile covered in chocolate. The smell of peanuts and caramel was intoxicating.

I'm not hungry.

When she finally reached her gate, she was out of breath and dizzy and felt her brain pounding on the inside of her skull, as if her skull weren't big enough to accommodate her brain. As soon as she sat down, she instinctively checked her cell phone for any validations. She was a frequent user of social media. She shared every aspect of her life at any given opportunity. She was pleased to see that people were responding to her '*Bye-bye Seattle*' comment.

She was never proud of her own achievements though. She had no need for it. As long as someone else was impressed by her, then she would keep neglecting herself. The validation she received from other people helped her to ignore her own perception of herself. If only someone else admired any aspect of her life, however small, then the reflection in the mirror was wrong.

"Are these seats taken?"

She shook her head in response to the woman's question. The woman who sat down next to her had short hair, and the color of her hair was as dark as her skin. Except for a small amount of eyeliner and mascara, the woman didn't appear to be wearing any makeup. She, on the other hand, always wore a lot of makeup, especially on her cheekbones. She hated her round cheeks, as they made her look bloated.

The woman put on a pair of glasses that made her look like a darker and taller version of Harry Potter. The woman seemed totally happy and at ease, very confident about herself. As the Harry Potter woman solved her sudoku challenges with incredible speed, she couldn't help but stare at the spellbinding numbers. She felt enchanted by them. Math had been her strongest subject in high school. Before she got expelled, that was. She never went to college.

She glanced at the sudoku puzzle once more and noticed how the woman tapped the empty box with her pen.

The answer is two, she thought, but didn't dare say.

She noticed the two men across the room. A father and son eating bananas, and they appeared to eat at the same pace and with the same gestures. The image brought a slight smile to her face. She reached into her purse. This was her second banana today, and she planned to have a third one, at the end of her flight. Suddenly, her jaw dropped. She wasn't used to seeing the pilots board the plane. The tall and handsome pilot reminded her of her father, and much like him, he completely ignored her. His only focus was on the plane. He paid no attention to any of the passengers.

Her father was a man of faith, and unlike her, he was a good Christian. God couldn't accept her weakness, and neither would her father. Her lust was her weakness. Her father would never speak to her again, and he would never walk her down the aisle. She had no children, and the mere thought of having any gave her a guilty conscience. For her to expose a child to her own emotional mayhem would be irresponsible.

The air bridge was cold and dark. She wasn't afraid of flying. She was, however, afraid of the dark. The bright fluorescent light from the airplane cabin brought her relief, and so did the warm and dry air, which radiated out across the plane interior.

The first thing she noticed when sitting down was the menu on the back of the seat in front of her. She stared at the menu for several minutes, then she reminded herself that she wasn't hungry. Once again, she reassured herself that the numbers were correct, and that her plan would prevail.

Today's count is now nine hundred.

30 C

7 RESENTMENT

Friday evening

My name is Matt Damon.

No, I'm not the famous actor. And I'm definitely not the sexiest man on earth, and I don't have the most exciting job in the world. Actually, my job is quite boring, I sit in my office most of the day and I mostly handle paperwork. But at the end of the day, I'm happy. Because I have my health and a family who loves me.

I really wanted to be a veterinarian. I love animals almost as much as I love children. I married my high school sweetheart, but we drifted apart and we got divorced this year. We never had children. She didn't want any. I think that was the main reason our marriage failed. I just couldn't image a life without children. I couldn't live like that. To live without the love of a child.

Perhaps that's why I do so much volunteer work at the local youth center. I probably have a longing to be someone's role model. And it also gives me the opportunity to share my wealth with others less fortunate, even if my father would turn in his grave. My father wouldn't spend a penny on anything that didn't give him a return. But I don't need any more houses, or cars, or whatever. Sharing my wealth with others brings me more joy than any object could ever do.

The person I admire most in my life is my mother. Not only did she give birth to me, she's the glue that holds our family to-

gether. She guided us through the bad times and healed us through the worst of times. She's such a strong and courageous woman. I wouldn't be the man I am today without the inspiration from my mother.

My mother loves animals as much as I do, and we actually adopted a cat from an animal shelter together. We had to keep the cat at her place on account of my ex-wife's allergies, but I would visit Smiley every chance I got. We decided on the name when we saw how happy the cat looked when we took him out of his cage. If I didn't know any better, I'd think the cat cried from joy. When my ex-wife left six months ago, Smiley moved in with me. In the beginning, I had a hard time just locating him, because my house is so big, but then I started to tap the jar with a spoon, and he would come running to the kitchen to eat. We have a lot of fun together, Smiley and I.

"Mr. Townsend... Excuse me, Mr. Townsend?"

He turned his attention to the female employee behind the check-in counter.

"I'm afraid your bag exceeds the weight limit. There will be an additional cost of fifty dollars. Would you like me to charge the same credit card you purchased the ticket with?"

"Whatever." He shrugged.

"Your gate is nine C and we start boarding at nine o'clock. Please don't be late. I hope you have a pleasant flight, sir."

The thought of Matt Damon reminded Mr. Townsend of how much he resented his own mother. His mother was the most pathetic person he'd ever met. She completely lacked self-knowledge, and she'd blame every misfortune in her life on somebody else, and especially on men. When he was growing up, his mother constantly reminded him of what a bad person his father was, and how much he reminded her of his father. At every opportunity, she would speak maliciously of both of them, ridiculing and laughing at him every chance she got. Mr. Townsend never met his father. Growing up, his mother was his only role model, and he swore he'd become nothing like her—and he wasn't. Instead, he had become the complete opposite of his mother.

The thought of his mother made him feel small and inadequate. His posture gradually decreased as he made his way to the security checkpoint. He noticed the fat man standing in line. Even if the man was several places in front of him in line, he could still smell the man's sweat.

"Do you smell that?" he asked the young man standing behind him.

The young man smiled his way, and shrugged his nose.

"This is an emergency! Does anyone have soap?" he yelled.

The young man burst into laughter and gave him a look of admiration. Mr. Townsend straightened his back slightly. As the fat man was about to pass through the metal detector, he came up with another witty remark.

"I hope he doesn't get stuck in there, and ruin it for the rest of us," he said loudly.

The young man laughed and rewarded him with another look of admiration.

Mr. Townsend straightened his back even more.

Seeing the other passengers removing their belongings reminded him of his wedding ring. Mr. Townsend took the ring off his neck chain, and placed the ring in his pants pocket. He'd told his wife that he could lose his finger if he forgot to take the ring off at work. She was reluctant at first, but he convinced her when he'd told her he preferred to wear the ring on the chain around his neck because that way she would be closer to his heart. The truth was he didn't want the ring to leave an imprint on his finger. He hated his wedding ring almost as much as he hated being alone.

The café was overcrowded and just to his liking. He smelled the fresh apple pie and coffee he held as he took in the scenery of the playing field. He noticed the man occupying a large table by himself, and a woman in the background, sitting alone at a smaller table.

He stood between the two tables, turned his eyes back and forth, waiting patiently for the woman to notice him.

"Do you mind?" he eventually asked.

The woman looked across the café. "No, I don't mind."

"Thanks," he said. "That guy over there is almost finished, but I hate to take up an entire table when a group of people is waiting by the counter."

As he sat down, he noticed the woman smiling when she glanced toward the counter.

His eyes were now focused on the apple pie, but in his peripheral vision, he detected the woman glancing at him. Yet as soon as he raised his eyes, she lowered hers.

"Oh my, this apple pie is amazing," he said.

"It looks good."

"You want a piece? I got plenty for both of us."

"No, I couldn't do that."

"Don't be silly. I'll get you a plate," he said, and quickly got up and left the table before she could say anything else.

When he returned to the table, he cut the slice of apple pie in half.

"No. I'll just have a small piece," the woman said.

"Trust me, it's delicious. The crust is so crispy, they must have brushed it with egg whites."

She eventually and hesitantly took a slice of apple pie.

"It's delicious," she said after having a taste. "Sounds like you know your way around a kitchen."

"Oh yeah, I love cooking. I used to cook with my mother as a child. She taught me. I owe so much to her. I used to cook for two people, but I got divorced this year. You know, it's actually hard to cook for just one person. I hate to throw away food, and *Smiley*—that's my cat, by the way—he can only eat so much. Actually, he starts a diet next week, cause he's getting kind of chubby," he said, making the woman laugh.

The woman suddenly extended her arm across the table. "I'm Rebecca Walters."

He felt surprised by the sudden gesture. He was used

to introducing himself first. He felt as he'd suddenly lost his script, and for a second he wasn't sure what to say.

"Rebecca... That's a lovely name."

"Thank you." Rebecca Walters blushed and a curious expression crossed her face. "So, what might your name be?"

"My name is Matt Damon," he lied. "No, I'm not the famous actor."

Rebecca Walters was a thirty-four-year-old single parent with two sons. Neither of the fathers had any contact with their children. She lived in a middle-range suburb in Seattle, and in order to pay the mortgage on her house, she had to juggle two different jobs. Her cat's name was apparently Simba, and needless to say, her favorite movie was *The Lion King*. Rebecca didn't enjoy cooking at all. She thought cooking was just a necessary chore in life. She did, however, enjoy long walks, weekend getaways, concerts, dancing, listening to a specific type of music, and ... some other nonsense.

Mr. Townsend made sure to give Rebecca Walters "Matt Damon's" business card before he excused himself. Then he left the restaurant with a straight back and a feeling of accomplishment.

Seeing the heavily armed guards reminded him of one of his greatest accomplishments in life. The shoot was easy. The hard part was to track down the prey. All those days of traveling in exchange for one second of joy, but in the end, it was all worth it. Before he pulled the trigger, he gazed into the eyes of his prey. The strong recoil didn't prevent him from admiring the view as the legs collapsed beneath the animal.

Seeing how the legs collapsed always fascinated him. In the same second that the bullet entered the prey, it looked as though the legs suddenly disappeared. He thought it was one of the greatest feelings' life had to offer. Hitting the target was easy. The head was about the size of an opened newspaper. And it didn't matter if the bullet shattered the skull since they had to burn the carcass anyway. He only kept a single claw, but he felt it was enough to remind him of his greatness.

Mr. Townsend straightened his back even more.

Then he thought of Rebecca Walters, and as he realized the irony, he began to smile. *Her cat's name is Simba,* he thought.

He'd made sure to hide the claw from his wife. He knew she'd never approve. She thought he'd gone to Europe on business. His wife was still upset over the time he'd killed the smaller, domestic version. It didn't look like a stray cat, but it didn't have a collar, and it kept soiling Jason's sandbox. So, the cat had to go. The cat swirled in the air as the twelve-gauge ammunition ripped its lungs apart. But the cat never saw it coming, and probably didn't feel much agony or pain. It wasn't as if he'd glued the cat to the floor and then bludgeoned it to death with a hammer.

According to his wife, killing a rat using a glue trap and a hammer, wasn't as bad as shooting a cat. He explained to his wife that the perception of pain corresponds with intelligence of the animal—that the rat is far more intelligent than the cuddly cat. This edification made his wife even angrier.

Mr. Townsend suddenly began to feel guilty about killing the cat. Not the cat he'd shot to pieces last year, but the cat he'd tortured to death as a child. He didn't hate the cat, but his mother loved it. Therefore, he'd stopped the cycle and put the cat in the washing machine. His mother thought she'd left the door open, and blamed herself for the death of the cat. But it only shut her up for a week or so, then she got a new cat, and forgot about the old one. And as always, his mother replaced the empty bottle of wine with a full one.

Mr. Townsend ordered a beer and noticed the loser standing by the bar.

"Drowning our sorrows, are we?" he asked the loser. "Forty-eight points. That had to hurt."

The loser didn't respond to his witty remark.

"Cheer up, bro. It's just preseason, and it can't get much worse, am I right?" he added, and then smirked.

The loser finally acknowledged his existence

"What did you do on Sunday?" the loser asked.

The question confused Mr. Townsend, and he didn't know how to respond.

"Didn't you watch the same game as the rest of us?" the loser added.

The truth was he hadn't even watched the game on Sunday, but he knew his team had won by a landslide. He assumed the loser referred to something that'd happened during the game. Probably an unjust call by the referee, or possibly a stroke of bad luck. *Typical loser, always blaming it on something else,* he thought.

"You going to blame the ref now?" Mr. Townsend asked.

"No, of course not. The Hawks won the game because they were the better team. Simple as that. But what did you do?"

Again, he wasn't sure how to respond, because he didn't understand the question.

"Didn't you just watch the game like the rest of us? Yet you seem so proud of your own performance," the loser added.

"You're telling me that you don't feel proud when your team wins?"

"I feel joy when the Chargers win. When I feel proud in life, it's only due to my own achievements. I don't leech onto other people's accomplishments."

Both men stared aggressively at one another. Then, the loser looked him up and down a few times.

"I don't have to," the loser added.

"Whatever."

Mr. Townsend grabbed his beer and began walking away from the bar, but then he came up with another witty remark.

"I think you're just used to losing," he said with a smirk.

The loser responded by smiling nonchalantly at him.

Some people can't stand to lose. Like arguing would make a difference. Your team lost, now get over it. Sorry, but my team kicked the crap out of your team.

He kept reminding himself that the man was just a sore

and pathetic loser. But the more he argued, the smaller he felt, and when he reached the opposite side of the room, he felt just as small and inadequate as he had when he was a child. His posture dropped even more when he heard the sound from the group of women laughing by the bar.

He noticed an elderly woman enjoying a glass of wine by herself, and how she kept glancing at him. She was far below his standards, and he would never consider going anywhere near her body. But her admiration, still gave him the validation he so sorely needed. But then suddenly, she devoted her attention elsewhere. He turned his head to his left. Seeing the two pilots passing by the bar reminded him the time had come to go to the gate.

His timing was perfect. People had begun to form a line by the counter. Mr. Townsend picked a lonely seat in the corner of the room to give him some privacy. As he waited for his laptop to start up, he noticed the young woman standing in line. He thought she looked familiar. Something about her. He was convinced he'd seen her before.

Could it be? Is that her?

A quick search on the internet confirmed his suspicion. She'd obviously lost a lot of weight, but it was definitely her. He downloaded her picture, but he didn't label it with her name. Instead, he came up with a name of his own, and it was a clever one.

It rhymes, he thought, as he read the name on the screen.

CANDY WHORE

Staring at the picture of her naked body and simultaneously looking at her in real life gave him a tremendous rush. He'd never paid for sex before, but now he felt as he didn't have a choice. He had to have her, and at any cost. He always had plenty of cash, and he always made sure to withdraw the cash from stores. He never used a bank ATM. He had about six hundred dollars in cash, and he'd assumed it would be enough.

Mr. Townsend decided to add to his excitement by

viewing his—or more accurately, Matt Damon's—impressive portfolio. The pictures were taken by a camera hidden in a smoke detector, so the quality wasn't perfect, but he had no trouble recognizing the women. None of the women ever noticed the extra smoke detector in the hotel room. Looking at the pictures made him feel superior.

Mr. Townsend straightened his back.

He felt the heat slowly descending and pressing down on his inner thigh. He knew he had to stand up soon, so he closed the portfolio and tried his best to focus on something else. The thought of the old woman in the bar did the trick. Then, he thought of the pilots and the reaction they got as they walked by the bar.

Do pilots carry business cards?

Renting a pilot's uniform online would be easy. But all he really needed to impersonate a pilot was a black blazer with some stripes on the sleeves, and some matching stripes to attach to the shoulders of a white shirt. All of those products were easy to purchase online. After doing a little bit of research, he quickly learned it wasn't against the law to impersonate a pilot as long as one wasn't attempting to fly an airplane.

Who would be dumb enough to impersonate a pilot in order to fly a plane?

As he entered the aircraft, he was greeted by a once beautiful female flight attendant. The mileage had caught up with her, and she'd lost her quality a long time before. Especially when compared with the younger model standing next to her. He made sure to widen his eyes, and gaze into the eyes of the younger version, hoping she'd reward him with a confidence boost. But just as he passed her, she suddenly giggled, and trained her eyes to the floor. At that, he felt small and insecure about himself.

Why are you laughing at me?

Is it the way I walk? Is it my size? What's so funny?

By the time he reached his seat, his chest had caved in,

and he felt even smaller than before. And when seated, he noticed she glanced at him, and once again she smiled and diverted her eyes to the floor.

If I smashed your teeth, then I bet you wouldn't be laughing any more.

Would you?

Mr. Townsend straightened his back.

29 D

8 THE ROLLERCOASTER

Friday evening

The sound of a microwave. A triangle-shaped sponge with a cheddar aroma. Who wants to eat that? I can see my reflection now. Oh no, I forgot to put on makeup this morning. Where is he? The passenger who ordered the "grilled" cheese sandwich is gone. All the passengers are gone. The air cabin is empty. Where did everybody go? I see the sky and clouds through the windows. The train. Hurry. Run. The train is leaving the platform. I'm in the cockpit now. Where did the pilots go? I see stars now. Use the radio. *Mayday. Mayday. This is Susan Olsen speaking. I'm trapped in space.* I hear my own voice. The sound of static noise. *This is Stephen King speaking. It's not supposed to make sense.* I hear a male voice on the radio. The train. Run, Susan. The train is leaving. Run. Now he's back. The man who ordered the sandwich is staring at me. *Well, it's cold now. And it's been on the floor. Do you still want it?*

Why is he staring at me? *Sir, put your seat belt on—we're about to crash.* He's not moving. He's in shock. Page thirty-seven of the employee manual states: *Do not panic, sir. There's no need to panic. Please remain calm.* I hear my own voice. He's still staring at me. He's still in shock. Why? Oh no, I'm naked.

Why did I forget to put on clothes this morning? Don't cry. Right arm across chest. Left hand between thighs. *Sir, put your seat belt on. And I thank you for not staring.* Sandwich man looks across the aisle. *He's not wearing a seat belt.* I hear a male voice.

There aren't any passengers on the other side. All the seats are empty. No, wait. It's him. I see him now. It's Ivanhoe. And he's looks so angry. *Well, he's a cat, so he doesn't have to wear a seat belt.* I hear my own voice. Why do you always have to look so angry, Ivan? It's not my fault. *I'm sorry, Ivan, but they told me it was the right thing to do.* My own voice trembles. He jumps. His claw is in my eye. Help.

***

Susan Olsen woke up screaming and covered in sweat that morning, and she'd scratched herself just above her left eye. After a quick shower, it had been too late for her to go back to sleep. She'd used the extra time to prepare a large breakfast feast for her son to enjoy, but still leaving her with plenty of time to put on her clothes and makeup. And she had no trouble catching the train to her first shift ever as a flight attendant. Her shift had started at 3 p.m., so her mother had to pick up her son from school.

As Susan greeted the passengers for today's last journey, she felt a tension in her chest. Even if the dream had faded away, the emotion hadn't, and she sensed something was wrong. She gently stroked the skin above her left eyebrow, making sure the cut from her dreamy encounter with Ivanhoe hadn't started bleeding again.

Ivanhoe wasn't the same after suffering from meningitis. The cat was terrified of every movement. Whenever Susan had company, Ivan would hide under the bathtub, shaking in fear. The Persian cat was in desperate need of therapy, but instead he got a shot of toxin.

Susan Olsen always thought being a flight attendant would be a glamorous job, but so far, there was no glamour in it whatsoever. The cabin was noisy, the air was dry, her throat was sore, and her vocal cords were on fire. As encouraged by the flight menu, she made sure to drink plenty of water, hoping it would insure her a pleasant flight, but if anything, it seemed to do the opposite. The more water she drank, the worse she felt. She had a pounding headache, her face was hot and bloated, and her cheeks felt dry.

Where's the glamour? She asked herself. Probably not in Anchorage. *The Reindeer Motel* certainly didn't have a glamorous ring to it.

Susan's throat had been sore to begin with, and saying the same mandatory phrase about one-hundred-eighty times made it even worse. As the second to last passenger boarded the plane, Susan was just about to say "welcome." But as the incredibly handsome man gazed into her eyes, she felt overwhelmed and lost for words. She felt embarrassed, and she couldn't help giggling as she broke eye contact.

Susan watched the handsome man walk down the aisle, and as he sat, their eyes met again. She made sure to smile once more, hoping he would notice. To her delight, the handsome man did notice, and once again, he gazed at her. This time, he appeared to be admiring her smile. She sneaked yet another glance at him, and made sure to smile as wide as possible, but then she felt embarrassed again, and diverted her gaze to the floor.

The last passenger to board the plane was the anticipated double-seater. As Susan mumbled the mandatory phrase for the last time, she reminded herself not to stare at the man, so once again she averted her eyes to the floor, but this time she didn't smile.

Why would anyone do that to themselves?

Susan's first customer when serving really provoked her. The young woman, who appeared to be in her early twenties, had purchased four blueberry-flavored muffins, which she minutes later exchanged for chocolate-flavored ones. However, it wasn't the inconvenience of exchanging products that provoked Susan, it was rather the fact the woman (who appeared cut and pasted from a fashion magazine) seemingly could eat anything without gaining any unnecessary weight.

That's so unfair.

For a brief moment, Susan considered asking the woman if she could be so polite as to enjoy her excessive amount of pastry in a secluded area, suggestively in one of the facilities in the back of the plane. And therefore, the rest of the people on this flight, could assume the woman was doing something entirely different than consuming a massive number of delicious calories. But for obvious reasons, Susan decided not to. Coincidentally, the provoking woman did go to the lavatory just a few minutes later.

To further add to Susan's frustration, the handsome man who seemingly checked her out when boarding, and who she hoped to engage in conversation with while serving him, paid no further attention to her whatsoever. Instead, the handsome man devoted all his attention to the woman sitting a few rows behind him—who appeared cut and pasted from a *different* kind of magazine.

The woman's makeup was excessive (but perfectly crafted), and her slim waist was about the same size as one of Susan's thighs. The woman appeared to have surgically integrated a pair of floating devices where her breasts no doubt used to be. For a brief moment, Susan considered enlightening the handsome man, that he was probably a victim of fraud, as the objects in question, the ones he couldn't take his eyes off, were most likely fake—as if that would've made a difference. But for obvious reasons, Susan decided not to say a word.

Her headache was just as tormenting as previously, and drinking water certainly didn't help. If anything, it seemed to make it worse. She felt as if she could explode at any moment, and just then, she did.

"Sir, don't write on the menu," she said harshly.

Susan pointed to the back of the seat, and rolled her eyes in a condescending way.

"Use a napkin or something," she added.

"I didn't write that." The man had a startled look.

Susan responded by staring angrily.

"Seriously, those numbers were here when I sat down. I didn't write that." This time, the man had a look of innocence.

Susan thought the man looked sincere, and she was just about to apologize for her little outburst, when someone tapped her on the right shoulder.

"I think someone is having sex in the bathroom. There are two of them in there," said a concerned female passenger.

Susan sighted and looked across the food cart.

"On your first day," Craig said, and gesticulated, indicating that the event was taking place on her side of the food cart.

As Susan made her way down the aisle, she tried to remember what the employee manual stated regarding public fornication onboard a flying vessel.

"You're breaking the law!" she yelled, and pounded the door with her fist. "What you're doing is illegal!"

Susan felt all eyes were on her, judging her performance. Just as she was about to raise the lavatory sign and unlock the door, the door suddenly opened, and a man emerged with his eyes focused on the floor as he quickly made his way up the aisle. Susan froze when she saw the other man. The man had a blank look, his face was plastered with hostility, and his hair was as dark as his eyebrows. The man mumbled a few words she didn't understand before he returned to his seat with his head held high.

Again, Susan felt a tension in her chest, and she sensed something was wrong. She checked the bathroom briefly before she rushed back to alert Craig. However, Craig just smiled and winked at her. But when Susan pointed out that both of the participants were men and suggested he should alert the captain, Craig's smile vanished, and he was obviously offended.

"Sorry, I didn't..."

Susan didn't know how to finish the sentence, so she just smiled and hoped Craig would accept her *apology,* and forgive her clumsy remark. Susan's headache had gotten even worse. She felt as though her brain was pounding on the inside of her skull, almost as if her skull weren't big enough to accommodate her brain.

"Can a person drink too much water?" she asked Craig, and hoped for a sign of forgiveness.

"I only drink herbal tea."

"But isn't that the same thing?"

"Water is so plain and boring."

That didn't answer Susan's question, but she saw an opportunity to patch things up with Craig. "Herbal tea sounds good. I'll try that."

Her last potential customer didn't seem to want anything and completely ignored her every inquiry. Susan wasn't sure whether the man understood English. She'd noticed him writing in a foreign language on his laptop. She couldn't understand any of the letters, and to add to her confusion, the sentences the man wrote went from right to left.

The herbal tea didn't stop Susan's brain from trying to escape her skull, and neither did two aspirin. To add to her discomfort, her ears kept popping, and she had to help several passengers who were enduring the same problem. As Susan told the elderly woman seated by the window to inhale, close her mouth, clamp her nose and exhale, she noticed the raindrops on the window. The plane had obviously descended below the clouds and had started to initiate landing. But the seatbelt light wasn't on. The pain in Susan's chest was back, and she felt that something was horribly wrong.

Suddenly, Susan's weight shifted. It went from approximately one hundred and seventy pounds to zero. She was weightless. Gravity had all at once ceased to exist; she felt as if she was floating around in space.

Her mind identified the perception of her body and produced a pleasant memory for her to enjoy: They were at the top of the rollercoaster, and just as the car was about to plummet, he'd grabbed her hand and together they'd embraced the emotional ride with cheers of joy. This time, however, no cheers of joy awaited at the end of the rollercoaster ride. But as Susan plunged into eternal darkness, she could actually feel his presence. As if he were right there, holding her hand. And just before the picture went black, she could actually smell him.

The scent of her only child.

9 LIFE

Friday night

His body was numb from the crash. He felt paralyzed. But the terrible situation didn't make a difference to him. He was determined to remain in his seat. He didn't want to live anymore, and he'd rather die sooner than later.

But as the cold water rose above his neck, he started to panic, and he was overpowered by the urge to live. Every fiber in his body told him he had to live.

Only life mattered.

He knew he had to move quickly. He coughed up water from his lungs while he desperately tried to unfasten his seat belt. His body was still numb from the crash, and his lungs felt as if they were on fire. He finally broke free, reached the ceiling, coughed up more water, and gasped for air in the remaining shallow air pocket. Then he half-swam, half-groped his way through the interior of the air cabin, and discovered the cabin door was already open.

The plane had stopped sinking, and the swim to the water surface wasn't far. He reached the surface just as he ran out of air. His vision went black. Nothing could be seen but darkness and the pitch-black night. The heavy rain collided with the water surface, causing the water to splash into his eyes. He closed his eyes and tried to listen instead.

Then he heard her name.

And just then, he believed he was dead. He thought he'd died in the crash, and this was the afterlife. He thought God shouted her name to remind him of his betrayal. As if God had taken her side, and left him in the darkness as a punishment for his crime.

But then he heard her name again.

And just then, he realized a man was shouting her name.

He knew he was alive, and God was nowhere to be found.

10 HUDSON RIVER

Friday night

The chocolate had lost most of its impact on his taste buds. The spike in his blood sugar made him nauseous, and so did the increased blood pressure from all the salt in the potato chips. But he was determined to finish this week's quota of unhealthy calories, since next Friday was a week away.

Tom Hanks was just about to land an airplane on the Hudson River, but the sound of a phone ringing interrupted the heroic landing. He paused the movie just as the plane was about to make contact with the water's surface. He expected a call from his mother regarding the next day's visit to see his sister in the hospital. He dreaded seeing his sister. Not because he didn't care about her, but something about the tubes upset him.

When he read the caller ID, however, he felt his heart stop—at least metaphorically.

CEO Michael Williams

"George Stanton speaking," he answered.

George rose to his feet as soon as he realized what the conversation was about, and his eyes opened wide while he tried to process the information given to him.

"Could you repeat that?" he asked in disbelief. George

had a hard time trusting what he'd just heard. "How is that even possible?"

How could both pilots have died?

"Yes, sir," George said, and then reminded himself to address his boss by his first name. "I'll see you soon, Mike."

George Stanton's plan for the weekend had just drastically changed.

As the public relations manager at Fare Airlines, George Stanton was also the spokesperson for the emergency crisis team. In case of an emergency, he was the one assigned to deal with any inquiries from the press. In his to-date six-months-long career at the company, he'd only attended one crisis team meeting.

The airline itself had only been operational for six months, in fact, and George got the impression that the other members of the crisis team took the task lightly, as the atmosphere in that one meeting had been extraordinarily relaxed. The airline was obligated to have a contingency plan in case of an emergency, but the team members didn't really seem to have considered the possibility of an actual plane crash. George also thought the crisis management plan itself appeared unprofessional, and perhaps even a bit childish, as the document had poor sentence structure and several misspelled words. George had wondered if the financial plan for the company was just as weak.

The CEO, Michael Williams, had just informed George that flight 7-1-9 from Seattle to Anchorage was missing. Apparently, it had deviated from its route, and then disappeared from radar somewhere in the Northwest Territories of Canada. The last known transmission from the aircraft was a text message a female flight attendant had sent to her husband in which she'd pleaded for help, claiming both pilots had died.

During his six months as the public relations manager at Fare Airlines, George hadn't accomplished anything significant. In fact, he wondered if he had done anything at all, except show up for work. The closest he came to performing any real duties had been when he'd dealt with the repercussions of the dumbest contest ever in American corporate history.

The board of the newly founded airline had announced a contest on the internet, through which the public not only could suggest the name for the unnamed airline, but also vote for the best suggestion. Needless to say, the contest ended as a complete and utter fiasco, with the idea and name that received the most votes being "Swirly Mcflies a lot."

The same board had quickly changed the parameters of the contest so that the award of one year of free domestic airline travel would go to the person who came up with the best name regardless of number of votes. The only proposal close to a name one could support for an airline was "Fairline."

The name had inspired the board to pitch several slogans, such as "fair prices at Fairline" and "great service at a fair price." In their state of euphoria, none of the board members ever contemplated the repercussions of putting the letter "F" in front of the word "airline" or the potential verbal abuse the employees might endure whenever a flight was cancelled or luggage was misplaced.

Fortunately, the name was already a registered trademark. But the name did, however, inspire one board member to come up with the name "Fare Airlines." That way, the company website would appear on search results whenever a potential customer searched for the words "airlines" and "fare."

As the name *Swirly Mcflies a lot* was rejected for obvious reasons, the mother (of the child who came up with the clever suggestion) insisted her son should receive some sort of award, or compensation. Despite the silly name, her son, though later disqualified, had actually won the originally announced contest. George Stanton then made sure to provoke the mother just enough for her to go to the press. After a few articles by the local paper, the wider media got wind of the controversy, and George did as many interviews as possible, and made sure to conduct each one in a professional, but also slightly irritating manner.

After the media finally moved on to pursue other stories of equally great importance, George patched things up with the family by giving them an all-expense-covered trip to Florida and passes to several amusement parks. The parents were so pleased, they once again contacted the media, which then made sure to run a follow-up and brag about how they'd helped. In the end, everyone was happy, and George had provided Fare Airlines with media exposure worth millions of dollars.

As George now stared at the frozen image on his television, he suddenly realized he was most likely to appear on TV over the vanishing of the plane. He had no significant background as a public relations manager, and like most people in their thirties with an inadequate resume, he'd exaggerated his skills and experience when he'd applied for the job. However, George felt he had people skills, and he was convinced he could talk his way out of anything.

He knew what to say.

As he made his way to his wardrobe closet, George began to question what might have happened to the plane. How could both pilots have died on the same flight? The odds on both pilots dying simultaneously of natural causes must be of astronomical, if not impossible, proportions.

The flight attendant had apparently sent a text message to her husband, urging him to seek help for them. Why didn't she use the radio? Why did the plane deviate from its route? What terrorists in their right minds would ever hijack a plane and fly into the outskirts of Canada? Had something been wrong with the plane? And was that what had killed the pilots? Had some kind of accident taken place on board? Could a flight attendant land an airplane? Could she land the plane on water?

Tom Hanks made landing on water look easy, and he did it without engines. George hoped the story of their own crash might have a happy ending, after all.

As he was about to exit his apartment, his phone alerted

him of another call. This time, the caller was as expected, and George knew he was in trouble.

"Hi, Mom." He swallowed once. "Listen, I have to work tomorrow, but we..."

George extended his arm far enough to protect his eardrums. The phone was half a yard away from his ear, but he had no trouble hearing every word his mother shouted while he made his way down to the garage.

11 PAMELA

Friday night

In the pitch-black darkness, a man yelled a woman's name.

Then came the sound of a person coughing up water.

The man stopped yelling, and instead asked, "Who's there?"

"I'm Andrew," another man said, and kept coughing.

"I'm Jack. Are you, all right?" Jack asked.

"Yeah, I'm all right. Is Pamela your wife?"

"No, but I heard someone yelling for Pamela."

"That was you."

"Excuse me?"

"You yelled Pamela," Andrew said and coughed.

"I'm aware of that. But before that, someone else was yelling her name. Nobody answered when I yelled for help, so instead I began yelling Pamela. So, the person would understand I heard them in the first place," Jack explained. "You didn't hear a male voice yelling for Pamela earlier?"

"That was you," Andrew said, and then coughed some more.

"No, it wasn't me the first time. It was a different voice, I'm telling you."

"Whatever," Andrew mumbled.

"Hello!" Jack suddenly yelled. "Is anyone out there?"

"Help!" a female voice called. "Help me!"

"Keep talking, and we'll come to you!" Jack responded.

The sound of stumbling could be heard as the two men seemingly made their way along the shore in the dark, while a woman continued screaming for help, and the rain kept pouring down in the pitch black of the night.

One of the men must have made contact with the woman, as she suddenly screamed in fear.

"Calm down, it's just us," Jack said in a soft voice.

"What do you want from me?" Her voice trembled.

"What do you mean?" Jack asked, sounding confused. "I want to help you. That's all. I'm Jack."

"I don't know any Jack."

"Listen, you've been in an accident. But you're safe now. Are you all right?"

"Yes."

"Can you walk?" Jack asked.

"Yes."

"Can I help you stand up?

"Yes."

"Say, is your name Pamela?"

"Yes."

"What's your husband's name?" Jack asked.

"I don't have a husband," Pamela mumbled.

"I mean the person who yelled your name?"

"I don't know. I didn't hear anything."

"You didn't hear a male voice yelling for Pamela?"

"Oh, him. Yes, I heard him."

"So, who is he?" Jack asked.

"She means you," Andrew said sarcastically.

"No, I meant, before that. Didn't you hear a different voice, Pamela?"

Jack was met with silence.

"Pamela? Hello," Jack said. "Can you hear me, Pamela?"

Jack must have brushed up against Pamela, because once again, she screamed.

"Calm down, Pamela."

"I'm not Pamela, I'm Nancy," she responded.

"What?" Jack sounded astonished. "Then where did Pamela go?"

"It's the same person, Jack," Andrew said, and sounded annoyed. "You're confusing her. You're confusing us all with that Pamela nonsense, including yourself. Maybe you should check your head. I'm guessing you have a pretty big bump on it."

After a short pause, Jack said, "No, I'm all right."

"You actually checked?" Andrew chuckled.

"Are you sure you're all right, Nancy? You should check your head for blood."

"My hair is wet," Nancy mumbled.

"But it's just water, right? There's no blood?"

"I can't tell," Nancy said in a quivering tone.

"Let me help you," Jack said, and must have ran his fingers through Nancy's hair. "You got quite a bump on your head, but I don't think there's any blood... Say, does anyone have a lighter?"

"I don't smoke."

"I smoke," Nancy claimed.

"Check your pockets. Maybe you have a lighter on you," Jack said.

Nancy seemingly searched her pockets, and then started to cry. "I lost my keys. I can't get into my apartment now."

"I wouldn't worry about that, Nancy," Jack said in a reassuring tone.

"That's easy for you to say. I can't get into my apartment now," Nancy cried out.

"I have a cell phone, but I'm afraid to turn it on. It's better to wait until tomorrow when it's dry. We might need it to call for help," Andrew said.

"Yes, that's probably wise," Jack agreed. "Don't worry, Nancy. They'll come for us soon. Everything is going to be all right. Let's move away from the shore, and see if we can find a tree where we can shelter from the rain."

A while later, the heavy rain was replaced by a light drizzle and dripping water from the trees. The group was silent, wrapped within the dark surroundings. The wind lessened, though tree branches still scratched about, and a person could be heard moving around. Suddenly, Nancy screamed in panic.

"What's wrong," Jack asked her.

"Get out!" Nancy screamed distraught. "Help me!"

"Calm down, Nancy!"

"How do you know my name?"

"It's me, Jack."

"I don't know any Jack."

"Listen to me, Nancy. You've been in an accident. I think you're suffering from head trauma, and that's why you don't remember me. But you're safe here with me and Andrew. So try to calm down. We're just going to sit here and wait for the rescue team to find us. Everything is going to be all right."

"I've been in an accident?" Nancy sounded confused.

"Yes, the plane crashed."

"What plane?"

"We were on a plane, remember?" Jack asked, but didn't get a response. "We flew from Anchorage to—"

"No, we departed from Seattle and flew to Anchorage."

"Yes, you're right, Andrew. I got confused. We flew from Seattle, but the plane crashed into the ocean—"

"No, this isn't the ocean, the water is fresh. In fact, I don't think we're anywhere near the ocean. I've lived in Seattle my whole life, and this doesn't smell like the Pacific. It smells different here."

The group sat in silence for a while, but again, the silence was interrupted, this time, by the screams of another woman in pain.

"Hello!" Jack yelled.

"Help! I think I broke my leg!"

"Stay there! I'll come to you! Where are you?"

Andrew chuckled sarcastically.

"I'll follow the sound of your voice! Sing a song!"

"Take a branch with you, it will help you feel the terrain."

Jack must have taken Andrew's advice, and the sound of a branch breaking was then followed by the sound of a person stumbling across the terrain, accompanied by a woman singing.

Several songs later, Jack said, "I'm right here. We should make a traction splint to keep the leg steady. I have a shirt we could use."

"Actually, it's my ankle that's broken. I misspoke. Sorry."

"I think we should just leave it be then."

"Sorry you had to come all this way for nothing."

"No, don't be. It's better if we pair up. I'd hate for you to be all alone."

"So more people are gathered over there?"

"Yes, Andrew and Nancy, and I'm Jack by the way... Say, your name wouldn't happen to be Pamela, would it?"

"No, why do you ask?"

"I heard a man yelling for Pamela earlier. Did you hear that?"

"No, I don't think so."

"I'm sorry, I didn't mean to be rude. What might your name be?"

The woman coughed a few times. "My name is Julie."

Jack suggested the two of them should get out of the rain, and they crawled a short distance to the nearest tree. Jack yelled to inform the others that he would spend the night alongside Julie.

"You should wring your clothes out—they'll dry faster. I can help you," Jack said.

"No, that's all right. My jacket isn't that wet really, and I'm afraid to take my pants off—Because of my ankle, that is,"

Julie quickly added.

"Good thing you brought a jacket. I wish I'd thought of that."

"You're not wearing a jacket?"

"No. I just have a shirt on. I left my jacket on the plane."

"I never take my jacket off when flying. I'm always cold," Julie said. "You can use my sweater if you like. I think I can do with just my jacket."

"I'm sure it wouldn't fit me. But thank you just the same."

"I think it's a size medium."

"Well, in that case, it definitely wouldn't fit me."

"Perhaps you can use the sweater as a blanket?"

"No, it's too small either way. I'm a very large man. Trust me, you'll get better use of it," Jack said. "Say, you wouldn't happen to have a lighter, would you?"

"No, afraid not."

"Don't people smoke anymore? It's as if everyone suddenly stopped smoking."

"I only smoke when I'm nervous," Julie said. "So I could use a cigarette, right about now."

"You and me both."

"So, you smoke?"

"For the last thirty years. But my lighter is in my jacket."

"How old are you, Jack? If you don't mind me asking?"

"I'm forty-two."

"Twelve is a good age to start smoking. How did you manage that? I'm smiling by the way."

"I don't know. Perhaps I watched too much television back in the eighties or something. You know, smoking wasn't dangerous back then. Too bad they changed it." Jack chuckled. "So how old are you?"

"I'm twenty-ten."

Jack chuckled once more.

"Too bad I lost my purse on the plane, or we'd have a phone to call for help."

"Andrew has a phone, but he said he'll wait until tomorrow to turn it on."

"Yeah, that's wise. If the phone is wet inside, then the battery will destroy the circuits." Julie sniffed. "The water came so fast, I completely forgot about the life vest."

"I think the plane broke in half. That's why it sank so quickly."

"They'll come for us, right?" Julie asked anxiously.

"There's a transmitter on the plane. They'll find us for sure. We just have to get through the night."

Later, during the night, a woman screamed for help.

"That's just Nancy," Jack said. "I recognize her voice. She gets confused and forgets where she is. I think she's suffering from head trauma."

"Help me!"

12 OXYGEN

Friday night

George Stanton arrived at the F.A. headquarters in San Francisco forty-five minutes after he'd gotten the call from the CEO about the plane crash. He felt as though he should have gotten there sooner and feared that he was the last of the five-member crisis team to arrive at the office.

As always, George wore a jacket and tie to work, and this time he'd gone with a beige blazer, black pants, and a black shirt. His beige, brown-striped silk tie blended perfectly with his jacket.

As he entered the designated conference room, he felt relieved to discover that he wasn't the last member to arrive. Cayla, with a "C" and a squeaky voice, wasn't present, and neither was the jolly fellow who resembled the Michelin man.

CEO Michael Williams stood up and greeted George as he entered the office. The CEO wore a light-gray suit and a white shirt with an open collar. His clothes brought out the dark color of his skin and created a lovely contrast. He appeared to be in his early fifties, but despite Mike's age, George still thought Williams looked handsome.

George recognized the man on the other side of the table, and he was pretty sure the man's role in the crisis team was to function as the emergency crisis coordinator, also known as the ECC. However, he wasn't certain of the man's name, but he vaguely recalled a first name something like Jeff.

George always had difficulties remembering people's names, and he regretted not to have skimmed through the crisis contingency plan before he left home. That way, he would've known everybody's names and designated roles and responsibilities.

He felt slightly overdressed for the occasion, and also lamented putting on a tie. But on the other hand, how long does it take to put on a tie? The man across from him, the ECC (probably named Jeff) was, however, admirably dressed for the occasion; his entire outfit spelled out EMERGENCY. The man wore a red and blue flannel shirt, and a pair of genuinely washed-out jeans, and his shirt was actually tucked into his pants.

CEO Michael Williams cleared his throat. "Now that we're all here."

George's fear came again to life as he realized he was, in fact, the last one to arrive—and he also noticed how his boss briefly glanced at his necktie.

"It's just the three of us?" George blurted out.

"Cayla was out of the town, but she'll arrive before morning," Mike responded. "Until then, I'll carry out her responsibilities as the ECC. I've notified our emergency contacts at the FAA and the NTSB, and both representatives will join us in the morning. Needless to say, Jeff is still hospitalized from the injuries he sustained on Thursday. So, I'll also fill his role as human resources manager and ensure that our employees are taken care off in this precarious situation."

George felt his chest tightening, as he had no idea what had happened to Jeff "the Michelin man" on Thursday, and neither did he know the name or the role of the man across the table. But he assumed the man across the table in the ranching outfit had to be the security director because all other assignments were taken.

George didn't socialize with his colleagues. He usually

had his lunch at his desk, and he rarely engaged in a conversation unless he had to. Neither did he socialize much on his own time. He didn't have any close friends, and he spent most of his time in front of one screen or another.

"Is there any news about what happened to the plane?" he asked.

"No, the plane is still missing," Mike responded. "I thought I'd give a brief summary of what we know, and we can take it from there. Feel free to interrupt me. Flight seven one nine departed from Seattle at nine thirty p.m. yesterday. Then, about halfway to its destination, Anchorage, Alaska, it apparently deviated from its route. All attempts to make radio contact failed, and the plane disappeared from radar near Great Slave Lake in the Northwest Territories of Canada."

Despite George's limited geographical knowledge of Canada, he concluded the plane must have disappeared a long way from its intended destination.

"If the plane flew that far after it deviated from its route, then shouldn't fighter planes have intercepted the aircraft?" he asked.

"If a plane is hijacked and flies close to a major city, fighter planes either intercept, or—in a worst-case scenario —dispose of the potential threat before it reaches a populated area," the security director said from across the table. "However, when a plane flies into the Canadian wilderness, I imagine they simply don't do that, or perhaps they did, but didn't get there in time."

"How do you lose an airplane?" George asked Michael Williams.

"Pardon?" Mike responded.

"I mean, the black box must have a transmitter."

"The Emergency Locator Transmitter provides the signal," the security director said. "The device you're referring to only records flight data and sounds from the cockpit." He raised his eyebrows. "It doesn't send out a signal. And neither is it black or shaped as a box."

George detected more than a hint of sarcasm from the security director and felt as though he'd been corrected by an authority figure.

"Either way, the plane has a tracking device," he pointed out.

"The ELT is used to locate the plane, but at this point, locating the plane isn't a priority," the security director responded.

"Excuse me?" George had trouble believing what he'd just heard.

"The only priority at this stage is to locate survivors, and they won't find survivors at the bottom of the lake."

"Do we even know for a fact that the plane actually crashed into the lake?" George asked, and made sure to address the CEO Michael Williams.

"Well, the plane disappeared from radar over the Great Slave Lake, so..." Mike turned his head and looked at the security director. "The pilots are trained to land on water in case of an emergency, Cliff. Perhaps the plane didn't crash and sink."

"As I told you before, Mike, the Canadian authorities have assured me that every boat available are searching the lake," Cliff said. "Public, commercial, and even private boats—and several helicopters are in the air."

"Yes, that is encouraging," Mike said. "Perhaps this story will have a happy ending after all."

"No, you're not hearing me, Mike. If the plane landed on the lake's surface, then they would have located the plane by now. Besides, if this had been a planned emergency landing, then the pilots would have notified the air controllers." Cliff shook his head. "I doubt they'll find any survivors, but if there are any, they'll likely have hypothermia and drown if the search and rescue team doesn't get to them before morning. This story won't have a happy ending, Mike."

"They could be wearing life jackets," George argued.

"I doubt it," Cliff responded somberly. "If the plane broke on impact, then the air cabin would have immediately filled with water. And if the plane was still intact when it sank, then the distance to swim to reach the water surface would have been long and tiring."

"It's still possible that survivors might be floating in the lake, clinging to wreckage," George added. He didn't like this man, Cliff, or his negative attitude.

"It's possible," Cliff agreed. "But my point being, if they don't find any survivors during the night or at least as soon as the sun rises, then..." The security director trailed off and shrugged toward the CEO. "After that, the task is merely a matter of locating the plane. Even if the ELT provides a signal, the searchers will probably need days, if not weeks, to locate the plane at the bottom of the lake."

"Why wouldn't it provide a signal?" Mike asked.

The security director sighed, possibly in light of Mike's ignorance. "Even though the ELT should transmit a signal, unfortunately, that's not always the case. The failure of the device to transmit has occurred before, notably when planes were lost at sea," Cliff answered. "But either way, it usually takes months before the investigation reveals what actually happened."

"What do you think happened, Cliff?" Mike asked.

"Somebody breached the cockpit, and it must have happened swiftly," Cliff responded without hesitation. "Under other circumstances, one could assume the pilots opened the cockpit to save the life of a crew member, even if it's against protocol. But in this case, that theory doesn't make any sense. The pilots would have called it in on the radio before opening the door. And given the fact that more or less every passenger has a cell phone these days, a lot more text messages would be circling around in the media."

In his fatigue, George had completely forgotten about the text message sent by a female flight attendant on board the actual plane.

"She sent a text message to her husband, did she?" he asked Mike.

"Yes, Elisabeth McAllister sent her husband a text message." Michael Williams looked down at the paper in front of him. "And I quote, Help-both-pilots-dead."

"Isn't it strange she sent the message to her husband?" George asked Mike.

"According to Canadian authorities, she tried to call the police on several occasions, but each time the call was cut off before she spoke. Presumably due to poor reception," Cliff cut in. "Her husband called nine one one, and then, apparently, someone notified the media."

Once again, George felt he was in over his head, and he had no intention of making a fool out of himself on national television.

He knew what to say.

George looked at his boss. "Make sure you don't answer any questions regarding what might have happened to the plane. Just refer to the ongoing search and investigation, and put the focus on the NTSB, instead of us. *Do not* speculate on what happened to the plane, Mike."

"Me?" Mike mumbled, and looked surprised "I thought you were going to hold the press conference. You're the designated spokesperson in this crisis team."

George nodded in acceptance of his boss's statement. "I am aware of that, but I'm also just the public relations manager of this company. Trust me, it looks better if the CEO holds the press conference. Your handling that shows the public this matter has the highest priority." George used a diplomatic tone. "Don't worry, you'll do fine. I'll write a brief statement for you to read."

"The kid's got a point, Mike," Cliff said.

George didn't care for the 'kid' remark, as he was a bit sensitive about his height, or more accurately, his lack of height. But he was also relieved that the man across the table agreed with him and helped argue his case to CEO Williams.

"I suggest you not shave before the press conference." George paused a few seconds to add more drama—he was good at that. "It shows the public you're upset about what happened," he added. "In fact, don't change your clothes between press conferences for the same reason."

George noticed Cliff staring at him, but he wasn't sure if the man was disgusted or impressed by his strategy. He assumed it was the latter.

Michael Williams reluctantly nodded in agreement, and then looked at Cliff.

"What do you make of all of this, Cliff? What do you think happened?"

George noticed the distinctive expression on Cliff's face. His eyebrows had almost merged with his nose.

"My guess is that one pilot went to the bathroom," Cliff said. "Protocol states a pilot can't be alone in the cockpit, so the stewardess you mentioned must have taken the pilot's place in the cockpit. At that point, someone ambushed the pilot in the bathroom, killed him, and took his uniform. The stewardess then opened the door, to let who she believed was the pilot back into the cockpit. Then, the same person killed the other pilot and threw the stewardess out of the cockpit. Leaving the stewardess with two dead pilots, and none of the passengers noticed what happened."

"That doesn't make any sense," George said, and shook his head in disbelief.

Cliff's face dropped. "Why not?"

"Took his uniform. Come on, that's preposterous."

"Simplicity is the ultimate sophistication," Cliff quickly responded.

What does that even mean?

"Besides, how do you plan for something like that?" George asked.

"You don't," Cliff responded. "The plan was probably to threaten the life of a crew member, but as the pilot went to the bathroom, the plan must have changed."

"Isn't the cockpit secured by a pin-code door lock?" George asked, and looked at his boss. "In addition to a manual lockdown from within the cockpit?"

"Either way, the pilot could have given up the code. Following protocol when the blade is on your neck and fear takes hold is hard," Cliff asserted.

"What blade?" George looked at Cliff in puzzlement. "You can't bring a knife through security," he quickly added.

"Son..." Cliff mumbled in a patronizing tone. "In my younger years, I worked as a correctional officer at a federal prison, and I learned one thing from back then—an inmate can make a knife out of just about anything. An inmate could probably produce thousands of shivs from the materials in a departure hall. There's glass, metal, razor blades, toothbrushes, you name it..." Cliff trailed off.

How do you kill a person with a toothbrush?

"What kind of terrorist hijacks a plane and flies into the Canadian wilderness?" George asked with a hint of sarcasm.

Cliff nodded and looked across the desk.

"The kid's got a point, Mike," Cliff said. "I don't think this is terrorism. At least not in a traditional sense. Terrorists want to draw attention to their cause and spread as much fear as possible. Crashing a plane into the Canadian wilderness doesn't spread fear, it only raises a lot of questions. Besides, why go through the trouble of breaching the cockpit?"

"What do you mean?" Mike frowned.

"If they just wanted to bring the plane down one way or another, why go to the trouble of breaching the cockpit?"

So they could crash the plane. Obviously.

"How to you crash a plane without accessing the cockpit?" George asked.

"I can think of numerous ways," Cliff said. "For instance, a minor explosion is probably enough to bring the plane down, or at least make landing impossible."

"How do you get a bomb through security?"

George's voice had grown more condescending, and he could tell that his colleague was provoked by his aggressive line of questioning.

"You can't bring a bomb through security, son, but you can easily bring the components and the ingredients though security. Then you assemble the bomb in the bathroom."

"You're referring to nitroglycerin, are you not? You think three points four ounces is enough to bring down a plane?" George questioned in an assertive tone.

"Son..." Cliff sighed. "First of all, the limit of liquid you're referring to is per item and not per person. And second, you don't need explosive oil to cause an explosion. Come to think of it, you could use oxygen, for example. You would have no trouble getting oxygen through security."

"What do you mean by oxygen? As in the air we breathe?"

"Son..." Another sigh. "We breathe nitrogen, mixed with a little bit of oxygen, just to keep our flame going." Cliff tapped his chest. "It's the oxygen that burns, and if no oxygen is in the room, there can't be a fire."

Tell me something I don't know.

"I'm talking about pure oxygen," Cliff said. "Trust me, it's highly flammable, and when contained and exposed to sudden temperature change, it will explode. For example, one could cause an explosion by short-circuiting a cell phone battery."

Oxygen?

Cliff cleared his throat. "TSA only looks for bottles with liquid in them. An *empty* water bottle filled with oxygen would easily pass through security. Come to think of it, if sealed properly, perhaps an entire carry-on could be filled with oxygen, and when passing through the x-ray, the carry-on would appear as empty. And it's easy to start a fire on board the plane. You could simply stick a handkerchief down a bottle of booze and light it with a lighter. A few Molotov cocktails would set the entire plane on fire in no time. You're permitted to bring a lighter with you on the plane, and they sell plenty of alcohol in the departure hall." Cliff chuckled.

You can't bring a lighter through security... Can you?

Cliff's eyebrows plunged into another undesirable frown. "Come to think of it, you might as well just check in your luggage. All you need is something that ignites, or produces enough heat to start a fire. For example, you could alter the battery on a laptop, and then program the laptop to turn itself on once the plane is in the air. When the battery gets too hot, it'll explode and ignite the oxygen. And there's no limit to the size or volume of liquid items for checked baggage. You could easily hide explosive oil within other liquid bottles. An *empty...*" Cliff put his hands in the air and gesticulated air quotes. "...suitcase with a laptop, and a few bottles of liquid would do the trick."

"That can't be accurate," George said in a brusque tone.

"Son..." the man said in a gloomy tone. "I know for a fact that alcohol burns, oxygen is highly flammable, and a defective battery can explode. So, what specifically don't you agree with?"

I don't agree with that outfit you're wearing. Did you just tuck your pajamas down your pants and walk out the front door? Doesn't your hallway have mirrors?

An awkward silence filled the room.

"But like I said, Mike. This isn't terrorism," Cliff added. "This is something else. Perhaps a person with a mental disorder, or someone with a personal vendetta."

George thought his boss suddenly looked uncomfortable.

"Has Jeff fired anyone recently?" Cliff asked Mike.

"I don't have that information," Mike said hesitantly.

"Gentlemen, aren't we getting ahead of ourselves here?" George blurted out. "I mean, shouldn't we focus on our assignments, and instead let the authorities handle the investigation?"

CEO Michael Williams and security director Cliff both looked at him in annoyance. George felt as though he'd just interrupted his parents.

"Fair enough," Mike eventually said. "Let's get to work

then."

Mike suddenly stood up. Cliff looked surprised by the sudden gesture, but then hesitantly rose from his chair. Mike gestured to George to remain in his seat, and George assumed it was because of the planned press conference. But as soon as Cliff had left the conference room, his boss sat down in the chair next to George. The CEO swallowed once, and seemed to be hesitating as to what to say.

George began to feel nervous and thought that perhaps he was about to reprimanded for not getting to the crisis meeting fast enough. George was a very cautious driver; he always kept the speed limit, no matter what.

"I didn't think it was appropriate to mention over the phone. I thought speaking in person would be better," Mike finally said. "I heard about what happened to your sister, and I want to express my deepest concern, and assure you that she will be in my prayers."

"Thank you, sir. My family and I appreciate your thoughts."

"Call me Mike, please," Mike said. "So, how is she?"

"She's still in a coma."

Another silence filled the room before George finally spoke.

"I'll get started on that statement, and I'll call a press conference as soon as possible."

Both men rose to their feet. Then Michael Williams suddenly took a step closer to George and extended both his arms. At first, George imagined that his boss was about to approach him with a hug. But instead, Michael Williams put his hands, on top of George's shoulders.

"I'll pray for her," Mike said, again expressing his intent.

13 BIGFOOT

Saturday morning

The wind had settled, and the few remaining leaves that had fought so persistently through the night grasping on to the remaining days of summer were finally at peace. The light rain and the thick clouds turned the surroundings of the lake gray and dull. Except for some small pieces of debris in the middle of the wide lake, no sign would alert someone that an airplane crash had ever taken place.

A large man stood at the top of the hillside and gazed down across the lake and the shore. Then he looked up toward the sky and moved his head methodically in each direction, back and forth.

"Any sign of the cavalry?" the woman who had introduced herself as Julie asked the large man.

The large man shook his head and then turned around and faced her.

"You weren't exaggerating, were you?" Julie said. "You're huge. Look at your arms. They look like they've been photoshopped."

The large man frowned at Julie.

"You've heard of Photoshop, haven't you?"

The large man kept frowning and shook his head slightly.

"Seriously? You never heard of *Photoshop*?" Julie's eyebrows rose. "It's a software program that allows you to alter a photo digitally. So one could pretend to have arms as big as yours, I mean." Julie smiled. "It's a compliment, Jack."

"I think I understand what you mean," the large man by the name of Jack said. "You should have seen me a few months ago when I was still lifting weights. I was a lot bigger back then."

"Is that even possible?"

Jack kept staring at Julie.

"What?" Julie asked.

"I'm sorry. I didn't mean to stare. It's just that… You know… Like when you talk to someone on the phone, and you imagine a face, but when you actually meet the person, the image doesn't match," Jack said hesitantly. "You know what I mean?"

"So how did you imagine me then?"

"Well, for starters, you look a lot younger than I imagined. You look closer to twenty, than thirty."

"That's nice of you to say, Jack."

"And I pictured you with dark hair for some reason," Jack added.

"What, I didn't sound blonde enough to you? Is that a compliment or an insult?" Julie smiled.

"No, I didn't mean it like that. I just imagined I would have seen your bright hair last night. But on the other hand, I couldn't see my own hands in front of me, and I'm as white as a ghost, and so is my shirt." Jack kept staring at Julie. "Are you, all right? I noticed you have a bump on your forehead."

Julie touched her forehead. "Oh, that. That's nothing."

"And there's blood on the sleeve of your jacket."

Julie looked at her sleeve. "I must have wiped my forehead with it. I think I hit my head on the seat in front of me when the plane went down. But I'm all right. Thank you for asking, Jack."

"How's your ankle?"

"I'd completely forgotten about it," Julie said, and focused on her feet. "No, it doesn't move. But it doesn't hurt, either. So, I think I'm all right as long as I don't put any weight on it."

"You just sit there, and I'll go and get the others."

"What?" Julie looked startled.

"There are two more of us. Nancy and Andrew, remember? It's better if we stay together as a group."

"But isn't it better if we go down to them? We might need to drink water eventually."

"That's true." Jack nodded. "So how do you want me to carry you?"

Julie climbed up on Jack's back, and the two of them carefully descended the steep hillside.

They eventually met up with a man who was resting his back up against a tree. The man squinted, and then rose to his feet. Julie climbed off Jack's back, and they both shook hands with the man, who introduced himself as Andrew.

"So, how's your leg?" Andrew asked.

"I think my ankle is broken, but I'm all right."

"You climbed that hillside with a broken ankle?"

"No, I didn't break my ankle when the plane went down," Julie said. "But I lost my footing as I ran into the woods."

"Why did you run into the woods in the first place?"

"I don't know," Julie said. "I guess I was confused after the crash."

"So, where's Nancy?" Jack asked, and looked at Andrew.

"Who?"

"I thought her name was Nancy."

"Who are you talking about?" Andrew asked.

"The woman from last night."

"What woman?" Andrew looked confused.

"The woman who was here last night," Jack said loudly.

"What did she look like?"

"What do you mean, what did she look like!" Jack yelled.

"It was dark."

"Well, I haven't seen her." Andrew shrugged.

"The woman you talked to last night," Jack said harshly. "Where is she?"

"I don't know what you're talking about," Andrew claimed. "I only talked to you last night."

Jack's jaw dropped, and he kept staring at Andrew with wide eyes. Then suddenly, Andrew burst into laughter.

"You should see your face, Jack."

Jack didn't laugh; instead he kept staring Andrew in the eyes. Andrew turned his head and pointed toward the lake.

"You see that purple *rock* by the water? The one with the blonde hair attached to it? That's Nancy. She's on her knees, washing away her makeup," Andrew said, and then looked at Julie.

"I picked a good day not to wear makeup." Julie smiled.

"So, is she all right?"

"She has some swelling by her temple, and she keeps forgetting where she is. I had to calm her down a few times last night. She got confused, and started talking to people who weren't there. You and she have a lot in common." Andrew smirked.

"Oh, now I see." Jack had a stiff smile. "I know what I heard."

"Did you hear someone yelling for Pamela last night? I mean, besides Jack?"

"I didn't hear any yelling at all," Julie answered. "But I ran into the woods."

"I heard a male voice yelling for Pamela last night."

"A male voice you say." Andrew nodded. "Did the voice say anything else?"

Jack frowned. "No, he just yelled her name."

"But the voice didn't command you to eat the other passengers, or anything, did he?"

Jack gave Andrew a sharp stare before he picked up Julie in his arms, and began walking toward the lake.

"It was a joke," Andrew said, and then casually followed in Jack's footsteps.

The group met up with Nancy down by the lakeside. She'd washed away her makeup and was now drinking water from the palm of her hand. When she noticed them, she rose quickly, and then, she looked at Jack, and suddenly, her face lit up with joy.

"It's you," Nancy said with a tremendous smile.

Andrew looked surprised. "You two know each other?"

"No." Jack sounded doubtful, and then looked at Nancy. "I think you're confusing me with someone else. I'm not the person you think I am. I'm Jack, from last night. Do you remember talking to me last night?"

Nancy suddenly looked sad and bowed her head. "I'm so sorry."

"You two know each other?" Andrew asked once more.

"This here is Julie. The woman who screamed for help last night. Do you remember her?" Jack asked Nancy.

Nancy looked at Julie, but never spoke.

"How are you feeling, Nancy? Are you all right? How's your head?" Julie asked.

Nancy kept staring at Julie, but didn't respond to the question.

Eventually, Julie looked across the shore in the opposite direction of where she and Jack had spent the night. Then she pointed at a tree close to the shore. The tree had the same shape as a crooked Chanterelle mushroom. The branches seemed to be drawn to the water, and the whole tree appeared to be sloping.

"You wanna go over there? We can sit by that tree. Would you like that?" Julie asked Nancy in a soft and gentle voice.

"Okay," Nancy said, and then suddenly walked toward the tree on her own.

"It looks like a good place to sit and wait for the cavalry, wouldn't you say?" Julie looked at Jack. "I mean, in case the rain picks up again."

"So you'd never seen her before?" Andrew decisively asked Jack. "Is that what you're saying, Jack?"

"I told you, I don't know her," Jack insisted.

"You've *never* seen her before?"

"No, I've never seen her before today."

"You expect me to believe that?" Andrew smirked, and began walking toward the *Chanterelle* tree by the shore.

"Do you two know each other?" Julie asked.

"I don't know who she is." Jack shook his head. "She probably saw me boarding the plane and is confusing me with someone else."

"No, I meant, do you and Andrew know each other?"

"No." Jack frowned. "Why would you ask that?"

"Well, you kind of argue like an old married couple." Julie smiled.

"I don't know him. In fact, I don't remember seeing him or Nancy boarding the plane," Jack maintained. "I noticed you though."

"Oh, did you?" Julie smiled. "It's nice to be noticed."

The group sat in silence under the odd-shaped tree. The ground under the tree was dry; the pine branches were thick and worked as an umbrella. Julie had her hands in her jacket. Andrew and Nancy had their hands tucked into the sleeves of their sweaters. Jack had his shirt up to his elbows. The group looked mostly at the sky, but occasionally they looked at each other, never speaking.

Finally, Andrew broke the silence.

"So, what do you guys do for a living?"

The others acknowledged his question, but none of them seemed eager to respond.

"I'm a welder myself, and I'm thirty-six years old," Andrew added.

The others stared down in silence, and seemed reluctant to answer.

"How about you, Julie, what do you do?" Andrew asked.

"I'm thirty years old, and I clean people's houses."

"There's no shame in that." Andrew shrugged. "You look younger by the way."

Julie looked at Andrew with a stiff and artificial smile.

"How about you, Jack?"

"I'm forty-two, and I'm currently unemployed," Jack said. "But I used to drive a truck."

"I thought all truck drivers were fat and out of shape. I figured you for a bouncer or something," Andrew said. "How about you, Nancy? What you do for a living?"

"I do some modeling," Nancy mumbled, and bowed her head.

"I bet you do," Andrew said.

Nancy looked suspiciously at Andrew. "What do you mean by that?"

"I mean, you look hot," Andrew responded. "Hot enough to be a model."

Jack looked at Andrew as if annoyed.

"What?" Andrew mumbled and looked at Jack. "It's a compliment."

"Do you remember how old you are, Nancy?" Jack asked.

Nancy took her time before answering. "I'm not sure..."

"You look no more than twenty-five," Jack said. "Were you born in ninety-two perhaps? Does that sound right?"

"I was born the same year as Nelson Mandela," Nancy blurted out.

Andrew chuckled. "That makes sense."

"She means the election," Julie said in a ridiculing tone.

"Oh, yeah," Andrew mumbled. "When was that? Mid-nineties? Ninety-five?"

"Ninety-four," Nancy quickly responded. "Ninety-four was a good year, I've been told."

"Do you remember when your birthday is?" Jack asked. "Is it summer or winter?"

"It's Christmas," Nancy said. "I always got fewer presents on my birthday."

"Well, there you go, you're twenty-two years old then," Jack said. "Do you remember my name?"

"You're Jack." Nancy hesitated.

"And do you remember seeing me boarding the plane?"

"What plane?" Nancy looked confused.

Jack explain in details to Nancy about the accident, and then the group didn't speak much after that. Nancy slept on and off.

Afternoon

"Where are they?" Julie asked without addressing anyone in particular. "It's been hours."

Jack suddenly twitched. "Wait a minute, didn't you have a phone, Andrew?"

"Oh, yeah." Andrew took his phone out of his front pants pocket. "I forgot to tell you guys. I turned the phone on this morning, and it started up just fine. But when I tried to get a signal, the screen suddenly turned all blue, and shortly after that, it turned black, and I couldn't get it going."

Julie rose to her feet, and slowly limped away from the group; seemingly in pain.

"Where are you going, Julie?" Jack asked.

"I have to go to the ladies' room."

Jake stood up. "I'll carry you, Julie. You shouldn't walk on your ankle."

"No, I'm fine," Julie said. "Just stay there, please."

"I won't look, Julie. I just want to help you."

"No, just stay there, please," Julie said once more. "I *do not* want you to see what I'm about to do."

"It's nothing to be embarrassed about," Jack said, and took a step closer to Julie.

"I said no!" Julie yelled.

"Okay." Jack put his palms up in the air.

Just then, Nancy woke up. “Is she leaving?”

“No, she has to... pee,” Jack hesitated.

“So, what’s your name?” Nancy looked at Andrew.

Andrew didn’t answer either; instead, he tilted his head and looked at Jack.

“His name is Andrew, and I’m Jack.”

Eventually, Julie emerged from the nearby bushes, and limped slowly, as she made her way back under the sloping tree. She glanced at Jack, but when their eyes met, she quickly trained her eyes toward the ground.

“Any sign of the cavalry?” Julie asked and looked at Jack’s chest.

“No, I’m afraid not.”

“You’re sure there was a transmitter on the plane?” Julie asked.

“Yes, I’m sure of it,” Jack responded.

“Can it transmit through water? I mean, the plane is at the bottom of the lake.”

“They would have thought of that,” Jack said. “Don’t worry, Julie. They’ll come for us sooner or later.”

Jack stood up and began pacing randomly toward the lake. Andrew shook his head a few times, then he walked the short distance to the lakeside, and joined Jack down by the water.

Julie squinted and focused on the two men standing by the lakeside.

“Do you have a headache or something? Is that why we’re just sitting here?”

“I lost my contacts,” Julie answered hesitantly.

“So, are you going to fuck those guys or what?” Nancy asked casually.

“Excuse me?” Julie looked astonished.

“The tall one is kind of hot. I like a man with muscles. But the short one is cuter,” Nancy said. “Wouldn’t it be great if you could put the little guy’s face on the big guy’s body. You know what I’m saying?” Nancy smiled, and winked at Julie.

"I'm not going to have sex with either of them."

Nancy smiled and brushed up against Julie. "Yeah, me neither."

Then Julie squinted again. "Are they fighting?"

Nancy looked at the men by the lakeside. "The big guy is grabbing the little one by the neck. But I think they're just playing around. Guys do that all the time," Nancy said. "Guys are weird that way."

Julie kept squinting.

"So, do you want to get out of here or what?"

"Of course, I..." Julie trailed off, and then looked cautiously at Nancy. "Do you know where you are, Nancy?"

Nancy face plummeted; suddenly she looked furious. "What did you call me?"

"I thought your name was Nancy?"

"Who told you that?" Nancy yelled.

"Jack called you Nancy." Julie sounded startled.

"He told you my real name?" Nancy muttered, and looked toward the lake. "He shouldn't have done that."

"Do you know where you are right now?"

Nancy looked confused and blinked a few times before answering. "No, where are we?"

"The plane crashed in the lake, and we're waiting for help."

"What plane?"

Julie took her time and explained what had happened. Nancy seemed confused by all the information, and eventually she fell asleep. Shortly after that, Andrew joined them.

Julie squinted toward the lake. "What happened to Jack?"

"He got pissed off, and said he'd walk home."

"What?" Julie looked terrified. "What happened between you two?"

Andrew's face shifted. Now, he looked surprised. "I was just kidding, Julie."

"So, where is he?"

"He thought he saw some movement on the other side of the lake," Andrew claimed. "So he went there to check it out."

"But the sun is about to set. It'll be dark soon."

"That's exactly what I said, but he wouldn't listen." Andrew shook his head, and then said. "The shadows are moving." It sounded like a quote.

"He thought it might be other survivors?" Julie asked. "That doesn't make any sense. They would've seen us. We're out in the open."

"Maybe they can't see us." Andrew shrugged. "I lost my glasses in the crash. I can't see across the lake."

"I know what you mean. I lost my contacts when I swam to shore."

"Well, there you go, "Andrew said. "Other survivors might be sitting there, right in front of us."

"But why didn't he just yell?"

"Oh yeah." Andrew suddenly looked concerned. "Why didn't he yell?"

Julie's posture dropped. "You don't think he left, do you?"

"No, staying together as a group is better."

"You can't see. I can't walk, and Nancy can't even stay awake," Julie said. "He doesn't need us, Andrew. We need him."

"He wouldn't leave the crash site." Andrew shrugged. "It's the first day."

"If the plane was transmitting a signal, they should've been here by now," Julie said in a trembling voice. "Something's wrong, and Jack knows it."

Andrew looked across the lake and kept squinting.

Julie broke out in tears. "This can't be happening."

Evening

The sun had set, and darkness surrounded the three remaining residents of the *Chanterelle* tree down by the shore. Jack hadn't returned. Nancy was still asleep, and Julie had just checked Nancy's pulse.

"Did you hear something just now?" Andrew asked.

"It sounded like an owl."

"That's a big owl," Andrew mumbled.

"So, what was the fight about?"

Andrew sighed. "I told you, it was just two guys blowing off steam."

"So you said," Julie answered. "But what was the argument about?"

"What difference does it make?" Andrew responded. "Besides, he left well after that. It's not like I scared him away or anything."

"What was the argument about?"

Andrew took a few breaths before answering.

"He made some demeaning comments about Nancy, and I responded rather harshly, and he grabbed me by the collar," Andrew claimed. "It's no big deal."

Julie exhaled loudly. "Are you sure it wasn't the other way around?"

"I didn't grab him."

"No, I meant." Julie exhaled. "Never mind. Did Jack specifically say that he saw people on the other side of the lake?"

"No, he said he saw movement," Andrew answered. "Something black moving behind a cliff or something."

"Maybe he meant debris from the plane. Perhaps he saw something we could use," Julie said. "That could explain why he didn't yell."

"No, I don't think that's what he meant. He saw something dark moving in the shadows by a cliff close to the water. It had to be something big for him to notice." Andrew chuckled. "Perhaps it's Bigfoot."

14 BIRTHDAYS

Sunday morning

George Stanton had a pounding headache—which he assumed was due to the lack of sleep—and he almost dozed off listening to the advice from a board member telling his boss, Michael Williams, how important using proper language, having a pleasant demeanor along with a professional appearance, and seeming as concerned and sympathetic as possible was when dealing with the press.

George wondered if the depressing atmosphere in the boardroom was due to the loss of lives, or the loss of financial potential. He assumed most of the board members were also shareholders.

Even though the Canadian authorities still searched for survivors, no one had much hope of finding any. Boats, helicopters, and drones had searched the entire Great Slave Lake that Saturday. Experts now presumed that the plane had sunk intact and nobody had survived the crash. The main focus had shifted on Sunday to being more a matter of locating the plane.

George had written several press statements the day before, and his boss had held a couple of further press briefings, but the media didn't seem that interested in what little information the airline had provided. Instead, the media was focused on the Imam who not only was a passenger on the plane, but also had been highlighted in the media on several previous occasions arguing that Sharia law should be enforced in the American legal system.

In contrast to his colleagues, George managed to restrain himself from taking part in the many discussions of what might have happened on board the plane. He thought it was counterproductive to speculate at this stage. But he also knew it would be weeks, if not months, before the investigation finally revealed what had actually happened. The expected wait made him feel powerless.

The feeling made him think of his sister, who had recently been in a car crash and was now lying in the hospital in a coma. George was supposed to visit her with his parents this weekend, but due to the missing plane, he had no real alternative but to cancel the visit.

That thought reminded George of his father's birthday this coming week, and he made a mental note not to congratulate him. He wasn't going to repeat his mistake ever again. His father didn't celebrate his birthday; instead, he celebrated the day he became an American citizen. The two occasions were only a few days apart. One year, George got the dates mixed up, and his father didn't speak to him that day. His father rarely spoke at all, but when he did, he tried his best to hide his Japanese accent. However, on the day in question, his father had spoken more than ever—just not to George.

His father was a strange man.

15 ANGELA

Sunday morning

It didn't rain, though the sun couldn't break through the clouds.

Jack stood by the oddly shaped tree and looked at the sky, moving his head back and forth. Nancy and Andrew were still asleep. Julie had just woken up.

Julie blinked several times, then squinted, and smiled. "You came back."

"It was too dark too walk last night, so we slept on the other side of the lake," Jack said." I yelled your names, but you didn't hear me."

"That was you," Julie said. "I thought it was an owl."

"That's a big owl," Jack said with a modest smile.

Julie's jaw dropped. "Did you say we?"

"Me and Kevin."

Jack pointed at the man who sat up against the sloping tree trunk and had his hands in his jacket pockets. Julie turned her head around and stared at the man with wide eyes.

"Hi. I'm Julie."

"He told me your names."

"So, how old are you, Kevin?" Julie asked.

"Forty," Kevin mumbled.

"I'm twenty-ten myself." Julie smiled.

"You're thirty?" Kevin sounded surprised.

"No, I'm twenty-ten." Julie smiled even bigger. "Are you married?"

Kevin barely shook his head.

"Kids?"

"What, are you writing a book?" Kevin sounded harsh.

"No, I'm just making small talk." Julie seemed disappointed.

Jack looked at Julie then shrugged his nose and shook his head slightly.

"You wouldn't happen to have a lighter, would you?" Jack asked Kevin.

"If I had a lighter, don't you think I would have told you by now?"

Jack sniffed. "I just thought you might have a lighter since you're wearing a jacket."

"You think I should feel guilty for wearing a jacket?"

"I didn't say that," Jack responded.

"Are you cold, Jack?" Julie asked.

Jack shrugged. "I'm okay."

"Perhaps we can make a fire? If you get me a couple of branches, and if I rub them long enough, I might be able to start a fire."

"It's too wet, Julie."

"I don't mind trying, Jack. Besides, I filled my pockets with grass yesterday. That's why my pockets are so full." Julie took a handful of grass from her pocket. "See, it will dry eventually."

Jack focused on Julie's jacket pockets. "It's better if you hold the grass up against the wind. Your pockets will just preserve the moisture."

Julie put her hand up, and the grass straws began to *dance* in the wind.

"Can you get me a couple of branches?" Julie asked.

Jack shrugged "Okay."

"Make sure they break off easily. If the branch bends

without breaking, it's because it's full of water."

Jack took a few steps in the direction of the hillside and the nearby bushes.

"Could you perhaps go the other way?" Julie asked. "I was just about to go to the ladies' room."

Jack looked at the nearby bushes and then shrugged. "Okay."

Jack walked in the opposite direction. Julie rose to her feet and slowly limped toward the bushes.

"You're all right?" Kevin asked.

"It's just my ankle. I'm fine."

Kevin rolled his body forward, and put his left knee on the ground.

"What you're doing?" Julie asked.

"I thought I'd give you a helping hand."

"I don't need help," Julie said in a loud decisive tone. "Just stay where you are."

"Whatever," Kevin mumbled and then leaned back against the tree trunk.

Just then, Andrew and Nancy woke up. Andrew squinted in each direction, before his face suddenly froze; his eyes locked in on Kevin.

"I'm Kevin. You're Andrew—am I right?"

"Oh yeah." Andrew exhaled. "You swam the other way, did you?"

Kevin nodded.

"So, where are Jack and Julie?"

"Jack went to get some branches, and Julie had to... pee." Kevin hesitated.

Nancy kept staring at Kevin for a long time.

"Can I help you?" Kevin eventually asked.

"I had a black boyfriend in college," Nancy claimed. "I mean, he was in college. I was in high school."

"Good for you." Kevin said hesitantly and then looked at Andrew.

Andrew scratched his temple and then he indicated

Nancy's temple.

Kevin looked at Nancy. "She shouldn't be moving around too much."

Soon after that, Jack returned with a couple of branches, and Julie, who had also come back, began to peel off the tree bark.

"What're you doing there, Julie?" Andrew asked.

"I'm gonna try to start a fire," Julie said enthusiastically.

"That's never going to work." Andrew sneered. "You're wasting your time."

"Wasting my time," Julie said in a mocking voice. "What else am I gonna do?"

Andrew rolled his eyes and looked the other way.

"Didn't you ever see Cast Away? Tom Hanks started a fire," Julie added.

"Tom Hanks wasn't stuck in the Canadian wilderness," Andrew said. "You have a better chance of finding a coconut."

Kevin focused on the branch in Julie's hand. "We could gather branches, and spell out SOS on the shore."

"That's a good idea," Andrew said. "You know, there might be hikers in these mountains, and they just see us sitting here and don't think twice about it."

"Okay." Jack shrugged. "Let's gather rocks and branches then."

The men rose, and began walking toward the woods. Julie had just finished peeling the bark off the one branch and was just about to start on the other. Andrew looked down as he walked past her, and their eyes met.

"That-a girl." Andrew chuckled.

Julie kept peeling, this time more intensely than before.

"Why are we just sitting here?" Nancy asked.

"I broke my ankle, remember?"

"Oh, we're waiting for a doctor?"

Julie sighed. "Do you remember the plane crash?"

"What plane?"

Julie sighed deeply, and then explained the recent

events to Nancy, who fell asleep shortly after.

Afternoon

The three men had gathered branches and spelled out the famous distress signal across the shore; they'd placed several rocks on top of the branches. When they returned to the crooked tree, Julie had her hands in the air.

"I thought you'd have started a fire by now," Andrew said.

"I have to dry the grass first," Julie said, and looked at the grass in her hands.

"Jack ate worms," Kevin suddenly blurted out. "A whole bunch of them."

"What!" Julie yelled in a high-pitched tone.

Just then, Nancy woke up and looked disorientated.

"What did it taste like?" Julie asked.

"I don't know." Jack sniffed. "Greasy, and a bit salty perhaps. It wasn't that bad, really."

Nancy suddenly walked away from the group.

Jack followed. "Where are you going, Nancy?"

"Nowhere," Nancy quickly responded.

"You shouldn't walk too much," Jack said. "It's better if you stay here."

Nancy took a few steps backward while her eyes focused on Jack, who then took a few steps closer to her. For each step Jack took, Nancy backed up accordingly. And then suddenly, she dashed and ran toward the woods, Jack in hot pursuit. Nancy didn't get far; the pursuit was over within seconds. Jack had a firm grip around Nancy's waist as she desperately tried to break free, her elbows swinging and her legs kicking. When Kevin came up and grabbed her legs, she howled even more, pleading with them both to let her go.

The sobbing wore her out, and Nancy soon fell asleep

crying, rolled up like a small child clinging to her knees in a fetal position. The atmosphere was as depressing as the lack of rescue. The group hardly looked at each other; rather, they stared at the ripples caused by the rain colliding with the dark-gray surface of the lake. Eventually, Julie broke the long-lasting silence.

"Hey, Kevin."

Kevin turned his head nonchalantly. "What?"

"How to lose weight by eating nothing but worms," Julie said, unusually slowly.

"What?"

"That's the title." Julie smiled.

"What title?"

"The title of the book I'm writing." Julie winked at Kevin.

Kevin raised his eyebrows, but never smiled back. Jack smiled briefly though.

Andrew looked confused. "What book?"

"Haven't you heard, Andrew? I'm writing a book, and I'm gonna call it How to Lose Weight by Eating Nothing but Worms."

"That's a shitty title."

"I think it might work," Julie said. "What *won't* people do to lose weight?"

"Eat worms," Andrew said sarcastically. "I'm going to write a book of my own, and call it How I Became a Millionaire."

"You're a millionaire?" Julie sounded astonished.

"No, but I will be, once I sue the airline for forcing us to eat worms in order to survive," Andrew said, sounding annoyed. "And making us wait out here in the cold."

"Well, In that case, we're all millionaires then." Julie smiled.

"*If* we ever get out of here." Andrew grinned. "Maybe that's why they're not coming for us. They can't afford the lawsuit."

"It's not the airline's responsibility to find us," Jack told them.

"I know that," Andrew said harshly. "Don't you think I know that?"

Jack sniffed. "Besides, you didn't have any worms."

"They don't know that. I remember reading about this woman who got a million-dollar settlement after eating a burger with a rat tail in it. Hell, I'll eat a few worms if it gets me a million dollars."

Julie's face suddenly shifted, and she kept staring at Andrew with a cold and empty expression. She looked as though she'd seen a ghost.

"Yeah. Can you imagine that?" Andrew looked at Julie. "To suddenly realize you're chewing on a rat tail."

Julie kept staring at Andrew with the same awkward expression.

"But at least she got a million dollars out of it," Andrew added.

"You mean that thing in L.A.?" Kevin asked. "Angela something?"

"I don't remember her name," Andrew replied. "But I think it was in L.A."

"That's how I remember her name," Kevin said. "Angela, as in Los Angeles. No, she didn't get a penny. In fact, I think she got twelve to eighteen months."

"She faked it?" Andrew sounded surprised.

"She sure did, but she used too much meat in the burger," Kevin responded. "Burger joints usually advertise their burger contains one hundred percent beef. Then people naturally assume they're getting one hundred percent meat. But in reality, they add other ingredients to the meat in order to cut the cost, or to enrich the flavor or whatever. But she didn't know that, so she made the burger purely out of ground beef. And when they examined the burger, they figured out she must have planted the burger with the rat's tail and charged her with attempted fraud."

Andrew chuckled. "Serves her right for being that stupid."

"Let me get this straight," Julie said in a diplomatic tone. "What you're saying, Kevin, is that the company fooled their customers into buying a product, different from what they were led to believe. And the same company probably made millions of dollars in the process. And in the end, that's what saved the company from a million-dollar lawsuit."

"I get what you're saying, Julie, and I guess there is some irony to this story," Kevin said. "But Angela is the villain in this story. She didn't deserve that money. She only thought of herself, and a lot of people could have lost their jobs because of her. In the end, she was just a charlatan." Kevin shook his head. "And apparently, she'd staged a car accident a few years before that. You know, for the insurance claim."

"What *won't* people do to gain wealth." Kevin actually smiled. He didn't show his teeth, but nevertheless, he did smile.

Jack and Andrew laughed, seemingly at Kevin's remark. Julie didn't smile though.

"Amen, brother," Jack said, and looked at Kevin.

The modest smile on Kevin's face suddenly vanished. Now, his eyebrows were low and sharp as he kept his focus on Jack.

Jack turned his head and looked at Julie. "I like the title of your book, Julie. I think it's funny. Come to think of it, I could give you a deeper insight on the subject. But make sure you don't use my real name." Jack winked at Julie.

Julie smiled back at Jack, and looked both humbled and embarrassed. Jack seemed to be staring at Julie's ears.

"You wouldn't happen to have any piercing do you, Julie?"

Julie shook her head. "Why do you ask?"

"If I had a hook, then perhaps I could catch a fish."

"There's a steel wire in my bra. You think that'll work?"

"It's worth a shot. If you don't mind."

"It's not going to work. The hook has to be thin and sharp enough to get stuck in the fish's mouth," Andrew quickly responded. "You're wasting your time."

Julie rolled her eyes. Then she turned her back on them and extracted her bra from under her sweater.

"There you go." Julie handed her bra to Jack. "Thirty-four B. Have fun."

Jack smiled briefly and looked a bit embarrassed. "I have to ruin it."

"I'll be sure to add it to my claim when I sue the airline." Julie had a clever smile.

A few hours later, after the rain had stopped, Jack stood in the lake with water almost up to his knees. He'd pulled his black suit pants above his kneecaps and was holding a long branch with both his hands. He'd tied his shoelaces together, and used them as a fishing line with a small rock at the end and then something that resembled a fishing hook with a worm attached to it. Kevin and Andrew stood by the lakeside, and both of them shook their heads while they focused on Jack. Julie sat by Nancy's side under the *Chanterelle* tree; Nancy was still asleep.

"Check if the worm is still there!" Andrew yelled.

Jack checked his line. The hook was still there, but the tempting bait had vanished; he replaced it with another worm from his pocket.

"It's not going to work, Jack!" Andrew yelled.

Just then, Nancy woke up, and she looked just as disorientated as before. "Look." She pointed at Jack. "He's in the water now."

"I know," Julie responded. "He's fishing."

"He doesn't have his shoes on, see..." Nancy pointed at a pair of black dress shoes by the lakeside. "He can't run fast enough if he's barefoot."

"Why would he run?" Julie asked.

"And the short one is squinting, see..." Nancy pointed at Andrew. "He can't see, and the fat one can't run that fast. We can break free now."

"What on earth are you talking about, Nancy? Those men are helping us."

"No, they're not. They're dangerous," Nancy said. "You're not thinking straight."

"No, you're not thinking straight, Nancy. You're confusing yourself."

"No, you're the one that's confused," Nancy argued. "You think they're your friends, because you're scared of them. That's what happens when you're scared. You have that *disease*... Your mind is fooling you."

Andrew turned around, and squinted as he looked at Julie and Nancy.

"We have to run." Nancy grabbed Julie's arm.

"I can't walk, Nancy. I broke my ankle. Remember?"

"They broke your ankle," Nancy said and looked at Julie with wide eyes.

"Is everything all right, back there?" Andrew asked.

"Yes, we're fine," Nancy immediately replied.

Andrew turned his attention toward the lake, and shook his head once more. "That man is too optimistic."

"I think he's religious," Kevin said. "Perhaps he thinks God is on his side."

"You mean because of that *amen* remark?" Andrew asked. "I don't think that's what he meant."

"I think I saw him praying the other day," Kevin claimed. "That's why I reacted to the amen remark. Christian people usually don't use that word except when praying."

Andrew lifted his left eyebrow. "Well, it would explain his annoying optimism."

Then Andrew glanced back at Julie and Nancy by the tree before he leaned in closer to Kevin with a cunning smile on his face.

"I know a secret too."

Kevin didn't react to Andrew's claim.

"Let's just say I know one of us isn't exactly who they

claim to be." Andrew winked his left eye as he looked at Kevin.

Kevin, suddenly looking furious, grabbed Andrew by the neck and squished his throat with his right arm.

"You shut your mouth! You hear me? This doesn't concern you."

Kevin pushed Andrew by the neck, and Andrew lost his footage and fell to the ground. Andrew stared back at Kevin with a startled and confused expression.

"They're fighting," Nancy said. "I'll get help. I promise."

Then Nancy jumped to her feet and ran toward the woods.

"Nancy's running!" Julie shouted.

Andrew was still on the ground, and squinted toward the woods. Kevin stood still and looked confused, before he eventually began to walk at a fast pace toward the woods. Then Andrew rose and ran past Kevin. Jack ran quickly to shore, trudging in water, and still holding onto his fishing pole. He put on his black dress shoes, only to lose them as soon as he started to run. His hands shook as he bent and attached his shoelaces.

Eventually, Jack ran fast and with determination into the surrounding forest, screaming Nancy's name, pleading with her to stop running.

Evening

The men and Nancy had been gone for hours. Julie was all alone, her eyes tracking back and forth across the shore. Occasionally, she yelled their names. She'd spent most of her time trying to get the branches hot enough by rubbing them against each other, but her effort seemed hopeless. Julie showed a sense of resignation as her eyes wandered between the empty sky and the distress signal written across the shoreline. The sun was about to set, and the woods grew darker as each minute passed.

Eventually, three men emerged from the shadows of the woods. Jack carried Nancy in his arms, her head tilted backward, and her left arm hanging down.

The three men seemed exhausted, and were breathing heavily. Nancy, however, wasn't moving at all.

"Is she dead?" Julie asked, a shiver in her voice.

"No, she's just sleeping," Jack said, and took another deep breath. "I found her curled up underneath a tree. She begged me to take her home. We all need to keep a better eye on her from now on."

"I'm sorry. It all happened so fast. I couldn't get hold of her."

"It's not your fault, Julie," Jack said. "We all need to keep a better eye on her."

Andrew nodded. "I'll stay closer from now on."

"Why aren't they coming for us?" Julie's voice quavered.

"I don't think the black box is transmitting a signal. If it was, they'd be here by now," Andrew said. "Something's wrong."

"They can locate planes at the bottom of the ocean," Jack said. "Finding a plane in a shallow lake shouldn't be a problem."

"Perhaps, that is the problem," Andrew responded. "The bottom of the ocean is hard, and the water's deep. However, the bottom of a shallow lake could be remarkably soft. Perhaps the transmitter's buried in mud."

"Is the transmitter located at the front or the back of the plane?" Julie asked and looked at Jack.

"How would I know?" Jack frowned.

"Well, you seem to know a lot about airplanes," Julie responded.

"I only know what's in the news," Jack claimed. "But I'm certain there's a transmitter on the plane."

"Something's wrong." Andrew shook his head. "They're not coming."

"You think we should leave?" Jack asked. "Is that what you're saying?"

"I'm just saying. If we're going to walk out of here, then we can't wait too long," Andrew said. "If it's this cold in late August, then imagine how cold it must be in October."

Jack looked across the shore. "Either way, they are looking for us. And if they fly over here, they're bound to see the sign."

"If they fly over here," Andrew replied. "But we're not where we're supposed to be. I don't think we're anywhere close to the ocean."

"Satellites are everywhere these days. Someone's always watching."

"Have you looked at a map recently, Jack? That sign is fifty feet wide, and the Canadian wilderness is half a continent."

"It's only been two days, Andrew."

"I'm not saying we should leave tomorrow, but we should at least get a better view of the surroundings," Andrew said. "A road could be within close proximity. Cars could be passing by us as we speak."

"That's true." Jack nodded.

"We should get a good view from the top of that mountain over there."

Andrew pointed at the dark silhouette of a mountain, slowly fading away in the sunset. Jack looked in the same direction.

"When you say we, I take it you mean me." Jack looked at Andrew.

"Well, there's no point in me going up there, I can only see a road if I'm standing on it. Julie can't walk, and *Candy* shouldn't walk. So, that leaves you and Bigfoot."

"What did you call me?" Kevin yelled, and looked aggressively at Andrew.

Andrew twitched. "Take it easy, Kevin. I meant it as a compliment."

“How is being referred to a hairy ape, a compliment?”

“He’s not an ape, he’s...” Andrew shrugged. “...Bigfoot.”

Kevin kept staring aggressively at Andrew.

“I just meant you’re a big guy. No more.” Andrew looked cautiously at Jack.

“He’s right, Kevin. We should pair up. There could be wolves in these woods.”

“Wolves?” Julie said in a trembling voice.

“I wouldn’t worry about that, Julie. If they come too close, just stand back to back and wave a branch at them. They’ll go away,” Jack said. “Wolves hardly ever attack people. That’s just in the movies.”

“What if we come across a bear?” Kevin asked.

“Don’t run.”

“That’s the best you got, Jack?” Kevin looked appalled. “Don’t run.”

“If we come across a bear, then we walk slowly in each direction...” Jack bowed his head. “...and we let the bear decide.”

Kevin slumped his shoulders.

16 PARADISE

Monday morning

The office landscape was buzzing, as more or less all employees were still busy keeping in touch with the passengers' families. However, George thought the word cloud that filled the room seemed slightly diminished from the loud furor over the weekend, and he assumed less screaming and crying could be heard on the other side of the lines. He felt thankful that he was a part of the crisis team, and therefore in charge of press relations, relieving him having to call the distraught and angry relatives.

Emergency crisis coordinator Cayla Marsh kept herself busy, constantly keeping in touch with the various agencies involved in the missing plane search and investigation. But the same authorities also communicated directly with the press, so whatever information Cayla received was presented on the news shortly after she had announced it to the crisis team. George's work seemed pointless, as the information on each of the press releases he'd written only stated the obvious, all the facts already known to the general public.

George wondered if he'd overestimated what part an airline played in a search for a missing airplane, or if he perhaps had overestimated this particular airline's capability in doing so. The company didn't comply with his idea of an airline, and he thought the way the company was run showed too many irregularities. However, he didn't think the mistakes were due to corruption; the errors were more a matter of incompetence.

George noticed how his boss, the CEO, sometimes stared at him through the glass walls of the man's office, and he also observed that now Williams was actually alone for once. George opened the crisis contingency plan and tried his best to give the impression that he was working. Once again, he couldn't help but notice how Cayla Marsh had wrongly used the word "personal" for the word "personnel."

The CEO kept staring at him, and then suddenly Mike gestured with his hand that George should join him in his office.

"What's the latest?" George asked.

"The ELT isn't providing a signal. They've found some debris in the lake, but it doesn't necessarily derive from the plane. It could just be garbage."

Mike Williams hadn't disclosed anything that George didn't already know.

"In addition to being the spokesperson for this crisis team, I also fill in for Jeff as human resources manager," Mike said, sounding a bit annoyed. "And I also have responsibilities as the CEO of this company."

George felt his boss had just accused him of laziness.

"How can I help?"

"I thought you could visit the captain's mother tomorrow, and make sure she's taken care off. Mrs. Daniels lives on the outskirts of Paradise, only a few hours' drive."

"What about tomorrow's press release?"

"I can handle the press release just fine," Mike responded in a short tone.

George felt that his boss had come to realize what little workload George had at this time of calamity.

"Okay then," George said. "You want me to visit the co-pilot parents also?"

"That won't be necessary," Mike responded. "His parents live in Calgary. Besides, I've already talked to his father. He has yelled at me on and off throughout the entire weekend."

"Do any of the flight attendants' families live near San Francisco?"

"Yes, but I've already scheduled a meeting for tomorrow with the mother of the flight attendant Susan Olsen."

"Is she the one who sent the text message to her husband?"

"No, that's Elisabeth McAllister," Mike said, and sounded even more annoyed.

George felt embarrassed since he realized he should've known her name by now. George always had a hard time remembering people's names.

"Elisabeth's family lives in Alaska," Mike added. "Her husband has been on just about every news channel there is."

"That text message really helped us."

"What do you mean?" Mike's eyes narrowing.

"Now the press is focusing on the terror angle. If not for the text message, the crash could have been an accident, and then the press would be all over us, instead of blaming the rest of the world," George explained.

It didn't seem as Mike Williams cared for George's analysis.

"Susan Olsen is a twenty-six-year-old single mom. No siblings, and her father passed away last year—and it was her first day on the job," Mike said in a sharp tone.

Her first day? George felt a tension in his chest.

17 HUNGER

Monday morning

The sunlight broke through the dark silhouette of the forest and illuminated the lake's surface. At the same time, the wind ruffled the water, breaking up the sun's hypnotic radiance.

Julie woke, blinked several times, and then squinted across the shoreline. Kevin walked fast and determinedly toward the mountain. Jack tried to catch up with him, and when he finally did, he put his arms on Kevin's shoulder. Kevin then lashed out with his right arm in Jack's direction.

"Get away from me!" Kevin roared, and then picked up the pace.

"Jack!" Julie shouted.

Jack stopped, and looked toward Julie with a startled expression.

"Is everything all right between you two?"

"We're heading for the mountain. We'll be back before sunset," Jack said loudly. "Take good care of Nancy. Make sure she doesn't run away."

"Are you on bad terms with Kevin?"

"It's nothing, Julie. Everything is fine."

Jack ran fast to intercept Kevin, and then the two of them disappeared into the woods. Eventually, Julie turned her attention toward the lake, and then suddenly, she burst into tears, covering her face with the palm of her hands.

"This can't be happening," she mumbled.

"Are you all right, Julie?" Andrew asked in a groggy morning voice.

Julie jolted and quickly wiped the tears away. "I was just thinking of all the people who died in the crash. It's so sad."

"Did you know any of the other passengers?"

"No, it was just me."

"Don't get me wrong, I think it's tragic too, but at the same time, people are dying every day."

"What do you mean by that?"

"I mean, I didn't know any of the passengers. They were all strangers to me," Andrew said. "Thousands of people die each day, but I don't feel sorry for them, because I didn't know any of them."

"Children are waiting in vain for their parents to return, and you don't find that sad?" Julie stared at Andrew. "What a selfish and careless thing to say."

"Don't get me wrong, Julie. I think it's sad, but I don't find it sadder than knowing that unknown people are dying across the country as we speak, or across the world for that matter. I'm not selfish. I'm only human, and I'm glad it wasn't me who died in the crash."

"You're glad? Seriously, Andrew?"

"You're telling me you don't feel relieved to be alive?"

"No, I feel nothing of the kind. I'm not like you, Andrew. Do you even hear yourself? Can't you hear, how wrong it sounds?"

Andrew got up, and walked in the direction of the hillside, and toward the tree where he'd spent the first night.

"Where are you going?" Julie yelled.

"I'm going to take a piss!"

"Don't walk too far. You need to be close to Nancy!"

Just then, Nancy woke up, and the two women went the opposite way of Andrew, but with the same purpose. Before they returned to the *Chanterelle* tree (which they had referred to as home) they drank plenty of water from the lake. Andrew was already "home."

"What did you mean when you said that you're not like me?"

"I just pointed out that we're different from one another," Julie said.

"So, you think you're better than me?"

Julie rolled her eyes. "No, I didn't say that. I just pointed out that we're different. If you take offense, then it's due to your own perception of yourself. I imagine a person with high self-esteem would probably take that as a compliment. So, the real question you should be asking is why you have such a low opinion of yourself?"

Andrew looked uncomfortable and never answered Julie's question.

"And when, or if, you ever find the answer to that question, then, you can change your ways and become a different person," Julie added.

"So, you're a psychologist all the sudden." Andrew smirked. "I thought you were a cleaning woman?"

"Yes, I'm a cleaning *woman*. Thank you for pointing that out. It makes all the difference," Julie said, and rolled her eyes again. "But I'm also a human being. You wouldn't happen to know what that's like, do you, Andy?"

"Stop calling me Andy. My name is Andrew."

"Why did Kevin push you to the ground yesterday *Andrew*?"

Andrew seemed startled by the sudden question. "It was just two guys blowing off steam. We're all hungry and frustrated."

"What do you mean by that? Did you argue about food?"

"I don't have any food," Andrew responded quickly.

"What was the argument about, then?"

"I made a comment about his size, and he took offense." Andrew shrugged.

Julie shook her head. "Jack wouldn't have teased Kevin

about his size."

"Jack..." Andrew frowned. "What's he got to do with anything?"

"They got into an argument this morning. Jack grabbed Kevin by his shoulder. Then Kevin lashed out at him, and Kevin looked really upset."

"Maybe Jack wanted to borrow his jacket." Andrew shrugged. "Can't blame Jack for being pissed off at Kevin for hogging the jacket."

"But it's his jacket," Julie said hesitantly. "Besides, it's just a blazer."

"Jack is just wearing a shirt. A blazer would make a huge difference."

"I asked him if he wanted to borrow my sweater, but he didn't seem eager at all."

"That's because your sweater would look like a handkerchief on him," Andrew said. "But Kevin is almost as big as Jack. That blazer would fit Jack perfectly."

"Did you notice Jack boarding the plane?"

"No, I only noticed Nancy."

"I bet you did." Julie sighed.

"Okay, what is that supposed to mean?"

"It means you're using every chance you get to look at Nancy's breasts. Must you do that?" Julie asked. "All the time?"

"I'm a man." Andrew shrugged.

Julie looked Andrew up and down a few times. "Are you sure about that?"

"It's not my fault I was born a man. It's not as though I had a choice."

"What's that supposed to mean?"

"It means, you're basically blaming evolution."

"Excuse me," Julie said sarcastically.

"When evolution took place, both genders looked more or less the same, except women had breasts. So, men are supposed to look for people with breasts. In order to procreate, and to secure the survival of our species, and all that." Andrew shrugged.

"So you're blaming it on instinct? Is that it?"

"Well, that too, I suppose. But the main reason men look for breast is because they are rewarded with a good sensation when doing so. Kind of like when you eat something high in calories, such as fat and sugar. To encourage you to keep eating, your brain rewards you with dopamine and such."

"Just because something brings you delight, doesn't mean you have to do it. Either way, you still have a choice. I enjoy chocolate, but I don't stuff myself every chance I get. I can control my urges," Julie said. "You still control your eyes, don't you?"

Andrew took a few deep breaths before answering. "Why don't you?"

"Why don't I what?"

"Why don't you eat chocolate every chance you get?"

"Because I care about my health." Julie shrugged. "What do you want me to say?"

"Exactly, that's my point. But when men stare at breasts, they don't endanger their health," Andrew said. "If you could eat unlimited amounts of chocolate without, endangering your health, then wouldn't you eat chocolate every chance you got?"

"I know I would," Nancy suddenly said.

Julie arched her eyebrows. "You're such a pig, Andy."

"Yeah…" Andrew sighed loudly. "Men are pigs."

"No, I didn't say that." Julie raised her index finger in the air. "Not all men, just you, Andy. You're the pig."

"Stop calling me Andy. I told you, my name is Andrew."

Julie arched her eyebrows once more. "You're such a pig —Andrew."

Andrew sighed heavily before he rose to his feet and walked determinedly along the shore. This time, toward the mountain.

"That's a little harsh," Nancy said.

"I don't care for him. He's a misogynist."

"What does that got to do with anything?" Nancy asked. "People should be free to have sex any way they please. Just because you're boring in bed, doesn't mean the rest of us have to be. Besides, most of these guys just do it for the money."

Julie looked clueless. "What on earth are you talking about?"

"And you didn't answer the question," Nancy added.

"What question?"

"If you could eat anything you wanted without gaining any weight. Then wouldn't you stuff yourself?" Nancy asked. "I know I would."

"I know what you mean. I'm hungry too."

Nancy made an attempt to rise, but Julie grabbed her arm.

"Where you're going?" Julie asked.

"I'm going to talk to him before he disappears into the woods."

"No, you shouldn't walk," Julie said. "Let's just sit here, and wait for Jack."

"Who?"

"You remember Jack, don't you? The big guy."

"The black guy?"

"No, that's Kevin." Julie exhaled heavily. "The other guy. The pale one with, all the muscles."

"Oh, him. I don't know his name."

Julie sighed and also shook her head. "Jack is his name."

"I meant I don't know his real name."

Julie frowned. "What did you say?"

"Jack isn't his real name," Nancy mumbled.

Julie's face plummeted, and she kept staring at Nancy with wide eyes.

"We're not supposed to use our real names," Nancy said. "Your real name isn't Julie, is it?"

Julie's face dropped once more, and she took her time before answering.

"I don't know what you're talking about," Julie said.

"You're not making any sense, Nancy."

"What did you call me?"

Julie exhaled deeply. "Did you board the plane with Jack? Or whatever his name is. Do you two know each other? Is that what you're saying?"

Nancy blinked a few times and looked as though she was about to fall asleep.

"What plane?"

Julie closed her eyes, and rubbed her forehead. Then she explained to Nancy all that had happened over the past few days. For the next several hours, Nancy dozed on and off, and each time she woke up, she drank a substantial amount of water from the lake.

Afternoon

A few hours later, Andrew finally returned to the sloping tree, and when he saw Nancy; he looked mortified.

"Is she all right? She looks drunk."

"Of course, she's not all right. She needs a hospital," Julie responded harshly. "She's delusional, and the swelling on her temple is even worse."

Nancy kept leaning forward, and her body had the same posture as the notorious tree; her pupils were dilated, and she kept focusing on Andrew.

"I'm Andrew."

Nancy didn't respond, but eventually she extended her arm, and pointed at Andrew's crotch, her eyes flickering.

Andrew took his cell phone out of his pants pocket. "It's just my phone."

"Did you find any food?" Julie asked.

"I found some mushrooms, but I was afraid to have any."

Julie sighed heavily.

"How's it going with those chopsticks?" Andrew

pointed at the branches without bark. "I thought you were going to start a fire?"

Julie rolled her eyes, then looked at Nancy.

"As I was saying, some people have such low self-esteem, they feel the need to humiliate and ridicule other people in order to feel better about themselves. That way, they don't have to think poorly of themselves—instead they can think poorly of others."

Andrew smirked. "Subtle. That's real subtle, Julie."

Julie kept her eyes on Nancy. "A person with good self-esteem can see the beauty in others, and especially in people who can't see the beauty in themselves. They care—"

"That's from Harry Potter," Andrew interrupted.

Julie swallowed once, and looked uncomfortable "So what? I can't quote someone else, is that what you're saying?"

"You make it sound like it's something you thought of." Andrew chuckled. "What, you just quote others, then try to pass their wisdom off as your own. That's so weak."

Julie kept staring Andrew in the eyes, but eventually she turned her head around and whispered a few words to Nancy, who then briefly looked at Andrew before she burst into laughter. At that, the two women looked at each other and then laughed even louder. Then something happened to Andrew's face. He didn't look like the same person anymore. His facial muscles appeared all cramped up. His profile didn't look the same. His eyes held an empty, metallic stare, and his eyes locked in on Nancy.

Andrew suddenly jumped to his feet and lashed out with his arm toward Nancy. He grabbed onto her forearm, which she seemingly was using to protect her face.

"I know who you are!" Andrew screamed in Nancy's face.

"You're hurting her, Andrew."

"I know who you really are." Andrew squeezed Nancy's forearm.

"Let go of her, Andrew. You're hurting her!" Julie's voice

trembled.

"You're just a dirty whore! Aren't you, Candy?"

Andrew pushed Nancy's arm toward her before he let her go and then he began walking away, this time toward the hillside, in the opposite direction of the mountain.

"What's wrong with you? Are you *insane*?" Julie's voice cracked.

Nancy cracked altogether and started to sob as if overwhelmed. "He hates me."

"Never mind what he thinks."

"But I'm a whore. That's why he hates me," Nancy mumbled while gasping for air.

"You're not a whore. Don't say that, Nancy."

"I fuck people for money. That's why he hates me," Nancy blurted out, and then she sobbed endlessly while drool ran down her jaw.

A few minutes later, Nancy began to calm down.

"You're a prostitute?" Julie eventually asked.

"Yes," Nancy said, trembling.

Julie brushed Nancy's hair over her ear. "It's okay, Nancy."

"No, I'm disgusting." Nancy kept crying, though not as intensely as before.

"No, you're not disgusting. Don't you ever say that about yourself," Julie told her. "I'm sure you have your reasons, and I'm sure most people would have done the same if they were ever in the same situation."

"What do you mean?" Nancy swallowed and stopped crying.

"Just because a person is rich and privileged, doesn't make them of higher morals. And if you're poor and desperate, it doesn't make you a person of lesser morals," Julie said. "There's no shame in being poor and desperate, Nancy."

"But I'm not poor. I have lots of money."

"What?" Julie looked surprised.

"I'm very good with money. I have lots of money. And

I own my apartment," Nancy asserted. "I mean, I'm already done paying the mortgage."

"Oh..." Julie mumbled. "Good for you."

Julie turned her head, and looked the other way. Then suddenly, her expression shifted. Now, she looked angry, and she kept staring at the hillside.

Evening

Darkness had cast its spell on the last two residents of the odd-shaped tree down by the shore. Julie and Nancy slept back to back, both of them clinging onto a large branch. Andrew slept by the same tree where he'd seemingly spent the first night. Julie had pleaded for him to join them by the *Chanterelle* tree, but the stubborn man stood his ground. Not even the prospect of wolves attacking made him change his mind.

Jack and Kevin hadn't returned.

18 THE TRUCK

Any other day

I did everything right, yet my life is ruined.

I stayed in school. I never did drugs. I had goals in life, and I worked ambitiously to reach them. I just made one little mistake. I was brave when I should have been scared, and I was scared when I should have been brave. I never contemplated the risk. I was in a hurry—it was almost 10 p.m.

Oh, how I wish I had been a scared person, a careful and wary person. I was never afraid. My little brother told me I was the bravest person he knew. And I was always in a hurry. If only I'd had more time, then perhaps my life wouldn't have been ruined. Now all I have is time. Minutes feel like hours... Especially when I'm in pain.

No one can hear me scream. I scream in silence. Every day is the same. Hours of physical and emotional agony. But the remorse is worse than the pain. I wake up every morning, and I feel furious with myself. I can never forgive myself. I had one life, and I ruined it. I had one bad moment. I made one little mistake, and now my life is forever squandered.

I used to be strong. My baby brother called me Pippi when we were young. But, now I can't even move my legs. I just lie in bed and wait for my life to end. My body doesn't move. All it does is produce pain. Waves and waves of agonizing pain. I'm trapped in my own body, in my own consciousness, and I have no way to escape. Only death can set me free.

Oh, how I hope they'll kill me soon, and put me out of my misery.

Sometimes, I actually think I'm dead. The sunlight, makes the white walls shine so bright. But when I try to step into the light, I realize I'm still trapped in this bed with nothing to do but to wait for my life to pass me by.

There's a TV on the wall. They leave it on for the most of the day. I think they do it for my sake, but all it does is to remind me of all the things I'm missing out on in life. All the dreams I had, all the places to travel, all the children to bear, and all the food to taste. They feed me something, but all food has lost its flavor. Just like my life.

I might as well be dead.

I feel like I died a long time ago but no one noticed.

I don't remember when, but I remember the truck.

19 ECHOES

Tuesday morning

"Help!"

The light, misty rain swirled through the air, and the wind silenced most sounds, except the cries of a lonesome woman screaming her lungs out in a voice that sounded terrified.

"Andrew!" Julie yelled. "Please!"

Julie sat on her knees and stared at the tree where Andrew had spent the night alone. She rose to her feet, and limped a few yards down the shore.

"Andrew! Why won't you answer me?" Julie's voice sounded raspy.

Julie limped in the direction of the hillside where she and Jack had spent the first night. She took her eyes off the slippery terrain and looked at the tree.

"Andrew! You have to wake up!"

Julie lost her footage and slipped in the mud, and her knee collided with a small rock. Her hands shook as she clasped her kneecap. She crawled on her hands and knees toward the tree where Andrew had spent the night. Then suddenly, she stopped, and her lower lip began to tremble as her tears mixed with the raindrops running down her forehead.

"Andrew! Where are you?"

Julie looked up the steep hillside and into the surrounding woods.

"Andrew! I need your help! Nancy's missing!" Her voice echoed across the landscape.

20 CRASH SITE

Tuesday morning

The initial plan was to visit Captain David Daniels's mother in Paradise and then return to San Francisco the same day. However, George's car had barely made it across the bridge to Oakland. So the plan was now to visit the widow Mrs. Irene Daniels in the afternoon, and then spend the night at a hotel in Paradise. After several hours in Oakland, they decided to leave George's car behind, and instead replace it with a new model rental car with all possible features—all at the expense of Fare Airlines.

Mike Williams had directed that his young assistant, Trisha Boyle, join George on his trip to Paradise. Not only could she assist him by offering a female touch with Mrs. Daniels, but she'd also help him pass the time driving. At first, George hadn't thought twice about the remark from his boss. However, after spending just a few minutes with Trisha Boyle, he came to realize why 'time would fly in her presence.' She hadn't stopped talking since they'd left San Francisco this morning; until, just now.

Trisha Boyle had suddenly stopped talking, and was now staring at George.

What is the safest response? he asked himself.

"I'm not sure I follow," he mumbled.

"You know what a steamroller is, don't you, George?"

George felt oblivious to what the conversation was about.

"To flatten the road," he said hesitantly.

"And they drive really slow," Trisha said with a witty smile.

George nodded in agreement.

"So, have you ever been rear-ended by a steamroller?"

George felt a sense of relief. "Now, I get it. You think I'm driving too slow?"

"Oh, come on, mister," Trisha said. "I spent like two hours on that joke. The least you can do is pretend to laugh."

Two hours? That is funny, George thought, then began to laugh, and so did Trisha Boyle. But contrary to him (or any other person he'd ever met), she actually pronounced the laughter. A loud series of "H"s and "A"s echoed in the car. George began to wonder if Trisha Boyle was experiencing some sort of seizure. He stopped laughing and looked at her vigilantly.

Suddenly, Trisha Boyle stopped laughing. "You're not offended, are you, George? Because I didn't mean to imply Asian people suck at driving, or anything."

To George's relief, Trisha Boyle had resumed normal breathing, and no longer seemed to require a trip to the emergency room.

"No, of course not," he said, and made sure to smile. "In fact, I think my mother might have invented that stereotype. That's probably why I'm such a cautious driver, I'm still traumatized from riding in a car with her as a child. Still to this day, she stops the car in the middle of the intersection whenever she's making a left turn." He shook his head in disbelief.

"She stops in the middle of the intersection?"

"If the intersection has a traffic light. You see, when the light turns green, my mother turns left. But once she's on the road she's crossed to, she stops, because there, the light is red. Then, she waits for that traffic light to turn green as well."

"Where did she learn how to drive?"

"Her parents are from China, but she was born and raised in America. My father was born and raised in Japan, but he doesn't drive that way. Except for when he's driving with my mom. Then he stops in the intersection to avoid her yelling at him—red means stop," he said in an elderly female voice.

"I'm Scotch-Irish by the way," Trisha said. "This basically means that I'm constantly drunk."

George felt a bit surprised by the sudden remark and didn't know how to respond, except to nod his head slightly and smile.

"I'm drunk right now. Can't you tell?" Trisha bit her lower lip.

"Well, that would explain all the talking."

George braced himself for another series of laughter. But to his surprise, Trisha didn't laugh at his clever remark. Instead, she looked the other way.

"Fine, I won't say another word for the rest of the trip, I'll just sit here, and be totally quiet," Trisha said, and then crossed her arms.

George tried to think of the best way to apologize, but before he could, Trisha Boyle rendered his attempt unnecessary.

"Okay, I was bluffing," Trisha said in a tone of defeat. "One of us has to say something, and until a few minutes ago, you hadn't said anything at all."

George Stanton restrained himself from explaining the reason why.

"If you think I'm talking too much, then you should meet my mom. She talks a lot more than I do," Trisha told him. "Whenever we have dinner, the food usually gets cold before we finish eating."

"Well, that would explain why you're so thin," he said, and winked.

"Oh, nice save, mister." Trisha tilted her head. "You're one of those smooth talkers, aren't you? You think you can talk your way out of anything, am I right?"

For a brief second George felt exposed as he was somehow caught in the act. "Well, I am the public relations manager, so I have—"

"Oh, is that what you are? Mike never told me what you did. I thought you were some kind of lawyer or something," Trisha said, and smiled. "I'm glad to go on this trip with you, George."

He was taken aback by her tone of voice. Trisha Boyle made it sound as if they were on a vacation getaway.

"Getting out of the office feels good. My head is still numb from all those phone calls, and I'm glad Mike didn't send me to Yellowknife. I'd much rather join you in Paradise," Trisha added and kept staring at him with an amused smile.

George was well aware that the crisis team had ignored his advice against escorting the passengers' families to Yellowknife, and their doing so still annoyed him.

"Did all the families accept the invitation to Yellowknife?" he asked even though he knew the answer.

"No, most of them declined the offer."

"I wonder why," he mumbled and shook his head.

"I don't know. Maybe they're too upset to travel, it could—"

"No, I meant, why would they want to travel to Yellowknife?" He cut her off.

"To be near the crash site," Trisha replied, and sounded slightly insulted.

"What crash site?"

"The lake," Trisha said. "Yellowknife is right by the Great Slave."

"But no one knows for certain that the plane crashed into the lake," he argued.

"The plane has to be in the lake, George. Where else would it be?"

George thought of the German plane that had crashed into the French Alps, and how the entire plane had simply crumbled after the explosion. The debris from the plane had appeared as ordinary garbage spread across the mountainside. Looking at the landscape, no one would have guessed that a plane crash had ever taken place there.

"Just because the plane dropped below radar near the lake, that doesn't necessarily mean it crashed into the lake," he said. "It could have kept going. Perhaps it crashed into a mountain."

"But someone would have noticed the debris by now," Trisha argued.

George didn't see the need to bring up the German plane.

"Besides, what are the families going to do in Yellowknife?" he asked. "Except stare at the lake, I mean."

"Perhaps they'll find comfort in being around other victims' families," Trisha said. "And maybe they'll feel a sense of relief at being close to the crash site."

What crash site? he thought, and then imagined a scene in which the families had scattered flowers across the shore and said their goodbyes to their loved ones, only to learn that the actual crash had occurred at an entirely different location.

"Either way, it can't hurt," Trisha added.

It can't hurt to have the victims' families running around a potential crash site? Then he imagined another scene in which the families stumbled across the remains of their relatives scattered across a nearby mountain.

"No, it can't hurt," he said, and tried his best to disguise the sarcasm in his voice, as he had no desire to argue further.

George wondered if the dangerous idea was a result of people in general not thinking rationally in a time of crisis, or if the airlines company itself was the problem. Either way, he thought the company had catastrophe written all over it, and a guided tour to a potential crash site for the families—who were to be plaintiffs in a future lawsuit against the airlines—only emphasized the problem in management. Even the name Fare Airlines was a stupid one, not to mention the contest that had led to the name.

"Wait a minute!" Trisha twitched and suddenly pointed at him, her eyes wide. "You're the one who came up with that naming contest."

George sighed internally.

"That was totally awesome. I love the way you tricked the media into giving the company millions of dollars' worth of advertising. Do you have any other strategies lined up?" Trisha asked, radiating enthusiasm.

The actual contest had never been George's idea. He was just left dealing with the repercussions of what must have been the dumbest contest ever in American corporate history. However, he didn't feel the need to set Trisha Boyle straight.

"Nope."

"I have an idea," Trisha said. "But you have to share credit if you use it, okay?"

"Okay."

"You could announce to the press that from now on female passengers will get a discount based on their cup sizes." Trisha gesticulated with her hands across her chest. "If you got double D's, then you'll get the double discount. Can you imagine the billboards, George?" Trisha asked, before she had a minor "seizure" while stuttering, "D.D. as in double discount. Get it, George?"

This time, hearing Trisha Boyle pronounce some tremendous laughter didn't scare him. Instead, he thought her laughter was quite amusing. At first, George couldn't restrain himself from laughing, but eventually, he began to feel guilty for laughing at her, rather than with her.

Trisha wiped the tears from her eyes. "That's good stuff. So, what you think?"

"I thought it was funny."

Didn't you hear me laughing—at you?

"I know it was funny," Trisha said. "But are you going to use it?"

"Use what?"

"My idea," Trisha said with a proud smile. "And you promised you'd share credit. Don't you forget that, George."

George wasn't sure if Trisha Boyle was seriously suggesting implementing a discount based on the size of women's breasts, or if her comment was just another attempt at humor. However, judging be her expression, she appeared to be serious.

"That would be illegal. I mean, we can't break the law," he said hesitantly.

"No, it can't be illegal, can it?"

Judging women by the size of their breasts, isn't illegal?

But on the other hand, men appear to be doing so on a regular basis.

Well, not all men. I mean, I do no such thing.

"Trust me, it has to be illegal."

"No, it can't be illegal to lie to the press. It's not as if we're lying to the cops or anything," Trisha said. "It's not our fault if they're gullible."

George just realized he'd somehow misinterpreted Trisha Boyle's plan.

"Wait, you didn't think I meant to actually implement the discount, did you, George?" Trisha asked, and then pronounced a short laugh.

George felt dumb, and now, ridiculed. "What exactly is your plan, Trisha?"

"I'm merely suggesting you trick the media into believing so. And once the news goes viral, you can disclose that you only did it for the media exposure."

"But that plan would solely depend on the media writing a retraction," he said. "I mean, why would the media set people straight, once they'd realized they've been manipulated?"

"Oh, yeah." Trisha slumped down. "I never thought of that."

Even if Trisha's suggestion was both absurd and inappropriate, the possibility of provoking people in order to get their attention was not. If George could get the press to misinterpret his intentions, then they'd have no choice but to write a retraction. And if the media didn't see the need to correct their mistake, then he could even threaten them with a potential lawsuit. George started to wonder as he thought of the possibilities of such a creative marketing strategy. Perhaps he could use words with different meaning in order to lure the media into drawing the wrong conclusion?

What words associated with airline travel can be misinterpreted?

As his mind wandered, he lost his focus on the road. Fortunately, the automatic braking system engaged and slowed down the car just enough, to avoid a collision with the other car crossing the intersection. George felt relieved with today's chain of events; his own car didn't have an automatic braking system.

Trisha, however, was boiling over with rage. George tried his best to keep her from sounding the horn, but his attempt was futile. As he carefully drove through the intersection, his much younger co-worker kept screaming out the passenger window even though the car in question was long gone.

"Why aren't you upset?" Trisha asked with wet eyes.

"I'm really sorry. I should have been paying better attention to the road."

"You shouldn't be sorry, George. You should be angry," Trisha said. "It's not your fault. It's his fault. You had the right of way."

"I prefer not to get angry." he said. "And I'm pretty sure it was a woman driving."

"What do you mean by you prefer not to be angry? You can't choose when to be angry. It's not possible to choose your emotions."

"I mean, why assume the worst?"

"What are you talking about?" Trisha asked loudly.

"I know I had the right of way, but I don't know the

reason why the other driver failed to give it. Perhaps the driver had a good reason."

"Like what?" Trisha yelled.

"Perhaps her son was bleeding out in the backseat, and they were on their way to the hospital. Or she could be chasing a person who abducted her child. I mean, who knows?"

Trisha Boyle suddenly went all quiet and looked out the passenger window.

"The point being, I'll never know why the driver didn't give the right of way. However, I can make one assumption and keep driving with a sense of compassion and understanding. Or I can make another assumption, and keep driving with a sense of anger and frustration," he said. "I prefer not to assume the worst, because it makes me feel better. I prefer not to get angry."

Trisha Boyle kept staring out the passenger window and didn't speak. George could tell by her reflection that she was really upset, but he wasn't sure why.

"I'm not saying we can control our emotions. I'm just saying we can choose how to think. You know what I mean?"

Trisha didn't respond to his question. George then went through a mental transcript of what he'd said in the past few minutes, but he didn't find any reason for why the so-talkative Trisha Boyle suddenly went quiet.

"I have a son," Trisha eventually said in a gentle voice.

"Yeah... Well, good for him," he said.

George noticed a smile in her reflection, but Trisha never turned around.

"I'm sure he's just fine, Trisha."

"He's with my mom," Trisha said and looked him in the eyes.

21 SOLITUDE

Tuesday afternoon

She had stopped screaming their names.

She was all alone.

As the rain had picked up, she'd curled up closer to the tree trunk under the odd-shaped tree that resembled a crooked mushroom. She had her arms around her legs, and she kept staring at her swollen ankle with puffy and tired eyes. Then she glanced at the branches free of tree bark, and just at that moment she burst into tears.

Eventually, she looked at the mountain, her eyes scanning endlessly across the terrain. She wondered if Kevin and Jack had found a road, and that was the reason for them not returning.

She felt vulnerable and scared. The feeling reminded her of her childhood, and how she'd had no other choice but to accept her life as it was—she'd had little or no possibility to change her life back then. But she didn't blame her parents for not being there. Instead, she blamed everyone else, and especially teachers and social workers whose job it was to keep her safe. She thought of all the pain she'd had to endure because people didn't do their jobs properly. Now, sitting in solitude, she felt just the same way. Her pain was yet again caused by people not conducting their jobs properly. People who weren't able to perform the simple tasks they'd been trained to do.

"I hate you!" she screamed at the top of her lungs.

Then she picked up a stone about the same size as her hand and threw it across at the lake, in the same direction as the hillside and the tree where Andrew had spent the night.

"I hate you!" she screamed again while her lips trembled and spit was dripping from her mouth. "It's all your fault," she mumbled and resumed crying.

22 THE PASSENGER

Tuesday afternoon

After being lost in Paradise for quite some time, George and Trisha finally found their way to the home of the widow, Mrs. Irene Daniels, on the outskirts of town. The red house was wedged in between a mountain and a road. The white picket fence and the perfect green lawn made the property look picturesque. Several apple trees were growing in the yard, but none with apples. On the front lawn was a massively over-proportioned bronze statue of a horse attacking a man, the horse ready to strike with its hooves against the man lying on the ground with a frightened look on his face.

George and Trisha were greeted by a resident of German descent. The dog obediently performed its duties and made sure the visitors stayed outside the fence. However, as soon as Mrs. Daniels opened the gate, the dog lost all interest, and was happy to resume his prior engagement—which seemed to be slacking off on the porch.

After the usual mandatory greeting, and following small talk, George couldn't help but ask Mrs. Daniels about the enormous statue.

"My late husband made it to remind us all to be humble in his presence," Irene said. "And to honor him."

He made a statue in his own honor?

"To honor your husband?" he asked, feeling confused.

"To honor our Lord," Irene said in a decisive tone.

Mrs. Daniels gave George a reprimanding stare before she turned her back on him and proceeded down the perfectly crafted gravel aisle that led to the house. George looked at Trisha, and for a split second he wondered if perhaps she was a religious person also. However, he quickly dismissed the thought as soon as he saw her expression; Trisha Boyle ground her teeth, and her shoulders almost touched her ears.

Trisha quickly joined Irene in walking down the path, and the two of them seemed to talk about the flowers Trisha had bought for Mrs. Daniels. Again, George felt relieved regarding today's chain of events, and was glad Michael Williams had talked him into including Trisha Boyle on his journey. Before he joined the two women on the gravel path, he took another look at the massive statue. This time, he noticed the inscription on the pedestal.

JEHOVAH

The hours flew by as Mrs. Irene Daniels and Trisha Boyle had at least one thing in common. George, however, hardly spoke at all. Mrs. Daniels didn't seem to be interested in finance or liability claims. She did, however, enjoy talking about her son. She explained to Trisha how captain David Daniels never got to know his father, as her late husband had died not long after David was born. And she explained how her son had been a fighter pilot for the US Air Force, and how he'd served in Afghanistan. For at least an hour, the widow Mrs. Irene Daniels had displayed several albums with pictures of her son in uniform. George thought Captain Daniels very much matched his own mental image of a typical US soldier. The man was tall and muscular. The captain reminded George of the G.I. Joe doll he'd played with as a child.

Mrs. Daniels also disclosed it was she who'd convinced her son to quit the Air Force, and pursue a safer career as a commercial airline pilot. George felt uncomfortable as he thought of the irony, and he got the impression Trisha must have felt the same way, because suddenly, the so-loquacious Trisha Boyle had nothing to say.

However, after a long and awkward silence, the German resident of the house unintentionally provided the group with entertainment. The German shepherd not only pushed his bowl of food out of the kitchen, but he also managed to cross the long hallway and most of the living room. But then, the dog suddenly stopped eating and tilted his head, while he kept staring at Trisha Boyle who "pronounced" some tremendously high-pitched laughter; Mrs. Daniels, on the other hand, appeared to be in shock.

"Are you all right, dear?" Irene asked Trisha.

Trisha Boyle wiped the tears from her eyes, before she stuttered, "Yes, I'm fine."

Mrs. Daniels seemed relieved. "I'm glad, dear."

"What a lovely dog you have," Trisha said. "And what a great name by the way."

George realized he must have dozed off sometime during the previous conversation because he had no idea what the dog's name was.

"It's not my dog," Irene said, and kept her eyes on the dog.

"Oh, is it David's dog?" Trisha asked.

"No, the dog belongs to her."

George detected a deeper tone in Mrs. Daniels's voice, and Trisha Boyle looked startled by the drastic change in the elderly woman's mood.

"She didn't care about the dog before, but now, she suddenly wants him back," Irene said in the same deep tone. "She never cared about David either. She lured him. She's the devil in disguise and sinks her claws into whatever comes her way."

Trisha looked genuinely frightened. "Are you all right, Irene?"

"There will come a day when she can't hide no more. Hide behind all her lies. She can lie in court, but she can't lie in front of our Lord," Irene said, and kept her focus on the dog. "There will be a reckoning, and on that day, she will get all she deserves."

George felt as if he'd witnessed a reverse exorcism, and a demon was now in possession of Mrs. Daniels' body. Trisha looked at him as though she asking for his assistance. George cleared his throat before he spoke for the first time in the past hour.

"His ex-wife gets the dog?" he asked the *demon*.

"They're still married. The divorce isn't final." Mrs. Daniels turned her head slowly and looked at George. "Oh, I bet she's having a laugh now."

George understood perfectly what Mrs. Daniels meant by the last remark. If the divorce wasn't final, then the wife could claim the insurance policy as well as any potential legal claims against the airline.

George swallowed. "David only listed you as his emergency contact. We didn't know about his wife. May I ask what her name is?" He tried his best to disguise his nervous tone.

"Sharon." Irene pronounced the name only with her lower lip.

"Sharon Daniels?" he asked.

"No, she'll go by her maiden name now," Irene responded. "Her name is Stone. Much like her heart."

Trisha looked as if she'd have seen a ghost. "Sharon's maiden name is Stone?"

George got the impression the elderly woman didn't understand the reference to the famous American actress. He also thought Trisha Boyle looked as if she was about to be sick, or possibly burst into tears.

"Irene, may I please use your bathroom?" Trisha asked in a quivering voice.

And just like that, Mrs. Daniels was suddenly loosed from the demon's spell of hatred, and her nurturing side returned. Now, the elderly woman smiled at Trisha.

"Yes, certainly, dear. It's the second door on the right,

just past the hallway."

George watched Trisha walk through the living room. Then, she suddenly stopped in the hallway and desperately searched through her purse. At first, George felt curious as to why she would go through the content of her purse on her way to the bathroom. But then, he saw his reflection in the hallway mirror, and noticed Mrs. Daniels' condescending stare in the background. At that moment, he realized he was invading Trisha's privacy.

George quickly averted his eyes. "Thank you again for the apple pie. It was truly amazing, Mrs. Daniels. May I ask if you made it yourself?" George felt confident he already knew the answer to the question.

"Call me Irene. Yes, I made it from scratch. I use apples from my own garden," Irene said. "David loves apples. Even as a grown man, he loved to bake an apple pie with me, whenever he came to visit. At least when he came on his own."

For a second, it would appear that the demon was back. But then, Irene lowered her eyes, only to suddenly raise them again and look at George with a stiff smile.

"David used to sell apples by the side of the road when he was a young boy. He was very creative as a child. He'd always find some use for whatever came his way."

George's phone vibrated in his pocket. Even though tempted to read the text message, he decided not to when he saw the judgmental look on Irene's face. He made sure to smile politely at her, to underline his courteous manner.

"The secret is to brush the crust with egg whites. It makes the crust crispy."

George pretended to care and nodded his head accordingly. He was just about to ask for the recipe when his phone vibrated once more.

He reached for his phone. "Excuse me."

"Oh, I'm sure you're a busy man," Irene said.

George wondered if the last remark was meant as an insult, or as a gesture of understanding. However, as soon as he saw the message, he couldn't care less. He recognized the phone number from this morning. The message however, was blank, completely free of words.

George turned his head and saw Trisha standing in the hallway. She appeared to be hiding from Irene, and was out of the elderly woman's view. She had her cell phone in her hand, and the screen was facing George's way. It was too far away for him to make out the words, but he could tell she wanted him to see a list displayed on a white background. Trisha kept staring back at him with a face of horror and disbelief. She looked like a young child who'd stumbled into the wrong bedroom and caught her parents in the act. She seemed appalled and terrified at having discovered the truth. Then George noticed his reflection in the hallway mirror, and realized he had the same look on his face.

George then looked at the first text message Trisha Boyle had sent him.

I think I know what happened to the plane!!!

23 WOLVES

Tuesday evening

Her eyes were wide open, but she had nothing to see except for darkness; the moonlight couldn't penetrate the clouds.

She sat with her back against the sloping tree trunk, her hands tight around a large branch she held across her chest. Hearing a low, cracking sound escaping the dark woods, she shuddered and rose to her feet. The branch high up in the air, she was ready to swing.

She feared wolves were closing in on her, so she leaned directly against the tree trunk and kept swinging the branch back and forth.

"Go away!" she screamed as loudly as she could.

She eventually lowered the branch and sat down, her back once again against the rough embrace of the tree.

Suddenly, she heard another cracking sound, but this time, the sound was closer. She jolted once more and jumped to her feet, ignoring the sharp pain assaulting her ankle. The sound was too loud to have been caused by wolves.

"Is that you?" Her voice shook.

She was met with silence.

She dropped the branch on the ground as she knew she would have no chance to defeat him in a fight. And she couldn't run away from him—she could hardly walk. Her only chance was to swallow her pride and beg for her life, hoping he would forgive her.

"I'm sorry. I didn't mean to hurt you," she lied.

She tried her best to cry as loudly as possible, hoping he'd feel sorry for her.

"I was just so angry with you," she said in a quivering voice. "I wasn't thinking straight."

She made sure to breathe frantically, so she would sound as she were sobbing.

"I'm so sorry. Can you forgive me?" she said and kept pretending to cry.

24 RELATIONSHIPS

Tuesday evening

George Stanton and Trisha Boyle had enjoyed a fine meal together and were now occupying a table in the center of the hotel bar. George felt he was overdressed for the occasion. He regretted wearing the suit vest, as it made him look pretentious. George felt he was on display, and that he came off as a strange foreigner with a much younger wife. However, to his delight, Trisha Boyle was at least an inch shorter than he. George hardly ever had the pleasure of feeling tall in the presence of others. Trisha Boyle had insisted the two of them were to have a drink together—at the expense of Fare Airlines.

At first, he thought her behavior was inappropriate, as she seemed so happy and enthusiastic in this time of grief and concern. But on the other hand, why should people who lose their lives in plane crashes matter more than, for example, the people who perish in traffic accidents—which happens every day.

Not to mention all the people who die each year from the indirect cause of poverty. How many homeless people had lost their lives in the US this past year? George wondered if the only reason people felt empathy toward the victims of a plane crash was because they could identify with the situation and were glad their planes weren't the ones that had crashed. In that case, the extraordinary empathy toward aviation victims was merely a concern for one's own safety and welfare.

George pretended to look at the drink menu, but he wasn't contemplating what drink to order. He knew what to order, and he knew his choice would provoke the much more energetic Trisha Boyle.

"So, what are you having, George?"

"I'll just have a glass of water."

"What…" Trisha mumbled and looked as if she was about to cry.

George began to feel guilty. He felt he'd somehow wronged Trisha Boyle, who currently stared back at him with sad puppy eyes. "I don't drink alcohol."

Trisha's shoulders dropped. "Is it against your religion?"

George was puzzled by the question, and he wondered how the attentive Trisha Boyle could ever consider him as a religious person.

"No, it's against my better judgment."

"Screw that. You're having a drink, mister."

She got up and left the table before he had any chance to object. Seeing her order drinks at the bar (and apparently, engaging in small talk with the bartender) made him ask himself his reason for still being single.

Is it because I don't drink alcohol? Is that why I'm still single?

Trisha returned shortly after with two cocktails in her hands. The sight of the forest green liquid made George frown.

"What are we having?"

"It's a Fallen Angel," Trisha said with far too much enthusiasm.

"What's in it?"

"Alcohol."

"And?"

"And some green stuff. I don't know. I just liked the name. Would you have preferred if I'd gotten you a Black Russian? Have you ever had a Black Russian, George?"

George thought his co-worker had a cunning smile on

her face, so he made sure to say as little as possible.

"You ever had Sex on the Beach?" Trisha asked him with the same smile.

"It makes you wonder who came up with all those names, huh?" he asked.

Drunk people, George was just about to add.

"Fun people," Trisha said, beating him to the punch.

Trisha got her cell phone from her purse, and began typing rapidly.

About ten minutes later (and after too many sips of the sour green liquid), George reflected on what part he'd played in the exchange with Trisha Boyle. Against all odds, she hadn't spoken a single word since she took out her cell phone. For a brief second, George actually thought of leaving, and wondered if she'd even notice. But just then, she suddenly looked at him.

"How does my hair look?" Trisha asked him.

Well, since you're the one who brought it up, your haircut kind of reminds me of a Lego man. Did an actual hairdresser put you up to this?

"Your hair looks fine," he lied.

Trisha extended her arm and appeared to be taking a photo of herself; holding the cocktail glass close to her mouth. Then, she resumed typing, only to suddenly stop.

"You want me to tag you?"

George was very familiar with that particular question. "I don't have a profile."

"Of course, you don't... You're a strange man, George."

George didn't appreciate being called strange. He was, however, used to being referred to as boring, but that didn't bother him at all. His father was a strange man. Was he turning into his father? Was that how people saw him? George felt the sudden urge to defend himself.

"I don't need a profile." He shrugged his shoulders.

"Nobody needs..." Trisha's comment trailed off, and she shook her head slightly. "Why don't you have a profile,

George?"

George still felt the urge to defend himself.

"I guess I don't have self-esteem issues," he said, flat out lying to her face. The truth was he didn't have a profile, because he hardly had any friends.

Trisha put her phone down and looked at him with the same sad, puppy eyes as before. He immediately regretted his comment.

"Why would you say that, George?"

Yeah, why would you say that, George?

George felt as though he'd painted himself into a corner and tried to think of another lie.

"I think people who have low self-esteem are more likely to post on social media," he said and shrugged.

That's not even a lie, George. You only made things worse.

"Why would you say that?" Trisha asked, and looked even sadder.

"Well, they seem so eager to let other people know whenever something good happens in their life," he said. "Like they need the validation from others in order to feel good about themselves."

Trisha glanced at her phone. "I only use it because I think it's fun."

George Stanton made sure to bite down on his tongue.

"Pretty much everyone has a profile these days," Trisha argued.

Wonder why that is? he thought, and made sure to keep biting down on his tongue. *Wait, is that why I'm single? Because I don't use social media?*

After a few minutes of awkward silence, Trisha finally broke the deadlock.

"I didn't mean to eavesdrop on your phone call. But why did you thank Mike so much? Did he give you a raise or something?" Trisha asked with a smile. "Because, if he did, then I totally want one too."

George felt relieved to see Trisha smile again. "He expressed his concern for my sister, who's in the hospital... She recently was involved in a traffic accident."

"What?" The sad, puppy eyes had returned.

"She was hit in a head-on collision when she tried to pass another car."

"You should have stopped me, George." She gave him a sad and guilty look.

"It's just the way I drive, Trisha. It's not because of the accident," he said in a soft voice. "Besides, I was going the speed limit."

Trisha pronounced a chuckle. "Yeah, sure you were."

"No, I'm serious. I always set the cruise-control to whatever the speed limit is."

Trisha looked at him as she waited for the punch line.

"I guess, I'm the lunatic, then," Trisha muttered. "So, what did Mike say?"

"About what?"

"About the celebrity on board the plane."

"He thought it could just be a coincidence. I imagine, Sharon Stone is quite a common name." He shrugged.

"Do you believe that, George?"

"No, I think it's too much of a coincidence that a random passenger just happens to share the same name as the captain's ex-wife," he said, and shook his head. "I'm afraid your theory is correct."

"How so?"

"The captain was going through a bitter divorce, and his ex-wife was on—"

"No, I meant, why are you afraid my theory is true?"

"For obvious reasons." He hesitated and felt confused.

"But either way, the liability will cover the lawsuits and damages? Won't it?"

George got the impression Trisha Boyle was worried about her job. At first, he thought her chain of thoughts was a bit selfish, but a second later, he actually felt sorry for her. Something about a single mom always produced a sense of empathy in him. He hesitated as to whether he should lie to her or simply tell her the truth. If, in fact, Captain Daniels had crashed the plane in order to murder his ex-wife, then the company would have no chance to ever recuperate from such bad publicity, and Fare Airlines was likely to file for bankruptcy within the near future.

"I don't have that information."

Trisha pronounced another chuckle. "You're starting to sound like him."

"Who?" For some reason, George thought of his father.

"Mike... I don't have that information," Trisha added in a silly voice.

George made a mental note to himself not to use that particular phrase in the presence of his boss, CEO Michael Williams.

"I'm going to get us some more drinks," Trisha said and got up from her chair. "This time, something less sour."

"None for me please."

"What?" Her puppy eyes prodded at him again.

"I shouldn't drink any more. I mean, one of us has to drive in the morning."

"Mike gave us the day off, remember? I thought we could have lunch, and enjoy Paradise before we leave. Besides, it's a free bar," Trisha said, and winked, while she waved the same credit card that she'd so enthusiastically used all day.

As George watched his younger colleague eagerly order another round of drinks, he felt a growing sense of concern. But he found some comfort in asking himself how much a woman of Trisha Boyle's small stature could possible drink?

A few hours later, George Stanton was shocked by the answer to that question. He wondered if perhaps Trisha's humorous remark about her ethnic descent was actually a cry for help. Perhaps she was constantly drunk. George felt as if his hotel room was spinning, and as he sat on the edge of the bed, he deliberated whether it was cautious or lazy of him, not to brush his teeth before going to sleep. Suddenly, he heard a strange noise coming from the hallway.

George got up and looked through the glass peephole where he saw his younger co-worker kicking the hotel door with the tip of her boot. When George opened the door, Trisha Boyle didn't wait for an invitation. Instead, she entered his room as soon as he opened the door, her hands full of miniature bottles.

"You found more alcohol." He sighed internally.

"It's a free mini bar. It comes with the room," Trisha claimed. "We'd be fools not to take advantage of it."

Trisha opened several bottles of a well-known whiskey from Tennessee, and poured them into a glass she'd picked up from the table near the window.

"It's our duty to empty both mini bars. If we don't, then my ancestors would turn in their graves," Trisha said with a witty smile.

Trisha kicked off her boots, casually climbed onto the bed, and rearranged the pillows to her liking, the drink still in her hand.

George saw his chance and pretended to pour one of the empty whiskey bottles into a coffee cup, only to fill the cup with soda.

"Jack and Coke," Trisha said. "Good choice, mister."

He raised his cup to salute his deceitful plan. He felt only pride in his invention, and no shame.

"So, how old are you, George?"

"I'm thirty-two."

"Then we're practically the same age."

He thought Trisha Boyle looked as if she were in the middle of her teenage years, but for obvious reason, he assumed she was older than she appeared.

"I seriously doubt that."

"I'm twenty-three, get it?" Trisha had a big smile.

"You look younger," he said, and felt a tension in his chest as he began to wonder if Trisha had passed the age when appearing younger was considered a compliment.

"Yeah, I get that a lot," Trisha said, and sounded disappointed. "You know, you don't look like a George."

"Yeah, I get that a lot."

Trisha pronounced a short laugh. "You don't look like a Stanton, either."

"Actually, it's just a random name my father selected when he immigrated to America. The person who handed him the form had a name tag with Stanton written on it," he said, and shrugged. "That's my family legacy, right there."

"Really?" Trisha frowned. "Did he change his first name too?"

"He changed it to Robert, on account of Robert Redford. My father..." George restrained himself from calling his father a lunatic. "...is a strange man."

"You're a strange man, George."

Again, George didn't care for being associated with his father.

"If you think I'm strange, then you should meet him."

"I love to meet your father." Trisha looked sincere.

He swallowed once, and tried to come up with an appropriate lie. But before he could come up with a decent excuse, Trisha Boyle released him from her wicked spell.

"I'm just messing with you," Trisha blurted out. "But I totally got you, didn't I?"

George made sure to smile her way, even though he felt the whole scene was more horrifying than amusing.

Trisha had her back against the headboard and her arms stretched out on top of the many pillows; her drink was on the night table. George sat at the nearby desk.

"Are you always on autopilot, George?"

"What do you mean?"

"Don't you ever let loose, and just go with it? You know, just ignore social protocol and so on," Trisha said and slapped the palms of her outstretched hands against the many pillows on the bed.

"No, I'm pretty much boring all the time."

Is that why I'm single? Because I'm such a boring person?

"You're not boring. You're just shy." She gave him a wink.

Again, George felt puzzled by Trisha's perception of him. He never considered himself as shy. If anything, he was more ignorant than most people. He didn't talk much because he didn't have much interest in other people's lives.

Is that why I'm single?

"When was the last time you did something outrageous, George?"

"I spent a night in jail once."

"Really?" Trisha looked astonished.

Then, Trisha pronounced a tremendous laugh, rolled around on the bed, and gasped for air. She appeared as if she was trying to speak, but she was laughing too hard to utter a word. George began to feel uncomfortable and was curious what had brought out her reaction.

"For driving too slow?" Trisha eventually said and then her face twitched and twisted before she began laughing even harder.

George couldn't keep himself from laughing as well. But this time he didn't feel bad for laughing at her rather than with her. He did, however, restrain himself from bringing up the cruise control again.

Trisha's distinctive laughter eventually faded away.

"That's good stuff." Trisha wiped the tears from her eyes. "Go on then and tell me what you were in for."

"I flipped over a cop car."

"Really?" Trisha's jaw dropped. "Were you in a gang or something?"

He felt confused. "No, I acted on my own."

"Did you use a forklift or something?"

Why would I use a forklift?

"No, I didn't flip over a cop car. I flipped over a cop car..."

George hesitated, considering what he could say.

"I mean, I ran up the hood of the car, stepped on the rooftop lights, and made a double tuck over the car. And the landing was perfect, by the way."

"Are you crazy, George? You could have broken your neck."

"No, I was a professional gymnast back then. The flip was easy. However, getting away from the cops was not."

"You were a professional gymnast?" Trisha had a deadpan look.

"I won state championship when I was eighteen. On that very day actually. I was out on the town celebrating with my friends, and I wanted to impress them. So, at the time, the flip seemed like a clever thing to do. Unfortunately, the San Francisco Police Department didn't share my sense of humor."

"So they chased after you?"

"Half the precinct chased me for at least an hour or so."

"And they eventually caught up with you?"

"Actually, I more or less surrendered."

"How so?"

"Well, I was full of adrenaline and shaking all over. I remember feeling I couldn't breathe. I had so much anxiety because I wondered when, how, and if they were going to catch me. But as soon as I gave up running, that anxiety went away. Like the thought of them catching me felt worse than them actually catching me."

To George's astonishment, Trisha Boyle appeared to be speechless.

"Come to think of it, that night in jail did something to me. I think it changed me somehow," he added.

"Did something happen to you in jail?"

"No, nothing happened. I just waited for the time to pass."

"How did that change you?"

"Go sit in the closet for the entire night," he responded, and pointed at the closet door. "Just sit there and wait for the morning to come. You'll see what I'm talking about."

"That's just silly, George."

"No, I'm serious. Try it, and you'll see what I mean."

"No, I couldn't do that. I would just feel like an idiot."

"Exactly."

Trisha looked thoughtful and kept gazing into his eyes. At that point, she slowly got off the bed and came toward him. Then, she ran past him and made her way into the bathroom. George could hear the sound of liquid colliding with water surface.

"Are you all right in there?"

Trisha didn't respond. But the familiar erupting sound from the toilet bowl answered his question just as well.

About fifteen minutes later, Trisha made her way back to the bed, only to slide down onto the floor a few seconds later. Once on the floor, she crawled on her hands and knees, then grabbed the garbage can under the desk, put half her face in it, but did nothing more. Trisha made a sad sound like the cry of a dog who's been left on its own, and the sound was emphasized by the echo from the empty garbage can. George thought the sound of echoing tears was heartbreaking, and felt he should say something to ease her discomfort.

"It'll pass soon enough, Trisha. You'll feel better in the morning... I mean, you'll feel better on Thursday," he added with a smile meant to poke fun at her.

Trisha's face emerged from the garbage can, her mascara running. "It's not funny, George."

"Are you all right?"

She didn't answer him. Instead, she crawled away from him, pushing the garbage can in front of her with half her face in it—much the way a dog might move its food bowl.

What was the dog's name?

"You remember the dog from the visit to Mrs. Daniels? What was his name?

"Jack," Trisha mumbled, her head still in the garbage can. "Jack Daniels."

"You remember how Jack moved the food bowl all around the house?"

Trisha's face slowly emerged, and her makeup ran even more. "It's not funny, George."

Trisha crawled up on to the bed, and lay down on her stomach.

"I just wanted to let loose for once," Trisha murmured with her lips pressed up against a pillow. "Stop being a mom for just one night."

Trisha looked as she was about to fall asleep.

"I hope this doesn't change your impression of the Scotch-Irish community?" Trisha mumbled into the pillow.

"No, it's pretty much the same as before," he said and laughed internally.

George noticed Trisha's breathing pattern had decelerated, and shortly after, her leg suddenly twitched. He came to think of how he cured his insomnia.

Just as the human body is about to fall asleep, the brain is destined to misinterpret the experience as the sense of actually falling. The sense of falling, and the sudden twitch used to keep George from falling asleep. So, in order to lure his mind, he would actually imagine and embrace the sensation of falling. He would imagine falling into something delightful, something that made him feel safe—therefore, luring his mind into interpreting the experience of falling as pleasant, instead of alarming. As George had grown accustomed to the sense of falling, his insomnia had slowly faded away.

To George's concern, he soon came to realize that Trisha had carried her arsenal of booze in her bare hands; she hadn't brought a purse. His head dropped as he thought of the consequences. He contemplated whether getting into her pockets was the right thing to do. Even though Trisha looked as if she was passed out for the night, there was always a slight risk of her waking up screaming as soon his hands were in her pants.

After a short deliberation and evaluation of all the alternatives, George decided getting into her pants pockets was the right thing to do. Trisha Boyle was still passed out and lying on her stomach. To his frustration, he quickly discovered her back pants pocket was empty. He hesitated once more before he fished out a card from her front pocket.

Trisha Boyle slept in his bed that night, and he slept in hers.

25 THE OCEAN

Wednesday afternoon

Jack walked toward the sloping tree down by the shore, and then casually brought up his arm as Julie rose to her feet.

"Hey," Julie called out in a hoarse voice.

Julie squinted, and then her smile suddenly vanished.

"Where's Kevin?" Julie eventually asked Jack.

"I haven't seen him."

"But he left with you, Jack."

Jack frowned. "He didn't come back?"

"No," Julie almost yelled. "What happened between you two?"

"He got upset and left."

"Why? What happened?"

Jack coughed into his fist. "I saw Kevin board the plane with his wife."

"But he said he wasn't married..." Julie's voice trailed off, and then she looked long and hard at the lake.

"I told him he shouldn't blame himself for what happened. I tried to get him to open up to me, but he just ignored me. Until he suddenly cracked. His face looked destroyed all of the sudden, and he ran back the way we came."

"Was he wearing a wedding ring?"

"He must have taken it off. I noticed the imprint on his

finger when we..."

Jack looked at the letters spelled out across the shore.

"...created the sign," Jack continued. "And before that, I noticed he had his hands in his pockets the whole time."

"I noticed that too, but I just thought he was cold."

"Guilt was eating him up," Jack said in a drowsy voice. "I think his wife's name was Pamela."

"What makes you say that?" Julie asked hesitantly.

"I heard someone yelling for Pamela when I swam to shore," Jack said. "Remember how I asked you if your name was Pamela?"

"I don't remember much from the crash."

"It must have been Kevin, yelling for his wife," Jack said. He looked around the nearby surroundings. "So, are Nancy and Andrew off looking for Kevin?"

"No, they're gone. I don't know where they went."

"Why did they leave?"

"I don't know," Julie said. "They were both gone when I woke up."

Jack took a few steps toward the forest. "I'm going to go look for Nancy. She shouldn't be moving around too much."

"But she could be anywhere by now," Julie responded quickly.

"When did you wake up?"

"They've been gone since yesterday morning."

"They've been gone for more than a day?"

"Yes, so she could be anywhere by now," Julie said. "Please, don't leave, Jack."

Julie tilted her head, and looked sad as she kept staring at Jack.

"Have you tried calling out for them?"

"I screamed all day yesterday," Julie said. "Can't you tell by my voice."

"That doesn't make any sense, Julie." Jack shook his head and coughed. "If Andrew ran after Nancy, then why didn't he wake you?"

"Well, he slept over there." Julie pointed at the tree by the hillside.

"Why?" Jack asked in a hushed tone.

"He was angry with me, and he didn't want to sleep next to me."

"Why not?"

Julie trained her eyes down. "We had an altercation, and I hurt his feelings."

"What happened?"

"He called Nancy a whore."

"What?" Jack frowned.

"Yeah, he called her a whore, Jack. I can't stand people like that," Julie said. "You know what I'm talking about. You almost strangled him the other day. What was that about?"

"I didn't strangle him. I just grabbed him by his collar. That's all."

"Why?"

Jack shrugged and coughed. "He made some remarks about Nancy."

"Did he call her a whore?"

"No, nothing like that," Jack said and shrugged again. "He told me how Nancy made some sexual references when she talked in her sleep during the first night, and it sounded like he enjoyed it."

"I bet he did. He was probably jacking off. That's disgusting."

Then suddenly Julie looked alarmed and waved her hands at Jack, looking as if she were trying to wave down a cab. "I didn't mean to imply men are disgusting. It's okay, Jack. I masturbate too."

Jack looked confused. "What do you mean?"

"I mean, you shouldn't feel bad if you *jack* off... No pun indented, by the way," Julie quickly added.

Jack chuckled. "What are you talking about, Julie?"

"I don't know anymore." Julie's shoulders slumped. "I talk too much when I'm nervous. My son always tells me so."

Julie looked at her feet, and then a teardrop slowly ran down her cheek.

"Please don't leave," Julie said, and wiped a tear. "I can't be alone again."

Jack sat down next to Julie, under the *chanterelle* tree.

"I'm not leaving," Jack said. "You're right, Nancy could be anywhere by now."

"I thought you and Kevin were gone for good." Julie sniffed. "I was all alone." Julie wiped another tear off her cheek, the blood still showing on her jacket sleeve.

"How's your head?" Jack asked, and looked at Julie's forehead.

Julie looked puzzled. "Oh, that. That's nothing. It's just a bump, I'd forgotten all about it. But I think my ankle is broken. I can't walk."

"Does it hurt?"

"Only when I walk."

"You don't have to walk. I'll carry you. I'll carry you home, if I have to."

"To the nearest road will do just fine." Julie smiled. "Did you see any roads?"

Jack began coughing severely then stood up and put his hands against his knees.

"Are you cold, Jack?"

"I wish I had some more clothes."

"You want to borrow my jacket for a while?"

"No, it won't make any difference, it's too small. You'll get better use out of it. No point in both of us getting sick." Jack coughed once more. "But thank you just the same."

"So, did you see any roads?"

Jack smiled at Julie before he cleared his throat.

"You saw a road?" Julie's face lit up.

"Nope." Jack shook his head but kept smiling. "But I saw the ocean."

"You saw the ocean?" Julie looked puzzled. "But Andrew said—"

"Andrew was wrong. I could see the ocean on the horizon," Jack said. "It's a long walk, but it shouldn't take more than a week. And if we get to the ocean, then we're bound to come across something."

Jack coughed some more while he looked at the forest.

"If Andrew ran after Nancy, then why didn't he return?" Jack asked.

"Perhaps he thought you and Kevin had left for good, and he couldn't care less what happens to me. So..." Julie shrugged. "Perhaps he just kept walking."

"He wouldn't do that," Jack said. "Maybe he's lost in the woods. Andrew lost his glasses when the plane went down, and he can't see very well."

Jack convulsed and suddenly diverted his eyes toward the lake. "You can't see very well without your contacts, am I right?"

Julie shook her head slightly and looked bewildered.

"Perhaps he went back to the other side of the lake."

"You mean, Andrew?"

"No, Kevin."

"He wouldn't just sit there. I screamed for help all yesterday."

"No, he wouldn't do that," Jack said and kept his focus on the lake. "We shouldn't drink any more water from the lake. It could be contaminated. You know, like cholera, and such."

"Nancy drank a lot of water the other day," Julie said. "You think she's all right?"

"No, she's not all right, either way," Jack responded. "She needs to get to a hospital."

"Do you two know each other?" Julie asked.

"No, I told you, she must be confusing me with someone else," Jack responded. "Why do you ask?"

"It sounded like she knew who you are."

"Who I am?" Jack frowned. "Who did she say I am?"

"She didn't specify." Julie looked at her feet.

"She's delusional, Julie. I'm not certain she even knows who she is, or where she is, for that matter."

"I know," Julie said, and kept looking at her feet.

Jack looked at the distress sign written across the shore.

"There's another lake not far from here. If we leave now, we'll get there before dark, and we'll have access to fresh water."

Julie looked at the SOS sign.

"I can go back, once a day, and check if the search and rescue team have arrived."

Julie nodded, and then climbed up on Jack's back.

They didn't walk very far before they discovered a dead body.

26 DANNY

Wednesday evening

As George Stanton stopped his car in front of Trisha Boyle's house, he reflected on how strange he felt driving his own car again. Despite driving the same car almost every day for the past four years, his car all of the sudden didn't feel the same after just a couple of days driving a rental.

Trisha just sat and looked at him and didn't seem to make any attempt to leave the car. She'd been quiet for most of the journey, and she hadn't taken off her sunglasses, until they'd changed cars in Oakland. Now, she kept breaking eye contact, back and forth. George wondered if she expected him to say something.

He noticed the woman staring at them from the porch. "Is that your mom?"

"Yeah, that's her," Trisha said, and briefly glanced at the porch. "I would introduce you to Danny, but he should be in bed by now."

George felt relieved the journey to San Francisco had taken longer than expected and he wouldn't have to greet the boy.

"She has a lovely house," he said.

"No, the house is mine. She lives with me," Trisha said. "I don't live with my mom. My mom lives with me. So make sure you get the office gossip right, George."

George felt he understood what Trisha was getting at.

"I don't gossip, Trisha," he said. "I don't care for it."

"I don't care for it either," Trisha said. "Sorry about last night. I'm not used to drinking, and I guess I went a bit overboard."

"What happens in Paradise..." George never finished the sentence—instead, he gave her a wink.

"Thanks, George." Trisha smiled. "And thanks for not taking advantage of me last night. A lot of guys would have."

Once again, George felt astonished by how wrong the otherwise so perceptive Trisha Boyle was. He was just about to set her straight, but decided not to, as she was well on her way out of the car.

27 THE BODY

Thursday afternoon

Jack and Julie sat next to each other on top of a pile of pine tree branches, which resembled a bed. Julie stroked her hand across the sweater on his back, the sweater Jack wore as a cape.

"Did the sweater make a difference?"

"Not so much." Jack coughed repeatedly. "I wish I had a jacket."

"If you go back and get his pants, then perhaps you could use them as a blanket or something," Julie said. "It might not be much, but it could make a difference."

Jack nodded slightly before he coughed hard and then shook his head.

"Are you all right, Jack?"

"I'm just so sick of it all. I just want it to be over."

"You don't think they're coming for us?"

Jack shook his head and kept coughing.

"Perhaps we should just leave then," Julie said. "Like you said, if we can get to the ocean, then we're bound to come across something, sooner or later."

"If we leave, then they'll probably be here the next day."

"Yeah, that's the irony of life," Julie agreed. "But they'll see the SOS sign, and keep searching for us. I'm sure they can track us with dogs."

"I suppose." Jack coughed. "You want to leave?"

"That's up to you, Jack. I'm just a passenger."

"Today's Thursday. How about if we wait until Monday. That's ten days from when we crashed, a nice round number. How does that sound?"

"I prefer round numbers, too. I don't care for odd or dodgy numbers. They don't look right to me," Julie said and smiled. "Or we could leave tomorrow. Then, we waited a week before leaving."

"You want to leave tomorrow, Julie?"

"I could leave tomorrow." Julie looked at her feet. "But like I said, it's your call. I'm just a passenger on this journey."

"Okay then, we'll leave tomorrow, as soon as the sun rises. I'll get Andrew's pants today, and check the crash site to see if Nancy or Kevin has returned," Jack said. "And fill up on worms. You should eat, Julie."

"No, don't eat Julie." She giggled.

Jack chuckled at first, but then he kept coughing.

"*It's been a week*," Jack eventually stuttered.

"I have low metabolism, and I'm just sitting still. You need it more than I do."

Jack chuckled and cleared his throat. "They're plenty of worms to go around."

Jack pointed at the rocks by the shore of the small and narrow lake. Julie never turned her head. Instead, she made an awkward face, and focused on the sweater, the sweater Jack wore as a cape.

"You still think Nancy killed him?" Julie asked.

"The back of his head was smashed in, so somebody killed him," Jack responded. "He probably startled her, and she got confused, and hit him with a rock. Why do you ask? What do you think happened?"

"Andrew didn't see very well. So, perhaps it was just an accident."

"But he was on his stomach, when we found him."

"I know." Julie swallowed. "But perhaps he ran into a

branch, and hit his head when he fell backward. Then walked until he collapsed and fell on his stomach."

"That make sense." Jack sneezed. "Perhaps it was just an accident then."

Jack kept coughing, and Julie patted him on his back.

"So you have a son?" Jack eventually asked.

"Yes, I have *a* son."

"How old is he?"

"I didn't mention him before because I get so worried when thinking about him," Julie responded, and then suddenly twitched. "He's seven."

Jack nodded and kept coughing.

"He's with my mom," Julie said and looked Jack in the eyes.

"So, what's his name?"

"*Geronimo*," Julie said in a Spanish accent.

"Named after a great warrior. I like that."

"No, he's named after his father. A great imbecile." Julie shook her head. "He's the reason I'm in this mess."

"What do you mean?"

"He's the reason I flew to Alaska. I was supposed to testify against him in court on Monday. If it wasn't for him, I wouldn't be here," Julie said. "After all this time, he still manages to ruin my life somehow."

"He sounds like a real charming fellow." Jack coughed. "But you can't blame him for what happened to the plane, Julie. It's not his fault we're stuck out here."

"But if it wasn't for him, then I wouldn't have been on this flight," Julie said in a slightly deeper tone. "I hate him so much."

"You can't think like that, Julie."

"Don't tell me what to think, Jack. You don't know him like I do."

"I know." Jack coughed a few times. "But sometimes these things just happen, and nobody's to blame. Like what happened to Andrew. Either way it was an accident."

"You think it was an accident?"

"Even if Nancy hit him over the head—"

"No, I meant the plane crash," Julie interrupted.

"It must have been something wrong with the plane," Jack said. "Why, what do you think happened?"

"I think it was just an accident," Julie said. "No one's to blame."

"Okay." Jack said in confusion.

"No wait," Julie said. "The NTSB is to blame."

"Who?"

"The National Transportation Safety Board," Julie pronounced clearly.

"Why are they to blame?"

"It's their job to find us," Julie said. "It's their fault we're in this mess. Someone isn't doing their job properly."

Jack looked mystified, then coughed a few times before he cleared his throat. "So, how did you end up with a guy from Alaska? If you don't mind me asking?"

"No, he's from L.A. We both are. I recently moved to Seattle. Finding work in Los Angeles was hard for me," Julie said. "They just caught up with him in Alaska."

"At least you have a valid reason for not showing up in court." Jack smiled. "I think the judge will show leniency."

"You think?" Julie chuckled once, but then bowed her head. "It's my own fault, really. I always fall for the wrong guys, and now Geronimo has to grow up without a male role model in his life."

"I can relate to that." Jack coughed some more.

"You didn't have a male role model growing up?"

"I never knew my father," Jack said, and his shoulders dropped. "It was just me and my mom. There were no one else."

"That must have been tough on you."

Jack bowed his head, and nodded slightly. "I think a child needs a role model of the same gender. I remember feeling weird and out of place. I didn't have anyone to relate to, and I felt I couldn't be the person my mother wanted or expected me to be. My childhood was very confusing. I always..."

Jack never finished the sentence. Then he looked at Julie with an apologetic expression. Julie trained her eyes down.

"I like your son's name," Jack said. "It makes me think of him as a great warrior."

"It's just a name." Julie shrugged.

"It's strange how the mind works that way. You think of one thing, and then you automatically think of another," Jack said. "Like your name for instance. When people hear Julie, they think of July, and then automatically think of summer."

Julie smiled and gazed at Jack for a long time.

"What? Did I say something?" Jack asked.

"I was born in July." Julie shrugged.

"Oh, so you were almost named June, then?"

"Almost." Julie's smile grew, and she kept gazing at Jack.

"It's a good name. People associate your name with something they enjoy."

"I like your name too, Jack."

"It's strange how attached people are to their names," Jack said. "I mean, it's just a random word."

"Well, addressing one another without names would be hard."

"I understand why we need names for practical reasons. But I think it's strange, how much we identify with a specific word, which doesn't say anything about us. Jack isn't who I am," Jack said. "At least names like, Sitting Bull, or Crazy Horse, describes some aspect of a person's life."

Julie suddenly burst into laughter.

"What?" Jack looked baffled.

"I just thought of a perfect name for you, Jack."

"Okay."

"Man who eats worms," Julie announced slowly.

Jack began to laugh, but again, he ended up coughing.

"Maybe I'll change my name when this is all over. At least then, I won't have to be associated with masturbation,"

Jack said, and rolled his eyes.

"I'm sorry for bringing that to your attention," Julie said. "I don't understand why masturbation is considered a bad thing. After all, you are having sex with a person that you care about."

Jack laughed, and then cleared his throat. Then he smiled briefly before he suddenly rose to his feet. "I'm going to get his pants before it gets dark."

Jack walked toward the woods, and Julie looked frightened as she watched him leave.

"Jack!" Julie yelled and swallowed once. "You're coming back, right?"

"Of course, I'm coming back." Jack frowned.

Julie kept her eyes on Jack as he disappeared into the woods.

Evening

Julie spent most of the afternoon staring at the sky. But as the sun had started to descend, so did her face. She wiped the tears with her sleeve, and stared at her feet.

A small cracking sound escaped the woods. Julie shuddered and turned her head around before, her jaw dropped.

"Kevin!"

Julie smiled and squinted toward the woods, but then, suddenly, her smile vanished quickly. She looked terrified.

"Kevin too?" Julie's voice shook.

"No, I haven't seen him," Jack eventually said.

"But you're wearing his jacket."

Jack averted his eyes and looked at the black blazer he wore. "I took the jacket off a dead guy floating in the lake," Jack claimed. "You should have seen this guy. He was huge. See it's still wet." Jack extended his arms. "When did everybody get so fat all of the sudden? Have you noticed that?"

Julie didn't respond to Jack's question. She just kept staring at her feet.

"Everything is based on portions these days, and the portions are way off. It seems today's restaurant portions are measured against the biggest customer, rather than the average one." Jack shook his head. "And this guy never missed a meal in his life."

Jack looked at Julie as if he anticipated a response. She kept staring at her feet.

"I found the steel wire I got from your bra. I thought we might find some use for it along the way. That reminds me." Jack reached into the jacket pocket and took out a see-through plastic wrapper. "See what I found."

Julie's jaw dropped once more, and her eyes grew wide.

Jack extended his arms toward Julie. "Take it."

Julie slowly reached for the plastic wrapper, her hand trembling.

"Smell it," Jack said.

Julie brought the wrapper close to her nose. "It smells like chocolate."

"Some hikers must have left it behind," Jack said.

Julie's face lit up. "You think hikers left it?"

"I thought you could use it to eat worms."

Julie's smile vanished. "Excuse me?"

"The sense of taste is strongly connected to the sense of smell," Jack said. "So, if you smell chocolate while you're chewing, you might not detect the taste from the worm."

Julie's shoulders sagged. "Jack..."

"You have to eat, Julie," Jack said, and then he walked down by the shore, and systematically turned over rocks.

A while later, Jack came back with a handful of worms, his hands wet.

"They're still moving," Julie blurted out, sounding nervous.

"How do you kill a worm?"

"Excuse me?"

"I tried drowning them, but that didn't work. So, I ripped one in half, but that didn't work either. I just ended up with two worms sprawling around instead of one," Jack said. "Chew a few times and swallow fast. They'll stop moving once you swallow. The stomach acid kills them."

Julie looked at the plastic wrapper and then shook her head. "I can't do this, Jack. I'm sorry. I'm just not there yet."

"Okay." Jack dropped the worms on the ground.

"You're not gonna have any?"

"I had plenty before," Jack said with a crooked smile.

A while later, Jack and Julie sat next to each other on top of the pile of pine tree branches and watched the sun disappear behind the silhouette of the forest. Then they smiled at each other and kept eye contact. Julie closed her eyes, and leaned in toward Jack, her lips close to his mouth.

Jack cleared his throat and looked the other way.

"Sorry," Julie said, and her face grew red.

"That's okay."

They sat in silence as darkness began absorbing the last contours of their faces. Jack still wore the sweater as a cape under the newly obtained blazer. They used Andrew's pants as a seat cushion on top of the pile of pine tree branches.

"Sorry, I took so long before," Jack eventually said. "I struggled getting the jacket off the fat guy."

"I'm just glad you found a jacket."

"They're going to need a crane to lift this guy out of the water." Jack chuckled. "Why would anyone do that to themselves?"

"Have you noticed you're not coughing as much as before?"

"And I feel better too," Jack said. "I saw another body floating in the lake also. It was far from shore, but I think it was a woman."

"Could it have been Nancy?"

"No, this woman had dark hair. It couldn't have been Nancy."

"But if her hair was wet, then it would have had a darker look to it," Julie said. "I'm as blonde as Nancy, but my hair looks a lot darker when it's wet."

"No, it couldn't have been Nancy. At first, I thought it might have been Kevin's wife, but I remembered she had short hair. This woman had long, dark hair, and she wore a red fluffy jacket," Jack said, and bowed his head. "A lot of people died in that lake."

Julie stared at her feet, and looked apprehensive.

"I'm not leaving you, Julie." Jack sniffed. "You know that, right?"

"I know," Julie muttered.

"I'm not leaving you," Jack said decisively.

"You're sure about that, Jack?"

"I'm positive."

"It's a long walk, Jack. Perhaps I could use a big branch as a cane."

"No. We'll move much faster if I carry you," Jack said. "Don't you worry about that. I'm as strong as an ox, and you're as light as a feather. When you're on my back, I hardly notice your weight."

"Somehow I doubt that's true."

"No, I'm serious, I can hardly notice you back there," Jack said. "Feels like I'm carrying a backpack."

"Well, I have been dieting for the past week."

"How to Lose Weight by Not Eating Worms," Jack said laughing.

"That's a better title. I give you that."

"You'll have to eat eventually," Jack said. "It'll be at least another week before we reach the ocean."

"A week sounds fine," Julie said. "I just wanna go home."

Jack took a few breaths. "I'll get you home. I promise."

"You shouldn't make promises you can't keep."

"I'll get you home to your boy no matter what."

28 STOCKHOLM

Friday morning

As George Stanton looked across the office landscape, he noticed that the loud, buzzing noise of multiple conversations was no longer present. People seemed more at ease with the situation and didn't rush around as much anymore. If anything, people seemed to have stopped working and instead were watching the news.

The ECC, Cayla Marsh, had been doing her best to keep the rest of the crisis team updated, but she had no new developments to report. The Emergency Location Transmitter still wasn't providing a signal, and the Canadian authorities hadn't managed to locate the missing plane. Security director Cliff Henderson seemed to enjoy talking to his former colleagues and friends at different branches of US law enforcement, but his efforts all appeared to be a complete waste of time.

George, on the other hand, wasted the days updating press releases. He produced more or less the same sentimental dribble as in his previous press announcements, except he made sure to move a few words around to give the illusion of working and producing fresh news. CEO Michael Williams had spent all day in the presence of a substantial number of lawyers and insurance representatives, which made George wonder if someone had already filed a lawsuit against the airline.

In his small (but also windowed) office across the floor, George noticed how Mike was finally alone in his domain, and how he kept staring at a particular document on his desk. George thought his boss had a look of defeat on his face. Suddenly, it occurred to him that perhaps the company was filing for bankruptcy, and that was the reason for the meeting with legal representatives earlier this day, and it might also explain the long meeting the day before with a few large shareholders.

George lingered on his way to Mike's office where he gently tapped on the open door. "I've written a new statement. I thought I'd run it by you before I update the website."

The CEO seemed surprised by the unusual gesture.

"I'm sure it's fine," Mike said.

Yes, it's just the same usual nonsense.

George glanced at the paper sheet lying between Mike's elbows. He was curious as to what it said, but he struggled to find an appropriate way of asking.

"Any new development?" he asked hesitantly.

Mike obviously understood George's intentions, as he glanced down at the sheet before he gestured to George to close the door and sit down. Then the CEO returned his focus to the sheet of paper on his desk. George thought his boss didn't look like the handsome man from the week before. This man appeared to have aged at least a decade since then, and the black suit he wore brought out the gray color of his hair.

George began to wonder if his boss had developed gray hair within the past week, or if the gray suit he wore the previous week had disguised the true color of his hair. Either way, George now thought, the man appeared to be in his sixties, rather than his fifties.

As George sat, he began to feel uneasy when he realized his own choice of clothing might be interpreted as inappropriate. He wore a casual, light-blue blazer and a white shirt. His boss, on the other hand, looked as if he was about to attend a funeral.

George waited patiently, but the man sitting across

from him didn't speak; instead, Mike Williams kept staring at the paper. Once again, George thought of bankruptcy, and for some reason he immediately thought of Trisha Boyle and her ability to support her son.

"What do you have there, Mike?"

"Are you aware employees get discount tickets for families and relatives?"

George first thought was that he'd somehow abused the program. But he quickly dismissed the thought since he hardly had any family or friends.

"Yes," he agreed.

"Sharon Stone had a discount ticket."

George felt as if his boss had sucker-punched him. His gut suddenly ached.

So much for this just being a coincidence, he thought.

"Captain Daniels got his ex-wife the ticket?" George asked in disbelief.

Michael Williams nodded. "And it gets worse."

How could this possibly get any worse?

"Did Daniels pay for the ticket, or did she?"

The CEO looked surprised by his question. "He must have paid for the ticket in order for her to get the discount," Mike said. "But that's not the worst part."

"How could this possibly get any worse, Mike?"

"He got her two tickets," Mike said, and sighed. "One for her, and one for the man seated next to her."

"The guy she replaced him with?"

"It might appear so," Mike said.

"Did he know who the other ticket was for?"

"I don't have that information. Why do you ask?"

"If he didn't know who she was traveling with, then perhaps he didn't plan for this to happen. Perhaps he left the cockpit to say hello, and then had an emotional meltdown as he realized who she was traveling with."

"Is that somehow preferable?" his boss asked.

"Then it's not premeditated," George said, and realized

such a circumstance wasn't much better.

George also realized he'd heard no mention in the media regarding Captain Daniels' possible murder of his ex-wife and her partner—not to mention the rest of the passengers.

"Did you share this information with the authorities?" he asked cautiously.

"I most certainly did," Mike affirmed. "But the feds didn't seem very interested. However, they did tell me not to interfere with the investigation."

"Well, they can't prohibit us from visiting the emergency contacts of our employees," George said. "And the reason they're not that interested is probably because they're working the terror angle. People usually seek out information corresponding with their own feelings."

"What do you mean?" Mike asked.

"It feels better to fear terrorists rather than fearing pilots," he said, and shrugged. "Did you hear about the Imam who was on the plane? He who wanted to introduce Sharia law into the American legal system."

George just realized how stupid his question was, given that the Imam had been the media's focus all week.

Mike looked uncomfortable, but eventually nodded in response.

"That text message from the stewardess makes a big difference," George added. "In many ways, it exonerates us."

"About that... that text message doesn't make any sense," Mike said.

"It indicates the pilots were murdered, and therefore people assume it's terror—"

"I understand that part," Mike said, cutting him off. "But if in fact Captain Daniels crashed the plane on purpose, then that text message doesn't make any sense. Elisabeth McAllister claimed both pilots had died. How could she possibly have known that?"

"She couldn't." George paused for a few seconds as he liked to do to add more drama. "The only way she could've known for certain the pilots had died is if she was in the cockpit at the time. And if so, I imagine she would've used the radio instead of her cell phone. I don't believe she was in the cockpit." He shook his head to emphasize his point.

Michael Williams looked bewildered. "It still doesn't explain the text message."

"Perhaps she noticed the plane was off course," George said. "I mean, she'd flown the same route all day. She must have been used to seeing certain surroundings. And when the pilots didn't respond to her every request, she assumed they'd died."

George felt as he'd forgotten about something.

"Wait a minute, didn't she send the text message around midnight, you say?"

"Yes, I believe so," Mike responded.

"The plane was scheduled to land in Anchorage around midnight, am I right?"

"Yes, that's right."

"Well, there you go." George shrugged. "She must have realized something was wrong when the pilots never initiated landing. And when the pilots didn't respond to her at the door, she tried to call the police, but was cut off due to poor reception. Then she panicked, and sent her husband a text message."

"It takes a cold person to ignore someone pleading for their life," Mike said, and shook his head firmly.

"I'm not sure I follow. What do you mean by that, Mike?"

"I mean, Captain Daniels must have ignored Elisabeth McAllister pleading for him to open the door."

"He was most likely dead already."

"I beg your pardon?" Mike said.

"Ironically, at the time she sent the text message, both pilots were most likely dead. Elisabeth McAllister's assumption was probably true."

"You think Captain Daniels killed himself before the plane crashed?"

"Suicide would spare him from the pain and agony of enduring a plane crash. Perhaps he killed himself as soon as he'd changed the destination."

"Destination," Mike muttered, and sounded baffled.

George thought his boss looked clueless, and at that moment, he felt quite pleased with himself.

"The plane deviated from its route. He probably changed the destination of the aircraft, and then killed himself. I mean, the plane was bound to run out of fuel sooner or later. An altered destination might also explain why the plane flew into the Canadian wilderness. Perhaps he tried to avoid crashing into a populated area."

At least he showed a shred of decency.

"Wouldn't it be better to head for the ocean?" Mike asked.

"If the plane crashed into the ocean, then perhaps there would be a slim chance of his wife actually surviving the crash. But if the plane crashed into the Canadian mountains..." George didn't finish the sentence, but shrugged his shoulders.

So much for a shred of decency, he added to his thoughts.

"But the plane crashed into the Great Slave Lake," Mike pointed out.

"Allegedly," George responded. "Or, perhaps he simply miscalculated and the plane crashed into the lake instead of a mountain."

"What do you mean by allegedly?"

"Just because the plane disappeared from radar near the lake, doesn't necessarily mean it crashed into the lake," George said. "It could have kept going. Perhaps it did crash into a mountain."

"They're searching the surroundings with drones, and they have satellite images also. They would've noticed the debris if the plane crashed into the woods."

Once again, George thought of the German plane that had crashed into the French Alps, and how the entire plane had turned into bits and pieces.

"But he had to have killed his co-pilot," Mike said. "And the pilots go through the same type of screening as the passengers. He couldn't have brought a weapon on board."

"He could have strangled him, I suppose," George said, and winced. "Captain Daniels was a very large and muscular man. And his mother told me he was ex-military. It wouldn't have been hard for him to kill his co-pilot with his bare hands."

"You really think he could've strangled his colleague to death?" Mike asked.

"Perhaps they weren't that close, or maybe they didn't care for each other. Besides, he was going to kill every other person on that flight, so—"

"It's not the same." Mike interrupted. "Killing his co-worker in cold blood would be much harder."

"Perhaps he was psychotic at the time."

"Each pilot has to go through a mental health evaluation," Mike retorted.

"A psychologist can only tell so much. Besides, healthy people can suddenly snap. Perhaps he snapped when he saw his ex-wife with another man."

Michael Williams looked appalled; the side of his mouth kept pulsing.

"Or perhaps the co-pilot was in on it," George added. "It could have been a suicide pact. Depression is contagious. Perhaps the co-pilot had his own reasons to end his life."

"No, they didn't fly together on a regular basis."

George thought his boss looked as he was about to be sick, and he figured changing the subject would be a good idea.

"I hate to sound cynical. But do you know if the passenger load factor has increased or decreased in the past week?" George asked.

"Actually, the load factor has increased in the last week," Mike said. "We're selling more tickets than ever."

"Fly F.A. or the terrorists have won," George said, and quoted a man on the street, who had been interviewed on TV the day before.

"This doesn't feel right," Mike said and bowed his head.

"Well, it could have been a coincidence for all we know. I mean, Captain Daniels could've purchased the tickets for his ex-wife and her companion from the goodness of his heart."

"Do you believe that, George?"

Of course not.

"It doesn't matter what I believe. The only thing that matters is what you can prove. You need evidence to convict someone. Even a dead man."

After an awkward pause, Mike Williams eventually shook his head and spoke.

"I find it incomprehensible a Christian person would do such a thing. Mrs. Daniels told me her son was raised in a home with Christian values."

Once again, George felt as he had been sucker-punched.

"You didn't tell her, did you?" He stared at his boss with wide eyes.

"No, of course not, George," Mike responded firmly. "I just can't believe a Christian person would cause the death of all those people."

"Going through a divorce can be devastating. I remember reading about this woman who committed suicide the same day her husband filed for a divorce..." George paused for a few seconds, again to add more drama. "...and she killed their children the same day. Drowned them in the bathtub. One at a time, and placed them in each of their beds. She left a note explaining how killing her children was truly an act of mercy."

"To protect the children from their father?" Mike looked mystified.

What? Why would you make that assumption?

"No, according to the psychologist who read the suicide letter, she killed her children because they no longer filled a purpose in life. Normally, a parent is supposed to be there to promote the welfare of a child, but in this case, it was the other way around. Her children's only purpose was to enrich this woman's life. The children were merely an asset, and when you're dead, you no longer have a need for assets. So, in her mind, killing her children was an act of mercy."

The CEO looked horrified.

George shrugged. "I mean, what are the kids going to do when she's gone? Just wander around the earth without any purpose, with nothing to do, and no one to please? It's not as if her children had lives of their own or anything—in her mind."

George thought his boss looked as if he was about to have a stroke.

"She killed the cat too. Rat poison," he added, and then mentally prepared himself to dial 9-1-1.

"And this was a Christian woman?" Mike asked and sounded annoyed.

"I don't have that information," George said, immediately regretting his choice of words.

Why did you use that phrase, George?

After yet another awkward pause, George eventually rose to his feet. "Tell Trisha, I said hello."

"She didn't come in today. Her boy is in the hospital."

"What happened?"

"He's sick a lot. He has a disability."

George felt his chest tightening. Something about a single mom raising a child always got to him, and especially a child with a disability.

"That reminds me, how was the meeting..."

What was her name again?

"...with the mother of the flight attendant?"

"Mrs. Olsen went to visit her family in Stockholm," Mike said. "So, we had no meeting."

Stockholm? George thought it was strange that the mother of the flight attendant had suddenly decided to travel abroad, especially when the plane hadn't been located.

"Stockholm? As in the capital of Sweden?"

"Stockholm, Wisconsin," Mike responded.

"Never heard of it."

"I had my doubts too, but apparently it exists."

29 THE SOLDIER

Friday evening

They'd started walking early in the morning, and hardly made any stops along the way. Jack had carried Julie on his back for the entire journey. As the hours passed, and the woods grew darker, they'd stopped, and settled down beside a large pine tree. When Jack went looking for food, Julie kept staring in the direction in which he'd left; she never took her eyes off his trail.

When Jack finally emerged from the dark woods, Julie lit up and waved her arm for him to see. Jack never waved back but simply held his cupped hands close to his chest.

"What do you have there, Jack?"

Jack extended his arms, and held his hands close to Julie's face, the content still concealed in his cupped hands.

Julie looked wary. "It's not an animal is it?"

Jack smiled, and slowly opened his hands.

"Blueberries," Julie blurted out. "I love blueberries."

Julie consumed each blueberry, one at a time, moving her arm rapidly back and forth between Jack's cupped hands and her mouth. Then, Julie suddenly stopped eating, opened her mouth, and extended her tongue far.

"*Is aisle town glue,*" Julie mumbled ambiguously.

"I don't understand what you're trying to say."

"Seriously? You're not getting this? It's so obvious," Julie said. "I asked you, if my tongue is blue."

"Now I get it."

"So, is it blue?"

"Yes, it's blue," Jack responded hesitantly.

"*Yaayyy*... It's blue," Julie cheered, and sounded childish.

Jack appeared puzzled by Julie's remark, and looked dubiously at her as she kept consuming the blueberries one at a time. Then Julie began giggling and made an attempt to feed Jack a blueberry. However, Jack never opened his mouth. He merely kept frowning and looked quite skeptical of Julie.

"You don't like blueberries?"

"I had plenty before. These are for you, Julie."

"Stick your tongue out," Julie said enthusiastically.

Jack barely extended the tip of his tongue.

"*Yaayyy*..." Julie cheered in a way that one could expect from a small child. "We're like blueberries you and I," Julie said with, the same enthusiasm.

"Okay."

"We're two of a kind, me and you," Julie said in a high-pitched tone.

Jack looked both baffled and appalled.

Suddenly, Julie looked sad and frightened. "What's wrong?"

"Nothing, I was only thinking that you're probably right," Jack said. "Just me and you are left to tell the story."

"What story?"

"We're the only ones who know where the plane is," Jack said. "That lake will freeze soon enough. It could be years before the plane is discovered."

"Well, there's the SOS sign. Somebody is bound to notice it, sooner or later."

"I suppose," Jack said.

"And then there's Kevin," Julie said. "He can take care of himself."

"I think Kevin quit."

"What do you mean he quit?"

"I think he just gave up," Jack said. "I felt sorry for him at first because of what happened to his wife and all. But now, I'm not so sure about him. He knew your ankle was broken, and he knew Nancy suffered from head trauma. But it didn't stop him from leaving. He was too scared to face the truth. He ran away from his problems, instead of facing them. That's not very noble is it?"

"No, it's not." Julie looked at her feet. "But either way, he's still out there. He could be on his way to the ocean. Perhaps he's in front of us?"

"I doubt it," Jack responded. "I think he's gone."

"Is Kevin a foreigner?" Julie blurted out. "His accent sounded so strange. Like he tried to disguise his voice or something."

"I noticed that too." Jack nodded. "But I thought he sounded like an American pretending to pass himself off as a foreigner."

"Why would he do that?"

"Perhaps his wife was foreign and her accent rubbed off on him. I remember switching to a Southern accent when I served with a guy from Texas. I actually had trouble getting rid of the accent after he left. I remember I had to concentrate really hard whenever I spoke."

"So, you were in the military?" Julie asked. "Is that where you got those muscles?"

Jack nodded slightly.

"Did you get that scar on your neck in battle?"

Jack exhaled.

"I'm sorry," Julie quickly added. "I didn't mean to pry."

"I'd rather not talk about it. I'm done with that part of my life."

Julie put her arm through Jack's arm, and curled up close to him, much the way a small child clings to a parent.

30 THE LETTER

Friday evening

George struggled to finish the letter to his sister. He didn't think it sounded right. It sounded like something a public relations manager had written, and not someone's brother. He decided to take a cold shower, hoping the cold water would reset his mind.

George had requested a few hours off from work to visit his sister in the hospital the next morning. Truth be told, he hoped Mike would deny his request, as he dreaded visiting his sister. Not because he didn't care about her, but seeing his sister's apparently lifeless body was unsettling. He felt as if a mannequin had replaced his sister. Her body was present, but the person was gone.

A shower later, he was back in his living room, and he noticed how the blue light kept flashing on his cell phone. He had two missed calls from his boss and also a text message.

Things just got worse! Can you meet me in my office at 8 a.m. tomorrow?

George hesitated as to whether he should call his boss or not, given the late hour, but his curiosity took the upper hand. However, Mike didn't answer his call. George sent a text message instead, confirming the next day's meeting. Then he swallowed hard and dialed a different number.

"Hi, Mom," he said, and swallowed once more. "Listen, I have to go to work in the morning, but we—"

George extended his arm far enough to protect his eardrums.

As he listened to his mother's endless shouting, he focused on the letter on his living room table, the letter that he'd written to his sister.

How could things possibly get any worse?

He kept staring at the letter.

31 THE RING

Saturday morning

They'd walked since early morning. Eventually, they'd stopped by a high, flowing creek with shallow waters. Jack gathered worms under the nearby rocks, as Julie drank from the creek. Julie was on her knees, but she'd stopped drinking to stare at her reflection in the water. For a brief second, her lips almost touched the surface.

Jack came up behind her, and focused on the back of her neck. Julie twitched when she noticed him, appearing startled by his sudden appearance. Jack sat down next to her, and washed the worms in water.

"You know, I'm not wearing any makeup, right?"

Jack didn't respond. He just kept chewing his food.

"Women look a lot different without makeup. You know that, right?"

"Good for you, Julie," Jack muttered, and kept chewing.

"Excuse me?" Julie looked puzzled.

"I mean, women wear so much makeup these days," Jack mumbled. "And some women even have surgery."

"So you prefer women who aren't wearing makeup?"

"I guess." Jack shrugged.

Julie looked disappointed and then turned her head away from Jack. Then she closed her eyes for a brief second and exhaled before she turned her head around and faced Jack with a stiff smile.

"So what gets you going, Jack? Is it the wrinkles? The tired eyes? The pimples?"

"I don't know." Jack sniffed. "It feels closer, I guess."

"Closer? You mean, as in intimate?"

"And genuine," Jack added.

Julie glanced at the water surface before she turned her head away from Jack. Then she closed her eyes and took a deep breath. Jack briefly glanced at the water surface, but then he kept staring at the back of Julie's neck.

"Nowadays, it seems as though women strive to appear less human. Like being human, isn't fashionable anymore," Jack said. "Nowadays, women don't have wrinkles and they smell like pastry."

Julie turned around and made a face. "You don't like pastry?"

"No, I like pastry."

"Then you should like the perfume I'm wearing," Julie said with a modest smile. "It's apple pie and cinnamon."

"No, that's not it."

"I'm pretty sure it is, Jack."

"No, you don't smell like apple pie."

"I think I know my own perfume." Julie leaned into Jack. "Smell me."

"I can't smell your perfume now, but when I carried you around for the first couple of days, I thought you smelled like chocolate or something, but now you smell—"

"Careful now Jack," Julie interrupted, and looked Jack in the eyes. "I believe the word you're looking for is genuine."

Jack chuckled, and then coughed a few times. "I was about to say, like a human being, but I guess genuine is just as true."

Jack focused on the worm that sprawled around between his fingers.

"Can I interest you in a worm?"

"I'm more in the mood for apple pie, now." Julie smiled.

Jack chuckled. "Me too."

Jack threw the worm into the creek. Then suddenly he jumped to his feet and ran out into the middle of the creek; with water up to his knees.

"What's wrong?"

"There's fish in the creek."

Jack dashed a yard to his left and tried to catch a fish with his bare hands.

"That's not going to work, Jack. Even if you catch one, you'd lose it just as fast. It's too slippery," Julie said. "Do you still have the steel wire from my bra?"

Jack pointed at Julie as a sign of acknowledgement and then reached into his inside jacket pocket. But he didn't take out a wire—he took out a note. Jack read the note with a puzzled look on his face. Then, he turned his head all the way back, and looked at the sky; he looked defeated.

"What's wrong?" Julie asked. "What does it say?"

"I shouldn't have made those remarks." Jack shook his head. "Now, I feel bad."

"Why, what did the note say?"

"Read it yourself." Jack said, and handed Julie the note. "I'll find a branch to attach the wire to."

Jack came back a few minutes later with something that resembled a spear.

"You shouldn't feel bad, Jack."

"I shouldn't have made those remarks."

"Well, you didn't know."

Julie extended her arm toward Jack, the note still in her hand.

"You hold onto it, Julie. Your pocket has a zipper."

Jack reached into his left pants pocket and took out a gold ring.

"Hold onto this too, so I don't lose it while fishing."

Jack handed Julie the ring before he walked out into the middle of the flowing creek. Julie carefully studied the ring before she put the ring in her right pocket along with the note; she closed the zipper.

Jack moved several rocks around in the shallow creek.

"Are you searching for gold?" Julie smiled.

"I'm building a horseshoe out of rocks, so I can lure the fish into a dead end."

A while later, after several disappointing stabbing attempts, Jack lifted the spear in the air, and smiled triumphantly; the fish sprawled at the end of the spear. They had plenty of fish for the next couple of hours, and they picked the fish to the bones.

Jack stood up. "We should get a move on."

"So, you're married?" Julie suddenly asked while she rose to her feet.

"No, I'm not married," Jack responded.

Julie took the ring out of her pocket. The note fell to the ground, but she didn't notice. Julie held the ring up for Jack to see.

"You're telling me this isn't a wedding ring."

"No, it's a wedding ring all right." Jack nodded. "But it's not mine. The ring belongs to Andrew. I checked his pockets when I took his pants. I put the ring in my pocket, so it wouldn't get lost."

Julie put the ring in her pocket and closed the zipper.

"So Andrew had his wedding ring in his pocket?"

Jack nodded, and raised his left eyebrow.

"That sounds about right." Julie shook her head. "So, do you have a girlfriend, perhaps?"

"No, it's just me."

Julie bowed her head as she climbed on Jack's back; she looked just as disappointed and confused as previously.

They walked along the creek, the note still on the ground.

32 PREJUDICES

Saturday morning

George expected Mike Williams to be alone in his office this morning, but instead he was in the company of two men George recognized as legal representatives. Mike gestured through the glass windows that George should wait outside the office. He noticed the envelope lying on Mike's desk and he feared that his assumption was right—Captain Daniels had left a suicide letter.

George wondered if the company had already begun the process of filing for bankruptcy, as he assumed the insurance company wouldn't cover the damage if the crash was deliberately caused by one of the F.A. employees.

The two legal representatives had looks of defeat as they left the office.

By now, George Stanton had grown accustomed to the CEO's office, which didn't feel as intimidating as it had the week before. However, the envelope lying on his boss's desk did look menacing. George felt a tension in his chest.

"What do you have there, Mike?"

George felt certain he knew the answer to his question.

But Mike Williams didn't provide his employee with an answer right away. He just handed George the envelope. George thought his boss had a look of resignation.

George opened the envelope and sprinted his way through the single sheet of paper. To his relief, the envelope didn't contain a suicide letter from Captain Daniels. Rather it was a formal complaint about Daniels from one of his co-workers, from a man named Isaac Gregorian.

"Have you talked to this Gregorian fellow about the complaint?"

Michael Williams tilted his head, and his eyes appeared as they were about to fall out of his eye sockets. "He's the co-pilot, George."

George quickly scanned the document once more, and then focused on the name at the bottom of the sheet.

"I thought the co-pilot's name was Gregory."

"Isaac Gregorian." Mike sounded annoyed.

George noticed the envelope didn't have a stamp on it.

"Tell me you got this in the mail, Mike."

"No, it was delivered to the office reception on Friday morning, seemingly by Mr. Gregorian himself," Mike said, and exhaled deeply. "Opening internal mail hasn't been on my agenda for the past week. Especially not any mail addressed to Jeff—until last night, that is."

"As long as the complaint was delivered on the same day the plane crashed, then we couldn't have acted any differently. Besides, the co-pilot never claimed Captain Daniels was suicidal. He just wrote he was uncomfortable working with him. This doesn't change much. I think we're all right here, Mike."

"What do you mean we're all right?"

"I mean, the terror angle is still intact," George said, and shrugged. "Did you tell the feds about the complaint?"

"Of course, I did," Mike responded. "I called them yesterday evening, as soon as I read the letter."

George placed the envelope and the letter on the desk. "How did they react?"

"They requested a copy, but they didn't seem that interested."

"Well, there you go. They're probably still focusing on

the Imam."

"Blaming the Imam certainly seems to be the consensus in the media," Mike said.

"Thank God for prejudices, am I right?"

Mike Williams suddenly looked infuriated. George got the feeling his boss was about to leap over the desk and strangle him.

"I beg your pardon," Mike said in a lethal tone.

George wondered what part of the last sentence had provoked his boss the most. Was it that he'd used the Lord's name in vain? Or because he might have insinuated religion was a source of prejudice?

"It's fortunate that everyone is focusing on terrorism," George said.

Mike didn't seem pleased with George's response, but he did however, lean back against his chair, which made George feel more at ease. He dismissed the thought of his boss leaping over the desk.

"This whole thing could still be a coincidence," George said, and tried his best to keep a straight face. "Perhaps the captain did buy the tickets for his ex-wife out of the goodness of his heart, and the co-pilot misinterpreted the experience of going through a divorce as signs of depressions."

George reached for the letter on the desk.

"He wrote that the captain showed signs of depression, and that he gave the co-pilot the creeps." George shrugged his shoulders. "I mean, what does that prove?"

The CEO didn't make any attempt to answer George's rhetorical question.

"Wait a minute. Didn't you say they hardly ever flew together?"

"They flew together fourteen days prior to the crash. Same route, Seattle, Anchorage. And a few times, during the summer holidays," Mike said in a low voice. The man sounded as if he was still struggling to rid himself of the insult.

"And the co-pilot is the only one who noticed the signs

of depression?" George asked. Again, the question sounded rhetorical, and he didn't get any response from the man across the desk. "Wait a minute. When did Captain Daniels buy the tickets for his ex-wife?"

Michael Williams quickly located the paper from the day before. Then suddenly, his face shifted. He didn't look angry anymore; instead, he looked humble.

"The same day that they flew together. Fourteen days prior to the crash."

"Well, there you go. Captain Daniels probably was blowing off steam for having to buy the tickets for his ex-wife, and..."

What was his name again?

"The co-pilot probably misinterpreted it as signs of depression. This could just be coincidence, Mike. Perhaps the Imam is responsible for the crash."

"Do you believe that, George?"

Of course not.

"Let the authorities do the investigation, Mike. It's not our job to speculate."

George didn't believe in coincidences. He was convinced Captain Daniels had crashed the plane on purpose. But even though his opinion of what had happened was firm, he was determined to keep it to himself. For some reason, he felt Trisha Boyle's welfare was more important than the possibility of justice. Something about Trisha and her ability to support her handicapped son made George forget about the other aspects of the tragedy.

"I called you in this morning because I want you to help me prepare a press release, and to announce a press conference today," Mike then said.

George was about to concur when he suddenly realized that his boss wouldn't have called this meeting simply to ask him to release the usual nonsense to the press. Mike Williams must have something else in mind. George's heart rate accelerated.

"And say what, Mike?"

"The truth."

"What truth might that be?"

"That Captain Daniels showed signs of depression, and he was aware that his ex-wife would be on this particular flight."

George shook his head. "You can't say that, Mike."

"I'm a Christian, George. I believe in telling the truth."

"You're also the CEO of this company, and you have a responsibility to its employees and shareholders. If you share that information with the media, then you might as well file for bankruptcy at the same time," George told him, and thought he sounded like a lawyer.

Mike Williams leaned forward, and once again, George got the feeling that his boss was about to leap over his desk.

"You're right about one thing," Mike said and stared George in the eyes. "I'm the CEO of this company."

George just realized why the two legal representatives had such a look of defeat when they left the office, and he imagined that he had the same look on his face right now. He decided on a different approach.

"What about his mother, Mike. This will destroy her."

The idea of Mrs. Daniels suffering seemed to have struck a nerve. The CEO leaned back in his chair with a look of shame.

"I'm not passing any judgment on her son. I'm merely stating the facts."

"But the media will pass judgment, for sure, and so will the public," George said. "When I visited Mrs. Daniels, she wasn't interested in any potential insurance claims or money. All she wanted was for us to know what a great man her son was."

Mike diverted his eyes toward his desk.

"Besides, how do you expect the feds to react when we release potential evidence to the press the day after we provided them with a copy," George said, and then cautiously added. "Didn't the feds tell you not to interfere with the investigation?"

George seemed to have struck another nerve, although Mike Williams made no attempt to answer his question.

"Let's at least wait until the plane is located, and we know more about what actually happened."

"The ELT isn't providing a signal, George. It could be months until the plane is finally located."

George saw an opportunity to change the subject, and hopefully get Mike's mind off the press conference.

"Are the victims' families still up there?" he asked.

The CEO seemed surprised by the sudden change in the conversation.

"They had a ceremony yesterday," Mike said hesitantly. "Janet is traveling home today, and I imagine most of the families will do the same."

George was just about to steer the conversation further away from the press conference by asking who Janet was, but when he noticed Mike's hostile stare, he assumed his boss had understood his attempt at changing the subject.

"Let's wait a few days at least, and give the feds time to release the information before we do. We can coordinate on Monday, and if you still see the need to disclose the complaint against Captain Daniels, then we can call a press conference on Tuesday."

George had no intention of helping his boss prepare for a press conference on Tuesday. In fact, he'd rather resign as public relations manager. But he hoped his boss would change his mind before Monday. Once again, George thought of Trisha Boyle and how desperate she'd sounded to keep her job.

Mike Williams nodded hesitantly, seeming to reluctantly agree. "That'll be all, George. Thanks for coming in early. I hope it didn't interfere with your plan to visit your sister in the hospital this morning."

"The plan is to visit her tomorrow morning instead. I won't be gone for more than a few hours."

"Take your time," Mike told him. "Also, Cayla won't be

coming in today. I'll conduct her job as the ECC for now, and I'll let you know if we have any new developments."

Or I could just watch the news, George thought before saying, "Sure."

George didn't plan to do much work the rest of the day, except for updating the company website with the information already known to the public. He imagined he'd spend most of his time writing a letter to his sister—the letter he'd promised his mom he would read to his sister during the next day's visit to the hospital.

"I'll be attending tomorrow's early morning mass," Mike suddenly announced as George was about to leave the office.

George thought his boss sounded guilty for having skipped church last Sunday, and it made him wonder if Mike had even left his office at all for the past seven days.

"I'll be sure to include your sister in my prayers."

George tilted his head and forced a polite smile before he left.

33 THE BEAR

Saturday afternoon

They'd followed the creek, which eventually merged with a lake.

The sky was clear. Julie unzipped her jacket, and closed her eyes as she faced the sun. She took the elastic band from her hair, put it on her wrist, and ruffled her long hair in the small breeze from the lake. Julie was alone, as Jack had gone up the hill to get a better view of the surroundings.

"Help!" A male voice echoed across the landscape.

Julie rose to her feet and yelled, "What's happening?"

Julie looked anxiously toward the steep hillside.

"Help!" Jack yelled from the top of the hill.

Julie looked terrified as Jack ran down the hillside in panic. His legs got tangled up and he lost his footage, and began rolling down the hill, desperately trying to get back on his feet. Julie took a few steps backward and fell to the ground.

"What's wrong?" Julie's voice cracked.

Julie had her eyes fixed on the surroundings behind Jack, squinting at the terrain. Jack ran toward her, waving his hand and encouraging her to stand up.

"We have to leave now," Jack said, as soon as he reached Julie.

Julie looked petrified and out of breath. Her nostrils

kept flaring. She remained on the ground and made no attempt to move.

"There are people on the other side of the lake."

"People?"

"A woman sunbathing," Jack said. "We need to get to the other side before she leaves."

"Sunbathing?"

"She's tanning," Jack responded. "We need to leave right away."

"There's no bear?"

Jack frowned, and looked up the hill. "I'm sorry, Julie."

"I thought it was a bear, Jack."

Julie wiped her tears with her jacket sleeve, her tears mixing with the bloodstains.

"We have to go," Jack said, and focused on Julie's sleeve. Then he glanced at her forehead, but said nothing more.

34 THE NOTE

I am a liar. (pause) I lied to you for almost as long as I knew you, but I only did it to protect you. I didn't want him to ruin your life the way he ruined mine. That's why I stayed away for so long, because I couldn't lie to you anymore, Mamma. He was your friend, and he broke me when I was eight years old. He said it was the only way I could ever learn, and (say his name) made sure I'd swallowed every time. (pause) I had to lie to protect you, and I had to hide to protect myself. That's why I ate so much, I didn't want to be the victim. I can't be the victim, Mamma. I don't know how. (pause) I'd rather be the fat guy. (pause) I'm sorry for not being there, and I'm sorry you died alone. (pause) I hope you can forgive me.

35 THE CELL PHONE

Saturday afternoon

Jack looked enraged as he stared at Nancy's remains, Julie still on his back.

"Why is she naked?" Jack mumbled.

There was a sound of dry heaves. Julie appeared to be gagging.

Jack looked over his shoulder. "Don't throw up, Julie. You'll just be worse off. Look the other way."

"It's the smell." Julie clamped her nose.

Jack set Julie down by a distant rock, both of them staring at Nancy's remains.

"Why is she naked?"

"Perhaps Kevin took her clothes," Julie said. "We took Andrew's clothes."

"He didn't have to take her bra." Jack grimaced. "I mean, he could've at least turned her over."

"I'm pretty sure she wasn't wearing a bra," Julie responded. "But you're right. Kevin wouldn't have left her like that. Perhaps she died naked."

"Why would she take of her clothes?"

"People who suffer from hypothermia often take their clothes off. Just before they freeze to death, they actually feel warm," Julie said. "Or, perhaps she was confused, and just took off her clothes, for some reason. Perhaps she was sunbathing."

"I'll have a look around, and see if I can find her clothes." Jack walked a few steps, but then suddenly stopped. "I heard someone yell."

Julie looked around. "I didn't hear anything."

"No, I meant before, when I screamed for help from the other side of the lake."

Julie's shoulders collapsed. "That was me. I heard you yell, so I yelled back."

Jack took a deep breath, exhaled loudly, and looked a bit embarrassed.

He was only gone for a few minutes, then he returned with a purple cable knit sweater and a pair of white denim jeans. He sat down next to Julie, and handed her a cell phone.

"Where did you find this?"

"It was in her pants' pocket."

"She had a phone all along?"

"No, she said her phone was in her purse, which she left in the plane."

"No, that was me, Jack. I told you that, remember?"

"I remember, but Nancy told me the same thing."

"Then where did she get the..." Julie trailed off, and sighed. "Andrew must have startled her. Or perhaps, he hurt his head when he tripped, and she found him that way. Perhaps she took his phone to call for help."

"Either way, it was an accident," Jack said in a decisive tone. "Perhaps we can start a fire if we reflect the sun rays from the phone screen."

After some deliberation, they decided to leave Nancy's remains the way they found them. They kept walking southwest, and left the lake behind them. Just as the forest began to thin out, the sun started to descend. They settled down by a large pine tree next to a giant rock. However, every attempt to make a fire failed.

Jack suddenly rose to his feet and hurled the phone into a tree. Then, he raised his arms and folded his hands on top of his head, his massive biceps stretching the fabric of the black blazer.

"Are you all right, Jack?"

"I failed," Jack mumbled.

"They make those screens to reflect as little sunlight as possible."

Jack looked at Julie and frowned. "I wasn't there for her."

Julie bowed her head. "It's not your fault, Jack."

"I should have been there for her."

"It's not your fault, Jack."

"I should've protected her," Jack said. "She was too weak to make it on her own."

Julie kept staring at Jack. "Did you two know each other?"

Jack gave Julie a sharp stare.

"Sorry," Julie said and trained her eyes down. "You're a good man, Jack."

"I'm *broken*," Jack said vaguely with a sad expression.

"You and me both. But not for long."

Jack looked baffled. "What?"

"Not once we sue the airline."

"Oh." Jack nodded slightly, but then shook his head firmly. "Money won't make a difference."

"That's just something rich people say," Julie responded. "Money doesn't make a difference if you have more than you need."

"Time is all that matters." Jack shrugged. "And when your time is up, then your life is over. Money won't make a difference."

"What are you talking about?" Julie said. "You're starting to sound like an eccentric millionaire."

"Wealth won't make you happy, Julie."

"Are you sure you're not an eccentric millionaire? You kind of dress like one," Julie said and looked Jack up and down.

Jack looked down at the suit he wore. "I never had much money, and I didn't have much growing up."

"And were you happy?" Julie quickly responded in a slightly sarcastic tone.

Jack shook his head. "No, I wasn't."

Evening

Once again, they'd used pine branches to protect themselves from the moist soil. Julie wore two sweaters, and one of them was purple. She curled up close to Jack, her hair band still on her wrist.

"I like your clothes," Julie said. "I don't think you look pretentious, or anything."

"That's okay." Jack tone was as short as his response.

"You dress well for a truck driver," Julie said. "I'm smiling by the way."

"I'm not a truck driver, Julie. I just drove a truck when I was younger. That's all," Jack said. "I'm currently unemployed."

"Is that why you wore a suit?" Julie asked enthusiastically. "Did you have a job interview in Anchorage?"

"No, I just wanted to look good. That's all."

"For a date?" Julie sounded overly cute and curious.

"No, I was..." Jack hesitated. "...to attend a funeral."

"I'm so sorry, Jack. I didn't mean to pry."

"That's okay. But I rather not talk about it."

36 HELL

Just another day

There's a fly on the ceiling. It moves back and forth, and I can't help looking at it. The fly almost distracts me from the pain I'm in. I try to adjust my body, but I can't move. My body doesn't comply with my attempts. The waves keep coming. Waves and waves of agonizing pain.

I'm not present. I'm somewhere else. Even if the pain is present, my mind is elsewhere. Nothing's real anymore. Dreaming is the little joy I have left in life. Whenever I dream, I'm somewhere else, and not trapped in this bed. But as soon as I wake up, I realize I'm still trapped in my own version of hell.

I wish they'd kill me, grant me the honor of dying. But, instead, they nurture me. They're making an effort to preserve my body. They wash me with a sponge, and they insist on shaving my legs. They each have their own routines, and their own schedules, but my day never changes. Every day is the same.

Oh, how I hope to die during the night.

Sometimes, they actually speak to me. But usually, they speak about me. Either way, they never address me as a person. They don't view me as a human being. To them, I am something else. I'm not a person anymore. I'm only alive to please others. I don't have any other function in life.

Oh, how I wish they'd let me die, and put me out of my

misery.

But I'm not blaming them for my misfortune. I brought this on myself. Every day I wake up furious with myself. I try to forgive myself, show leniency toward myself. But I never forgive myself.

I had one life, and I ruined it.

I don't remember when it was, but I remember seeing the truck.

37 THE SIGN

Sunday morning

George's throat felt dry from reading the letter out loud to his sister. The letter didn't sound like anything a brother would have written; it sounded like something a public relations manager had written. However, the lack of authenticity didn't stop his mother from crying her eyes out while stroking his sister's hair in a nurturing and frantic manner. His father, however, didn't cry at all, and he hadn't uttered a single word during the entire visit.

His father kept staring at the face of the lifeless manikin who once was George's sister. But then, suddenly, his father averted his eyes, and instead focused on the television mounted on the wall.

The whole scene made him nauseous, and George asked himself if he really knew any of the people in this room. He certainly didn't understand any of them.

"*Luke,*" his father said in a thick Japanese accent while pointing at the television.

As George read the letters on the television, he felt even more nauseous.

SOS

38 THE MOTHER

Sunday morning

Julie struggled to get the pine needles out of her hair. At first, Jack didn't pay much attention to her. But when she put her hair up, he wouldn't stop staring at her.

"Do I have something in my hair?"

"No, it looks fine."

"Yeah. Sure, it does."

Jack kept eyeing Julie.

"What?" Julie sounded concerned.

"I'm sorry. I didn't mean to stare."

"I don't mind," Julie said. "I just wondered why."

"It's just that you remind me of someone else wearing your hair like that."

"You mean the ponytail?" Julie pulled her hair to the side, across her shoulder. "Well, who do I remind you of? An old girlfriend? A high school sweetheart who got away?"

"Actually, you remind me of my mother."

"Oh really." Julie sighed.

"Yes, there is something about you that keeps reminding me of her. I can't place my finger on it, though."

Julies made a face. "Well, that explains it."

"Explains what?"

"Why you wouldn't kiss me the other day."

"No, that's not why."

Julie's smile quickly vanished. "Why then?"

"It wasn't genuine, Julie."

"Excuse me?"

"It was obvious you didn't really want to kiss me."

"Then why do you think I tried to kiss you?" Julie looked startled.

"Why do you think you wanted to kiss me?"

"Spare me the psychology and just answer the question," Julie said harshly.

"Okay." Jack raised his palms. "Your mind can be quite deceitful, Julie. It's hard to distinguish between impressions and emotions."

"I told you to spare me the psycho mumbo-jumbo, Jack."

"You're out here all alone, and you can't walk. You feel scared and vulnerable. But when I come along, that anxiety goes away. And when I leave, the anxiety returns. Therefore, you will feel a longing to be with me because it's feels good to be around me."

"So, you didn't want to take advantage of me. Is that what you're saying?"

"I guess you could say that."

"You're a good man, Jack," Julie said. "I think you're my guardian angel and sent to earth to protect me."

"I'll get you home to your boy, Julie. I promise, no matter what."

"When this is all over, then perhaps the three of us can go out for pizza, and get to know each other better. My son could sure use a male role model in his life," Julie said, and put her hand on Jack's forearm.

"I'd like that very much. We can all go out for pizza—with worms on it."

"No, with ham and pepperoni," Julie blurted out, sounding childish.

Afternoon

They kept a faster pace than the previous days since the terrain was flatter. They kept walking southwest. Jack stopped to rest and find something to eat. He pulled the sleeves of his white dress shirt up to his elbows, and began turning over rocks. Julie sat on her jacket, her hair band was on her wrist.

"My hair is such a mess."

Jack didn't respond to Julie's remark. He just kept consuming whatever came his way in a rapid motion and without any hesitation.

"I wish I had a hairbrush."

Jack kept turning rocks.

"I don't usually look like such a mess."

Jack straightened his back. "I think you look just fine. Lovely."

Julie smiled, and her focus fell to the ground. "I'm not used to compliments."

"I find that hard to believe," Jack said and turned another rock.

Julie looked suspicious. "I'm serious. I don't get a lot of compliments."

Jack smiled and shook his head slightly. "I'm not buying it, Julie."

"No, it's true, Jack," Julie responded. "Even as a child, I never got any compliments. No one ever told me they loved me or even gave me a pat on the back. And no one ever stood up for me. I had to make it all on my own."

"I'm sorry to hear that, Julie."

There was an awkward pause as the two of them looked at each other; each one as humble as the other. Then Jack suddenly flinched and slapped his forearm.

"What's wrong?"

"I think a mosquito got me," Jack responded. "I can't remember the last time I got a mosquito bite."

"That's because you smoke, Jack. They can't stand the cigarette smoke."

"Yet people say nothing good ever comes from smoking."

Julie laughed briefly. "That's one way of looking at it."

"And I'm not used to the outdoors. I'm more used to concrete."

"I don't care for the outdoors either." Julie shook her head and had a serious look on her face. "I don't understand why anyone in their right mind would want to wander around in the woods and eat whatever comes their way, and relieve themselves behind a bush."

"I think most people are wise enough to bring food," Jack said and looked at the worm in his hand. "You're hungry?"

"No," Julie quickly responded. "I filled up on sushi yesterday."

Jack took another look at the worm before he dropped it to the ground.

"I used to be jealous of men for being able to eat more calories, but now I'm actually glad."

Jack frowned. "What do you mean?"

"Men can eat more calories without gaining weight. But as a woman, I have to eat fewer calories, or I'd jeopardize my health," Julie said. "That's so unfair—am I right?"

Jack didn't respond to Julie's question. Instead, he arched his eyebrows, and kept staring at her.

"What?"

"Nothing." Jack shrugged, and looked the other way.

"What you're thinking, Jack?"

"We should get a move on. Are you good to go?"

Before Julie climbed on his back, she put her jacket on, the same jacket she'd used as a seat pad. The jacket had a tear on the back of it.

Evening

They didn't get far before the sun disappeared behind the horizon. They had to abandon their quest for water as darkness eventually made it impossible for them to keep moving. They spent the night under yet another pine tree. This one, however, was different from the rest. The branches sloped all the way down to the ground, and the tree appeared to be practically a tent. They slept on the dry ground. Julie had her arm across Jack's chest, and her head on his shoulder. Jack brushed Julie's hair over her ear.

39 CALGARY

Sunday evening

As George packed his bag, he thought of the advice his boss had given him to bring a helmet or perhaps even a bulletproof vest, on his journey. George had neither of those things, but, he did, however, have the ability to talk his way out of any predicament—or at least, he thought he did.

His boss had assigned him to travel to Yellowknife and hopefully meet the passengers who'd survived the crash—and if so, express the airlines' deepest concern and apologies before any of them were interviewed by the media.

However, the suggestion of safety measures by his boss was not due to any anticipated hostility from any of the passengers. Since George had to switch planes in Calgary in order to reach his final destination in Yellowknife, he thought he might as well stop by and talk to the angry father of the co-pilot and hopefully calm him down. The man apparently had made it a daily routine to yell at George's boss over the phone.

George had agreed with the mother of the co-pilot to arrive at her house at precisely 6 p.m. The timing suited George since his plane left at 9 p.m., therefore providing him with an excuse for cutting the meeting short.

40 APPLES & BEEF

Monday morning

They'd slept late, the sun not breaking through the thick, sloping branches of the pine tree, which resembled a tent. However, the sound of a gunshot echoing across the landscape and the following sound of birds fleeing the scene woke them up.

"Wait here, Julie. I'll climb up the hill, and scream for help."

Jack left before Julie had a chance to respond.

Julie eventually peered out of her hive, her head sticking out of the thick pine tree. She looked up the hillside and kept squinting. The second gunshot seemed to have startled her. Obscured by the sunlight, a tall silhouette of a person emerged and slowly descended the slippery hill. Julie squinted once more.

"Is that you, Jack?" Julie used her hand to shade the bright sunlight. "I didn't hear you yell," Julie said. "Did you see any hunters up there?"

"No, but there's a road at the top of the hill," Jack responded, coming close. "We're safe, Julie."

Julie made a gasping sound, and her eyes turned wet. Jack picked her up and carried her in his arms, as the two of them ascended the hill, both of them with tremendous smiles.

When Jack set her down, Julie fell to her knees and practically embraced the compressed gravel of the narrow dirt road.

They then waited patiently, but there wasn't any traffic. Their postures slowly sagged as the hours passed. Jack's stomach kept rumbling.

"Perhaps we should start walking," Julie said.

"I just thought there would be more traffic."

Jack rose, and Julie climbed on his back.

"Left, or right?"

"Left is closer to the heart," Julie said, and gently tapped Jack's left chest.

Afternoon

After an hour of walking, they finally came to a halt; a fence blocked their path. They both stared at the sign on the massive steel gate blocking the narrow road.

Trespassers will be shot!
(seriously)

"Who would write that?" Jack sounded annoyed.

"Even if we're trespassing, they can't shoot us. Can they?"

"Seriously, who writes that?"

"Well, at least they wrote the serious part in parentheses." Julie squinted at the sign. "They can't shoot us? Can they?"

Jack turned his head, and looked back at the long road behind him. Then, he opened the massive steel gate that blocked the narrow road, the loud squeaking noise of the heavy gate echoing across the otherwise so-silent surroundings.

They didn't walk far before they came to a house at the

end of the road. The large house had seen better days, and so had the barn and the small house next to the barn. The sun and the rain had taken their toll on the property, and the red paint had begun to flake off all the structures. A porch was attached to the main house next to a lawn with several apple trees. A large semi-trailer truck was parked by the side of the house. Jack stopped about fifty yards from the main house.

"We're just going to stand here, Jack?"

"I saw some movement in the window. I think they've seen us. I don't want to startle them. Especially if they're armed."

A large man came out of the house, and then stood in the middle of the road, his legs wide and his back straight. With his left arm, he pointed toward the road behind Jack and Julie. The man had a rifle in his hand, the barrel pointed toward the ground.

"We need help!" Jack yelled.

The large man lowered his arm only to raise it up again, and once more he pointed toward the distant road. Then, a second man emerged from the house. Aside from the rifle, the two men had the exact same appearance.

Julie climbed off Jack's back and yelled, "We're survivors of flight seven one nine from Seattle to Anchorage! Can you please help us?"

The large men glanced at each other, and then began walking down the road toward Julie and Jack. They both wore the same type of jumpsuit, and their large stomachs wobbled as they walked along the sloping road. The armed man held the rifle casually over his shoulders, the barrel touching the back of his neck.

"*They even dress alike,*" Julie whispered.

Julie extended her hand, but the large twins stopped a few yards away and looked her up and down. Julie placed her palm across her chest.

"I'm Julie, and this here is Jack."

The twins stared at Julie's chest, but neither of them

spoke.

"Jean," the unarmed man, eventually mumbled, and then tilted his head. *"Adam."*

"Nice to meet you, John. Can you please call the police?" Julie asked Jean.

"Phone, no work out here," Jean said in a French accent.

"Oh..." Julie gasped. "We've been walking for days. You're the first people we've met since the plane crashed. Is there any chance you can give us something to eat, and drive us to the nearest town? I'm sure the press will salute your every effort."

The twins looked at each other, but neither of them spoke.

"So where are we exactly?" Julie asked.

Once again, the twins looked Julie up and down.

"Where is this?" Julie pointed toward the ground.

Adam mumbled a word in French, making his twin brother laugh.

"Did you say, Layfair," Julie asked Adam.

"Oui ... Layfair," Jean responded, and pronounced the name in an English accent.

"I don't think I ever heard of that," Julie said. "Is it far to the ocean?"

"What ocean?" Jean responded in a French accent.

"The Pacific." Julie hesitated and looked at Jack.

"I thought I saw the ocean on the horizon," Jack said.

"No ocean," Jean said, and shook his head. *"Great Slave."*

"The great what?" Jack asked.

"One of biggest lakes in world," Jean said, staring provocatively at Jack.

"Are we close to Yellowknife?" Julie asked.

Jean responded with a single nod.

"Can you please drive us to Yellowknife?" Julie asked Jean.

"You shower and eat, and then we take you."

"Thank you, John," Julie said. "Much obliged."

Jean walked toward the house, but his brother didn't move. Jack picked Julie up and carried her in his arms as they made their way toward the house. Adam walked behind Jack, the rifle still resting casually across his shoulders.

The interior of the house that greeted them was shabby, but not entirely untidy. Julie was given a towel and limped her way into the bathroom, while Jack awkwardly remained alone with Adam in the living room. Silence filled the space, and the atmosphere was as cold as ice. The only sound was the sound of a running shower. Jean remained in the kitchen where the man kept stirring a pot of beef stew while he casually leaned against the kitchen counter—as did the rifle next to him.

Jack broke the silence in the living room. "You wouldn't happen to smoke?"

Adam shook his head in response.

"I was afraid of that." Jack exhaled loudly. "Do you mind if I go and take a look at the truck? I used to drive one."

At first, Adam didn't respond. Instead, he looked Jack in the eyes. He appeared to be chewing, even though he had nothing in his mouth. Perhaps he was chewing on the question. Eventually, Adam stopped chewing, nodded, and then barked a few instructions in French to his brother in the kitchen. Then he pointed Jack toward the front door and walked behind him as the two men left the house.

Jack and Adam stood next to each other and gazed at the truck. But they didn't engage in a meaningful conversation with each other; their dialog mostly consisted of nouns. Jack pronounced several nouns in line with the vocabulary describing a large semi-trailer, and Adam responded by shaking or nodding his head and occasionally raising his eyebrows.

Jack looked at the small house next to the barn. "Do you guys have a house each, or does someone else live in the smaller house?"

"*Mother lives there,*" Adam said in a thick French accent. "*She sick.*"

After an awkward pause, Jack looked across the lawn, and then turned his eyes toward the barn. "Do you have pigs on the farm?"

Adam had a look of insult. "*No pigs*."

"I just thought you might have pigs on the farm on account of the apples." Jack pointed at the trees and all the fallen apples rotting away on the ground. "But the apples are only there to attract the thieves—am I right?"

Adam smiled wide and revealed his dirty and discolored teeth. "*Oui, I shoot one this morning, from kitchen window,*" Adam said enthusiastically, and tilted his head. "*You come see.*"

The moose hung upside down from the ceiling in the barn. The head was missing, and so was the skin. Adam slapped the side of the carcass and then formed a crooked smile. He appeared proud of his accomplishment.

"That's a big one," Jack said.

Jack took his eyes off the prey and focused on the wall in the background. At first, he smiled, but then his jaw dropped.

Beside a shelf with a few glass jars on it nothing was striking about the wall. One jar, however, was filled with soil.

"*Quoi*?" Adam looked Jack in the eyes.

"What?" Jack frowned.

"*What.*" Adam smiled and nodded once.

Jack looked Adam up and down and then swallowed hard. "I'm going to check on Julie."

Before Jack made his way out of the barn, he once again glanced at the glass jar.

Jack walked toward the main house with Adam a few yards behind him. Suddenly, he stopped. "Could you be so kind and ask your mother for some clothes? We've been wearing the same clothes for a week. Perhaps your mother has some clothes in Julie's size?"

Adam seemed agitated by the question, and once again, he appeared to be chewing, moving his jaw and wrestling his tongue. Eventually, he stopped chewing, and nodded slightly.

"*I will look,*" Adam said.

Adam pointed toward the main house, and seemed to encourage Jack not to follow him on his way to the small house next to the barn.

Julie sat by the dining room table, and as Jack entered the room, she smiled. Jack came up behind her and placed both his hands on her shoulders.

"Is everything all right?"

"Yes, I'm fine, Jack." Julie sounded a bit bewildered. "I limped over here."

Jack looked at the bathroom door just a few yards away. "I'm going to take a shower and lose the beard. I won't be long. Don't go anywhere. Okay?"

"I didn't see a razor in there. I was..." Julie trailed off and looked embarrassed, while she glanced at her legs.

"There should be a razor," Jack said and focused on the kitchen.

"Both Adam and John have full-grown beards. I don't think they shave, Jack."

"They shave their heads," Jack responded quickly. "My good man! Do you have a razor I could borrow?"

Jean had stopped stirring the pot and had placed four deep porcelain bowls on the counter next to the stove. Now, he looked toward the dining room and frowned.

"Razor." Jack pronounced the word slowly, and scratched his beard.

Jean shook his head, and scratched his beard in response.

"Razor." Jack ran his hand through his hair.

Jean twitched and then stroked his bald head. Then, he went to the dresser next to the bathroom door and took out an old-fashioned razor along with a pack of blades from the top drawer.

"*Le rasoir,*" Jean said in a perfect French accent, and winked at Julie.

Jean walked sideways to the kitchen, his eyes focused on Jack.

"Is John the one in the kitchen?"

Jack shrugged his shoulders at Julie and then went into the bathroom.

When Jack emerged from the bathroom a few minutes later, the dining table was set and three out of four chairs were occupied. The twins had their backs toward the kitchen. Jack sat down next to Julie in the chair furthest away from the kitchen. No knives or forks had been placed on the table, only spoons. Jack had shaved his beard. However, his hair wasn't wet.

"Look at you, Jack. You look like a new man." Julie smiled, and touched her chin.

"No, I'm back to the old one."

"You look great, Jack." Julie leaned in closer to Jack and whispered, "*And you smell great too.*"

"*I put on some aftershave,*" Jack whispered.

"Look, their mother was kind enough to lend me some clothes."

Julie pointed at the dresser next to the bathroom door, and then looked at Jean.

"What is your mother's name?" Julie asked Jean.

"Melinda," Adam eventually answered.

"Be sure to thank Melinda for me, and I do hope she'll get well soon."

"*Bon appetite,*" Adam said, and extended his palms across the table.

Jean was just about to pour Jack a glass of red wine.

"No, thank you. I'd rather have a glass of milk." Jack got up from his chair.

Adam rose quickly. "*I get you milk.*"

Jack unwillingly sat down, and while he did, he glanced toward the kitchen.

"You don't drink alcohol, Jack?"

"Red wine is quite sour, and you shouldn't drink it on an empty stomach."

Adam returned to the table, and put the glass with milk down with excessive force. Then he picked up the wine bottle and was just about to poor Julie a glass of wine.

"I'll get you some milk," Jack said, and prepared to rise to his feet.

The twins gave Jack a hostile look, as both almost rose.

"No, I want wine. I can take it. Hit me." Julie smiled, and extended her glass across the table.

"*Bon appetite*," Jean said, after he'd filled the glass with wine.

"*Mer-see*," Julie said, pronouncing the French word awkwardly.

Jean gazed into Julie's eyes and then shook his head and smiled. "*Nope*," he mumbled.

"Pardon my French," Julie said, and smiled back at Jean.

Jack stared at Julie with wide eyes.

"What's wrong, Jack?"

Jack swallowed hard and eventually blurted out, "I want to say grace."

Julie looked confused. "Okay."

Jack folded his hands, bowed his head and closed his eyes; Julie did just the same. However, Adam and Jean kept their hands apart and their eyes wide open, as they stared suspiciously at Jack.

"Thank you, Lord, for the food we're about to receive, and thank you for helping us find shelter in our hour of need."

Jack opened his eyes briefly and glanced across the table.

"Amen," Jack added, looking disappointed.

He drank all his milk at once. Then he brought the bowl with stew close to his face, and began eating in a fast and frantic manner. The brothers looked at each other, and then they focused on Jack before they eventually began eating.

A few moments later, Jack stopped eating and placed the bowl down on the table, the bowl almost full. He placed his hands on the table surface and spread his fingers apart. He sniffed his nose louder than usual. Then his breathing accelerated, and he was breathing deeper each breath he took.

Both brothers looked curious as they focused on Jack.

"Are you all right, Jack?" she asked.

Jack didn't speak. He appeared to be hyperventilating, and his eyes were fixated on the bowl in front of him. Then his head collided with the hardwood table top, and he collapsed on the floor.

Julie slid down onto the floor, shook Jack's shoulder and asked him what was wrong. Adam rose to his feet, and as he stood next to Jack's lifeless body, he started to yell in French. He kept repeating the same phrase, while he pointed at his brother, who had a look of defeat.

"*Yes. You told me,*" Jean eventually said, and seemed provoked by his brother, since he avoided eye contact with him. "*You win.*"

Adam walked up to Jack's lifeless body and kicked Jack in the head. Not much force was behind the kick, but it was enough to make Julie cry.

"What are you doing, John?" Julie asked in a quivering voice, and embraced Jack's head with her arms.

Adam lifted Julie up by her armpits, but she didn't move from there at all. She just hung still in the air with a befuddled look on her face. The same look remained on her face as Adam carried her across the hall, but when she noticed the bed, she started to scream, and once on her back, she started to kick. As Julie kept screaming and kicking, Adam began choking her. But he didn't put his hands around her neck; instead, he put his fist in her mouth and his fingers deep down her throat. Seemingly, grabbing and squeezing her tongue, Adam kept smiling her way, as though encouraging Julie to try to bite down on his hand.

Julie stopped kicking.

When Adam finally took his fist out of her mouth, Julie tilted her head to the side, and began hurling and spitting up a mix of saliva and stew. After that, she coughed and gasped for air. Adam pulled off her pants in one rapid motion—Julie wasn't wearing any underwear.

"Please, John," she pleaded in a soft, calm voice.

Adam suddenly burst into laughter. But it wasn't a raw, or a cruel laugh. He sounded genuinely amused. As Adam kept laughing, Julie looked just as confused as previously, and for a brief second, she actually smiled. However, Julie's face shifted as soon as she looked Adam in the eyes. Suddenly, she looked defeated and weak. Adam kept staring at the hair on her legs, and he wouldn't stop laughing.

Julie turned her head away from Adam and looked at the window. It was a beautiful day outside. The sun was shining. The sky was a clear blue, and the birds spread across the ground were eating apples. Inside came a heavy and deep moaning sound, and the sound kept increasing.

Julie didn't make a sound, though—she just kept her focus on the window. However, as the warm liquid landed on Julie's stomach, she turned her head and screamed. A massive flow of blood had begun gushing out of Adam's neck. Jack stood behind him, and held Adam's head back with his left hand. In his right hand, Jack held a bar of soap with a couple of razor blades attached to it, the soap bar functioning as a handle. Julie crawled on her back out of the bed, backpedaling across the floor, until she reached the corner of the room.

"I'm so sorry, Julie. I didn't mean to actually faint. My blood sugar must've been low," Jack whimpered. "I figured the poison was in the stew. So, I thought I'd fake fainting and perhaps catch them off guard, so I could get to the rifle in the kitchen. I'm so sorry, Julie. I never meant for this to happen."

Julie stood up, but kept staring down at the floor with her arms hanging down and her shoulders low. The blood on her lower stomach had merged with her sweater. She kept her eyes on the floor, and held her head down.

Then Julie walked out of the room—she didn't limp.

Jack's jaw began to shake, but before he spoke, Julie had already left the room.

Julie didn't make any noise as she passed through the dining room. She just took the clothes from the dresser, and then locked herself in the bathroom.

Jack took off the blood-drenched blazer he wore, and used it to cover the other dead body in the living room. The dining table had a big pile of blood on it, and Jean's face was in the center of that. Jack kept his eyes on the bathroom door as he paced back and forth across the dining room. Then suddenly, he stopped, and with a miserable expression on his face stared out the window. His eyes focused on the apple trees on the overgrown lawn, and his jaw began to shake once more. As Julie emerged from the bathroom, Jack startled.

"How... I mean," Julie hesitated. "Did you see him put poison in the stew?"

"No, but I saw a glass jar in the barn. I think they were planting beef."

"Excuse me?"

"They were making toxin, or at least attempting to."

"You can make toxin out of beef?"

"But the jar had air in it. I don't think they knew what they were doing. I don't think the stew was poisonous." Jack glanced at the pile of vomit on the floor. "I think I'm all right."

"You can make poison from beef?"

"You can make poison out of more or less everything organic." Jack looked out the window. "You can even make cyanide from apples."

"You can make cyanide from apples?" Julie looked overwhelmed.

"From apple seeds. But you need a lot of them."

"But they're not very hard to come by."

Julie kept staring out the window with empty eyes and a catatonic stare. Suddenly, a tear escaped her eye, but she wiped it away just as fast.

"We should leave. We'll take the truck," Jack said. "How's your ankle?"

"I don't notice the pain anymore."

"Either way, you shouldn't walk on it. Let me carry you from now on."

Jack picked Julie up in his arms and carried her past the hallway. But then he froze and kept staring at the wall, as he set her down.

Julie looked mystified. “What’s wrong?”

“This guy.” Jack pointed at one of the many pictures on the wall. “He’s in all of the pictures. I think there’re three of them.”

Julie looked frightened, and stared intensely at the man in the picture.

“I’ll get the rifle from the kitchen,” Jack said.

On his way back from to the kitchen, Jack exhaled loudly and shook his head, as he looked down at the rifle he was holding.

“What’s wrong?”

“It’s not loaded. They tried to trick me into the kitchen.”

Jack walked back to the kitchen, and opened several kitchen drawers.

“There’re no knives either!” Jack yelled.

Then Jack went into the dining room, and opened the top draw in the dresser next to the bathroom door, and his face lit up with joy.

“Did you find the ammo or the knives?”

“Neither,” Jack responded. He picked up a cell phone out of the drawer, but then, his smile vanished. “I don’t think it’s working. The screen is all black. No, wait, it’s working now.”

Julie seemed relieved as Jack brought the phone to his ear. But a few seconds later, Jack looked back at Julie, dejected.

“It’s not ringing,” Jack said. “What’s nine one one in Canada?”

“It has to be nine one one. Right?”

“It’s not ringing.” Jack looked at the screen.

“Try triple nine.”

Jack kept his eyes on the screen. “How do I hang up? There’s no hang up button.”

“Let me see,” Julie said, and extended her right arm.

Jack handed her the phone.

Julie sighed. "That's where to punch the pin code, Jack. Did you just punch nine one one on the screen? You have to unlock the phone first. You know how to use a smart phone, don't you?"

"So, how do we unlock it?"

Julie shook her head. "You need a code to unlock it, and the code could be anything." She sighed deeply. "Let's just get out of here. You got the keys, right?"

"What keys?"

"For the truck." Julie looked frightened.

"The keys are in the ignition. I checked."

Jack grabbed the bar of soap from the dining table and placed it in his pants pocket. Then he picked Julie up in his arms. Once at the door, he looked cautiously in all directions, scanning the terrain before he quickly ran across the courtyard toward the truck. The blood in the center of his white shirt rubbed off on Julie's elbow.

Julie climbed into the truck on the driver side and scooted over to the passenger side. Jack pressed the starter button and the engine started accordingly, but then he turned it off just as quickly. His eyes wandered across the windshield.

"What's wrong?"

"This doesn't feel right," Jack said. "Something's wrong."

"You mean the truck sounded wrong?" Julie seemed frightened.

"No, the image is wrong. I'm forgetting something. It doesn't feel right."

"Are you all right, Jack?" Julie asked warily.

Jack turned his head and looked at Julie. His pupils were more dilated than usual. Then he kept turning his head until his eyes were locked in on the curtain that separated the driving cabin from the trailer mattress—Julie did just the same.

Jack took the bar of soap out from his pocket, and swallowed once before he pulled the curtains apart and dashed into the back of the truck. His eyes briefly took in the scenery, and then he returned to the driver's seat.

Except for a mattress, a few bed accessories, a baseball cap, and a crumpled-up pornographic magazine, nothing and no one was in the back of the truck. Julie looked relieved when she saw the empty sleeping cabin, but when she looked at Jack, who kept staring at the windshield, she appeared just as frightened as before.

"Are you all right, Jack?"

Once again, the deep sound of a massive engine filled the cabin. Jack kept his eyes on the road in front of him, but his hands never moved.

"You know how to drive this thing, right?"

Jack kept staring at the windshield and never blinked.

"Are you really a truck driver, Jack?"

"No, I was never a truck driver. But I drove a truck when I was younger," Jack looked at her. "But trust me. I have no trouble driving this truck, Julie."

"Well, let's go then. What are you waiting for?"

"It doesn't feel right."

"What, Jack?" Julie's tone said she had run out of patience. "What doesn't feel right?"

Jack turned off the ignition, and the heavy, vibrating sound came to a halt.

"It doesn't feel right. My intuition tells me something's wrong."

"That's because you're scared, Jack." Julie placed her hand on his shoulder. "It doesn't feel good to be scared. I feel scared too. But we have to go now."

Jack kept staring at the road ahead, his pupils even more dilated than before.

"The image is wrong." Jack sounded drowsy. "I'm forgetting something."

"What image?" Julie's eyes had turned wet. "Perhaps that guy was just visiting when the pictures were taken. Just because he's in the pictures doesn't necessarily mean he lives here."

Jack shuddered. "The pictures. She wasn't in any of the pictures."

"Who?"

"The mother."

Jack dashed out of the truck, and ran toward the small house next to the barn. Julie looked at the open truck door with a face of shock and disbelief. Another tear escaped her eye, but she didn't wipe it this time. She just locked the door and climbed into the sleeping cabin.

41 THE DOCTOR

An unusual day

What a strange day I'm having.

A strange man is trying to convince me everything is going to be all right, and he actually speaks to me, as though he's expecting me to answer his questions. He seems so different from the others, although he smells exactly the same. He looks like a doctor who just came out of surgery.

I'm outside now. The doctor is carrying me in his arms. The sun is in my eyes. It's burning my corneas. I make sure to close my eyes. But now I feel a shadow on my face, so I open my eyes again. I can see the truck, right in front of me.

42 L'ENFER

Monday afternoon

"Open the door, Julie! It's me!" Jack yelled.

Julie came out of her hiding place in the back of the truck and opened the driver's door. Then her jaw dropped and she looked disconcerted.

"Who is she?"

Jack glanced at the face of the young woman in his arms. "She doesn't talk. At first, I thought she was dead."

"Why is she naked?"

"She was strapped to the bed. She didn't have any sheets on the bed, just a plastic tarp," Jack responded. "But I think I saw a jumpsuit in the barn."

Jack climbed into the truck, now carrying the young woman over his shoulder, and then he laid her down on the mattress in the back of the truck.

"Can we leave now, Jack?"

"I'm just going to get the jumpsuit. It won't take long."

Jack returned a minute later with a large green jumpsuit.

"Can we go now, Jack?"

"Yes." Jack sounded baffled.

Jack handed Julie the jumpsuit, and she helped the young woman dress. Jack started the truck, and this time he didn't hesitate. He maneuvered the large semi-trailer perfectly down the narrow dirt road until it came to a complete and sudden stop, no more than a minute later.

"Why are you stopping?" Julie yelled from the back of the truck.

Jack didn't respond. He simply kept staring at the road in front of him.

"What the hell is..." Julie froze as she looked at the gate.

A man stood in front of the massive steel gate, which blocked the road. He had a leather strap across his chest. A shotgun barrel was pointing upward behind the man's back.

"Can you run him over?" Julie's eyes fixed on the target.

"That steel gate looks pretty solid," Jack responded. "It could damage the truck, or make me lose control and drive into the ditch."

"Why is he just standing there?"

Julie got the baseball cap from the back of the truck, and put it on Jack's head.

"Open the window and wave your arm. Perhaps he'll open the gate for us," Julie said. "But make sure he doesn't see your face."

Jack did as instructed, and lowered the window and waved his arm. The man waved back at Jack. However, the gesture didn't appear to be a sign of confirmation, it rather seemed a childish version of greeting someone. The man kept waving his hand for quite some time before he eventually made his way toward the truck.

"Hide, Julie," Jack said and lowered the cap all the way down to his eyebrows and held his left hand up to his face, seemingly to hide his profile.

The man, who appeared to be in his early twenties, approached the truck with a huge smile on his face. But then, suddenly, the man stopped and his smile vanished.

"*You're not uncle Adam*," the young man said in an English accent, but with a heavy stutter. "*Does Adam know you're driving his truck*?" The young man kept stuttering. "*He will slap you!"*

Jack took his hand away and looked the young man up and down. The man's legs appeared shorter than normal, and the distance between his eyes was unusually far.

"I bought the truck from Adam. Can you open the gate for me?" Jack asked.

The young man shook his head. *"No, I'm not allowed to open the gate. I don't want to get slapped."*

"Is that rifle loaded?" Jack's voice had an authoritarian ring to it.

"No, sir," the young man quickly responded without a stutter, then he took the rifle off his shoulder and opened the bolt. *"See, no bullets. I'm just a pretender."*

"You mean you pretend to hunt?"

"I pretended a deer yesterday," the young man stuttered, and smiled. *"It was a difficult shot. The sun was in my eyes."*

Jack leaned out of the window. "Listen... Adam's dead."

The young man filled his mouth with air, then blew it out and created a large noise. *"How did that happen?"*

"I killed him, and I killed his brother too."

The young man stared intensely at the truck's cabin, as Julie emerged through the curtains from the back of the truck.

"Because of them girls?" The young man sounded guilty and sad.

Jack frowned. "How many girls were there?"

"I don't know. He wouldn't let me talk to them." Now the young man sounded rebellious, much as one could expect from a reluctant child.

"Where did they come from?"

"They can trick me with their love."

"Where did they come from?" Jack kept his voice firm.

"From Quebec. They moved here a long time ago. Took the furniture and everything. I don't remember much from back then."

"No, the girls." Jack sounded annoyed. "Where did the girls come from?"

"Adam brought them back trucking."

Jack frowned. "You want to take a ride with us. We can get something to eat. Would you like that?"

"I don't want him in the truck, Jack."

Jack looked at Julie. "He's not in his right mind, Julie. He's not his age."

"I don't care," Julie responded harshly. "I don't want him in the truck."

Jack leaned closer to Julie. "I just thought with all that blood..."

"No, I got chores to do!" the young man yelled, and then peered up the road. *"I have to go now. I don't want to get slapped."*

The young man walked up the road, then Jack got out and opened the massive steel gate.

They drove for about half-an-hour, the truck moving slowly on the narrow road. There were no other roads, or any houses on the horizon. Julie kept looking over her shoulder.

"She keeps staring at me," Julie said.

The young woman lay on her back with her head barely brushed up against the wall in the sleeping cabin. She kept staring at Julie and hardly ever blinked.

"She looks pissed off, like she could scratch my eyes out any second."

"You better keep an eye on her. She might attack you."

"Why?" Julie looked over her shoulder. "I helped her."

"I think she's psychotic, or catatonic, or something. Like she's dreaming, and she can't tell, if this is real or not."

"Either way, she has no reason to be angry at me." Julie looked over her shoulder once more. "I helped you get dressed."

Jack's eyes grew wider, and he looked as though he'd just had an epiphany. He leaned in toward Julie, and then whispered, *"You're wearing her clothes."*

Julie glanced over her shoulder once more. "You can have your clothes back. They don't fit me anyway."

A few minutes later, Julie emerged from the back of the truck. Now, she wore the green jumpsuit. Once in the passenger seat, she sniffed repeatedly.

"It was hanging next to a slaughtered moose," Jack said. "The jumpsuit, I mean. That's why it smells so bad."

"It smells like him," Julie said. "But you're right. It smells like an animal."

"A dead animal." Jack's voice was deep and aggressive.

Julie suddenly flinched. "My jacket!"

Julie lost her balance, and almost fell on the floor. Her face twisted, and her breathing accelerated as she appeared to be having a panic attack.

"I forgot my jacket back at the house. We have to go back for it."

"We can't go back, Julie. It's just a jacket."

"I need my jacket!"

"It's just a jacket, Julie. Calm down."

"I want my jacket!" Julie yelled even louder. "Turn the truck around."

"I can't turn the truck around," Jack said. "There aren't any exit roads."

"Well, put it in reverse, then!" Julie sounded furious.

"Are you crazy?"

Jack slowed the truck as Julie's eyes wandered across the interior of the driver's side of the cabin. It appeared that she was considering the possibility of maneuvering the large vehicle. Jack stopped the truck completely and looked Julie in the eyes.

"Now, think this through, Julie. That man could now be armed. He's probably scared, and he's not in his right mind. He could shoot us," Jack said. "Let the police handle this. They'll get you your jacket. Okay?"

Julie didn't respond. She just stared provocatively at Jack, her breathing still heavy, and her nostrils still flaring.

"Think of the potential consequences here, Julie."

Just then, it appeared that Julie's did, in fact, evaluate the risk and reward of retrieving her jacket from the house. Her pupils bounced around the interior of the truck, and her eyes wandered back and forth before they eventually trained down at the floor. Then Julie turned her body the other way and looked out the passenger window. She put her hair up and didn't speak a word until they reach the town of Yellowknife.

They stopped at the first diner they came across. Julie had insisted they eat and then contact the police.

The diner was small and intimate. It had a genuine and personal touch to it rather than a corporate and franchised feeling. The few customers who were visiting the diner this afternoon all glanced in the same direction—at the three individuals occupying the sofa in the corner of the room.

Julie sat closest to the window and was currently devouring a large stack of blueberry pancakes, using her entire mouth. The young woman who was wedged in between Jack and Julie had an unkempt appearance. Her red hair was thick and greasy, her complexion was pale white, and the number of pimples on her face almost exceeded the number of freckles. The young woman had her eyes fixed on the chocolate cupcake in front of her. Jack had a sad and disappointed look on his face. A glass of milk and a half-eaten chocolate cupcake sat on the table in front of him, but he didn't eat or drink at this particular time. Instead, he kept staring at Julie.

"Is this because of the jacket? Is that why you're not talking to me anymore?" Jack sighed. "It's just a jacket, Julie."

Julie ignored him and kept consuming her pancakes.

Jack focused on the young woman beside him. "You're not hungry?"

He removed the plastic wrapper from the chocolate cupcake and brought the cupcake close to her mouth, but the young women didn't take a bite. She did, however, all of the sudden stare directly into Jack's eyes.

"Is your name Melissa?" Jack asked.

The young woman didn't respond, but she kept staring into Jack's eyes.

"Melinda," Julie mumbled, and kept chewing.

At first, Jack seemed relieved by Julie's response, but

then his face turned sad just as fast. Julie kept eating, and never looked his way.

"Melinda, is that your name?" Jack asked. "Do you understand English?"

The young woman kept staring Jack in the eyes, then suddenly, she blinked and her eyes shut for longer than usual.

"You're safe now, Melinda. You're going home. It's all over," Jack said.

Then, something suddenly broke. The young women's facial expression appeared completely shattered. She began sobbing hard and loudly, choking for air, almost as if she were drowning in her tears. Jack flinched and looked frightened by the abrupt change in the young woman.

A waitress came to their table, an angry and concerned look on her face.

"What did you do to her, eh?" The waitress poked Jack's shoulder.

"What did *I* do to her?" Jack responded. "I think I just brought her back to reality."

"I'm calling the Mounties," the waitress said.

"Are you calling the police?"

"You bet I am," the waitress responded quickly.

"Thank you," Jack said in a soft voice.

The waitress looked confused.

"Please, call the police," Jack said and stared the waitress down.

"You just sit right there." The waitress pointed toward Jack in a hostile manner, and then walked away.

"What the hell is your problem, lady?" Julie yelled, and sprayed the tabletop with her blue saliva.

Not long after, the sound of sirens bounced across the interior of the diner. However, the sound vanished shortly after as the fire trucks passed by the diner in high velocity. Dark smoke rose up from the forest, far away on the horizon.

The police eventually came. Jack sat in the back of the police car. The young woman who sat next to him insisted on holding his hand, and her hand trembled for the entire ride to the hospital. Julie sat in the front seat. She never spoke, and she never turned her head around or even glanced at the people in the back seat of the car.

Both women were admitted into the local hospital. Jack however, was brought to Yellowknife police station.

Evening

Jack sat in an office, and a woman who appeared to be in her forties sat across the desk from him. She had a dark complexion, short curly black hair, and wore a black pantsuit along with a white shirt. The woman turned the computer screen around, so it could be viewed by Jack from the other side of the desk.

"Is that her?" A hint of French came through in the woman's accent.

On the screen was a picture of a young woman with red hair and lots of freckles. Above the picture was a large headline.

MISSING GIRL, MELINDA NORDSTROM, 16, IS PRESUMED TO HAVE BEEN ABDUCTED AS HER CAR WAS FOUND BY THE SIDE OF THE ROAD.

"Yes, that's her," Jack said, and then frowned at the screen. "She's been missing for three years?"

The woman nodded at Jack and seemed appalled.

"Did they find any more victims up there?" Jack asked.

"Everything burned to the ground. His son is still missing. We think he set the estate on fire once he discovered his dead father and uncle."

"It burned to the ground? The house too?"

The woman nodded. "It took a long time for the firefighters to get there."

"Julie left her jacket in the house," Jack said. "She

wanted to go back for it, but I assured her she'd get the jacket back once we contacted the police."

"It's just a jacket." The woman shrugged.

"That's what I said, but she was really upset," Jack said. "It must have had some sentimental value to her."

"Either way, it's just a jacket."

"I agree. I don't understand why she was so upset," Jack said. "Besides, the jacket was pretty much ruined anyway."

Jack exhaled deeply, then he shook his head, and his face turned sad.

"Julie wasn't the same person after we left the house. She was so different all of a sudden."

"People react differently to..." The woman seemed to be lost for words, and she looked uncomfortable. "When people's integrity is violated, they usually have a strong reaction."

Jack bowed his head, but then he raised it.

"Are you certain the main house went up in flames?" he asked.

"I was told the entire estate burned to the ground."

"And you're sure we're talking about the same farm?"

The woman's expression suddenly shifted from compassionate to alarmed. Then, she turned the monitor back her way and focused on the screen.

"He said the place was called Layfair," Jack said. "Does it sound familiar?"

The woman pouted her lower lip and shook her head.

"Perhaps it's a landmark, or the name of a road? Julie asked him where we were, and he said something in French that sounded a lot like *Layfair*," Jack pronounced the last word in a distorted French accent.

"*L'enfer*." She pronounced the word in a perfect French accent.

"That's it," Jack said and smiled.

"That's not a real place. At least not, as far as I know." The woman turned her eyes back to the screen. "That's the French word for Hell." The woman clicked hard on the mouse, and then turned the monitor around. "Is this the man who attacked you?"

On the screen was a picture of a bald man with a thick beard, his face plastered with hostility. It was obvious the man didn't appreciate being photographed.

"Yes, that's him." Jack nodded. "I see you met him before. I mean, the police, that is."

"We're familiar with all three of them. They're always causing problems, one way or another," the female police officer said. "I remember standing in line behind him at the pastry shop not long ago. I remember it clearly, because I noticed he bought four bear claws that day."

The female police officer clicked the mouse once, and then looked at the computer screen, a look of regret on her face.

"I think I know what you mean," Jack said hesitantly. "Who gets the fourth bear claw, am I right?"

"*Exact-lee*," the female police officer said, and her French accent became quite apparent.

"He could have bought an extra for himself to eat on his way home."

"That's what I convinced myself."

The female police officer turned her eyes back on the screen, and once again, she had a look of regret on her face.

"But I knew he was up to no good. I knew it."

Jack tilted his body forward and glanced at the monitor and at the large headline across the screen.

"You can't arrest a person for buying too much pastry, Sophia."

They then agreed to meet first thing in the morning. Sophia gave Jack a bag of clothes, and claimed they were the largest size she could find on such short notice. On the way to the hotel, she bought him a package of cigarettes.

43 HEADLINES

Monday evening

The house was located on the outskirts of Calgary. George could see the city lights on the horizon. The taxi driver appeared to be true to his word, as he'd parked the car by the curb and was now reading a newspaper. George noticed the cars passing by on the freeway, and he started to plan for a fast getaway in case things turned for the worse. The advice from his boss must have gotten to him. George felt nervous as he rang the doorbell for the third time, and as previously, he waited patiently for a response. He resisted the temptation to check his cell phone yet again to ensure the time was right. As instructed, he'd arrived precisely at 6 p.m. at the home of the co-pilot, Isaac Gregorian's parents.

"Go away!" A female voice called out from inside the house.

George startled at the sudden noise and immediately checked the number on the house, to once again assure himself he was at the right address—in this case a rundown wooden house next to a freeway.

"Is this the Gregorian residence?"

After a short pause, a female voice yelled, "What's it to you!"

"Is your name Magdalene Gregorian? My name is George

Stanton. I believe we spoke on the phone."

"You're not him."

The woman's statement had rendered George speechless, and he wasn't sure how to respond.

"I can assure you I most definitely am ... him."

"Do you have any credentials?"

Credentials, that's a good idea, he thought, and wondered why he didn't think of it in the first place. He took out his driver's license, held it up next to his face, and made sure not to smile. He could see a shadow moving behind the window curtain next to the front door.

"Slip it under the door."

George then realized the front door to the house was actually an interior door, the kind of door the lock could easily be opened with a screwdriver—or if one didn't have anything that resembled a screwdriver, one could just as easily kick the door in. The door framing had sloppy workmanship written all over it, and it was obvious the door hadn't been installed by a professional. As George slipped his driver's license under the door, he wondered if he ever was to see his license again.

To George's relief, the door opened, and a woman appeared. Magdalene Gregorian was a short woman, no more than five feet tall. Her hair was also short, no more than an inch, and the little hair she had was mostly gray. She was obviously a heavy woman, and she wore a gown that resembled a sheet rather than a dress. George assumed the woman was in her sixties even though she moved like an octogenarian.

"You don't look like a George," Magdalene said and handed his driver's license back to him.

"Yes, I get that a lot."

"We're not use to foreigners around here." She gave him a humble look.

George was unfamiliar with the demographics of Calgary, but he assumed the city had an Asian community, and therefore, he felt a bit puzzled by her remark. But then it occurred to him that Magdalene didn't appear to be a woman who left the house much, and probably had little, or no knowledge of the ethnicity of Calgary. He was just about to correct her on the subject, when he suddenly realized she was right all along.

I am a foreigner.

"It's my first time visiting Canada."

"Well, your English is very good, I must say," Magdalene said, and then looked him up and down.

George swallowed a couple of sentences. "Thanks."

As he entered the house, the first thing he noticed was the picture on the wall. Then he began contemplating why he was single. George had a bad habit of focusing on his physical dislikes in regard to the men he dated. At first, he thought they were attractive, but then he always managed to focus on some minor flaw in their physical appearance. However, he found absolutely nothing appealing about the man in the picture. George thought the man looked truly horrendous.

Am I superficial person? Is that why I'm single?

George just realized he was probably making his hostess uncomfortable by staring at the photo for too long. So he quickly reminded himself of his much-planned opening line. But then it occurred to him that pointing out what a lovely home she had was more likely to be interpreted as an insult, rather than a compliment. Again, George felt speechless, but he soon noticed how Magdalene Gregorian glanced at his left hand. That reminded him of the bouquet of flowers he was holding.

"These are for you Magdalene," he said, and added a genuine smile.

Mrs. Gregorian seemed completely overwhelmed by the gesture. She filled her lungs with air and created a trembling, moaning sound, and her eyes turned wet. George felt as though he'd just handed the woman a million dollars. And when he gave her the bouquet, she accepted it in a way one would expect a person to take delivery of a small child. Her face lit up with joy as she looked at the bouquet in her arms.

George started to feel uneasy, but he wasn't sure why; he thought her behavior was the strangest thing.

After a slow start, however, the two of them actually hit it off. Magdalene talked a lot about her childhood, and described in detail what sort of person she was as a child. However, she never mentioned any aspect of her adult life.

The interior of the house was truly awful. Every piece of furniture was worn down, and the ceiling appeared to be sloping. However, the house looked very clean and had a nice smell to it. The tablecloth was perfectly ironed, and the napkins were folded into beautiful origami. The bouquet of flowers was now the centerpiece on the dining table. Magdalene frequently glanced at the flowers, which she'd arranged to perfection in a glass vase, and when she did, she had a charming and modest smile on her face. A bowl of toffee sweets was also on the table, but neither of them had any sweets as they were too busy talking to each other. Neither of them noticed the time, either, and how it flew by.

Eventually, the phone rang, and as Magdalene answered it, she seemed perplexed. A few minutes later, she started yelling, and George wondered what the person on the other line had said. Magdalene kept yelling, and claiming she didn't know the answer to whatever question had been asked, and she kept repeating the word "taste." Then, she abruptly hung up the landline phone, which was mounted on the wall in the dining room, and joined George again by the dining table.

"Is everything all right, Magdalene?"

"It was the government—Does this taste, right?" Magdalene said in a ridiculing voice. "What kind of question is that?"

George tried his best to understand what the phone conversation had been about.

"They kept asking me if I recognized the voice on the phone. I told them no!" Magdalene yelled. "But they just kept on asking."

Mrs. Gregorian shook her head, and was obviously

upset. George tried his best to, once again, imagine what on earth the phone call was about, and the more he thought about it, the better the pieces started to fit.

"They asked you to identify a voice? Is that what you're saying?"

"It wasn't Isaac's voice," Magdalene said in a firm manner, and shook her head. "I'd recognize his voice anywhere."

Just then, the front door to the house was slammed against the hallway wall, and a large man appeared in the doorway to the dining room. The man appeared to be in his early sixties. The clothes on his back were clean and perfectly ironed. However, the rest of his appearance was untidy. George recognized the man's features from the horrendous picture on the wall, and just then, the horrific image of the actor Danny DeVito popped up in his head. The large man briefly glanced at the center of the dining room table, and then he turned his focus on George, and kept staring at him with the most aggressive look.

"Who the hell are you?"

George felt as if he couldn't speak. He began trembling inside, and he felt lightheaded, almost as though he was about to pass out. However, George eventually found enough composure to turn his head toward Magdalene and was expecting her to introduce him to her husband. But she did nothing of the kind. Instead, she just kept chewing, and her eyes were focused on the bowl of toffee sweets.

"*I'm George,*" he stuttered, sounding like a child waiting to be reprimanded. He swallowed. "I work for the airline."

"About time you people showed up," the man said, and seemed pleased with the response. "Why didn't you call ahead like normal people?"

George looked at Magdalene for a reply, but she just kept staring at the bowl of sweets. He began to wonder if the reason for her being so specific regarding what time he should arrive at the house was a way to prevent him from meeting her husband.

"My plane stopped in Calgary," he said. "I mean, I thought I'd stop by on my way to Yellowknife." His voice trembled.

The large man stared George in the eyes. "Did you bring a check?"

"I brought flowers," he blurted out.

The man's face dropped, and he looked enraged by the response. Then, he pointed toward George in a hostile manner.

"You better pay up, you hear me!"

George felt that fear had possessed his body and was squeezing his internal organs. He felt as if he couldn't breathe or speak properly. Something about the man in front of him scared him so intensely.

"I'm a public relations manager. I don't handle any legal issues."

The man walked toward the table; the hardwood floor squeaked with every step he took. He stopped right beside George.

"Then what good are you?" he asked in a condescending tone.

The man picked up the glass vase, and made his way over to the kitchen; George could hear the twigs breaking as the man forced the flowers into the trash can. Magdalene kept chewing and she was holding a toffee sweet close to her lips, as though to make certain to replace the one in her mouth as soon as it was gone.

"I think I'll be leaving now, Magdalene. My plane is departing shortly."

Mrs. Gregorian didn't respond. She just kept chewing, her eyes focused on the bowl of sweets. Even though George had lost track of the time, he felt certain he had plenty of time to get to the airport and make his connecting flight to Yellowknife. Fear was the true reason for his sudden departure. He felt absolutely petrified, his mind pleading with him to run away and hide.

George had never felt so small, not even as a child.

On his way to the hallway, he noticed how the smell of the house had changed, and the smell now reminded him of sulfur. George briefly glanced at the large mirror hanging in the hallway. He didn't care for his reflection. He saw a coward staring back at him. And as he turned his head, and peered into the dining room, he saw the other coward standing behind a woman who frantically consumed the little joy she had left in her life.

When he'd reached the curb, he realized the taxi was gone. But then, he saw a flash of lights, and a car slowly drove toward him. To his relief, the taxi had parked just down the road. As George got into the car, he felt an even greater sense of relief and felt he'd done the right thing. The anxiety and fear were gone, and he felt that he'd made the right choice by leaving, even though his mind told him the complete opposite.

"Godzilla made me park down the road. Apparently, he thinks the curb belongs to the house," the driver said and smiled over his shoulder.

George felt as though he were caught in a dream and nothing seemed real. His head was spinning, and he felt dizzy and nauseous.

"To the airport, right?"

"Yes, please," he mumbled.

George noticed the newspaper in the front passenger's seat, and once again, he read the headline.

MYSTERY PLANE FOUND IN A SMALL LAKE NEAR YELLOWKNIFE

George noticed the cup holder and the coffee cup with a flame design, and then, he thought of the phone call that Magdalene received. *Does this taste, right?* he kept chanting to himself, and then imagined a scene in which Captain Daniels handed a cup of coffee to his co-pilot and asked him to have a taste. Had Captain Daniels poisoned his co-pilot before crashing the plane? It would certainly have been easier to poison his colleague, rather than strangling him to death.

George assumed the phone call was from the National Transportation Safety Board or some other branch of the 'government' as Magdalene had put it. And the reason for the phone call must have been to identify the voices on the recording from the cockpit. But the question was why? Was it just standard procedure to establish who said what? Or was there something more to it? Was the terror angle still intact?

George suddenly thought of Trisha Boyle and her disabled boy.

Then it occurred to him, if in fact, Captain Daniels had poisoned his co-pilot, then the poison would probably appear on an autopsy. Or would it? The body had been in the water for more than a week. But why would they perform a toxicology? And did poison eventually disappear from a dead body? Perhaps that depended on the type of poison. If so, what kind of poison had Captain Daniels used?

George rolled his eyes, as he realized his line of questioning was nothing but absurdly ridiculous. He told himself to stop speculating and focus on his job instead of playing detective. But then his thoughts wandered back to Trisha Boyle, and he imagined her standing in the unemployment line and holding the hand of her disabled boy.

What was it with a single mother raising a child that always got to him? Was there something special about it? Something special he could relate to? Had it something to do with his own mother, and how she'd raised him? Or was it perhaps a biological urge? Did other men feel the same way?

He took out his cell phone and made a few searches online, mostly to satisfy his curiosity. To his astonishment, he discovered how easy making lethal poison out of the most common household products was. All one really needed was a simple coffee filter, and of course the necessary organic product.

His jaw dropped as he read the headline on the blog topic.

HOW TO MAKE CYANIDE FROM APPLES

His mind brought him back to the house in Paradise where Captain Daniels grew up. George thought of all the apple trees surrounding the house, and how Mrs. Daniels had described her son as creative.

George tried his best to find a definitive answer as to whether cyanide would appear while doing an autopsy, but the answer was inconclusive. He did, however, stumble over a news article regarding a group of scientists who had newly discovered a different type of the poison tetrodotoxin. According to the news article, the same scientists were now in possession of enough tetrodotoxin to theoretically kill eight billion people.

"Eight billion," he blurted out.

"What was that?" the taxi driver asked.

"I'm sorry. I was just thinking out loud."

Once again, he noticed the driver's coffee cup, and the distinctive flames on it.

"So, how's the season going?"

"The season hasn't started yet," the driver said and smiled over his right shoulder. "I take it you don't follow hockey much."

George didn't follow hockey at all, but he was still able to recognize the distinctive *Calgary Flames* logo, on the driver's coffee cup.

"I've lived in San Francisco my whole life," he said.

George was expecting a follow-up question, but the driver didn't seem too eager to prolong the conversation. George turned his attention to his phone and reminded himself to concentrate on the task at hand, rather than keep playing detective. He decided to look through the latest news articles regarding the crash.

Then it hit him.

He felt as he'd been sucker punched in the stomach, and his spleen was now blocking the air to his lungs. He kept staring at the news headline.

SEVERAL PASSENGERS MISSING FROM CRASH SITE—AND ONE PILOT!

44 THE PILOT

Tuesday morning

Jack sat at a table in what seemed to be a conference room, and two men sat across the table from him. The two men appeared to be the complete opposites of each other. The man to the right of Jack had a pale complexion and was almost as tall as Jack. This man wore a gray blazer, and he looked to be in his fifties. The man to the left of Jack had a dark complexion and was a lot shorter than Jack. This man wore a black blazer, and he seemed to be in his twenties. Jack wore sweatpants and a sweater with a police logo on it. Both articles of clothing were at least two sizes too small.

In addition, two other men were seated at the other end of the conference table, and they both wore black suits and matching black ties. The female police officer by the name of Sophia was also present in the room. She stood by the door and casually leaned up against the wall, her eyes focused on the windows.

Jack kept glancing at Sophia, but she appeared to be ignoring him.

"I think she's disappointed with you," the pale, tall man said, and looked at Jack. "She assumed you were just an average passenger."

Jack looked to his right and arched his eyebrows.

The pale man then turned his focus on Sophia. "I'm sure Detective Houllier didn't appreciate being lied to."

Detective Sophia Houllier took her eyes off the windows and peered at the pale man. Her eyeballs seemed about to poop out of her eye sockets; she looked absolutely furious.

"I didn't lie," Jack said.

"Withholding information is the same as lying," the short, dark man responded in a fast, sharp, and provocative tone. "You misrepresented yourself."

Jack looked at Detective Sophia Houllier once more, this time with an expression of shame. But she had her eyes focused on the windows and seemed to ignore his every gesture.

Jack looked at the man to the left of him. "Are we about done here, or what?"

"Done?" the dark, short man responded sarcastically. "What do you mean, we're done?"

"I told you everything I know," Jack said. "What more is there to say?"

"You mean that bullshit statement you just gave." The dark man sighed. "How about telling the truth?"

"I told you everything I know."

"No, you haven't," the same man quickly responded.

"What do you mean?"

"You haven't told us where to find the body, have you?"

"What body?" Jack said. "What are you talking about?"

"I'm talking about Kevin Anderson."

"Kevin's last name is Anderson?" Jack asked with a crooked smile.

"His last name was Anderson. Until you killed him."

"What?" Jack looked startled.

"His daughter and son are now orphans because of you. The very least you can do is to provide them with a decent funeral. So tell us where you hid the body."

"What are you talking about? I didn't hurt Kevin."

The tall, pale man appeared to be studying Jack's facial expression.

"Why did you kill him? What possible reason could you have for killing him? What's your excuse? Did he provoke you? Was it something he said? Was it something about his appearance that set you off?" The dark man kept staring Jack in the eyes. "You have a problem with black people? Is that it?"

Jack leaned forward and dragged his elbows across the large table. "What did you call me?"

"I didn't call you anything." The dark, short man had a superior smile.

Just then, the tall, pale man put his right arm across the table, similar to what a boxing referee would do when separating fighters. He cleared his throat loudly before he reached for a small notebook from the inside pocket of his jacket. "You were seen wearing Kevin's jacket."

"I get it. You've been talking to Julie, and she told you about the jacket," Jack said, and shook his head. "That information is inaccurate. I was not seen wearing Kevin's jacket. I was seen wearing a black blazer."

Jack looked to his left. "Much like the one you're wearing, Agent Coleman," Jack said, and tilted his head. "Well, except for the small size."

The superior smile on Agent Coleman's face suddenly vanished. The tall, pale man beside him appeared to be biting down on his lips.

"As I said before, I took the blazer off a dead body floating in the lake."

"Was there any blood on the jacket? Did the body have any sign of injuries?"

Jack looked to his right. "No, I don't think so."

"Where's the jacket now?" the tall, pale man asked.

"I left it at the house."

"In the house that so conveniently burned to the ground, and thereby destroying the evidence proving it was Kevin's jacket," Coleman said. "How convenient."

"No, it's inconvenient. Because it wasn't Kevin's jacket," Jack insisted.

"Why did you take it off in the first place?" the pale, tall man asked. "People usually wear blazers indoors. Much as you pointed out a minute ago."

"It was bloody." Jack sighed. "It wasn't Kevin's blood. The jacket didn't have any blood on it until..."

"Until you slit Jean Laponte's throat," Coleman quickly added.

"While his brother was about to rape, Julie." Jack's voice was firm and decisive.

Once more, the tall, pale man put his arm across the table, and cleared his throat loudly. "Did the blazer have any distinctive marks? Anything that might help us to identify the person it belonged to?"

"No, it was just a black blazer. I can't tell them apart. They all look alike to me."

"They all look alike to you," Coleman said and stared aggressively at Jack.

"Wait, there was a note in the inside pocket," Jack said.

"There was a note?" The tall, pale man looked surprised. What did the note say?"

"I think it was a funeral speech," Jack said. "I think the man who wrote the note was a victim of abuse. And it would appear that the man planned to reveal his secret at a funeral, and he made a reference to a man with no name. I think that's the man who abused him."

"A man with no name," the tall, pale man said. "Every person has a name."

"Yes, I'm aware every person has a name, Agent Smith," Jack responded. "But he didn't write the man's name, instead he wrote *say his name*. I figured the guy probably hated the man so much, he couldn't bring himself to write his name."

"I see. And was there any other reference to this man with no name?" Smith asked. "For example, did he describe the man's physical appearance?"

"No, but he described himself as an overeater." Jack had a look of shame.

"I see... But he didn't describe his own appearance in detail?" Smith asked.

"Why would he describe his own appearance?" Jack countered. "The note was intended for his eyes only."

"So, what you're saying is that you found a note in the inside pocket of the blazer you wore. And the note appeared to be a funeral speech written by an overweight man of unknown ethnicity, describing a secret he was about to reveal at a funeral," Smith said. "Does that sound accurate?"

"I guess." Jack looked uncertain.

"Tell me, Agent Coleman," Smith said. "Was Kevin Anderson a big fellow?"

"I believe he was, Agent Smith," Coleman responded in, a superior tone. "According to his family, he did have a problem with his weight, and his mother had apparently pleaded with him on numerous occasions to lose weight."

"I see. And tell me, Agent Coleman, did his family tell you the purpose of his trip to Anchorage?"

"Well, yes they did, Agent Smith. According to them, Kevin Anderson was on his way to attend a funeral."

"It wasn't Kevin's jacket," Jack said loudly. "Check the surveillance tapes from the airport and look for an enormous man with sweatpants and a black blazer."

"He could have taken his blazer off, once he boarded the plane," Smith said. "Just because he wore a black blazer when boarding doesn't mean the blazer isn't at the bottom of the lake."

"So, drag the lake," Jack said. "Make sure every blazer is accounted for, and you'll discover one is missing."

"But if even if one blazer is missing," Smith responded. "Who's to say, Kevin is still wearing his."

Jack displayed a look of defeat.

"What about Andrew Townsend?" Coleman addressed Jack.

"I told you, he's dead. Didn't you find his body?"

"I meant what you killed him for? He wasn't wearing

a jacket." Coleman quickly responded. "Please don't tell me, you killed him for his ring. Did you?"

"You were seen in possession of his wedding ring," Smith quickly added.

"The ring was in his pants, so I gave the ring to Julie for her to hold."

"His wedding ring was in his pants pocket?" Coleman asked.

"Yes, it was in his pants pocket," Jack responded. "And not on his finger."

"According to his wife," Smith said, "Andrew Townsend never wore his wedding ring on his finger."

"Well, there you go, then," Jack said. "Problem solved."

Agent Smith glanced at Jack's fingers before he flipped through a few pages of his notebook. "According to his wife, Andrew Townsend always wore the ring on a chain around his neck. That way, his wedding ring would be closer to his heart."

Jack chuckled. "That's sounds about right."

"So you admit to removing the ring from his neck chain?" Smith asked.

"What?" Jack looked startled. "No, I didn't say that."

"For a little piece of gold." Coleman shook his head.

"How would you describe your relationship to Mr. Townsend?"

"I didn't care for him," Jack said. "As I'm sure Julie already told you. And she didn't care for him, either, by the way. But I never laid a hand on him, and I certainly didn't kill him."

"You never laid a hand on him," Smith said slowly, and looked at his notebook. "So you deny grabbing Mr. Townsend by his neck?"

"I didn't grab him by his neck. I grabbed his collar. It was nothing."

"But you admit to having an altercation with him?"

"He made some demeaning remarks about Nancy, so I told him to stay away from her and to leave her alone." Jack exhaled heavily.

"So Nancy belonged to you?" Coleman quickly commented.

Jack frowned and looked to his left. "What did you say?"

"But Andrew wouldn't back off, so instead, you killed him," Coleman added.

Jack exhaled deeply and looked at Agent Smith. "As I told you before, when Julie and I found him, Andrew was already dead. It must have been an accident. Either he startled Nancy, and she hit him with a rock, or he could have slipped, and hit his head while he chased after her. And as I told you earlier, Nancy had his cell phone in her pocket."

Agent Smith flipped through his notebook. "Nancy's clothes weren't in the proximity of her body. Is that correct?"

"Yes." Jack sighed. "As I'm sure Julie told you, I was alone when I discovered Nancy's clothes, and Andrew's cell phone in her pants pocket."

"It sounds to me that you planted the phone on Nancy to draw the suspicion away from yourself," Coleman said with a superior smile on his face.

"No, I didn't plant the phone on Nancy, and I didn't kill Andrew, even though I didn't care for him." Jack looked at Coleman. "And before you ask me, Agent Coleman. I can assure you that I don't have a problem with short people."

The superior smile on Agent Coleman's face vanished just as quickly as the last time. And once more, Agent Smith appeared to be biting down on his lips, and so did Detective Sophia Houllier.

"A woman," Coleman said, and then tilted his head. "A woman. How could you? You had to force yourself on her? And to just leave her naked like that."

The stiff smile on Jack's face was replaced by a hostile stare. "You little shit."

Once again, Agent Smith put his right arm across the table, and cleared his throat. "Let's all calm down and handle this matter professionally."

Agent Coleman kept staring provocatively at Jack.

Agent Smith flipped another page in his notebook. "There is a substantial time gap between when you claimed to have climbed a mountain to get a better view, and when you allegedly noticed a woman sunbathing. Do you deny being alone for approximately two hours prior to your claim of seeing a woman sunbathing?"

Jack shook his head. "I can't believe you just asked me that, Agent Smith."

"You didn't answer the question," Coleman quickly replied.

"I told you where to find Nancy's body. Just do an autopsy," Jack said. "She must have died from natural causes. Possibly from head trauma. She hit her head pretty badly in the crash. Or perhaps she starved to death."

"People don't starve to death so easily."

"I know. But Nancy was so thin, I think she might have had an eating disorder. I didn't notice at first, on account of her thick sweater and her plump cheeks. But when I carried her, it felt as though I was carrying a small child." Jack paused and shook his head. "And when I saw her naked, I noticed she was all skin and bones. Her hipbones poked from her skin, and rainwater had gathered by her collarbones. Two puddles of water."

Agent Coleman frowned. "We're talking about Nancy Callahan?"

"I don't know her last name. We were all on a first-name-only basis," Jack said, and shrugged. "I'm not even sure her first name was Nancy. As I said, she suffered from head trauma, and at times, she appeared delusional."

Agent Smith looked startled. Then he opened his briefcase and took out a web tablet. At first, he typed rapidly, but he suddenly froze for a moment, as though he wasn't sure what choice to make. He glanced briefly at Detective Sophia Houllier before he looked at the screen again. At first, he had an awkward expression, but eventually, he tapped the screen, and placed the tablet on the table.

"Is that her?"

Jack's jaw dropped as he looked at the screen, his eyes wide.

On the screen was a picture of a young woman who appeared to be in her early twenties, even though the text on her T-shirt indicated she'd just turned eighteen. Her plump cheeks emphasized her huge smile, and her eyes were focused on the object in her hands: A ridiculously oversized plastic replica of male genitalia.

"Yes, that's her, but she must have lost a lot of weight. She looks nothing like herself in that picture. She must have developed an eating disorder." Jack frowned at Agent Smith. "She was a porn star?"

"She was an *adult* actress," Coleman responded and smiled wide, his bright teeth in sharp contrast to his face.

"But she wasn't a star?" Jack said.

"No, she wasn't a..." Agent Coleman trailed off, and his face grew red.

Once again, Agent Smith appeared to be biting down on his lips. Agent Coleman glanced at Detective Sophia Houllier, and as their eyes met, his face grew even redder. Then, he looked at Jack with accusing eyes.

"Do you even know how many people you've killed?" Coleman asked. "Do you, *Box*?" Agent Coleman's superior smile was back.

Jack's jaw dropped once more.

"That's right. I know all about you. They should've kept you looked up in that loony bin," Coleman said. "So, how many people have you killed? Or have you lost count recently?"

Jack rose to his feet and put his hands on the table top. His enormous biceps bulked through the tight sweater he wore. "Call me that name one more time, and see what happens."

"That sounded like a threat to a federal agent," Coleman

said and looked at Smith. "Wouldn't you agree, Agent Smith?"

Agent Smith remained silent while Agent Coleman looked at him as if seeking some sort of insurance. The two unidentified men in black suits rose from their seats, and judging by their posture, they appeared to be ready to engage in a fight. For the first time that day, Detective Sophia Houllier looked at Jack—or at least at his profile.

Jack kept staring at Agent Coleman. "I dare you."

Just then, Agent Smith rose to his feet and grabbed Agent Coleman by the elbow. "May I speak to you outside, Agent Coleman?"

The two agents then left the conference room.

Jack looked at the picture on the screen once more, and once again, he had a look of resignation. He appeared like a man with a broken heart or like a father who recently learned his only daughter had decided to pursue a career in pornography. He flipped over the web tablet and pushed it further away.

Shortly after, Agent Smith returned to the room, this time alone.

"Sorry about that," Smith said. "Between you and me, I think Agent Coleman is a little sensitive about his height—Among other things."

Jack shrugged. "Are we done here or what?"

"I know you didn't kill Nancy. I could tell by your reaction, and I'm sure the autopsy will reveal there was no foul play," Smith said, and sounded sincere. "I'm sorry for insinuating otherwise."

"Okay." Jack nodded once.

"I can only imagine what you've been through for the past week," Smith added. "It must have been hard not knowing whether help was coming, and it was freezing cold—"

"And Kevin wouldn't let you borrow his jacket, and so on," Jack interrupted. "I get it. You're the good cop?"

"No, of course not." Smith smiled, and glanced across the room. "There are no good cops. You know that. We're all bad."

Agent Smith chuckled, and the two men in black suits and matching ties smiled briefly, and then shook their heads slightly.

"You're a federal agent," Jack said in a brusque tone.

"That's right."

Smith seemed proud of the remark, and smiled Jack's way. But suddenly, his face changed, and his smile quickly vanished.

"You think you can hide in Canada? Is that it? I can have you extradited in no time," Smith said, and added a smile. "That is if my Canadian colleagues, for some strange reason don't charge you with mass murder."

Jack looked across the room at the two men in suits and then he glanced at Detective Sophia Houllier once more.

"Was it an accident?" Smith asked. "Did you fight over his blazer, and he slipped and fell? Is that it? If it was just an accident, then I can help you."

"I didn't kill Kevin!" Jack yelled.

"Calm down. I'm just trying to help you."

"Sure, you are."

"Either way, you're going to jail." Smith shrugged his shoulders. "So, why not come clean and tell us where you hid Kevin's body?"

Jack looked confused, and seemed puzzled by Agent Smith's question.

"Either way, you are going to prison," Smith said in, a diplomatic tone. "The only question is on what side of the boarder."

"I want an attorney."

"I told you, this is a debriefing. You can't have an attorney present."

"In that case, we're done." Jack rose.

"Sit down," Smith said in a tone of authority.

"No, we're done." Jack seemed about to leave the table.

"Wait! I want to show you something."

Agent Smith quickly grabbed the web tablet, and swiped the screen several times before he placed the tablet on the table for Jack to see.

"Remember him?"

Jack remained standing and briefly glanced at the screen. "He was dead when we found him."

Agent Smith appeared to be studying Jack's facial expression. "I'm sure he was, but why did you tried to conceal his body?"

"What are you talking about?" Jack looked confused. "I told you where to find his body. And the ring was in his pants pocket."

"That's not Andrew Townsend," Smith said.

Jack looked at the screen once more, and then he sat down, and kept staring at the screen with wide eyes. On the screen was a picture of the back of a man's head with blood running down his neck, coloring the collar of his white shirt red. The man appeared to be wearing a black jacket. He was on his stomach, his face against the forest ground.

"Is this from the crash site?" Jack asked.

"Do you recognize him?"

"No," Jack responded. "Is this from the crash site?"

Agent Smith swiped the screen once. "How about now? Do you recognize him now?"

Jack barely glanced at the screen, and at the profile picture of a man smiling. Then his posture changed, and he kept staring at Agent Smith with wide eyes.

"Where did you find him?" Jack asked.

"So, you do recognize him?"

"Yes," Jack answered, and swallowed hard. "Now I do."

"When did you last see him?"

"I saw him board the plane."

"But you haven't seen him since?"

Jack frowned. "No, I haven't."

"But you know who he is?"

Jack nodded.

"Well, who is he, then?" Smith asked.

"Well..." Jack's voice trembled. "He's the pilot, am I right?"

"That's right, Jack." Smith nodded. "He's the pilot."

"Where did you find him?"

Agent Smith appeared to be studying Jack's face. Then, suddenly, he relaxed, looking more at ease. "Not far from the SOS sign. A hundred yards south."

"But you asked me if I saw that man storm the cockpit," Jack said. "If that man killed the pilots, and crashed the plane, then how could the pilot end up in the woods? That doesn't make any sense."

"No, it makes perfect sense. I'll walk you through it," Smith said casually. "The Imam stormed the cockpit as the pilots opened the door to let the stewardess in. Then the Imam killed the pilots, or at least he thought he did, leaving the stewardess trapped in the cockpit along with the Imam. Maybe the Imam thought she was dead—I don't know. Either way, she managed to send a short text message to her husband, where she was pleading for help and claiming both pilots were dead. But just before the plane was set to collide with the mountain, the pilot woke up and saw the mountain ahead, therefore diverted the plane into the lake."

Jack looked suspiciously at Agent Smith.

"The Imam wasn't wearing a seat belt and neither was the stewardess, so neither of them survived the crash. The pilot, however, survived the crash, and then opened the door to the cockpit before he swam to shore. But he died during the first night due to the injuries he sustained from fighting the Imam. Then, when the plane was full of water, the remains of both the Imam and the stewardess floated out of the cockpit and into the air cabin."

"But why would the Imam fly the plane halfway across Canada only to crash it."

"Well, I'm not a pilot. Obviously." Smith chuckled. "But it has come to my attention, crashing an airplane isn't necessarily as easy as it sounds. If the plane functions properly, that is. You need pilot training in order to crash a plane, and as far as we can tell, the Imam didn't have any training. However, changing the intended destination on an aircraft doesn't require the same level of skill. So, we think the Imam simply changed the destination, and just waited for the plane to run out of fuel."

"Doesn't the cockpit record sound?"

"It sure does, and it's all over the Internet," Smith said, and shook his head. "You could hear how the pilots discussed how bad the coffee tasted, and then shortly after comes the sound of a commotion and sounds of kicking and gagging. We think that's when the Imam made his move. When the stewardess brought the pilots some fresh coffee, but just before the plane crashed, you can hear sounds of a fight in the cockpit. That's when the pilot must have woken up, and fought the Imam. But before that, you could actually hear crew members banging on the cockpit door, and pleading for him to open up."

"You got that information off the internet, you say?" Jack asked.

"Yes, can you believe that?" Smith shook his head. "Everything is on the Web. There're no such things as secrets these days, and nothing's sacred anymore."

"I'm sure," Jack said with a stiff smile. "But I find it a bit peculiar no one told you. It sounds as if your employer doesn't trust you with certain information."

"It's not like that. I just have a different assignment," Smith responded. "You see, I'm not here to investigate the actual crash. I'm here for a different reason. A lot of dead bodies are scattered across these woods. Wouldn't you say?"

"You're out of your jurisdiction," Jack said. "Why am I even talking to you?"

"It's Canada, Jack," Smith responded. "We're all working together to resolve this mess. I would suggest you do the same."

Jack's eyes started to wander.

"Besides, it's pretty obvious what happened to the plane. The only thing that doesn't make any sense is why someone would try to conceal the body of the pilot..."

Agent Smith's face suddenly changed, and he looked more at ease again.

"Or was it perhaps some sort of funeral act? Out of respect for the pilot?" Smith asked enthusiastically. "What do you say, Jack?"

Jack raised his left eyebrow. "What do you want me to say?"

"All I want is the truth."

"I never saw the pilot," Jack replied. "And I don't think anyone else did either, or they would have mentioned it."

Agent Smith looked disappointed.

"Did I get it wrong?" Jack raised his left eyebrow once more. "Wait a minute, how was the body concealed?"

"The body was covered with pine tree branches." Smith looked at ease, but didn't smile. "Like a little tent. Impossible for a human eye to notice. But the dogs had no trouble finding it."

"We did that every night."

Agent Smith shrugged his entire face, although he didn't look very surprised.

"We covered ourselves with pine tree branches to keep the cold out," Jack added. "The pilot must have been disoriented and confused after the crash. So he lay down and covered himself with branches to stay warm, but then he died during the night."

"That actually makes sense. Thank you for clearing that up, Jack," Smith said in a tone which sounded monotonous and well-rehearsed.

Agent Smith looked at Jack and nodded as if he was suggesting he was both proud and pleased with Jack's behavior.

"See what happens when we share information with each other. We find answers. Then we can help each other out. There's no need to be hostile to one another."

"I want to cooperate," Jack responded. "But it's hard to cooperate when you're accusing me of crimes I didn't commit."

"I know you didn't kill Nancy. I could tell by your reaction," Smith said. "So, let's talk about Andrew Townsend, and see if we can find some more answers together."

"Okay."

"You were seen grabbing his neck," Smith said. "Is that true?"

"No, that's inaccurate. I grabbed his collar," Jack asserted. "Julie can't see very well without her contacts."

Agent Smith face dropped. "Contact lenses?"

"Yes, she told me she couldn't see very far without her contact lenses, and I saw her squinting all the time. She probably lost them in the lake when swimming to shore."

"I see. But you're certain you didn't scratch Andrew's neck?" Smith asked, and glanced at Jack's fingers again. "I couldn't help noticing your nails are quite long."

Jack looked at his nails. "I've been living in the woods for almost two weeks. They weren't that long to begin with, and I'm absolutely certain I didn't scratch Andrew's neck. I grabbed his collar. That's all."

Agent Smith seemed to be studying Jack's face.

"I believe you, Jack. You see, Andrew had some scratch marks on his neck, and it would appear he'd been in a fight. So perhaps you're right, perhaps he did startle Nancy, and she scratched his neck and then hit him with a rock," Smith said, and nodded firmly. "In that case, we'll find his DNA under her fingernails once we've located her body. I think you're in the clear. I don't think you have anything to worry about."

Jack smiled.

"See..." Smith extended his hand toward Jack. "Now we're cooperating. We're sharing information, and we're finding answers."

"I want to cooperate, and I'm sorry for losing my temper before," Jack said, and glanced at the empty chair next to

Agent Smith.

"I don't blame you," Smith said. "He gets on my nerves too."

Both men smiled and looked at each other.

"So, let's talk about Kevin Anderson, and see if we can't resolve this matter, once and for all."

"Okay."

Agent Smith studied Jack's face. "Did you hurt him?"

"No, I didn't hurt him." Jack's eyes dropped slightly.

"You're lying to me, Jack," Smith said harshly. "I've been doing this for more than thirty years. You can't lie to me."

"It's not what you think. I didn't—"

"It was just an accident. I understand," Smith interrupted.

"Well, yes, it was an accident. But I didn't hurt him physically. I hurt his feelings," Jack replied in, a trembling voice. "Big time."

"What?" Smith sounded angry.

"I saw Kevin board the plane with his wife, and I saw guilt was eating him up. I felt sorry for him. So I told him, his wife's death wasn't his fault. And when he wouldn't talk to me, I kept pushing him, and then suddenly he cracked. His face looked completely destroyed all of a sudden. Then he walked away. I think he just gave up."

"What do you mean, he gave up?"

"I think he just gave up, and looked for a place to die."

"That doesn't make any sense, Jack. His daughter and son had just lost their mother. Why would he give up?"

"I agree, it doesn't make any sense," Jack responded. "But, I don't know what to tell you. Kevin had this look of resignation. Kind of like a dog who knows its time has come."

Agent Smith frowned, and appeared puzzled by the response. "You think he found a place to die? Kind of like an old dog?"

"Something like that."

"I see. And do you have any idea where we could find his

body? Are there any specific landmarks you can think of?"

Jack frowned. "What do you mean?"

"You are familiar with the terrain out there, so do you know of any places, Kevin might have gone, to seek his final resting place? For example, a cave or..."

Suddenly, Agent Smith's eyes widened and then he leaned forward.

"A cave? Is the body in a cave? Where's the cave, Jack?" Smith pointed at Jack. "Your twitch gave you away. Now, don't you lie to me. Tell me where the cave is."

"It's not what you think." Jack had a look of defeat. "The cave is in Alaska."

"What?"

"A cave is the reason I flew to Alaska," Jack said. "I wanted to see if I could find a cave I used to visit as a child."

Agent Smith's expression shifted, and he appeared more sad than angry.

"You violated your parole just to visit a cave from your childhood?"

Jack looked startled. "I didn't violate my parole. The plane was destined for Anchorage. It's not my fault I'm in Canada."

Agent Smith tilted his head. "You can't leave the state, Jack."

"I can't leave the country."

"No..." Smith sounded dejected. "You can't leave the state."

Jack had a look of resignation and appeared to be heartbroken, much as when he identified Nancy in the picture.

"You're all right?" Smith asked. "You didn't hurt yourself when you climbed that mountain, did you?"

Jack looked confused, and then he shook his head.

"You didn't sustain any injuries? You don't have any recent scars, do you?" Agent Smith asked, and then focused on the massive scar on Jack's neck.

Jack frowned. "I didn't bleed, if that's what you're asking?"

"That's exactly what I'm asking," Smith responded. "The thing is. There were no injuries or blood on the dead body that you allegedly took the blazer from, and if you didn't bleed, then where did the blood on the jacket come from?"

"What blood?"

Agent Smith looked at his notebook. "You were seen returning to the lake wearing a black blazer much like the one Kevin wore. The blazer had a significant amount of blood on one of the sleeves. How did the blood get there, Jack?"

"I didn't notice any blood," Jack answered. "And Julie never mentioned it."

"You find it peculiar that she didn't bring to your attention that you had blood on your sleeve?"

"No, I understand if she was scared. But I don't know how I got blood on my sleeve." Jack shivered. "Wait a minute—perhaps I got blood on the sleeve when I took Andrew's pants. The jacket was so big I almost lost it at times. Perhaps it was Andrew's blood on the sleeve."

"I see." Agent Smith studied his notebook. "Did you get Andrew's blood on your hands?"

Jack hesitated. "I didn't have any blood on my hands."

"You were seen washing blood off your hands in the lake."

"No, I didn't wash any blood off my hands. But I washed my hands frequently. Julie must have confused the soil on my hands with blood. Like I said, she didn't see that well without her..." Jack trailed off and never finished the sentence.

The two men kept staring at each other, and neither of them flinched. They appeared to be having a staring contest. Eventually, Jack began to smile.

"What lake?" Jack asked.

"What?" Agent Smith responded, and looked uncertain.

"In what lake did I allegedly wash blood of my hands?"

Agent Smith's eyes started to wander.

"You're lying, aren't you?" Jack said. "Julie didn't say any of this. You're just making it up as you go along. You never suspected me of killing Nancy or Andrew. You were just trying to get on my good side. And you shared the information about the pilot, hoping I would open up to you."

Agent Smith glanced at his notebook. "I'm not lying."

"I bet you're looking at a blank piece of paper, aren't you, Agent Smith? There are no notes, are there?" Jack raised his eyebrows. "Let me see the notes and prove me wrong, why don't you?"

Agent Smith looked at his notebook. Then, he sniffed once and raised his eyebrows in a casual manner and held up the notebook for Jack to see.

BLOOD - HANDS - WASH - LAKE
BLOOD - JACKET SLEEVE
JACKET IS THE EVIDENCE!
VOICES?

Jack stared at the notebook with wide eyes, and then, he shook his head. "That doesn't prove anything. Either you've taken her words out of context, or you wrote that just to fool me. You're trying to trick me into confessing a crime I didn't commit."

Jack suddenly rose to his feet and then pointed aggressively at Agent Smith.

"You're right, Agent Smith. You're not a *good* cop. You're an incompetent one." Jack kept eye contact with Agent Smith. "And you're a liar, Mister Smith, and I'm done talking to you."

Jack walked up to Detective Sophia Houllier who stood by the door.

"Am I under arrest?" Jack asked gently.

Sophia Houllier looked at Agent Smith as though waiting for an answer to the question. Agent Smith nodded firmly at her.

"No," Sophia said.

Agent Smith looked disappointed.

"The evidence is all circumstantial. It will never hold

up in court," Sophia said, and kept her eyes on Agent Smith.

Detective Sophia Houllier had the same hostile expression as when she previously stared at Agent Smith, but this time her eyeballs didn't seem about to poop out of their sockets. Agent Smith's eyeballs, however, did. He looked absolutely furious.

Detective Sophia Houllier looked at Jack. "But don't leave town. You hear me?"

"No, I'm not going anywhere. I promise."

"I'm sure they'll find Kevin within a day or two. So, don't leave town until we sort everything out," Sophia said decisively. "And *do not* go to the airport, Jack."

"I'm not going anywhere," Jack replied. "I don't have a dime in my pocket, and I'm done walking."

"You need some money?"

Detective Sophia Houllier briefly glanced at Agent Smith, but he had his eyes focused on the tablet in his hands.

"For food, I mean," Sophia added.

"I can eat at the hotel and charge it to my room. But thanks."

Detective Sophia Houllier and Jack looked each other in the eyes, and they both had regretful and apologetic expressions. Eventually, Jack broke eye contact, smiled, and almost walked out the door.

"Jack!"

Agent Smith pushed the tablet across the table for Jack to see. Then, he pointed at the screen, which was filled with words on a white background. He looked Jack in the eyes.

"You can't leave the state."

Jack stared at the screen from a distance that made reading impossible.

"You're going back prison," Smith said. "I'll see to it personally."

Jack had the same look of resignation as previously, and for each step he took down the narrow hallway of the police station, he appeared a little more dejected. When Jack reached the end of the hallway and the door that separated reception from the rest of the building, he found Agent Coleman standing by the door.

Agent Coleman shook his head, but he didn't say anything. Instead, he opened the door for Jack and politely waved him through in the same way a servant would open the door for a person of royalty.

"Don't go to the airport. You hear me?" Coleman said.

"Why would I go to the airport? I don't even have my passport."

"You're sure about that?"

"Why would I bring a passport?" Jack shrugged. "I mean, the plane was destined for Anchorage."

At first, Coleman didn't say anything else, but when Jack had almost reached the end of reception and was just about to walk out the entrance doors, Agent Coleman suddenly spoke in an absurd and high-pitched tone.

"*Pam-me-laaa*!" Coleman sounded as he was imitating a ghost.

Jack turned around, and looked at Agent Coleman. "What did you say?"

"I didn't hear anything," Coleman said, and looked genuinely baffled. "Did you hear something, Jack?"

Jack turned around and almost walked out the door.

"Hey, Box!" Coleman yelled. "You're not hearing any voices, are you?"

Jack stared intensely at Agent Coleman, then his head dropped and he came charging at Coleman; much as a bull locked in on its target. But Agent Coleman managed to shut the door fast enough. Jack's collision with the door created a loud noise that echoed across the reception room. Then, he punched the door once with his fist before he turned and walked out the entrance of the police station.

45 THE PENGUIN

Tuesday morning

George Stanton had woken up with a bad feeling this morning. Just as he'd anticipated, he'd developed a sore throat during the night. Whenever he flew, he always had a tendency to develop a cold.

However, watching the morning news had brightened George's mood. The media now reported that both pilots had perished in the crash. The authorities were convinced it had been a terrorist attack and that the frequently cited Imam had orchestrated the whole thing on his own.

George, however, thought differently.

When he'd heard the sound recording from the cockpit on the news this morning, he hadn't heard the Imam storming the cockpit, or the desperate attempts of a crew member pleading with the Imam to open the door right before the plane crashed. On the contrary, once he heard the recording, George was even more convinced Captain Daniels had crashed the plane on purpose. The sounds of fighting halfway through the flight, weren't from the Imam storming the cockpit, but rather the sounds of the co-pilot, Isaac Gregorian's fight for survival. And the kicking and gagging sound was him choking to death from whatever poison Captain Daniels had slipped into his coffee.

The fighting just before the crash must have been the co-pilot's unexpected awakening and his desperate attempt to stop Captain Daniels from crashing the plane into the nearby mountain. The sound of a crew member pleading with them to open the door was, however, accurate. Except, Elisabeth McAllister wasn't trapped inside the cockpit with the Imam and trying to phone for help while she pretended to be dead. She was the one outside the cockpit banging on the door.

According to the ECC, Cayla Marsh, two passengers had apparently walked out of the woods and at least one of them had now been admitted to the local hospital in Yellowknife. George's plan was to visit the passenger in the hospital, but he thought it was a good idea to contact the local police first and get their blessing before doing so.

Now, George was patiently waiting his turn in the reception area at the local police station when he overheard a conversation between two men. The larger man insisted that he hadn't brought a passport because his flight was destined for Anchorage. The hair on George's neck rose as he realized that the large man must be a survivor of flight 7-1-9. George kept his eyes on the large man as he passed by on his way toward the entrance doors, when suddenly, a strange voice called for someone named Pamela. He thought the cry was odd since no women were present in the reception area. George looked around the room, trying to locate the source of the strange voice.

Once more, George eavesdropped on the rather loud exchange between the two men. The large man's first name was apparently Jack, and his last name appeared to be Bosch. Suddenly, the colossal man made an honest attempt to run through a door. To George's astonishment, the door actually held.

The water bottle in George's hand had now, suddenly, turned into some sort of defensive weapon. He wasn't sure how to use this peculiar weapon, but his intuition told him to squeeze the bottle if necessary, and therefore render his assailant with the discomfort and shock of enduring wet clothes, and thereby leaving himself with enough time for a fast getaway. Needless to say, the water bottle was equipped with a sports cap.

As the enormous man came toward him, George was ready to squeeze and trigger the fearsome string of water. But the man walked straight past him and out the entrance doors. George first thought was not to bother the massive man as he was obviously upset. But on the other hand, the entire purpose of his flying to Yellowknife was to ease and calm the surviving passengers before they were interviewed by the press. George swallowed his fear and ran out the entrance—the water bottle still in his hand.

"Excuse me!" he yelled. "Mister Bosch!"

The large man stopped and turned his head, and looked angrily back at him. George hand tightened around the water bottle.

"Are you a survivor of flight seven one nine to Anchorage?"

The tall man looked him up and down.

"No comment."

"I'm not a reporter," George quickly added. "My name is George Stanton. I'm with the airline. I just wanted to make sure you're all right, and ask if there is something I could do for you in this time of need."

George wasn't at all impressed by his improvised speech, and by the looks of things, neither was the strong man. So he decided on a different approach.

"The cops aren't sharing any information with us. We just want to know what happened," he said, dejected. "How about if I buy you lunch? I noticed this great diner down the road. What do you say?"

Mr. Bosch eventually nodded in agreement.

As the two of them walked down the road, George never felt as small—literally, that was. He felt like a sidekick as he walked next to the tall, muscular man who wore training clothes at least two sizes too small. The tall man appeared like a stereotype of a comic book superhero. George felt as if he were walking beside the notorious Batman, and needless to say, he was Robin (or at least a smaller and skinnier version of Robin) and judging by people's reaction, it wouldn't have made a difference if George had actually worn a cape and a spandex suit.

George felt a chill run down his spine.

Suddenly, the horrific image of Danny DeVito popped up in his head.

Afternoon

Time flew by quickly as the two of them enjoyed a lunch together at a local diner. George was surprised by how much he enjoyed the company of Jack Bosch. Not only, was the tall, muscular man attractive, but he also had a gentle and nurturing side that blended perfectly with his raw and butch appearance. George wondered how the man had gotten the huge scar on his neck. Jack Bosch reminded George of his ex-boyfriend, Derrick, the only man he'd ever lived with.

Jack Bosch had been very open with George and told him an amazing but also a horrific story of what he and a woman by the name of Julie had gone through for the past ten days. And to George's relief, he'd also disclosed that Captain Daniels had died alone in the woods and no one had talked to him.

"So, did you see him put the poison in the stew?"

"No, but I noticed a jar in the barn when he showed me the moose," Jack Bosch said. "I think they were planting beef."

Planting beef? What's that supposed to mean?

George's jaw dropped. "Tetrodotoxin?"

Jack Bosch suddenly had a wary expression. "That's right, but I don't think they knew what they were doing. I think they were just experimenting, and I was their guinea pig. That's why they didn't shoot me right away."

George felt a morbid curiosity brewing, and he began to wonder how on earth a couple of hillbillies could possibly attempt to produce one of the most lethal poisons known to mankind. And even though it was obvious Jack Bosch possessed that knowledge, George didn't want to make a mistake and ask the man straight out, as he noticed Jack Bosch seemed quite wary and suspicious regarding George's curiosity.

"So, what made you notice the jar in the first place?"

"I noticed the label on the jar," Jack Bosch responded. "It said, *Lady Jane Marmalade*."

Jack Bosch looked intensely back at him, and George assumed the man had understood the real purpose of his asking.

"So you like marmalade?" George tried his best to sound casual.

"I don't think I ever had marmalade."

"Really." George astonished. "It's just jam, basically."

Suddenly, Jack Bosch's face lit up with joy, and he kept smiling for quite some time. George smiled back at first, but then he started to feel uneasy, and as he closed his mouth, he rubbed his tongue against his front teeth to make certain he didn't have any food wedged in between them.

After a moment of silence, George felt even more uneasy, and he tried his best to come up with something to say.

"Is the name Bosch of German descent perhaps?"

Jack Bosch's face shifted. Now, he looked angry and disconcerted. "What?"

"I didn't mean to eavesdrop," George lied. "But I couldn't help but overhear the man back at the police station call you Bosch, and you only introduced yourself as Jack to me, so I assumed your name was Jack Bosch."

"*Box*," Jack said, and pronounced the word clearly. "It's a nickname."

"Oh, yeah, I get it," George said. "Well, it's shorter than Jack I suppose."

George smiled wide and hoped the man would return the favor.

"I hate that name."

"I think it's cute."

Why did you have to use that word, George?

George felt his fever rising, and he struggled with thinking straight. Jack's expression shifted once more, but this time he looked more sad than angry.

"I tune out sometimes. I sort of escape reality. You know, like when the light is on, but no one is home," Jack said. "But this guy I served with told people I was insane, and he started a rumor about how I was locked up in a mental institution—Jack is in his box." The last sentence sounded like a quote.

"Sorry to hear that," George said. "Did you file a complaint against him?"

Jack frowned. "He died."

"He died in battle?"

"I guess you can say that," Jack responded in a drowsy voice.

"So, you were in the military?" George asked. "Is that where you got..." George was about to say 'that scar,' but he didn't dare. "...those muscles?"

Jack's expression changed once more, and this time he looked ashamed.

"Julie asked the exact same question." Jack bowed his head. "No, I was never in the military. But I did, however, spend twenty years in prison."

"That's a long stretch," George said, and thought he sounded like an idiot.

Do not tell him about the night you spent in jail. Don't you dare, George.

"I was young, and I needed some fast money. So, I thought it was a good idea to drive a truck filled with counterfeit booze across the Canadian border—the bottles even had my name on them." Jack had a crooked smile.

"They gave you twenty years for that?"

"No, they gave me two years, but I ended up serving twenty," Jack explained. "Manslaughter."

"I'm sorry to hear that."

"I'm sorry too. Every day," Jack maintained. "And the last name is Green by the way. Hey, speaking of names, the feds told me we had a celebrity on board." Jack Green winked and offered another crooked smile.

George felt as if the lump in his throat had just expanded. The mention of Captain Daniels ex-wife, Sharon Stone, scared him. But then again, it wasn't strange if her name had come up during Jack Green's debriefing. After all, Fare Airlines had provided the feds with the information, and it would only be natural for them to ask some questions. It doesn't necessarily mean they suspected Captain Daniels of crashing the plane on purpose. And according to the news, the investigators were certain the Imam was to blame. George felt more at ease again. However, the lump in his throat was still present, and he felt his fever rising.

George swallowed. "You mean the ex-wife?" he asked and tried his best to sound nonchalant.

"His ex-wife?" Jack sounded surprised. "I thought they were married?"

"Yes, you're right," George responded. "Technically, they were still married, but I was told they were going through a divorce."

"That's strange. They seemed so happy together."

"They talked to each other?" George asked. "Did this happen during the flight?"

"I only noticed them when boarding. But they looked very happy together, and very much in love," Jack claimed. "Perhaps they'd fallen back in love."

"No, that can't be right," George said. "His mother told me they hated each other."

"You talked to his mother?" Jack Green had a look of disbelief.

"It's just standard ... protocol," he mumbled. "I visited the co-pilot's parents also. It's just company policy." George made it all sound very nonchalant.

Jack Green kept staring at him with wide eyes.

"The pilot's ex-wife was on the plane, and they were going through a bitter divorce, and then the plane crashes. Is that what you're saying, Stanton? That's some coincidence, wouldn't you say?"

What just happened here?

"Did the pilot know his ex-wife was on the plane?"

Yeah, he even bought her the ticket.

"I don't have that information," George lied.

"That's too much of a coincidence if you ask me."

"It's just a coincidence," George said. "But I thought the feds mentioned that she was on the plane?"

Jack Green frowned. "No, they never mentioned it to me."

"But they mentioned her name?"

"I don't think so. What was her name?" Jack Green kept frowning.

"Sharon Stone," he almost yelled.

"The pilot's ex-wife was Sharon Stone?"

"Not the actress, obviously," George responded. "It's a common name. But, I don't understand. You told me there was a celebrity on board."

"I was referring to Pamela Anderson."

Pamela Anderson?

"Who's Pamela Anderson?" This time he yelled.

"She was on this TV show when I was young, she played this lifeguard—"

"I've heard of *Baywatch*, and I'm familiar with Pamela Anderson, the actress," George interrupted. "But who exactly are you talking about?"

"Kevin's wife was named Pamela, and the feds told me his last name was Anderson," Jack added. "I saw Kevin board the plane with his wife, and I noticed how happy the two looked. I was talking about her. I never heard of Sharon Stone."

"Kevin..." *The guy from the woods?*

George reached for his cell phone, and swiped the screen before he scrolled down to the bottom of the manifest.

"Kevin Anderson was seated next to..."

George hesitated on how to pronounce the name.

"...Aiglentina Anderson," he mumbled, and then scrolled through the list of names. "There was no passenger by the name of Pamela."

"Perhaps I did imagine it then."

"Imagine what?"

"I thought I heard a male voice yelling for Pamela."

"I heard that too."

Jack Green frowned. "Excuse me?"

You probably shouldn't frown so much, given how distinctive your eyebrows are.

"Back at the police station," George responded. "I heard someone chanting Pamela, but there weren't any women present."

"That was just Agent Coleman messing with me," Jack said. "After the crash, I kept asking the others if they'd heard someone yelling for Pamela. But no one else heard it, and I was getting on people's nerves for asking. Julie must have mentioned it to Coleman, and he used it as an opportunity to mock me."

"Is that why you tried to break down the door?"

"I lost my temper," Jack admitted. "Sorry about that."

"Don't be. It sounds to me as if that Coleman fellow had it coming."

"He's just young for his age. That's all," Jack said. "He'll grow out of it."

"I think that guy is done growing." George smiled.

Jack Green smiled back at him.

Seriously, George? Are you making fun of short people now?

"I thought it was Kevin who was shouting for his wife," Jack said. "But I guess I must have imagined it then. At first, I thought I heard God."

George hesitated. "God..."

"I was confused after the crash, and it was so dark, and I didn't know which way to swim. I thought I was about to die," Jack said. "My mother's name was Pamela, and I thought God shouted her name to remind me that I didn't attend her funeral. I thought God had forsaken me and left me in the darkness as a punishment."

"Sounds to me, as if you had a near death experience," George said. "They wouldn't let you out to attend your mother's funeral?"

Jack Green bowed his head. "I chose not to go."

There was an awkward silence before Jack Green finally spoke.

"That explains why the pilot checked out Julie before boarding. He probably noticed his ex-wife in the waiting area, and tried his best to make her jealous."

"He talked to Julie?" George asked. "The woman from the woods?"

"No, that's the thing, he wasn't really talking to her," Jack responded. "He just stood close to her, as if he was pretending to have a conversation with her or something. But Julie didn't show any interest in him. And why would she?" Jack chuckled. "As if a guy like that ever could have a chance with her."

"So, you find her attractive?"

"Julie," Jack responded. "Oh, she's gorgeous."

George sensed something about the way Jack Green had said her name; he was a man in love.

"On the other hand, you don't have to be gorgeous to turn that guy down," Jack added. "It makes me wonder what Sharon Stone looked like. You know, in comparison."

"You mean in comparison to the actual actress?" George felt puzzled.

"No, I mean in comparison to the pilot," Jack clarified. "She had to be pretty desperate to marry a guy like that. Am I right?"

Jack Green appeared to be waiting for a response, and George hesitated as to whether he should comment on Captain Daniels's physical appearance, which he thought was very delightful.

I like men who are tall and muscular... Oh, do NOT say that, George.

George Stanton made sure to bite down on his tongue.

Jack Green smiled and winked. "You didn't think he was attractive, did you?"

Yes, I thought he was attractive... Wait, did you just call me gay?

George tried to think of a safe response. "I don't follow."

Jack Green's face clouded over. "I didn't mean to sound shallow. But I just can't imagine most women would want to wake up, next to a bald eagle every morning."

"A bald eagle?" George asked and felt clueless. "Why would you say that?"

"I hate to sound shallow."

"No, a bald eagle—What do you mean by that?" The tension in George's chest was back, but he wasn't sure why.

"Well, his nose was shaped like a beak, and then there was the lack of hair. I don't know," Jack said and shrugged.

George felt the hairs on his neck rising.

"That's the co-pilot," he just about yelled. "You're describing the co-pilot, Isaac Gregorian. Was it him up in the woods? Captain Daniels was tall and handsome."

"Well, in that case it was the other way around," Jack said, and shrugged once more. "Then it was your co-pilot who died in the woods. That... Gregory fellow."

If Captain Daniels had poisoned his co-pilot, then how could the co-pilot, Isaac Gregorian, have ended up in the woods?

"I remember seeing the captain too," Jack added. "I remember him because he gave me the creeps. He was almost my size, and he looked pissed off, like he was depressed, or something. I guess he must have noticed his ex-wife in the waiting area. For a minute there, I almost freaked out, and my intuition told me not to board the plane. I was afraid he'd crash… Crash the plane or something."

Jack Green stared at George with wide eyes and then suddenly pointed at him.

"You think your captain crashed the plane on count of his ex-wife, don't you, Stanton?"

No, I don't.

"You thought your captain killed his co-pilot, didn't you?" Jack asked. "That's why you're so upset to learn it was the co-pilot who died in the woods."

I said: NO. Didn't you hear me the first time?

George felt as his lips were glued to his teeth. He couldn't speak anymore, and he was about to be sick, his fever still rising.

"Well, I guess it's better than the Imam theory, I give you that," Jack added. "But I think you're wrong, Stanton. I don't think your captain crashed the plane. Don't get me wrong, it's a good theory. But your theory has two major flaws in it."

George felt an ambivalent sense of relief. He didn't want to argue his case, but at the same time, he felt curious as to what the flaws in his theory could possibly be.

"How so?" he asked, and then immediately regretted asking.

"I'm going to tell you what my lawyer told me when he convinced me to plead guilty to manslaughter," Jack said. "It doesn't matter who started the fight. The guy in the coffin is the victim, and the guy standing trial is the murderer. It's that simple."

"I don't follow."

"The pilot in the lake is the victim, and the pilot in the woods is the killer," Jack said. "Your co-pilot killed his captain. It's that simple."

"He could've killed the captain in self-defense," George argued.

"Which brings me to the second flaw," Jack said. "For

the past twenty years I've witnessed a substantial number of fights, and I've participated in several as well. And if there's one thing I learned, it's that the big guy always wins. Except for when the other guy has a weapon."

Yeah, how could the much-smaller co-pilot, Isaac Gregorian, possibly have defeated Captain Daniels in a fight? Daniels even had military training.

"Trust me on this, Stanton," Jack added. "The only way that small turkey-shaped-looking co-pilot of yours ever could have killed a man of my size is if he had a weapon. And that means, he must have planned for it."

"Each pilot has to go through the same type of screening as a passenger would. No way he could have brought a weapon on board."

"You'd be surprised how easy it is to create a weapon out of more or less anything," Jack said. "You ever heard of a shiv, Stanton?"

"Yes, it's a sharp object that resembles a knife. I understand what you're saying, and I'm sure an inmate could produce thousands of shivs from the materials in a departure hall," George said, and shook his head slightly. "But how would the co-pilot ever explain why he was in possession of such a weapon. What? He just happened to have a toothbrush in his pocket that day? And he managed to break the toothbrush in half quickly enough for him to stab the captain in self-defense? How is he going to explain that?"

George felt proud of his last remark, especially when he noticed how Jack Green's eyebrows plunged deeper than ever. For some reason, George suddenly thought of Cliff Henderson, security director.

You really shouldn't frown so much, Jack. It's not a good look for you.

Jack Green kept frowning, and appeared to be scratching his beard, but he stopped as soon as he must have realized he didn't have a beard.

"Well, he could've drugged him, I suppose," Jack said.

"I'm sure the co-pilot would've been permitted to bring medicine through security. At least if the medicine had his prescription and name on it, am I right?"

George thought of the sound recording from the cockpit, and how the pilots discussed the way proper coffee should taste.

"Perhaps the co-pilot slipped some medicine into the captain's coffee, or perhaps he switched cups, or something," Jack said, and then made a noncommittal face. "Come to think of it, the feds mentioned something about coffee."

Does this taste, right? George thought of Magdalene Gregorian's phone call.

Could it be the other way around? Had the co-pilot, Isaac Gregorian, poisoned the captain by offering him a taste of his coffee? But his mother didn't recognize his voice. But then again, perhaps she was protecting her son? And he knew the cockpit recording was on, so perhaps he disguised his voice. But why would the co-pilot crash the plane? Was he depressed? Then why did he write a letter claiming Captain Daniels was depressed?

"Did the co-pilot seem depressed to you?"

"No, on the contrary," Jack responded. "Like I said, he flirted with Julie, and he seemed very happy, as he paraded through the waiting area. It looked as though he was having the best day of his life. He didn't look depressed at all."

"Then why would he crash the plane?"

"That's the million-dollar question." Jack Green winked, and stared at George with a mischievous smile.

"I don't follow..."

"During my twenty years of incarceration, I came across men with all kind of difference sentences. But in the end, each one of them was incarcerated for one of two reasons."

Jack Green paused and kept staring George in the eyes.

"It either involved a woman or the prospect of money. Or possibly a combination of the two," Jack added.

"I don't understand what you're trying to tell me," George said and felt dizzy.

"I don't think your co-pilot had a woman in his life. I hate to sound shallow, but I don't think that guy knew what love was," Jack said. "So, that leaves money."

"Money?" George almost yelled. "What money?"

"I don't want to alarm you, Stanton. But it has come to my attention that I might be entitled to a large sum of money within the near future."

"Call me, George. And I'm sure you will. In fact, I hope you receive the money. And not to worry, it won't come out of my paycheck. Our insurance will cover every claim."

At least, as long as the Imam gets the blame.

"But I imagine the co-pilot would be entitled to a claim of his own, would he not?" Jack asked. "I mean, if he prevented the captain from completing a suicide mission, thereby saving all the passengers. He wouldn't just be left with fame and glory? He would be entitled to an insurance claim also, don't you think?"

Suddenly the image of Tom Hanks landing his distressed plane on water popped up in George's head. Then he imagined a scene in which co-pilot Isaac Gregorian was interviewed by the media.

Captain Daniels was on a suicide mission on account of his divorce, but I managed to fight him off, just as he was about to crash the plane into the Canadian wilderness. Oh, I'm no hero, I only did what I'm trained to do, which is to safely land the plane on water. Besides, the Great Slave Lake is one of the biggest lakes in the world, so it was easy to land the plane safely. It's not like landing a plane on the Hudson River or anything. What was that? Yes, I'll be happy to sell you the movie rights to my story.

"This whole thing was about money?" George asked in disbelief.

"What won't people do to gain wealth?" It sounded like a quote.

To gain wealth? Who talks like that?

"He probably knew the captain was going through a divorce, and perhaps he even knew the ex-wife would be on this particular flight," Jack added. "That's a good setup. It would be easy for him to frame the captain."

Yeah, he even wrote a letter.

Just then, it occurred to George that this scenario was even worse. It would most definitely result in the complete bankruptcy of Fare Airlines and perhaps shatter Trisha Boyle's financial situation along with it.

"No, they never flew together before. In fact, I think it was the first time they ever met each other," George lied.

Jack Green seemed disappointed with the answer, and then diverted his attention to whatever was left of his lunch. However, as soon as he finished eating, Jack looked at him with the same mischievous smile as before. George braced himself for another wave of discomfort.

"So, what did his father look like?"

"Who?"

"The co-pilot," Jack clarified. "You told me you visited his parents. Did his father look like a bald eagle also?"

Again, the horrific image of Danny DeVito popped up in George's head.

"Did you ever see that Batman movie where Danny DeVito played the Penguin?"

"Yes, I remember seeing it in theater when I was young," Jack responded. "I enjoyed that."

"His father looked like the Penguin," George said. "But twice as big."

"A penguin..." Jack nodded. "That's a better description. I should've gone with penguin instead of bald eagle. To describe the co-pilot, I mean. You know, because of his black and white uniform."

Both men laughed briefly and shook their heads.

"Well, aren't we being shallow, George. I'm sure his father was a nice person. One shouldn't judge a book by its cover—am I right?"

"No, you're wrong," George responded. "His father was probably the worst person I've ever met. He treated his wife like garbage, and I imagine he treated his son just as bad."

"Well, there you go then," Jack said. "Perhaps money wasn't his only motive."

"I don't follow."

"Perhaps he sought his father's approval," Jack said. "If he achieved fame and fortune, then perhaps his father would finally stop treating him like garbage."

Jack Green suddenly bowed his head with an expression of shame.

"Children will go a long way to please their parents," Jack added.

George thought of how eager he'd been to please his own father, and how he'd begged his father to come to the state championship. But as always, his father was too busy reading his books. His father thought if he only read enough books in English then he'd finally lose his Japanese accent. George had told his father it would make more sense if he'd watch television instead—something his father hardly ever did.

When George had returned as state champion that night, his father had already gone to bed. So, instead of celebrating with his father, he'd celebrated a night on the town with friends. Then, his father came and got him out of jail the next morning, and he couldn't have been more disappointed with his son. His father told him it was the worst day of his life.

Is that what caused the crash? Was it just a son's desperate attempt to prove his worthiness to his father? Is it that simple?

The more George thought about it, the more sense the motive made. Now, he felt convinced the co-pilot was responsible for the crash. Just then, he came to realize the irony in it all. Even though Captain Daniels was innocent of any crime, he probably did cause the plane to crash. Unintentionally, but nonetheless, he probably caused the plane to crash when he woke up and engaged in a fight with his co-pilot. Who, then, overshot the landing and crashed the plane into the Canadian wilderness. If Captain Daniels hadn't woken up, then the plane probably would have landed safely on the huge water surface of the Great Slave Lake.

George felt nauseous as he once again realized how much things had started to make sense, and how much worse this scenario was.

"This doesn't much sense," he lied.

Jack Green looked at him with wary eyes. "That's your problem."

"Actually, it's not the airline's problem. It's not—"

"No," Jack interrupted. "I mean, your problem is you're trying to find a solution that makes sense. You're not going to find a rational explanation why someone would want to crash a plane. If people only acted rationally, then there would be no need for prisons."

"It still doesn't make any sense," George argued.

"I don't think it's supposed to make sense. Haven't you ever watched the news and asked yourself why anyone would do such a thing? What on earth were they thinking? What was going through their minds?"

"I know what you mean, but still..." George began to stress and had no idea how to finish the sentence.

"The way I see it," Jack said. "Four alternatives could each explain the crash. Either the crash was caused by the captain, or the co-pilot, or a passenger, or it was just a freak accident. But none of those alternatives makes much sense. But then again, I don't think it's supposed to. But if you eliminate the three alternatives that make the least sense, then the alternative remaining is most likely the truth."

Where have I heard that before?

"In that case, I think the Imam did it," George lied, and tried his best not to sound presumptuous.

"The Imam." Jack frowned. "I don't know, George. I have to agree with my ex-lawyer on this one. The guy on the bottom of the lake is the victim, and the guy in the woods is the killer. I think the co-pilot did it for fame and money."

George felt his fever rising, and he struggled to think

rationally.

"Are you aware the Imam tried to get us to enforce Sharia law in this country?"

"You mean in America?"

"Yes." George just realized he was in Canada.

"And how would crashing an airplane make a difference?" Jack asked. "It's hard to enforce any laws when you're dead. Don't you agree?"

"I'm just saying," George responded and felt as if he was about to throw up.

"I get what you're saying, George. Don't worry, I'm sure the Imam will get the blame, and then the airline will come out as the victim, rather than the problem."

Jack Green winked at him before he rose to his feet.

"You're leaving?"

"I'm going to the hospital to visit Julie, and make sure she's all right," Jack responded. "That is, if she'll even talk to me."

"Why wouldn't she talk to you?"

"I told her I was in the military." Jack had a look of shame.

"But you only did that to spare her feelings," George said. "Don't worry, I'm sure she'll understand."

"I don't know," Jack said. "I think Agent Coleman has made it abundantly clear to her that I can't be trusted."

"You still carried her out of the woods, Jack."

"I suppose..." Jack suddenly twitched. "Say, you wouldn't happen to know Julie's last name, do you?"

You don't know her last name?

"I never told her my last name," Jack added. "I was afraid she'd recognize my name from the news. My lawyer created quite the ruckus in the media prior to my parole hearing. So, I never asked for her last name. In fact, I tried my best to avoid the subject."

George swiped the screen of his cell phone, but he didn't have to scroll down the manifest this time.

"Julie Morrison," he said.

"Thank you, George, and thanks for lunch."

Jack tapped George's shoulders twice as he passed him, and as he did, George suddenly realized what was wrong, and the answer to the question that had been puzzling him for the past week suddenly became obvious.

George Stanton just realized why he was single.

The gentle but firm tap on his shoulder reminded him of Derrick, the only man he'd ever lived with. Whenever Derrick got upset, he would raise his voice, as one could expect from any person who's upset. But even though, Derrick never laid a hand on him, or even attempted to do so, George still felt vulnerable, every time they had a disagreement; his instincts told him to run away. And eventually, he did run away. He'd broken it off with Derrick because living with him didn't feel right. Living with a person who was physically superior to himself didn't feel good—which more or less ruled out every man on the planet.

George had come to realize the reason he was single wasn't because he was afraid of getting his feelings hurt, as he'd convinced himself so many times. He was single because he was literally afraid of men hurting him.

46 EXIT

Tuesday afternoon

He felt nervous as he entered the hospital; he felt he was about to stand trial.

"My name is Jack Green," he said. "I'm here to see Julie Morrison."

The female receptionist typed and then frowned at the screen.

"There's no patient here by that name."

"Actually, I'm not certain her last name is Morrison," he said. "Can you please check if there's a patient by the name of Julie."

Jack wondered if George Stanton had checked the entire list of passengers, and if there perhaps had been more than one passenger named Julie. He thought the receptionist looked suspiciously at him, and he noticed her name tag said Linda.

"Are you a relative or a friend of the family?" Linda asked him.

"I'm the guy who brought her in," he responded. "I carried her through the woods after the plane went down."

"Oh, her." Linda's face lit up. "She checked out a few hours ago. I called her a taxi myself."

Jack felt both surprised and relieved to learn Julie had checked out of the hospital.

"So, she's, all right?"

"She seemed fine to me," Linda said. "I mean, she was on crutches, but besides that, she seemed fine."

Linda the receptionist looked Jack up and down while biting her lower lip.

"It was a good thing you did, helping her out like that."

"You wouldn't happen to know where she was going?"

"To the airport."

The words felt hurtful. They made him feel rejected and abandoned. Why would Julie leave without saying goodbye? After all they'd been through. And now she'd left with not even a farewell? But on the other hand, Julie didn't know how to contact him. It wasn't as though he had a phone. And understandably, she must have been eager to get home to her son.

"So, are you on your way to the airport yourself? Or are you planning to stay in town for a while?" Linda asked him, and took a substantial chunk of her lower lip.

Jack leaned up against the reception desk.

"There was another woman who was brought in at the same time as Julie. I think her name is Melinda ... Nordstrom, I think," he said in, a low voice. "She has red hair and a very pale complexion. Do you know, if she's all right?"

"I heard she was transferred to the psychiatric ward."

Jack felt his chest tighten.

"What, they strapped her to a bed?"

His voice was harsher, and Linda the receptionist no longer looked at him with eyes of delight. On the contrary, she appeared frightened and lost for words. For the past twenty years, Jack had tried his best to be as intimidating as possible. Now, he struggled to do the opposite, and not scare people.

"Sorry," he said, and noticed the wary look from the doctor in the background. "I'll be leaving now. Thank you for your help, Linda."

Before Jack left the room, he turned around to see if the receptionist had recovered from the harsh tone in his voice. He saw the doctor standing next to her, and as the doctor whispered in her ear, Linda's jaw dropped and her face had a look of fear and contempt. Jack assumed the doctor had told the receptionist the same thing the police had told Julie, and he imagined Julie had the same expression on her face when she'd discovered the truth of who he really was.

He was a murderer, and a liar. He wasn't a soldier; he was a convict. He felt convinced he'd never hear from Julie ever again, and any attempt to contact her would only result in another interrogation, or possibly a restraining order.

At least I got her home to her boy, he comforted himself.

On his way out of the hospital, he noticed the exit sign, and added a sixth word to his French vocabulary.

EXIT / SORTIE

Jack couldn't help noticing his reflection in the glass door as he exited the building, and the enormous scar on his neck.

As Jack Green walked down the road, he felt the wind against the tender skin of his conspicuous scar, and he felt the sharp pain caused by the imaginary knife frantically stabbing his neck.

That excruciating pain.

After wandering around town for an hour, he came to realize he had nowhere to go. He was at a dead end. He'd violated his parole, and he was destined to serve the remaining seven years of his sentence. But this time, prison would break him for certain. Julie would never come to visit him and neither would anyone else. And whatever money he had coming his way would be paid to the family members of his former cellmate, the man he'd killed in battle. He'd made his decision prior to his flight to Anchorage. However, the cave from his childhood was now out of his reach. The hotel room in Yellowknife would have to be his final destination and the end of his journey.

Jack used the card to open the door, thereby granting him access to his hotel room, and as he did, he puzzled over the fact that a "card" could be used to open a door.

He placed the bucket containing ice and a chilled champagne bottle on the table, along with the salt shaker, which he'd taken from the hotel restaurant while he waited for the champagne.

Then, he went to the bathroom and removed his bloody shirt and pants from the bathtub before he turned on the hot water. He glanced at his pants on the bathroom floor, and especially at the bulk in the front pants pocket. Then he got a towel from the rack before he left the bathroom. Jack emptied the bucket with ice on the towel and wrapped his left forearm tight; the cold ice *burning* his skin.

A few minutes later, he returned to the bathroom. He turned off the water. Steam rose from the hot water in the tub. He used his right foot to open the toilet lid—just as he'd done for the past twenty years.

He felt dizzy as he began to urinate, and he accidentally peed on the floor.

On his way out of the bathroom, Jack glanced once more at his bloody pants lying on the floor. He filled a glass of champagne, and then added a substantial amount of salt to the sweet beverage. His face twisted as he swallowed the salty liquid he'd created. Then, he repeated the process until the champagne bottle was empty. He decided to leave a note to the person who had to clean the room. As he wrote, he felt overwhelmed by shame and remorse.

Jack placed the note on the floor in front of the bathroom door, and as he stared at the note, he asked himself why he used the word "lady." Was it because Julie had described herself as a "cleaning lady," was that why he wrote it? Was that an accurate description of Julie's occupation?

Cleaning lady!
Call the cops!
Don't open the door!

Jack Green worked methodically. He never stopped to think or to reflect on what he was about to do. He picked up his pants from the bathroom floor and took out the bar of soap with two razor blades attached to it. He didn't lock the bathroom door. He merely closed it. The skin on his forearm wasn't *burning* any more. The skin, rather, was entirely numb. Without hesitation, Jack climbed into the bathtub still wearing his clothes.

The bar of soap connected with his wrist, and the razor blade cut deep into his flesh and skin. Jack dragged the soap all the way down to his elbow. The skin opened up, layers of fat and tissue unfolded rapidly, and his blood colored the hot water red.

The view was horrific.

Jack closed his eyes and tried his best not to think. His threshold for pain was high, but the pain was much worse than he'd anticipated. The numb skin didn't make much difference; the sharp pain was still unbearable.

That excruciating pain.

Don't think. Nothing good ever comes from thinking.

Focus on something else.

Jack Green counted the tiles on the walls, first horizontally, and then he counted them vertically. For each number he chanted, his body temperature fell. Despite the hot water, he was still freezing, and he'd never felt as cold. Eventually, his head started to tilt and drop forward, but just then, a familiar smell woke him; the smell of urine and blood.

Jack turned his head and looked at the toilet, and toward the smell of his own urine on the floor. And in his state of drowsiness, he could actually see his mother sitting on the toilet, staring back at him with a look of disappointment. Now, he felt overwhelmed with regret.

What have I done? I had one life, and now I've wasted it.

Jack tried his best to move, but he was too weak. It was too late. He was going to die in that bathtub, drowning in his own blood and remorse. The salt on his tongue reminded him of his mother, and how he'd pleasured her out of guilt. The guilt of merely being born, and thereby ruining her life.

Before she gave birth to him, his mother was thin and beautiful, and desirable to men. But her body was ruined the day she gave birth to him. Men had stopped paying attention to her. She'd sacrificed her beauty for his sake, so she could grant him a life. A life that came with a price. Jack had ruined her for other men, and leaving her with only him. It was just the two of them; there was no one else.

As Jack's life slowly faded away, and just before the final image turned black, and just after Jack took his last breath, his mind mustered one last thought before he drifted off into eternal darkness.

The very last word he thought of was "Pamela."

47 THE SEARCH

Tuesday afternoon

It's just a coincidence, she reminded herself.

As expected, her flight to Los Angeles was a pleasant one. Flying was one of the things she enjoyed most in life. The plane crash didn't change anything; she wasn't afraid of flying now, and she never had been. She knew the odds were in her favor, and the risk of ever enduring a plane crash was remarkably low. Not only would she keep on flying, but in the near future, she would fly more than ever, and explore the world from a new perspective.

The irony brought a smile to her face.

She'd spend the money she would receive from the airline on the actual airline. Therefore, the airline wouldn't lose any money. They'd simply gain an additional passenger, and she would merely occupy an empty seat. No one would lose their jobs because of her settlement. On the contrary, because of her future spending on air travel, people's jobs were more secure now than before, she argued.

Of course, she wouldn't spend all the money on traveling. A large sum of her settlement would go to finally purchasing an apartment—in Los Angeles.

She cut to the front of the taxi queue.

"Excuse me, sir," she said, and held up her crutches for

the man to see. "My foot is killing me. Do you mind?"

"No, of course not," the man replied. "You go ahead and take the next one."

"Thank you, sir. That's very noble of you." She looked at the man once more before she entered the taxi. "You, my good sir, are a true gentleman."

She had no trouble remembering where she was going. She knew the address by heart.

She noticed her reflection in the rearview mirror. Suddenly, she felt overwhelmed with joy. She was finally going to see him again. The long wait was over. How long she'd dreamed and fantasized about this moment. She'd been chanting his name for the past five days, and now the time was finally here. Her perseverance had prevailed. But then, just as quickly, she felt nervous about meeting him again, and nervous about what to say.

What if he's angry with me? I've been gone for such a long time.

As she got out of the taxi in downtown Los Angeles, she felt the warm breeze on her arms, and it reminded her of how relieved she'd felt to learn that her jacket had been lost in the fire. The police had assured her that her jacket had gone up in flames and was forever lost—and so was the blood on the sleeve. The blood from when she'd smashed his head with a rock. She'd never indented to kill him, but she was so angry with him for crashing the plane. Despite all his training to safely land a plane on water in case of an emergency, he'd still managed to screw it up. Even if the Great Slave Lake was almost the size of an ocean, he'd still managed to miss the landing.

After the crash, the idiot kept shouting her name, and at that point, she was still angry at him for trying to engage in a conversation with her at the airport, even though she'd specifically told him never to greet her in public. She had explained to him how vital it was people never understand that they knew each other.

But on the other hand, she had obviously overestimated Isaac Gregorian's intelligence, and she would have had to dispose of him sooner or later. The investigators were apparently under the impression that the Imam had inflicted the injuries on his skull, so in the end, everything had turned out for the best.

It's all just a big coincidence, she chanted, while she kept smiling.

Now, alone in the elevator, she waited to reach the top floor, her eyes fixed on the mirror. She was mesmerized by her reflection. She smiled when she suddenly realized she still wasn't wearing any makeup. But then again, why would she wear makeup? It wasn't as if she needed makeup—or a bra, for that matter.

I'm perfect the way I am.

She moved closer to the mirror, still mesmerized by her reflection. Her lips almost touched the surface, but just as she was about to merge with her own image, the sound of the elevator door opening made her jolt. As she stepped out of the elevator, she recognized a familiar face. The old woman looked up and then greeted her with a smile.

"Welcome to Hernandez, Stein and Lebowich," the old woman said. "How may I help you today?"

"I was hoping to see Mr. Hernandez," she said. "I'm a former client of his."

"And what is your name, if I may ask?"

She felt slightly insulted that the receptionist didn't recognize her. Even though two years had passed since they had last seen each other, their final conversation then was a memorable one. The receptionist had lost her appetite that day. A story about a hamburger with a rat tail had seen to it. But on the other hand, it was probably better the receptionist didn't recognize her, given that the lawsuit against the restaurant eventually ended with her being convicted for attempted fraud.

Once convicted, she knew she could never file another

legal complaint against any other company. However, if she just happened to be on a plane with a suicidal captain, then her criminal record wouldn't be used against her.

It's all just a big coincidence, Geronimo.

At first, she hesitated, and she almost blurted out Julie.

"My name is Angela..."

And not Pamela, she thought and laughed internally.

"... Summer," she added.

As in June or July, she thought and almost laughed out loud.

The receptionist picked up a phone, and spoke in a low voice, then looked back at her and rewarded her with yet another smile. Angela made sure to smile politely at the old woman who was covered in wrinkles and could stand to lose a few pounds.

"And what is this regarding, if I may ask?" the wrinkly woman asked her.

"I'm a survivor of flight seven one nine to Anchorage. I plan to file a lawsuit with multiple damage claims against the airline, and several work and protection claims against my insurance company," Angela replied in a robotic tone. "And I would like the notorious Geronimo Hernandez to represent me in court."

Once again, the receptionist spoke in a low voice, and once again Angela made sure to keep smiling at the wrinkly woman. The receptionist's micro-expression didn't reveal a thing. Angela started to feel uncomfortable, and she felt as if her facial muscles might cramp up soon from all the false smiling. The feeling made her think of Jack, and how easy it was to manipulate men who seek women's approval. Jack's romantic side appeared to be nonexistent, but his nurturing side had craved her approval—and nothing is sadder than a single mom raising a son.

Angela questioned whether or not Jack would have been as eager to get her home if she'd told him she had a daughter instead of a son. She had neither, but Jack didn't know that.

When the investigators showed her Jack's mug shot as they interviewed her at the hospital, Angela had realized Jack wasn't the former soldier he presented himself to be. Instead, he was an ex-convict—and the perfect scapegoat at the time.

Angela had needed an explanation for how the co-pilot had died in the woods. She told the US agents that she had seen Jack wash blood off his hands, and she assumed they'd suspect Jack of killing the co-pilot in rage for causing the plane to crash. But to her astonishment, the agents thought Isaac had sustained his head injuries fighting with the Imam, who they suspected had stormed the cockpit.

Nonetheless, Angela still thought it best if Jack went back to prison. She didn't want to risk his contacting her, or telling his side of the story to the media. She made sure to invent a few racist remarks on Jack's behalf before she described Kevin's appearance in detail, and how cold Jack was before he conveniently had found a black blazer on one of his hikes into the woods. The chain of evidence she laid down amused her.

Jack had assumed that "hikers" had left the chocolate cupcake wrapper she hadn't hidden well enough.

Idiot.

Agent Smith was hard to read, but his younger colleague, Coleman, wasn't, and when Angela mentioned how Jack heard voices, and how he kept talking to someone named Pamela, who wasn't present. She quickly understood that Jack must have had a history of mental problems. The fact provided her with an explanation of why Jack would refer to her as Julie in his interrogation.

I didn't dare say that my name was Angela, because it's so close to Pamela. I was afraid he'd think that I was her. Also, he kept telling me how much I reminded him of his mother. Please don't tell him my real name. I don't want him to contact me, she'd told the agents while she cried her eyes out.

Angela's heart skipped a beat when the receptionist finally hung up the phone.

"He'll be right with you, Miss Summer."

It's all just a big coincidence, Geronimo. It's not like I crashed the plane or anything, she prepared herself to say.

Angela felt overwhelmed. She felt as if she'd just passed the finish line. She had rigged the lottery, and she had won. Now, it was finally her turn to experience happiness and all the benefits of a "carefree" life. She didn't have to clean people's houses any more—or Dr. Sherman's pharmacy.

Angela couldn't stop smiling. She felt flooded with joy.

Her search for happiness was finally over.

AFTERWORDS

I hope you've enjoyed reading this novel as much as I've enjoyed writing it. And if you did, please consider leaving a review on Amazon. Please keep in mind that authors depend on reviews in order to sell books. Thank you for your consideration, and thank you for reading my novel.

Sincerely,
Jordan Shore

Need clarification on the ending?

If you're struggling to fully grasp the ending, please follow the instructions below for better understanding:

1. The anonymous characters in the initial chapters are the same as the passengers who survived the plane crash.

2. To fully grasp the end, you need to identify the character in the last chapter, from the initial chapters. The Angela charac-

ter (or Julie, if you will) is first introduced in chapter 2 "LOVE."

Keywords to look for in this chapter:
Cleaning lady (not prostitute)
Pharmacy
Card (as in keycard)
Penguin
Coffee cup

3. Reading chapter 15 "ANGELA" will give you a clearer perspective on what kind of person she was. Please keep in mind that these chapters are written from a third-person point of view, therefore, the narrator doesn't have access to thoughts or emotions.

I hope these instructions help you to tie up any loose ends.

And thanks again for taking the time to read my novel.

Printed in Great Britain
by Amazon